ERIN HAWKINS

UNEXPECTEDLY IN LOVE SERIES BOOK TWO

Unexpectedly Mine

Copyright © 2023 by Erin Hawkins

ISBN: 978-1-7356883-7-4

This is a work of fiction. Names, characters, businesses, places, events and incidents are either the products of the author's imagination or used in a fictitious manner. Any resemblance to actual persons, living or dead, or actual events is purely coincidental.

Edited by Chelly Peeler inkedoutediting.com

Cover design by Cover Ever After covereverafter.com

Titles by Erin Hawkins

Reluctantly Yours
Not in the Plans
Best Laid Plans

CHAPTER 1

Emma

The needle pricks my finger and a red dot of blood immediately appears. Shit. There's no pain, just panic as I stick the punctured digit into my mouth to stop the bleeding. The last thing I need is blood spots on this dress. It's white, it's couture and it's hitting the runway in five minutes.

"Four minutes, everyone!" a voice calls out.

Make that four minutes.

"Models, take your places, please," Willow, the show coordinator, announces into her headset. She's on the far side of the room, waving her arms toward the stage. She's like the grounds crew at the airport, except instead of waving orange batons, she's flagging the women into position with a clipboard in one hand and a lint roller in the other.

The movement around me might seem chaotic to others, but I'm used to it. For many years I watched my mother take the runway at some of New York Fashion Week's top shows, her lithe figure donning some of fashion's iconic looks at the time, and that's where I fell in love with fashion.

I've been backstage at every couture fashion show you can imagine, brushing shoulders with names like Lagerfeld and Versace. Okay, maybe it was more like my shoulders to their waists, because I was six, but let's just say this environment is second nature.

The lights, the energy, the urgent countdown to the start of the show. The designer sewing a model into her dress and stabbing herself in the finger. That part is new but exhilarating all the same.

I tie off the thread, knot it and cut the excess.

"All right, Anna, you're in." Taking me for my word, she doesn't bother to look back as she rushes off to get in line with the other models. When I stand from where I was crouched on the floor to finish the detail on Anna's dress, I notice the dark black spots on my pink dress. Shit. I had been so focused on sewing the dress, so intent on getting it ready that I hadn't stopped to think about kneeling on the floor, the delicate hemline of my dress tucked under my knees. The hemline that is now smudged with dirt.

"Two minutes!" Willow shouts.

I hustle to a nearby hair and makeup station to look for a towel or wipe or something I can attempt to clean myself off with.

"What are you doing?" Jess, my personal assistant and friend, appears beside me. Her eyes go wide when I pull away the wipe that was not only unsuccessful in removing the dirt spots, but made them wet and splotchy.

"No one will notice, right?" I glance down and then back up to Jess's face. While I'm not modeling in the show, I am the designer and will be taking a walk down the runway at the end.

We're at the Blushing Bride Convention in Las Vegas for my first official runway show. The top five up-and-coming bridal gown designers were invited and I was asked to headline the show. According to the brochure they put out, I'm the hot new bridal gown designer that's got a flare for 'sassy, flirty gowns that are guaranteed to make you own your day.'

I would be panicking, but Jess is a fixer. Maybe because

she's had to be. Jess is my assistant, but also my publicist, my marketing assistant and head of branding. She wears a lot of hats at Emma Belle Bridal. She's used to these crunch time disasters and always has a solution to a problem.

"Hold on." Jess strikes her finger into the air. "We've got an extra."

"Dress?" I ask, quickly following her, and wondering why we would have a dress without a model.

By the time we get to the rack at the back of the convention space, I'm breathless. Jesus, this place is huge. Jess unzips the garment bag and immediately my jaw drops.

"No way." I shake my head in disbelief. "How did this get here?"

"It got mixed in with the other bags in New York. It's all we've got in your size." Jess slips off the garment bag, exposing the white slip-dress style gown that my mom wore when she and my dad got married. It's Dior haute couture circa 1991, and I'm obsessed with it. When my mom gave it to me, I'd envisioned making a few small adjustments to update it a bit and wear it at my own wedding.

My wedding.

I think about the secret Pinterest boards filled with inspiration. The binders of magazine clippings I've saved. The vision board I've kept on the top shelf of my closet. The years spent curating a dream for an event that up until two months ago I thought would be happening soon. A proposal was inevitable. I'd argue that's what most twenty-nine-year-old women living with their boyfriend of two years would think. We'd discussed it many times. I'd even had my ring finger sized and conveniently put on file at the top three jewelers in New York.

I was wrong.

Two months ago, my boyfriend, Alec, took me out to dinner to celebrate our anniversary. The sunset was breathtaking, the martinis were dry and although I was freezing in the white cocktail dress I'd put on, I was determined to be dressed for the occasion regardless of the thirty-five-degree temperature that evening. I thought he was going to propose over oysters and champagne.

Not only was he not proposing, he was breaking up with me.

I was completely caught off guard. It was an Elle Woods, *Legally Blonde,* moment. Maybe even more so. I'd just finished picking out a new dining room table for our apartment. One that would be host to our future dinner parties, and eventually family meals with our children. It was a beautiful reclaimed oak table. The saleswoman said it was great for families because it would resist dents and stand up to anything. What she failed to mention is that it was custom and therefore unreturnable. It now serves as a worktable at my rented boutique space in Brooklyn.

Now, I'm living with my parents, which isn't exactly a hardship. They're rarely in the city and it's a penthouse on Park Avenue, but still far from the life I thought I would be living at thirty.

That's right, today is my birthday. As of seven nineteen this morning, the time I was born and the exact moment when my parents called me from Barbados, I am thirty now.

My phone buzzes in my pocket.

"Aww. It's from Barrett and Chloe." I lift my phone is Jess's direction so she can see the electronic birthday card they sent me.

I've been getting texts and calls all day, but nothing from Alec yet. I would imagine he'd still send me a birthday text; we were together for two and a half years.

Although he is casually dating an Instagram influencer named Brecken right now.

But, it's super casual. That's what he said when I ran into him last week at our gym. Not 'our' gym, but the gym we both go to.

Sometimes, I stare at that dining table and imagine Alec walking into my boutique to tell me he made a mistake. He was wrong for breaking up with me and that we should give it another try. It still doesn't hurt any less, being dumped by the person you thought you were going to spend the rest of your life with. Then, watching them move on, casually or not.

"Are you thinking about the table again?" Jess asks.

"What? No." I shake my head, but Jess knows me too well.

Alec used to tease me about being in love with love, but how can I not be? Isn't it the most magical feeling in the world? And through my bridal gown designs, I get to see how that love is transformed into a union between two people that are going to spend the rest of their lives together. That's my favorite part. That my gowns get to be part of someone's memories on the most special day of their lives.

I want that. But I'm no closer to my special day than I was two years ago when Alec and I bumped into each other at the coffee shop between our apartments.

"Emma." Jess pulls me out of my spiral. "Put it on."

My gaze drops to my unsalvageable pink dress and I nod, knowing that as the minutes count down to the start of my show, I have no choice.

I turn to let Jess unzip my dress so I can shimmy out of it and quickly into Mr. Christian Dior. No one even bats an eye at my impromptu dress change as Jess starts to do up the buttons along the back.

"You don't think it's bad form to wear this now, do you?" I ask. "It's not going to bring me bad luck if I need to wear it in the future?" *In case Alec realizes he's made the biggest mistake of his life, dumps Brecken and proposes to me?*

I don't have to say it out loud, Jess knows what I'm thinking. What I'm hoping for.

"Let's not think about Alec right now. Tonight is about you and your hard work."

"Everyone on the team's hard work," I interject.

"Right, but without you there is no Emma Belle Bridal, so get moving, missy."

Jess swats at my butt to shoo me back toward the stage where I make it just in time to watch the first model step out onto the runway.

The venue is lit up with soft white lights that bounce off the shiny pink runway. The music, which is a classic bridal song remixed with an upbeat dance song, sets the perfect tone for the sophisticated, yet flirty gowns I have designed. While this isn't my first collection, it's the first that I'm showing to the world. My fingernail finds its way to my mouth automatically. It's a bad habit that prevents me from keeping a decent manicure. Alec always thought it was gross. He could never understand why I couldn't just quit biting them. Willpower, he said.

I see the buyers from Bloomingdale's and Bergman's. I watch anxiously as they point at the model walking by, then furiously write something down on their notepads, eyeing each other suspiciously before turning back to watch the next model advance. While I have always enjoyed designing custom pieces, and I have for some friends and social acquaintances, I love the idea of my gowns being available to the masses to shop in department stores and bridal boutiques across the country.

Anna, the model that I stitched into her dress, is the last one ahead of me. It is a bit funny to realize that the months and months of hard work have been for this two minute and twenty-six-second show.

When Anna makes her way back down the runway, the parade of models goes out again, and this time I follow. The audience is on their feet. At the sound of their applause, a wave of emotion hits me. It's beyond thrilling to be following models down the runway that are wearing my designs. I nervously tuck a strand of my shoulder-length hair behind my ear and step out into the lights. My gown might be a tad much for my neutral makeup and casual hair, but the gorgeous vintage gown fits like a glove and gives me a boost of confidence as I attempt to stay upright on this shiny stage.

The audience applause is deafening and the lights are blinding. I smile and wave, doing my best to soak in this moment. For a moment, a twinge of sadness settles over me. None of the faces in the audience are familiar. All of the Emma Belle Bridal team is backstage and my mom and dad weren't able to make it, their work schedules conflicting. I'd always imagined this moment with Alec in the audience cheering me on. But the reality is, even if we were still together, I'm not confident he would have shown up.

My gaze settles over the front row where the buyers from several department stores are seated. Their heads are down, pencils furiously jotting notes on the papers in their laps. I let the anticipation of hearing their feedback push my recently single status to the back of my mind.

The models finish their lap around the runway and I give a final wave and blow a kiss to the still cheering audience before disappearing backstage. My heart beating with excitement, I watch the models embrace each other, smiling and laughing. Then six sets of arms are embracing me. I take a breath, trying to calm down from the adrenaline rush of it all.

My phone buzzes. I expect to see another text or notification from a friend wishing me happy birthday. I scroll through the notifications.

Alec Mitchell has a new post.

I glance around, feeling guilty that I haven't taken Jess's advice and removed him from my contacts.

How can you move on if you're constantly checking up on him?

Somewhere in my brain I wonder if Alec's post is wishing me a happy birthday.

My curiosity is piqued. But the moment the post and photo come up, I regret it.

It's not a birthday post.

It's Alec smiling ear to ear with Brecken in his arms. He looks handsome in a crisp white button-down and slacks, while her long platinum locks spill over her shoulder and against her white mini dress. Their perfect, toothpaste-ad smiles are blinding.

Brecken's left hand is pressed against Alec's chest in the universal 'just engaged' photo pose. Her nails are manicured, painted light pink and buffed into a perfect almond shape. There, nestled onto her ring finger is a large, brilliant princess cut diamond.

Oh my God. I should close the app. Drop my phone back into my purse. Pretend like I never saw it. But my brain is already running wild with the unsettling image.

Maybe it's one of those parties where you try on the diamonds for fun.

I can make out the rooftop of the Gansevoort Hotel in the background. The same place Alec broke up with me. He must be insane. Or he's really into full circle moments. Except this doesn't feel like a full circle. It's more of an obtuse triangle where all points meet each other.

And because my brain is searching for answers to this *Twilight Zone* turn of events, I read the caption.

'SHE SAID YES!'

That's all it says. Oh, and #**loveofmylife**

He used a hashtag. Alec hates hashtags.

Love of his life?! They've known each other two months! Unless he was cheating on me and that most certainly does not make it better.

I'm trying to process the evidence.

Alec is engaged.

Two months after we broke up, he has proposed to his girlfriend.

On my birthday.

The juxtaposition of the smiling, celebratory faces that

surround me and the shocking news about Alec's engagement is overwhelming. I'm shook. Someone thrusts a champagne glass into my hand and clinks it with their own.

"Cheers! You killed it!" Leo, the social media manager for Emma Belle Bridal, shouts over the noise. "I need a shot for socials." He holds up his phone to take a picture. Shaking his head in disapproval, he shifts me sideways. "Better, but do something different with your face. Like smile."

I plaster on my best smile. Leo is a perfectionist and if he doesn't get the shot he wants, he'll be on me all night.

He looks at his phone and scrunches his face, but I'm saved by Kiara, Emma Belle Bridal's sales manager.

"Emma," Kiara rushes to my side, "I've got a proposal from Bergman's. They want exclusive and when Bloomingdale's got wind of it, they upped their offer. We're in a bidding war! Isn't that amazing?!"

Everyone from the models to the hair and makeup teams to the fashion show production staff and my team at Emma Belle Bridal are gathering around me.

"Wow," is all I can say because I'm still processing Alec's news.

Jess appears beside me.

"Tonight was a wild success and we couldn't have done it without our fearless leader, Emma." Jess raises her glass. "Your designs are officially out in the wild now, and we all know that with every thoughtful stitch, your exquisitely designed gowns will make every bride feel like a queen on her wedding day."

"Cheers to Emma Belle Bridal!" everyone shouts.

Jess hushes everyone with her hands. "And, even with all this excitement, we didn't forget that today is another special day."

The gathered group parts and a person from the venue's catering team wheels out a cart with a large white cake with sparklers on it. There's a topper with a gown similar to one in my collection. The icing work is impeccable. It's beautiful, but it also looks lonely on there. A bride without a groom.

The crowd around me sings a joyous and off-key happy birthday song that should make me giggle, but right now my brain is racing a mile a minute trying to process the highs and lows of the last ten minutes. It's giving me whiplash.

I manage to fill my lungs with enough air to blow out the candles and everyone cheers.

In a daze, I raise my glass and swallow back the entire contents. The group disperses to start breaking down the show, but Jess grabs my arm.

She must see the shock on my face.

"Are you freaking out? It's not crazy that everyone loved it. We knew they would. Now it's official." Her smile drops when she sees my non-reaction. "What's wrong?"

I hand her my phone, the screen still lit with Alec and Brecken's beaming faces.

Her eyes widen as she reads the caption. "Oh, fuck."

I reach for the champagne bottle she's holding, and begin to chug it.

CHAPTER 2

Griffin

"What do they put in this shit?" Reggie scrubs at his cheek with a makeup wipe. "Permanent marker?"

"It's a good thing it's not on your dick, then." Dallas laughs from where he's lacing up his boots.

"I'd take lipstick any day over the rash Kenny boy got from the last fan girl he slept with." Reggie grins, still scrubbing his red-stained cheek.

"It was an allergic reaction to the metal of her tongue ring," Ken pipes up from where he's buttoning his vest across the room.

"Fuck. That's messed up." Dallas chuckles. "Was it good at least? I've heard a tongue ring on your dick is fucking out of this world."

"Yeah, it was fucking cool until I broke out in hives." Ken laughs like it was no big deal his dick swelled up for hours and I had to take him to the hospital.

"Better make sure her mouth is pure platinum before you dive in next time, bro." Dallas claps Ken on the shoulder before jogging over to the vanity to check his hair.

"Yo, Griffin." He catches my eyes in the mirror. "You going to get ready or what?"

11

I drop my feet off the stool I've propped them up on and stand to move toward my locker. Even with the changes in routines and various costumes over the years, I could get ready in my sleep. Whether it be my solo teacher routine, the rough riders trio I perform with Dallas and Mike, or the group closing number with trench coats and umbrellas, Rainin' Men—it's the signature performance that our revue is known for. Five years ago, our choreographer, Rita, introduced the element of rain on stage. She had watched *Flashdance* a few too many times, and wanted to emulate the water bucket scene, except with rain constantly pouring down on us for nearly three minutes of the routine.

That first week we learned the routine, we had guys falling left and right. Romeo, who's now retired, shattered his tailbone, and Dax hurt his shoulder when he wiped out on the wet floor. It was made clear that if you couldn't dance the routine with the water safely, then this job wasn't cut out for you. While some of the guys dance because they like the attention, most of us are on the revue for the money, so I quickly worked to engineer a slip-proof sole that gives better traction that could fit onto our dance shoes and outfitted all the guys' shoes with it.

"Griffin doesn't have to primp like you clowns. He's naturally good-looking." Mike raises his chin to give me a kissy face and a wink.

All I can do is grin and shake my head at him. "Thanks, man. I always appreciate the compliments."

"Naturally good-looking and *straight*, Mike." Dallas smirks.

"I don't know." Mike grabs his trench coat from his locker and slides his muscular arms into it. "I haven't seen him take any girls home like the rest of you fools, so I'm still thinking there's a chance."

Before I can respond, Dallas stands up from the mirror. "That's because Griffin is too good for the fan girls."

He's right. Aside from Mike, who is gay, but gets his fair share of hookups from men that frequent our shows, I'm the only one of our crew that hasn't taken home a woman from a show. It's a rule of mine. A rule I put in place when I started dancing with the Rainin' Men male revue eight years ago. At that time, there was a girl in my life that took precedence over any biological urge I had—my sister, Sophie.

I pull off my t-shirt, ignore Mike's whistle and start the act of getting dressed for the group's opening number. Tear-away pants, an easy-open vest, Velcro bowtie and shirt cuffs.

For a lot of the guys, dancing is an extension of their social life. A way to start their night, before indulging in alcohol and women, or men, Mike's preference. They dance, hit The Strip to party, then nurse their hangover until they do it all over again the next night. I've never been a partier. Not bragging, because there were plenty of times in my early twenties that I wanted to be a normal guy with no responsibility to anyone but myself, but where my parents had failed us, I refused to fail Sophie.

When I'm in wardrobe for work, I become someone else. An alternate persona. The charming flirt that entertains the audience during every show isn't real. He's the façade that I developed to give them what they're here for—fantasy, escape, a good time.

A Saturday night in Vegas doesn't mean much because every night in Vegas is someone's birthday, girls' night out, or bachelorette party, but still, weekend audiences have an added intensity.

We perform Tuesday through Saturday nights with double feature shows on Friday and Saturday for three-month stints, and get two weeks off between productions. I'm ready for a break.

"But isn't every woman a fan of our show?" Dallas asks. "I mean we've got the muscles, the moves and if DJ Vince gets his head out of his ass, we've got the music."

"Are you talking about how you missed your curtain time last week? It's not Vince's fault you were hooking up with a woman from the previous show in the bathroom."

Listening to their antics, I shake my head, fasten my bowtie and cuffs, then close my locker. In years, I'm not that much older than most of the guys, but as the oldest now, and most experienced in the business, I've become the self-appointed big brother of the group. A role I'm familiar with.

It's not my personality to be rowdy like the other guys, constantly working each other up and trying to outdo one another. When Chad, Romeo as he was known on the stage, stopped dancing, I became the oldest and most experienced guy on the revue. I'm only thirty, but they give me shit about being the old man. I don't feel old, but to some of these young twenty-somethings, I am.

Since I started dancing with Rainin' Men, I've had a singular goal. To put Sophie through school. To see her graduate college and start her career.

The money I've made here over the years has afforded me that.

My eyes slide across the room to the guys horsing around. They've got Ken in a headlock trying to make him eat some weird looking substance from Dallas's bag just as Rita, the revue's manager and choreographer, bounds through the door.

"All right, guys, listen up. Jackson pulled his groin last night," Rita's words are interrupted by several hoots and hollers, *whoo, shit* and *yeah he did*, "and he won't be dancing tonight," Rita finishes, her eyes narrowed on the interrupters. "I know you're excited for your friend that he had a fun night, but now he's missing the bonus that goes with tonight's shows."

"Griffin." Rita's eyes find me. "You'll take point on the closer. Dallas, I need you to take Jackson's construction worker routine. Make sure Vince knows your music so we don't have an issue like last time."

Low chuckles fill the room until Dallas heads them off with a glare.

After the group disbands, Rita signals for me to follow her to the office.

She drops into the chair behind the desk, then pulls out an envelope and hands it to me.

My fingers grasp the paper, noticing my name scrawled across the front, before tucking it between my palm and my thigh.

"Open it now." She nods toward the envelope.

I groan like a teenager whose mom just told them to pick up their room. That's the kind of relationship Rita and I have. She mothers all the guys, but to me, she isn't a second mom, she's the mom I never had.

I slide a finger under the sealed flap, causing it to tear.

It's a card. And inside, a handful of one-hundred-dollar bills.

"What is this?" I ask.

"We took up a collection. We know you're not much for a goodbye party, but we figured you could use the money to buy a suit or something. High-powered lawyers need nice suits." She smiles. "Ones that don't tear away."

"I'm not a high-powered lawyer." Rita's projection of my future is premature.

"Yet," she argues.

"I haven't even gotten my results."

"You'll pass." She smiles. "Terrence won't live to hear that his best student didn't pass on the first try."

Terrence is Rita's husband. He's a lawyer, thirty years at his practice, and a tenured professor at Boyd School of Law at the University of Nevada-Las Vegas (UNLV). He's also been my mentor through law school.

I met Terrence eight years ago when I started at the revue. Rita likes to get all the guys together at her house for a monthly meal and what she calls team building. She cooks enough food for an army, enchiladas are her specialty and they're to die for.

Besides feeding us a homecooked meal, it's her way of checking in with everyone. She knows we're grown men, but some of us don't have families nearby or at all. Ken is from South Africa and isn't able to visit family during the holidays. Rita and Terrence have become surrogate parents for many of us. Terrence has become my mentor and if—when—I pass the bar exam, I've already got a position with his firm.

Rita stands and I follow suit.

"How are you feeling about tonight?" she asks.

"It's time to move on, but I can say I'll miss seeing you every day."

She motions me in for a hug.

"You are trading me for Terrence. That's enough of a reason to be melancholy."

She's teasing, but her warm embrace has my throat tightening. I can't see her face, but her body shakes and she sniffles against my chest. Rita's a tough lady so seeing her emotions get the best of her makes me even more grateful that I've had someone like her in my life.

We finally pull apart, both of us overwhelmed by the moment.

Rita shakes her head and laughs, wiping her tears. "You better get going."

"Yeah." I sniff and nod, moving toward the door.

"And Griffin?" My hand catches the door frame on my way out so I can turn back to see Rita. "Try to have fun out there tonight."

I nod, then hustle back to the locker room to put the card away.

Five minutes later, the curtain lifts on our opening number. The theater is dark, the audience cast out by the blinding stage lights, but I can still hear them. The women, and men, that are paying my bills, Sophie's college tuition, and keeping my aspirations for a different life alive. When the music starts, a loud thumping bass that pulses like a sexual climax, my body takes over. The dance moves I've rehearsed and performed a thousand times. I don't have to think about them anymore. My shirt comes off and the hours in the gym are immediately recognized by the crowd of screaming females donning sashes and tiaras, and sipping on their overpriced cocktails. My hips roll and thrust sugges-tively, one hand snakes down my bare chest, eliciting catcalls. I've learned over the years I can look past them, not seeing anyone in particular, yet look like I'm giving them each a personal caress with my eyes. It's a learned skill. One that Chad taught me. His ability to be aloof, just out of anyone's reach, is a honed skill. One that has served me well over the years. Not making any personal connections, in the audience or elsewhere, that was a life lesson courtesy of my parents.

Seventy-five minutes later, I'm half-naked and soaking wet. The final number behind us, we have forty-five minutes until we do it all over again. I grab a water bottle and protein bar off the snack table backstage. Rita insists we refuel between performances so we don't get a muscle cramp while dancing. It's happened a few times to guys over the years.

"Killer show, boys." Ken slings an arm over my shoulder. He's soaking wet and panting. "We were more on beat with you at the point tonight. Any chance we can convince you to stay?"

Rita's lips twitch before her eyes find mine. I give a shake of my head.

She gives me a small smile before she moves toward the

door and addresses the group. "Dry off and make sure those wet clothes get into the laundry hamper. I'm not your maid."

"Thanks, man." I pat Ken on the chest before I slip out of his hold. "It was nice to go out on top tonight."

On my way to the locker room, I twist open the cap on my water and chug the whole thing down. The locker room is always calmer after the first performance. Less talking and messing around. We've gotten a workout in now and need to rebuild our energy for the second show. Out of respect for the late show crowd, we strip down and shower, so we're fresh as daisies. Sounds bizarre, but one time a woman I was giving a lap dance shoved her nose in my armpit. People are fucking weird.

"Don't the ladies know you have to come to the late show if you want to party after? That woman in the red dress was fine as hell, but I can't make commitments at eight thirty," Dallas says. "The night is too young."

Once I've toweled off and dressed, I head for the stairs. I'm on the roof in two minutes, with the door propped open so I can get back in. The first few times I came up here I was nervous I would get stuck out here like the guy in *Hangover*. Von, the theater's custodian, found me up here once and gave me a key, just in case.

Even with the sun set, the ninety-degree day hasn't lessened much. It's got to be eighty degrees still, and I'm going to be sweating if I stay out too long, but I needed to get away from the group. I pull my phone out and call Sophie.

"Hey." She's breathless and there's shuffling in the background.

"Hey, how's packing going?" I ask.

She groans. "I'm sitting on my suitcase to make it close."

"It's two weeks, not two years."

"I know, but I want to be prepared for every occasion."

"The occasion is your final practicum and project presentation. Have you been studying for that?"

"Yes, Griffin. I'm an adult, I've got it under control."

This is the part I hate most about our situation. We're eight years apart, but sometimes it feels like twenty. I'd loved to have been the fun-loving big bro that snuck her into bars or covered for her when she was late for curfew, but instead I've had to be Grouchy Griffin, as she used to call me in high school, enforcing curfew and thwarting her dating efforts. Not because she was a troublemaker, the opposite in fact, but because I was terrified, and still am, that something might happen to her.

"And I can't study every minute of every day. Most of my exams are practical and I could only do a mock presentation in the mirror a certain number of times before I started to feel like a deranged person. I already have my final event board complete and I have one budget to edit."

I think about the hard work Sophie has put into her Hospitality and Event Planning degree. How having her graduate will take a small weight off my back and finally allow me to focus on something other than dancing to provide for us.

She continues. "And it's my last few weeks of college. Now that I know I'm going to graduate, I'm allowed to have some fun, right?"

"Fine. But not too much fun. You need to stay focused on graduating."

"Yes, sir." I think I can hear her saluting me through the phone. "How's The Strip tonight?"

I look out on The Strip. The flashing lights of the casinos. The Bellagio fountains dancing in the distance. There's so much going on, yet the visual is calming. It looks the same as it always does.

"Busy. Lots of bachelorette parties as usual. Should be a good night."

"Maybe you'll loosen up and have some fun yourself?" Sophie teases.

"Doubt it," I mutter. It's impossible to not feel like a grandpa around the other guys.

"You can try." She sighs. "I'm done packing for tonight. I'm going over to TK's. I love you, G."

"I love you, too. I'll see you in the morning."

I drop my phone back into my pocket.

Standing here in this moment, I know that after tonight things will change. It's a change I've been patiently waiting for. Since the day I took over guardianship of Sophie. The day my mom, six months sober, got T-boned by a drunk driver.

The silver lining being that I was eighteen, allowing Sophie and me to avoid foster care. My father was long gone, he hadn't made an appearance since my fifth birthday, and we never really knew who Sophie's dad was.

With Sophie only a few weeks from graduating college, I know that all the hard work and sacrifice I've made over the last twelve years has been worth it. And, for once, I'll be able to make decisions about my life that aren't reliant on someone else.

CHAPTER 3
Emma

I've never been a big gambler, but tonight, I've discovered I like penny slots. There's something so satisfying about pulling the lever on a slot machine. So much promise in those few seconds when the three lines of objects spin at speeds which make their shapes unrecognizable. I've been sitting at this machine for a good hour now. Dottie, the little blue-haired lady to my right, is from Cleveland, she's eighty-seven and she's on a roll.

After the birthday celebration backstage at my fashion show, I helped my team pack up the gowns, as much as they would let me, and then Jess and I had headed straight for the bar and slot machines. The rest of my team wanted to celebrate with a late dinner and drinks, and while I adore them, I just couldn't handle an evening of smiling and pretending everything was fine. I insisted they go ahead without me. Jess insisted that she stay with me and she's been watching me like a hawk.

Alec is engaged to another woman.

The taste in my mouth is bitter.

My feelings are all over the place.

It should have been me.

That's not right either.

Jess props herself up against the side of my machine. "Okay, I think we should call it a night. We can order up room service, put on our PJs and watch *Dirty Dancing*."

She's just listed all my favorite things, but honestly at this moment I'm afraid if I close the door on the chaos of the casino, the clinking of coins and pinging of machines, the flashing lights, and really process Alec's engagement, I'll lose my mind. That, and I'm a bottle of champagne in, and it's my birthday. I refuse to let this be the story of my thirtieth birthday, jilted and drunkenly watching Patrick Swayze gyrate.

The breakup with Alec had been hard, but every day since I'd found confidence that it was the right thing. We weren't meant to be. We wanted different things. But seeing him happy and engaged to someone else has ripped open that barely healed wound. It's the rejection that hits the hardest. The confirmation that for all of Alec's inability to commit to me, it wasn't commitment that he didn't want, it was *me*.

I know now that we weren't right for each other. I don't want him back, but was it necessary for him to turn around and propose to his girlfriend of two months...on my birthday?! Maybe that's what's hitting the hardest.

My birthday. Another year around the sun. I'm thirty and so much further from finding my happily ever after than I was a year ago.

"I'm not ready to give up yet," I tell her, then grip the neck of the champagne bottle I've got tucked between my legs and take a big gulp. I'm still wearing my mom's wedding dress. The hem hiked up and the excess material pooled between my legs. It's probably a wrinkled mess, but I don't care. Any hope I had of walking down the aisle in it is gone. It clearly did not bring me the luck that it brought my mom. It being vintage Dior, I can't exactly light it on fire, but after tonight it will need to be cleaned, saged and returned to its box in storage, never to be spoken of again.

In my clutch, my phone buzzes. Likely another birthday text from a friend or family member. There are three more hours left in this day. I might just spend them staring at this slot machine, drinking warm champagne and listening to Dottie ramble.

"My second husband was a lawyer. I helped him through law school, worked two jobs to pay his tuition. He ended up leaving me for his secretary."

"Lawyers are the worst," I commiserate.

I drop another penny into the slot and pull the lever. The wheels spin, cherries appear on the first two wheels, giving me hope, but a number seven appears on the last wheel, denying me a win.

"Love is like a playing a slot machine," Dottie chimes in. "You invest time and effort, not to mention money, and all you can do is hope that it eventually pays off. I hate to break it to you, dear, but the odds are against us." Dottie shares another philosophical anecdote about love. She's a love cynic, married and divorced three times. Her fourth husband just left her for a seventy-five-year-old water aerobics instructor, so she cleaned out his bank account and jumped on a plane to Vegas.

She's the perfect person to commiserate with. Dottie understands what it's like to put yourself out there time and time again only to have it end in disappointment. We're kindred spirits, her and I.

Jess narrows her eyes at the sweet old woman, then turns back to me.

"You and Alec were not meant to be. You said so yourself. The timing of his engagement is awful, but when you're ready you'll find someone."

I appreciate Jess's optimism.

After previous breakups, I've shared it. Instead of dwelling on a failed relationship, I've always been willing and ready to move forward, onto the next. Truth be told, I'm tired of it all. Dating. Love. Giving someone your heart just so they can hand it back to you with scars and bruises. Hearts should be like vacation rentals and require a damage deposit for use. Must return in original condition.

Alec is the latest in a string of committed relationships that I thought would last forever. It's because that's what I want, to find love and get married. Watching my parents' relationship, seeing the love they still have for each other over thirty years later, that's what I want. When I get married, it will be forever.

"Maybe it's time to let go of my dream."

Jess looks alarmed. "You can't let Alec moving on make you change what you want. That's not being true to yourself."

"No. I still want those things, but maybe I need to relax the timeline. Take the pressure off." I take another sip. "Date more than one guy at a time. Play the field." My hand holding the champagne bottle flings out to the side and some bubbly splashes out of it. "Sow my wild oats."

"Your oats are not wild, Emma. They're serial monogamists."

I look at Jess's concerned face.

"Well, that needs to change," I say, my attention drifting to the flashing billboard on the far side of the casino. The screen goes black and then a group of men wearing trench coats appear, their faces bowed to the ground as they tip their hats down. It flashes again and their chests are bare. There's another flash coordinated with hip thrusting and a final flash with Rainin' Men scrawled across the screen. A smile pulls at the corners of my mouth.

"I have an idea."

Jess's eyes narrow with doubt. "What can be better than room service and Patrick Swayze?"

I don't respond, I'm too busy dumping the rest of my pennies into Dottie's bucket. "Light 'em up, Dottie!" Her crooked fingers give me a wave of gratitude, before I grab

Jess's arm and lead her across the casino. A quick search on my phone indicates that there is a Rainin' Men show in twenty minutes, and lucky for us, the theater is an escalator ride away.

"What are we doing?" Jess calls from behind me, but I don't have to respond because a moment later we're in front of the theater. There's not much of a line. It appears most people have already purchased their tickets and been seated.

"Two, please." I slide my credit card under the plastic screen to the box office attendant. "You know how I feel about Mr. Swayze, but I think we need something new tonight."

"Are we seriously going to a male revue show?" Jess's eyes are wide, but I can tell by the way she's fighting a smile that she's enticed by the idea.

"Yes."

Jess nods in approval and accepts the ticket I hand her.

The man at the door tears off the end of our tickets, and after an ID check, fits a bracelet around each of our wrists. He motions us to go through the lobby and toward another door. Inside that door, the theater lights are low and thanks to the sconces on the walls, there's a red glow to the room.

"How many in your party?" the usher asks.

"Two," I announce.

The usher eyes me and Jess. Or at least I think he's looking at us collectively until I catch him checking out my dress.

"Bachelorette?" he asks.

"Um…" I hesitate, but then nod excitedly. "Yes!"

He motions toward the door. "Right this way."

"Emma," Jess hisses from behind as we follow the usher toward our seats.

"What? They give you free shit sometimes. We might as well see what they have to offer. Besides, it's my birthday."

I realize as we pass through the crowd that among the groups of women, there are others dressed similar to me, bachelorettes decked out in skimpy white cocktail dresses and sequined rompers wearing sashes and tiaras. Large groups of women here celebrating with brides-to-be.

Maybe it's because he feels sorry for me, a bachelorette with one friend at her party, or maybe they're the only seats left in the theater, but he points to a small table and two chairs at the center of the stage in the front row.

"See?" I beam at Jess. She looks less enthusiastic.

I glance around. The throngs of women there to celebrate their impending weddings hits me hard. That, and the bottle of champagne I drank. I'm suddenly feeling the need for fresh air. A waitress walks by with a tray and I wave to get her attention.

"I'll be with you in a minute, hun."

"Actually, I was wondering if there is a place to get fresh air." I wave my hand in front of my face, fanning myself. "Too much champagne."

The waitress's response is quick, she's probably afraid the longer I stand here the higher the chances she'll be cleaning up vomit off the floor. It's not even late but we're in Vegas, she's probably used to people drinking and partying all day. "Back through the lobby, last door on the left, there's a staircase."

"Thanks."

"Don't shut the door, it'll lock!" she calls from behind me.

The staircase is easy to find and once I'm outside, taking in fresh, non-circulated casino air, I take a deep breath. Heeding the waitress's advice, I keep my body positioned between the open door and the frame. Vegas is lit up around me, twinkling lights reminding me of the camera flashes at my fashion show, the elation I felt when I walked the runway behind my designs, and for a moment, I'm at peace. Then I ruin all the good feelings by pulling out my phone to look at Alec's post again.

Do I miss him or do I miss the thought that he was the one? That I had invested over two years of my life into a man that I thought was going to be my husband to find out that he didn't feel the same way? That starting over scares me more than being with the wrong person?

"Brecken. What kind of a name is that?" I mutter. That's all I can come up with. Making fun of her name that is actually kind of adorable.

"I should congratulate the happy couple." I tap on the comment bubble and start typing.

"TWO MONTHS!! WTF!!!" I say as I type it out.

From somewhere in front of me someone clears their throat.

Caught off guard, my phone slips out of my hand and I lunge forward in an attempt to catch it. With my body no longer being used as a door stop, the metal door slams closed behind me. The ominous sound of an automatic lock clicking into place doesn't stop me from checking the handle anyway. Yup, locked. Oh shit. The waitress said not to close the door. But then I remember the throat clearing and my attention is drawn behind me. A man has stepped from the dark corners of the rooftop toward the door where the single overhead bulb illuminates him just enough to display his large frame.

"Sorry, I didn't mean to startle you." He reaches out a hand. My brain isn't receiving messages as to what for because it's too distracted by the cords of muscle that make up this man's forearm. The light brown hair and the prominent vein that runs the length of said arm are the ultimate accessories to his god-like forearms. It's a body part that shouldn't make me flustered, but I've never seen forearms like his before. Surely this is some illusion, a trick of light or a flex pose made possible by the weight of my phone, a mere five ounces. That's the reason he's got his arm outstretched. "I thought you were talking to someone. I wanted you to know you weren't alone up here."

"I was talking to myself," I say, finally accepting my

phone. "Not in a weird way. I was processing out loud. I do that sometimes. Okay, a lot."

His response is a deep chuckle, which draws my attention upward to his face.

How have I not even looked at his face? Oh, that's right, I was too busy drooling over the forearm porn he was providing me with. My eyes roam up his body. And in case anyone's wondering, he's no Popeye. His forearms are perfectly proportionate to the rest of his muscular frame. He definitely works out. Maybe even plays a sport. Back to his face. It's good. Better than good. Square jaw, defined nose, enough scruff on his chin to tell the world he's got plenty of testosterone pumping through his veins. Thick, sandy brown hair that's long enough to have a slight wave in it. I can't tell what color his eyes are in the dim light, but when he smiles, they fill with humor and a dimple appears in his left cheek.

I know that because he's smiling at me right now.

"It's my birthday," I announce out of nowhere. He's probably thrilled that he's stuck out here with an excellent conversationalist like myself.

"Happy birthday."

"Thanks." The goofy smile that forms on my face is surprising. Why is this guy making me feel giddy? Maybe it's the champagne.

I realize that I'm a little too excited about being trapped on a rooftop with a stranger. A man with muscles like that could easily overpower me, yet there's nothing about this man's demeanor that makes me feel that way. In fact, it's the opposite. The way he stands with his hands buried in his front pockets, casual and sweet. I'd expect a guy that looks like him to be cocky and self-possessed. My eyes drop to his crotch, then quickly away. Why did I just do that? I was thinking about being cocky and that made me think of…my eyes lower again to the bulge in his jeans. The alcohol running through my veins apparently gives them free rein to ogle men's crotches.

"Did I just lock us out here?" I motion to the shut door behind me.

"Nah. I've got a key."

"Oh." I nod. That should be a relief, yet I'm suddenly disappointed that we aren't stuck out here together. That this isn't some fated romantic encounter destined for me on my birthday.

"So, we won't need to lie in each other's arms to stay warm when the desert temps fall later tonight?"

When I realize what I just said, my cheeks burn with embarrassment, or maybe that's the champagne gone to my head. And this guy's sexy smile has gone straight to my lady parts.

"Or use our phones to call someone to open the door?" I can hear the teasing in his voice.

"Yeah, that either." Should I start plotting how I'm going to capture his phone and throw it off the side of the building?

I walk farther out onto the roof, taking in the lights from The Strip all around us. He turns to follow my movement.

"I'm Emma."

"Griffin." He's watching me carefully.

"Nice to meet you, Griffin."

"Likewise." His kind eyes search mine. "You okay?"

It's the strangest feeling. The sudden urge to tell this man everything that has happened tonight. Maybe it's the alcohol, maybe it's loneliness. A feeling that has wrapped its way around my heart long before I found out about Alec's engagement. I can't explain it, but I force myself to keep quiet. The last thing this guy wants is to hear about my problems. He's in Vegas, and like most people, probably out looking for a good time.

"Oh, yeah. I'm not going to throw myself off the roof or anything."

"Glad to hear." He smiles, his eyes drifting over me with careful consideration, pausing at my lips for a moment longer than the rest.

"I just needed some air." I exhale, then take a deep inhale.

"Me, too." He takes a few steps forward until he's in line with me. I can feel his gaze on the side of my face now.

"I was brainstorming a response to my ex-boyfriend's engagement post." I tuck my phone back in my clutch. So much for not spilling my problems to a stranger.

"How about 'congratulations?'"

"We've been broken up for two months. And he chose to propose to her on my *birthday*?"

He grimaces. "How long were you together?"

"Over two years. I thought he was the one."

"Okay, yeah, that's shitty."

I sigh. "I need to forget about him. Not let it ruin my night. It's my birthday *and* I just had my first runway show."

"Are you a model?" Griffin looks me up and down, probably wondering how a shorty like me would be walking a runway. The five-inch heels I'd need to meet the standard height requirement would cause me to break both my ankles. It's a question I get asked a lot, with my mom being tall, but I got my dad's genes.

I shake my head. "A designer. Bridal gowns. I'm visiting from New York for the Blushing Bride Convention."

He points to my dress. "Did you design that?"

"No. This is my mom's wedding dress. It's vintage Dior." I look down and run a hand over the silk material at my hip. When I look back up, I expect to find him studying my dress, but instead, his eyes are back on my lips. A wave of desire washes over me at the thought of tilting my face up and letting his lips settle over mine.

"I don't know much about fashion."

"That's okay."

He pulls his gaze from me and back out to the city lights below.

"So, New York, huh?"

"Have you been?" I ask.

"No. I've barely been out of Nevada." He runs a hand through his hair and I'm captivated by the visual of his biceps flexing against his sleeve.

"Really?" My surprise is evident, my tone borderline condescending. Griffin laughs out of his nose. I can tell he's embarrassed.

I need to remember that not everyone grew up with a runway model mom and a dad who is a professional photographer. Their careers took us all over the world. I'd been to nine different countries before I was nine years old.

"I'm sorry, I didn't mean..." Instinctively my hand reaches for Griffin's arm in a comforting gesture. It's meant to be a reassuring gesture, but when my fingers meet his warm skin, feel the firm cords of muscle flex beneath them, my entire body starts to tingle.

I'm a nurturer by nature. That's probably why Alec stayed even when he realized we weren't right for each other. He liked being taken care of, his needs met and put first. He liked to brag to his friends that I was a chill, low-maintenance girlfriend. That it didn't take much to make me happy. I was always proud that I wasn't the needy girlfriend that he said his dating friends complained about, but that badge of honor made it hard for me to tell Alec what I needed from him. And when low maintenance turned into no maintenance, I felt like I was painted into a corner. After giving and giving, Alec had been shocked by my 'sudden' demand for more attention and care in our relationship.

I'd simply ask for Alec to show more affection when we were out to dinner or at an event. He'd say he wasn't into PDA. I'd argue that PDA and sweet gestures that acknowledge my presence are two different things. It's clear now, from his ability to move on so quickly, that he wasn't into *me.*

When Griffin's eyes lift from my hand to my face, I immediately pull my hand away.

"Sorry. I'm a handsy person." I realize how weird that sounds. "I gesture with my hands and touch people a lot." Not much better of an explanation. Griffin's eyebrows shoot up, but the rest of his face is unreadable. If his skin is tingling from our interaction, he's much better at hiding it than I am.

"It's fine." He turns his gaze back out to the city. "Everything that matters to me has always been right here."

He says it so reverently, I have to wonder if he's talking about a woman, someone he cares deeply for. The loving look on his face has my ribs tightening with jealousy, which is absurd because I just met this man and have absolutely no claim to him.

That pang of loneliness is back. It's a feeling I've had even before Alec and I broke up. There's nothing worse than being in a relationship, yet feeling completely alone.

Champagne and curiosity get the better of me. "A woman?"

Griffin smiles but shakes his head. "Well, I guess she is a woman. My sister, Sophie. We've been on our own since my mom died twelve years ago. She's in college at UNLV. She'll graduate in a few weeks." He runs a hand through his hair.

My eyes zero in on his empty ring finger. That doesn't mean he's not taken. But surely, he would have mentioned a girlfriend or fiancée when I asked.

I follow his gaze out to the lights below. The Bellagio fountains are going off in the distance. I take in another deep breath, enjoying the view and the quiet presence of Griffin beside me.

This view is captivating. It reminds me of why people come to Vegas. Other than gambling and its shows, Vegas is a symbol of letting loose, enjoying the moment and not worrying about tomorrow. I want that. I want to forget about Alec. Not worry about anything but tonight and the moment I'm in.

Griffin cuts through our comfortable silence. "I'm sorry you're having a rough night."

It's not a casual 'sorry' that someone would convey to a stranger. The way he's intently looking at me makes me feel like he truly cares. Like he would do everything in his power to fix it if he could. The warmth behind his green eyes—yes, they're green, like olives in a dirty martini—is overwhelming.

I shrug, not wanting his words to penetrate the champagne fog I've been operating under for the past few hours. "It's okay. I'm determined to have fun tonight."

My phone rings. It's Jess. Griffin pulls his gaze away, giving me privacy to answer.

"Where are you? The show is going to start in a few minutes."

"Oh, right. Yeah, I'll be there in a minute." I drop my phone back in my clutch.

Griffin glances at his watch.

"I've got to go," he says.

"Me, too."

We make our way over to the door and I wait while Griffin unlocks it.

I hesitate. Would asking what he's doing later be too forward? It is my night. I should be celebrating the success of my new line's launch. And then there's the fact that it's my birthday and I want to push Alec's engagement news as far away as possible. Griffin seems like a nice guy. The kind of guy I could have a little fun with. Before I can get the words out, he turns to say goodbye.

"Have a good night, Emma," his deep voice is smooth, like a caress. Then, he's moving quickly down the stairs.

"You, too," I finally call out when he's at the bottom, but he doesn't look back.

On my way back into the theater, I try to muster up the enthusiasm I previously had for the show. No matter how hard I try, as I walk through the lobby, my head is on a swivel looking for Griffin. Maybe he's one of the doormen and was taking a break on the roof? Maybe he's into half-naked men and he's here to watch the show? Could he be gay? Oh, no. Maybe I've been out of the dating scene for so long my ability to tell a straight man from a gay man is not intact.

After weaving through the crowd, I make it back to our table where Jess is waiting with our drinks.

"Geez, I thought you'd ditched me." She hands me a bottle of water, but I reach for her flute of champagne. I'm still buzzing from my interaction with Griffin.

The theater lights dim and a loud techno beat starts, drawing our attention to the stage in front of us.

"No, but I met a guy."

"What? Where?" She glances around the theater, but it's pointless because the audience is dark now. The only light is the spotlight pointing down on the center of the stage. "This place is filled with estrogen."

"Welcome to Rainin' Men. We hope you enjoy tonight's performance," the speaker announces overhead.

I feel antsy. I take a sip of champagne and try to muster up the enthusiasm I once had for this show.

The curtain lifts to reveal five men onstage, fog billowing around them, their bodies shadowed by the lighting backstage. Their heads are bowed. The music stops for a beat. The audience is quiet, with the exception of a few catcalls in the back, everyone is poised on the edge of their seat, waiting for the action they know is coming.

A second later the music drops back in, the spotlight pops and the men's heads lift. It only takes me a second to recognize him. There in the middle of the pack, rolling his hips to the music, is Griffin.

CHAPTER 4

Griffin

"Did you see that pretty little thing in the front row?" Dallas crows as soon as we hit backstage. "She thinks she wants to get married, but one night with me and she's going to change her mind."

There's no need to ask who he is talking about. I already know. It's Emma. The crazy thing is before the lights hit and I looked up, it was as if I could feel her presence. There was an awareness that pricked at my skin the moment I stepped out onstage. The same buzz of electricity I felt when she put her hand on my arm. The second I looked up, our gazes locked. I saw the way her eyes widened and her lips parted in surprise.

No matter how hard I tried, I couldn't keep my eyes off her. I figured she was here for the show, but I didn't expect her to be sitting up front, her eyes following my every move, her tongue darting out to wet her lips when I ripped my shirt off.

I don't get involved with Dallas's conquests. I come to work, perform, then go home. All of the women I've seen him take home after a show, ring or no ring, are more than willing, but having him talk about Emma makes my blood boil. *She's single*, I remind myself. *Maybe she would have a good time with*

35

Dallas. My jaw clenches at the thought. Playing devil's advocate is only making me hate the situation even more.

"You need to stop trying to sleep with married women," I grit out through clenched teeth. I'm facing my locker, getting changed for my solo routine. Dallas must not see how much I dislike the thought of him pursuing Emma.

"They're not married yet. And 'trying' would indicate I wasn't successful." Dallas smirks. "You've got to give me more credit than that."

"Lay off the bachelorettes," Ken tosses out. "There are a hundred women out there with no ring or white dress."

"You know I like a challenge." Dallas smirks again.

"Here's a challenge," I say, "don't sleep with a woman from the show tonight."

Dallas turns his attention to me. "Why do you care, G? You're never at the after parties anyways."

"I don't," I lie, because if there's anything that I know about Dallas, it is he's competitive as fuck. He'll pursue a woman another guy's into just for kicks. He's an immature prick that I try not to associate myself with other than our work on the show. "It makes the revue look bad."

"That's not what all the satisfied customers tell me," Dallas gloats.

Rita pops her head around the corner. "Griffin, you're on in five."

"Thanks, Rita." I tilt my head side to side, trying to ease the tension in my shoulders that arguing with Dallas has put there.

I slide on my blazer and button it, then grab the wire-framed glasses from the top shelf. I exit the locker room without saying another word to Dallas. There's no point in trying to reason with him. I know how he operates. Further discussion will only pique his interest more.

Backstage, Reggie greets me with a nod and a fist bump as

he exits after his fireman routine. The crew resets the stage for my performance, wrapping up the firehose Reggie used to tease his 'hot seat'—the audience member who is singled out by the performer to get a personal dance onstage—with and sliding my desk into place. Chad's voice booms onstage, the audience's laughter, and whistles, indications that he's doing his job as MC.

While Rita likes to freshen up routines from time to time, she hasn't changed mine. She knows I like the habit of it. And she knows how to play on our strengths when choreographing the routines. Giving a playful guy like Reggie props like the hose to bring his performance to life, having a shy guy like Ken do a slow strip tease that drives women wild, and having Dallas's routine move through the crowd to appease his overinflated ego. As for me, I've channeled Grouchy Griffin into a stern teacher, here to take disciplinary action.

Seconds later, I'm seated with my feet propped on the desk and a book in my hands, and the curtain goes up.

On most nights, I have the ushers pre-select the woman that I will put in the 'hot seat.' It makes it less personal. There's no connection, just a random woman that appears onstage.

Tonight, it's going to be different. I made the decision on the walk from the locker room to the stage.

I can see Chad now, moving through the audience to make his selection. With two fingers in my mouth, I whistle to get his attention. He turns around in time to see me stop in front of Emma. I've never done this before, but somehow Chad understands my intentions. I know this because he starts to move back toward the stage where he announces that I've made my selection.

My gaze returns to Emma and I reach for her hand.

Her eyes widen, and her head shakes slightly as she mouths the words 'what are you doing.' But after a glance at her eagerly nodding friend, she takes it and I help her up onstage.

"This is Emma," I announce with my mic. "And it's her birthday."

I glance over at Emma, her cheeks are flush, and though her eyes look like she might want to kill me right now, she's also biting back a smile.

"She is ready to go out and party. But, unfortunately," I say, my voice turning stern, "Emma has detention."

Wild cheers escape the audience. Cue "Bad Teacher."

"Emma didn't bring an apple for the teacher." I pause, letting the audience play up the situation with a chorus of boos. "Instead, she brought me a peach." Taking her elbow in my hand, I gently rotate her one hundred and eighty degrees, until her ass is facing the audience. "A juicy, ripe peach," I announce, waving a hand near Emma's gorgeous ass.

High-pitched screams fill the theater.

I turn my mic off, then lead a tipsy Emma over to the desk. She sways one way, but my firm grip on her elbow corrects her path. The music, which had faded to the background while I talked, returns to full volume.

"Is this okay?" I ask, uncertainty starting to edge into my brain.

Emma nods in approval. My hands wrap around her waist and lift her to the edge of the desk. "You can touch me if you want, but you don't have to."

It's the standard statement I've told every person I've danced for. It's always up to the woman or man, they can do what they're comfortable with. With Emma, I'm dying for her to touch me. To feel that same electricity I felt when she touched me on the roof.

"Okay." I see the word on her lips more than I hear it. The sound of Emma's voice is lost beneath the music and crowd noise.

Typically, I can do this three minute and thirty-two second

routine in my sleep. I do it twice a night, five nights a week. However, I've never danced for a woman that I know. And that's the strange part, I don't *know* Emma, but talking to her on the roof, hearing the excitement in her voice about her fashion show, and then the sadness about her ex-boyfriend getting engaged, on her birthday no less, I know she's feeling vulnerable right now, and all I want to do is protect her. It's the way I feel about Sophie, except that's not exactly right, because the protectiveness I feel toward Emma is in no way brotherly. The entire time she was talking to me on the roof, I couldn't stop staring at her lips.

That doesn't matter. I can't have her myself, I never cross that line, but the least I can do is prevent Dallas from preying on her tonight. After tonight, she'll be headed back to New York. She's got a successful career to look forward to and hopefully in time she'll find a guy worthy of her attention.

This dance is all I can offer her.

I pull my gaze away from Emma's distracting lips and focus on the routine.

Glasses discarded.

Blazer stripped off.

But when Emma gets playful pulling at my tie, I almost break character and crush my mouth to hers. It would be unprofessional and Rita would disapprove, but maybe it would be worth it since I'll be leaving soon anyway.

It takes me a moment to remember where I am in the routine. To clear the thoughts of what I imagine doing to Emma if there wasn't an audience.

I yank my tie off, followed by my shirt; the snap buttons easily release. This is the point where the women I dance for either giggle and seem shy or put their hands on me and flirt, but Emma looks confused. She's studying me, my face, not my naked torso, like she's trying to figure something out.

"You okay?" I call near her ear to be heard over the music.

A smile spreads across her face, and she nods. "Yeah."

A moment later, her hands find my chest, and the feel of her palms against my skin sends a shockwave of electricity through my body. Her fingers brush against my nipples, then lower, her fingernails lightly scraping against my abdominals. Below my waistband, my cock stirs. The jolt of arousal is surprising. I don't get aroused dancing for random women. This never happens.

The sensation of Emma's hands on me has somehow caused my brain to shut off. The part of my brain where this routine is stored has suddenly become inaccessible. My brain tells my eyes to look away from her, to look at something else to regain my focus, but my brain isn't in charge right now.

All my practiced moves are gone, chased out of my head by the brown-eyed beauty in front of me. Unable to look away from Emma, my rhythm falters.

There's nothing routine about dancing for Emma.

I move through the routine, rolling my hips slowly, leaning in toward Emma's body. Rita's choreography is sexy, designed to give women the fantasy of being with the man on stage, without the consequences of getting physical. It's embarrassing to admit how long it's been since I had sex.

By the time the track hits the last thirty seconds, I'm so turned on thinking about Emma's mouth on me, that I'm full on improvising this routine. I think I'm still dancing and I can vaguely hear the crowd screaming. Until the final chorus hits and I finally remember where I'm at.

"Lean back," I tell her as I move to hover over her.

Emma glances behind her at the wood desk, then slowly lowers her body until she's prone. If I wasn't already distracted by her, seeing her spread out on the desk has my brain working overtime to capture this moment. Her warm eyes on me, the innocent way she bites her lip. I will definitely be jerking off to the thought of Emma later, imagining what she tastes like, how soft her skin would be under my palm, how good it would feel to slide between her legs.

I try to pull my awareness away from her, to focus on the crowd, their excited cheers and screams. While Emma is getting a special dance, the crowd is here for the show, too. But I'm finding it impossible to look at her and not want to know more. To imagine her outside of this theater, in the light of day.

I easily climb on top of the desk, moving over Emma without touching her, into a plank position with my hands outside of her shoulders. My arm and shoulder muscles bear my body's weight. With my elbows bent, I slowly lower down until our faces are inches away. Emma's teeth capture her bottom lip and her eyes close.

"Open your eyes," I say urgently. I want to see her eyes, the way they look up into mine. I've got five seconds to memorize the way she looks underneath me. Before this dance is over and I have to pull away from her.

Emma's eyes pop open on my command and I feel her chest brush against mine with the deep inhale she takes.

It's absurd that I have a strong urge to tell Vince to cut the music and lights. Make everyone go home, so I can continue this moment with Emma in private. I'd tickle her sides, hoping to produce the same genuine laugh that I heard on the roof before I'd pin her arms above her head and devour her mouth, swallow up her infectious laughter so I could save it for a rainy day. Vegas gets less than five inches of rain annually, yet so many times over the years I've felt like I was drowning. Trying to stay afloat. Give Sophie everything our parents couldn't. Having something for myself has never been a priority, and yet I've never wanted anything so bad. Until now.

And just like that, the music fades away and the dance is over. There's no reason for me to remain above Emma, so I push back and off the desk, then help her sit up. The audience is clapping and cheering. Catcalls and whistles ring in my ears. I walk Emma back over to the edge of the stage and help her lower down to her seat.

"Happy Birthday, Emma." I give her a wink. It's what I would do with any other woman I dance for. It makes me feel like I've got the situation under control. That Emma, a woman I've known for ten minutes, hasn't gotten under my skin. Made me wonder what it would be like if I gave in to the urge to have something for myself, even if it was just for tonight.

I shake the thought and turn away from Emma. On my way backstage I run into Dallas. He's ready for his biker performance. I'm satisfied, knowing that he can't choose Emma for his dance.

"Hope you enjoyed that view." Dallas lifts his chin toward the stage. "I know I sure will, later tonight."

He knocks his shoulder into mine before heading out on stage. I'm not a violent man, but it takes everything I have to not yank him back and slam his body into the wall. From the side stage, I watch Chad pick out a woman from the crowd and lead her up to the stage to join Dallas.

Dallas is a punk. Most likely just trying to irk me. I shouldn't let him get under my skin. He's not worth it.

My gaze lands on Emma again. She giggles while her friend whispers something in her ear, then they both turn their attention back to the stage.

I turn away and start walking back to the dressing room, determined to let the moment go and move on.

"Griffin, you coming with us tonight?" Mike halts his movement toward the door.

"Why do you bother asking? He never comes with us." Reggie stops short behind Mike.

"There's a first time for everything." Mike shrugs.

"Besides, the company seems far better tonight. I'm excited to talk with the bridal gown designer. She's going to give me all the gossip on the New York fashion scene."

Mike's announcement catches my attention.

"What?" My brain stops working and my heart seizes in my chest.

"She's a designer and her friend is her assistant," Mike says, "she's the woman you picked for your solo dance. Gorgeous, curvy brunette." He motions his thumb out the door, indicating she's out in the hallway. Adrenaline seeps into my veins. I realize it doesn't matter what I told myself before. I do care that Dallas is trying to hook up with her. Not just because *I* want her, but because he's a jerk that will try to nail her just for the sport of it.

Fuck. Had I really thought that Dallas would drop his interest in Emma after I gave her a solo dance? No. If anything, my desire to make Emma off limits has only made things worse. Now, I imagine he is even more determined. I don't know Emma that well, but I would hope that she can see through his sleazy, fuck boy come ons.

I have two options. Go home, like I do every night after our shows, or go out with the guys with the plan to keep tabs on Emma and her friend, and keep Dallas away from them. I think about the comfort of my routine, how easy it has always been to tell the guys no, how most of them have stopped asking me to hang out. I'm like the parent no one wants chaperoning their school dance. Then, I imagine lying in bed tonight alone, torturing myself with images of Emma and Dallas, dancing together, him touching her.

My stomach roils with the thought. I already know it would be a sleepless night.

Even if I had no interest in Emma myself, I reason, cock-blocking Dallas sounds like a good time.

I grab my jacket. "I'm coming."

"Shit. For real?" Mike calls but I'm already exiting the

locker room. I don't have to go far to find Dallas and the other guys. The music and laughter travels from where they're gathered backstage. Mike was right. There, among the group of women talking with Dallas and Reggie, is Emma.

Her gaze finds mine, and I realize even though I'm annoyed with Dallas and his games, I'm excited to see her. To spend more time with her.

"Hey," I say to the group, running my hand through my freshly showered hair, but my eyes are trained on Emma.

"Hi," she responds, looking at me over the plastic cup she's drinking out of. "Griffin. This is my friend, Jess."

I shake her hand. "Hey, Jess."

"Nice to meet you." She smiles, then flicking her gaze between Emma and me, she replies, "Let's keep it that way."

I chuckle. Maybe Emma doesn't need me after all. It appears watch-dog Jess is on duty as well.

"I'm going to be right over there." Jess nods toward the rest of the group, then moves to join them.

"Are you headed home?" Emma's eyes land on the water bottle in my hands. "The other guys said you never go out after the show."

"They're right." I nod, then uncap my water bottle to take a drink.

"Oh." The disappointment in her voice is evident. "That's too bad."

She takes a drink from her cup, then raises it to me. "Do you want a drink?"

"No, thanks." I peer into her plastic cup, noting the heavy vodka smell. "Did you have fun at the show?"

"Yeah. This really hot guy pulled me up on stage and stripped for me." Her lips twitch with amusement before she leans in closer to whisper, "For a moment, I thought you were going to kiss me."

She's right there. Our faces even closer now than they were onstage. I could lean down and kiss her right now.

Claim her in front of everyone. Her eyes flutter closed, like she's anticipating it. My heart rate accelerates at the sight of her perfect lips parted and eager to be captured.

"It wouldn't have been professional of me to kiss you onstage."

The second the words leave my mouth I know that I've ruined the moment.

Fuck.

While Emma's trying to be fun and flirty, I'm reciting the rule book at her.

Emma's eyes pop open and she pulls back. "Yeah, I guess you're right."

"I—"

Dallas cuts into our conversation before I can rectify my misstep and tell her I'm dying to kiss her.

"Time to move, people." He signals toward the door.

"Where are we going?" Emma asks. "Am I dressed okay?" While she leans down to examine her dress, I catch Dallas staring at her breasts.

"You look smokin' hot," he says.

The desire to carve out both his eyes with a fork is strong.

"Don't worry, gorgeous. It's gonna be a fun night." Dallas smirks at me, his brows lifting in challenge. My hand goes around Emma's waist, protectively pulling her toward me. If she's surprised by the action after my awkward response to her flirting, she doesn't show it. Instead, she leans into me further, placing her hand on my chest.

My body immediately responds to her touch. Beneath her palm, my skin heats with awareness and my heart rate kicks up a notch. The rush of being near Emma is like nothing I've felt before. I'm already addicted.

"Are you sure you want to go out? You've had a long day." I'm alluding to what Emma told me on the roof. The stress of her fashion show that she'd been working on for months. The heartache of hearing her ex had gotten engaged so shortly after they broke up. She seems to be having fun, but I don't want her to do anything tonight that she's going to regret.

"Don't listen to this wet blanket over here. He's never up for fun. You should stick with me." Dallas chuckles, moving in closer.

I practically growl at Dallas, but when Emma's hand snakes its way up to my neck, I relax and turn my attention back to her.

"I think we'll have fun." Emma's eyes twinkle. Her cheeks are rosy, her lips pink and full. Everything about Emma screams at me to take notice, but I need to keep my guard up, too. She's everything I could ever want, but I've never gotten anything I've wanted.

I have one goal tonight. To keep Dallas's dick away from Emma. Unfortunately, the gleam in his eyes tells me he knows it and he's going to make me work for it.

Emma turns to me, her body presses further into mine and my chest expands with the closeness of her.

"I just want to have fun tonight. Can we do that?" she asks.

"Yeah." I nod, vowing to stick by Emma's side tonight and make sure she gets back to her hotel room safely. "We can do that."

CHAPTER 5
Emma

My arms whirl around my body, attempting to move to the music but the fast pop beat is a runaway train, impossible for me to catch. I watch Mike across from me, trying to mimic his smooth moves. He makes it look so easy.

I'm not the best dancer, but when alcohol is involved, I swear I'm Beyoncé, minus the outstanding choreography. Okay, I'm more like a contestant cast-off of *So You Think You Can Dance?* The one they put on between the superior dancers during auditions so the audience can gain some perspective. And have a good laugh.

Maybe that's why watching Griffin dance tonight was so thrilling. I mean all of the guys were excellent dancers, but my attention stayed on Griffin the entire time he was on stage. There's no way in a million years I could make my body move like that. I'm graceful in a walking in a straight line kind of way. My body doesn't tend to operate in multiple planes of movement at once.

My elbow knocks into a man close by and I wince my apologies.

"Are you having fun?" Jess yells in my ear even though we're only inches apart. The music in the club is deafening.

"Yeah!" I yell back. I am having fun but I could argue I'd be having more fun if Griffin were out here with us.

My eyes move to the last place I spotted Griffin, fifteen seconds ago when I was glancing in his direction for the millionth time. He's still sitting on a stool at the end of the high-top table the group has occupied talking to a few of the guys from the revue. His black t-shirt sleeves are taut against the muscles of his upper arms as he lifts a beer bottle to his lips.

Backstage at the revue, I could tell there was tension between Griffin and Dallas. The way Dallas spoke to Griffin, joking yet with an edge of hostility. And Griffin's hard stare aimed at Dallas whenever he talked to me. They work together, but it's clear they're not friends.

Dallas is more of an over-the-top kind of flirt, letting his interest be known with suggestive compliments and playful eye contact, while Griffin had simply put a possessive arm around my waist. The moment his fingers curved around my hip, I felt my body melt into him.

When we arrived at the club, it was clear there was a stand-off between Griffin and Dallas for my attention. While flattering, I don't want to be in the middle of two guys.

My eyes scan a few feet to the right where Dallas now has a leggy redhead sitting on his lap. Seeing them together does nothing to me. In fact, I'm glad he's found someone else to put his charming efforts into.

I'll admit, Dallas is attractive. He's got surfer guy vibes with shaggy blonde hair, and deeply tanned skin. His muscular arms are bulky, a sign he's done some serious weightlifting, with a large tattoo encircling his bicep. Earlier he was pointing out scars and telling me the dare devil stories behind each one. I'm seventy-five percent sure that the 'shark bite' on his leg is really from a lawn mower accident. He also seems very into himself. He kept looking over my shoulder, and I finally realized he was glancing in the mirror behind the bar…at himself.

As if on cue, Dallas briefly takes his attention off the redhead's breasts to look in the mirror behind her and run a hand through his hair.

I have to laugh. I have no interest in Dallas. He's not why I'm here. But it seems with Dallas's shift in attention, so went Griffin's.

While I was certain that there had been a connection between me and Griffin earlier, on the rooftop, during the dance he gave me, and even when we first arrived at the club, since I've been dancing with Jess and Mike, he's kept his distance.

"I need a break." Jess fans herself.

"Agree." Mike's tank top is drenched with sweat.

I nod in agreement and follow them back to the table where a waitress stops by to drop off a fresh round of drinks.

I shouldn't be intimidated to approach Griffin. After tonight, I won't see him again. I've got nothing to lose, but I feel out of practice. When I think about my past interactions with men, relationships or casual dates, I've never been the one to initiate anything. I've always waited for the guy to call, to text, to ask me out or move the relationship forward.

Just like I had been waiting for Alec to propose. And now he's engaged to someone else.

But that's not what tonight is about. If I want to make things happen, I'll have to put myself out there.

I take a sip of my champagne, trying to cool off when I see that a woman in a tight black dress has approached Griffin. Her blonde hair is styled in perfect waves, her skin is golden, her face flawless and when she leans into him, I'm immediately jealous of the abundance of cleavage she has to offer. I watch them, my stomach twisting anxiously while she whispers something into his ear. Clearly, she is willing to go after what she wants.

I can't see his face, but he shakes his head and with an annoyed twitch of her lips, she retreats.

I'm watching her leave when Griffin turns and catches me staring. The impact of his gaze has me nearly knocking my glass over. I recover quickly only to find his green eyes still taking me in, dropping from my face to my body, before turning away to take another drink of his beer.

If I was feeling uncertain before, with what seemed to be a rejection of a gorgeous blonde, now I'm shaking with nerves. From my side, Jess nudges me with her elbow, then tilts her head in Griffin's direction. 'Go,' I read the word on her lips more than I hear it. She's right. I need to put on my big girl panties and make a move. I'm single, it's my birthday and we're in Vegas.

It's the trifecta of reasons to approach Griffin. To not be afraid to put myself out there. I mean I'm looking for a one-night stand, not a husband.

I round the side of the long table, attempting to strut with confidence. My silk dress moves easily with every step I take. I may not have the impressive rack the blonde has, but I have to admit my small breasts are perky and fill out the triangle cut of my mom's deep V slip dress rather nicely. With the club music at an ear-splitting decibel, I know I'll have to get close to be heard, just like the blonde. I'm searching my brain for a witty opening line, maybe something suggestive to let him know I'm interested.

Suddenly, Griffin swivels on his stool. The movement catches me off guard and my legs wobble. In the next moment, the toe of my shoe bumps into the leg of the stool beside him, stopping my lower body's motion while pitching my top half forward, right into Griffin. With nothing to slow my momentum, I put out my hands to brace myself.

On Griffin's thighs.

Beneath my palms, his muscles contract, while his hands wrap around my elbows to steady me.

The shock of landing in Griffin's lap makes it impossible to come up with any casually cool conversation starters.

"Hi." The single syllable falls out.

The corner of his mouth twitches. "Hi."

I'm certain the music is still thumping around us, yet being this close to Griffin feels like being enclosed in sound-proof glass, shutting out the chaos of our surroundings. The lights from the dance floor flash and change colors, casting his strong jaw in pink, then blue, then red light. My fingers itch to reach up and touch the stubble across his jaw, run my thumb over his full lips, feel the contrast between the two.

His eyes search my face before lowering to where my hands are resting on his thighs, my fingers splayed over the black wash denim, only inches from his crotch.

They slowly move back up to mine, lingering for a moment at my chest. I don't bother looking down to see the view that Griffin has, but the fact that I barely feel the silk material against my nipples tells me he might be getting an eyeful.

"Um," I remember why I came over here but saying it out loud is harder than I imagined, so I ignore the fact that I left a mostly full drink at the table with Jess and use needing a drink as an excuse. "I need your assistance at the bar."

"Now?" he questions when I don't remove my hands.

"Um, yeah. Now would be good."

He stands, righting my angled body.

"Let's go." He takes my hand in his, then leads me through the crowded space, toward the bar.

Griffin is simply holding my hand so we don't get sepa-rated, but it still sends a rush of excitement through my body. He parts the crowd and keeps me tucked behind him until we make it to the bar. There, he promptly shifts me in front of him into a newly vacated spot.

He bends down to whisper in my ear. "What do you want?"

You, my brain answers automatically.

I know he's talking about a drink, but the way his breath tickles the shell of my ear and the huskiness of his voice has me wanting to turn around and pull his face down to mine.

I chicken out, though, and think about what he's really asking. What do I want to drink?

I turn to smile up at him, loving the way his arms bracket me in against the bar. Protective, yet not crowding me. My eyes drop to the wall of muscle around me. God, I wish he would crowd me.

"We should do birthday shots," I finally say.

He chuckles, shaking his head. "That seems like a bad idea. I don't want to have to carry you out of here."

The image of Griffin throwing me over his shoulder and walking out of the club sends a wave of arousal between my thighs.

"Oh, come on. You need to loosen up."

"This is me," he drops his hands from the bar to roll his shoulders back, "loose."

Now he's got his hands in his pockets, and he's a good six inches farther away.

"I feel like you're here, but you don't want to be."

He shrugs. "I'm not much of a partier." He lifts his hand to signal the bartender, so I turn around to give the guy my order.

"Two lemon drop shots, please."

The bartender nods and slides down the bar to start making the shots.

"So why did you come out tonight?" I ask.

"Honestly?" He bites his lip and looks away for a second. Jesus. Either I've never seen a man bite his lip before or I'm drunk and incredibly horny. Why is Griffin's contemplative gaze making me want to jump him? I'm starved for attention, clearly.

I'm trying to think when was the last time I had sex? I'd

had a few too many glasses of wine at one of Alec's client dinners and then I'd attempted to seduce him with lingerie and a tipsy strip tease. I'd been wanting to spice things up and had been practicing some seductive lap dance moves I'd found online. I thought the alcohol would help, and in my mind, I felt like I was sexy until Alec burst out laughing.

"Em, what are you doing?" He had bit back another laugh. "This is awkward. I can't take you seriously right now."

After that I felt too self-conscious to make a move, and Alec seemed content to roll to his side of the bed each night. That was months before we broke up.

I'm still waiting for Griffin's response when the bartender drops four shot glasses on the bar and starts pouring liquid from the shaker into them.

"How many did you order?" Griffin asks.

"I overmixed; extras are on me." The bartender winks in my direction.

"You can't take four shots," Griffin protests.

"I wasn't planning to." I pass one to him.

"Emma." My name on his lips is a playful scolding. It makes me want to do other naughty things to find out how he'd respond.

"Hmm?" I lift my brows innocently before clinking our shot glasses together and tossing the sweet, lemon-flavored liquid back.

Although the taste is nice, I can immediately feel the alcohol burn a path down my throat. The warming of my belly as it settles in my stomach soon follows.

I pick up the remaining two shots and as I rotate back toward Griffin, one of my spaghetti straps falls down my arm. Griffin's eyes shift from mine to the newly exposed skin. It would be the perfect moment for him to slide his thumb along my bare shoulder, push the strap farther down and trail his lips against my exposed collar bone. My skin is calling out, practically begging to be touched. But he doesn't do any of that. I have to settle for the light graze of his fingertips when he simply pinches the rogue strap between his fingers and guides it back to the top of my shoulder.

"I'm watching out for you tonight and you're making that increasingly harder."

I briefly drop my gaze below his waist.

"Is that so?" I'm surprised by my flirty response, but then again, it seems like I'm going to have to be the one to make this happen.

As the lemon drop shot settles into my blood stream, the realization that I can do whatever I want tonight makes me feel free. I don't need to feel self-conscious with Griffin. He can see all my quirks and messiness and it doesn't matter. We're having fun tonight.

Again, I clink my shot glass with Griffin's, but before I can down the second one, he whisks it out of my hand and throws it back.

"Hey," I pout.

"You want to have fun tonight? It's a marathon, not a sprint."

"Yeah, but if you saw my moves earlier, you'd know I'll need at least three more of those to really find my groove."

"You're not a bad dancer."

"No?" I laugh. "You're a bad liar."

"I saw you out there. You were having fun, that's what matters."

"You're not like the other guys." My eyes move to the table where the other revue dancers are drinking and laughing. Some are flirting with women, pouring on the charm. Griffin exudes the same confidence, but his is quiet, reserved. Nothing like the man that flirted and teased me onstage tonight.

"Is that a good thing?" he asks.

"Yeah." I nod.

He takes the final shot and sets the glass back on the bar.

CHAPTER 6

Griffin

I've managed to keep Emma's shot total to three by taking the additional shots she was gifted once the group beside us heard it was her birthday.

We're propped up against the bar watching the people on the dance floor.

I've been sipping on a beer while Emma tells me about her bridal gown business and life in New York.

"How did you get into dancing?" she asks.

"Rita, the revue's choreographer, scouted me at a hardware store."

"You worked there?"

"No, I was buying supplies for a contractor I worked with at the time."

"How'd she know you were a good dancer?"

"She didn't. She said I had the look. That she could teach me to dance." I laugh, recalling how terrible I was at first. How I was certain I wouldn't even make a call back, let alone the final cut. "I wasn't good. I could barely remember the steps."

"So, what you're saying is there is hope for me, I just need the right teacher?" Emma asks, taking my hand.

When I hesitate, she bites her lip and groans. "I know it's probably the last thing you want to do."

"That's not it. I—" How do I explain that I'm here to keep an eye on her, and there shouldn't be any more to it? That just watching her every move already has me in some kind of trance, that touching her would be dangerous for us both.

Emma licks her lips. "Please?"

I drain my beer, then set the bottle down on the bar. With her hand in mine, I let her pull me out onto the dance floor where we're quickly swallowed up by the crowd.

"Okay. Show me some moves. I need all the help I can get."

The upbeat house music transitions to a slower song. I can feel the bass pulsing in my chest. It's a seductive beat, similar to the music we play at the revue.

With bodies pressing in all around us, there's no way to keep my distance from Emma. Her hands grip my forearms to steady herself against the flow of the other dancers. When Emma looks up at me from under her lashes, I let myself give in to her.

Selfish, greedy, longing. I haven't allowed myself to feel any of it in way too long. It's intoxicating. Emma is intoxicating.

"Turn around." My words, pressed against her ear, come out hoarse.

She easily lets me guide her until her back is to my chest.

My hands move to her hips, the smooth silk of her dress makes it impossible to miss the soft curves of her body underneath. With my hands there guiding her, I start to move our hips in a slow rhythm to the music.

"It's about relaxing into the rhythm. Letting your body move naturally."

I relax my grip on her hips, and Emma continues moving in the slow, seductive rhythm I started.

"Just like that," I whisper in her ear. "Good girl."

Emma's ass presses into me, and she slowly grinds back against my dick. The feel of her against me there is both desire and agony. I'm quickly turning rigid beneath my zipper.

Dancing with Emma, my movements become lazy. When I'm onstage, even slow grinding hips are practiced and sharp, but here, with Emma in my arms, want has taken over. My pelvis grinds into her, wishing there was nothing between us, begging to press into her softness. It's like I'm floating. I pull her closer to me. We're so close, our bodies are nearly fused. If we were in private, there would be far more happening than dancing. The way I'm touching her, the way she's grinding into me, we shouldn't be in public. But we're packed in tight, surrounded by other dancers, and the bodies around us don't care. They're all similarly absorbed by the sensual beat of the music. Emma turns around to face me and our bodies still, while the crowd continues to pulse around us.

I can't help myself from moving one hand from Emma's hip up her ribcage. My fingers wrap around her side to her back, while my thumb hovers over her nipple. She arches into my touch, allowing the silk of her dress and her hardened nipple beneath it to graze against the pad of my thumb. And I swear even over the bass heavy music, I can hear her breathy moan. The sound sends a jolt of arousal to my cock. I've been hard since the first time she grinded her perfect ass against me. I'm beyond that now. I can feel the pre-cum leaking from my tip.

I haven't touched a woman like this in so long. It's nothing like the way I touch the women onstage.

This is pure want. No, *need*.

Conflict battles inside me. I'm supposed to be watching over Emma, not touching her like this. Her fingers tangle in the hair at the nape of my neck, her nails lightly scratching my scalp.

I have to take a moment to breathe. To remind myself why I'm here.

"We should take a break," I tell her, my rough cheek sliding against her soft one so she can hear me.

"Is there something else you'd rather be doing?" She slides her palm down my chest to cup my erection. I grab her hand and pull it back up to my chest. I refuse to come in my pants in the middle of this club.

"You're trouble," I tell her. She bites her lower lip and smiles. I can feel my own lazy smile take over my face.

"Let's be wild and spontaneous," she says.

"I'm neither of those things." I think about my life before tonight. Every night the same. Shower after the show, then late dinner alone. I'd be hours into an REM cycle by now. It's the same routine I've had for years.

"Me either." She laughs. "I just don't want the night to end."

She's smiling, but I can see the sadness creeping in behind her brown eyes. I want to blame the alcohol, the heady attraction to Emma for making it hard to tell her no, to walk away, but the truth is I felt this pull to her the moment I saw her on the rooftop.

I drop her hand and move mine to her chest.

"Me either," I echo.

My fingers trace along her collarbone, then up along her neck until I'm tilting her chin up toward me. Her eyes flutter closed, her lips part in preparation for what is to come. This time, I don't hesitate. When my lips meet hers, the last of my restraint melts away. Emma's soft mouth opens farther for me and I'm a goner.

Our tongues taste and lick. She tastes sweet, like honey, and a faint citrus, the lemon from the shots we took.

Somewhere in the back of my mind, the man that has been raising his little sister, worrying about her safety and wellbeing, paying insurance and bills, denying himself to set a good example for her, sags in relief. I let my hand tease into her hair and tighten my grip there. Putting my hands on Emma, letting myself touch her this way, taste her, has awakened something primal in me.

I pull back, still holding Emma close to me, and let our kiss linger between us. Her cheeks are pink. When her eyes open, they're glossy with lust. She's fucking perfect. Just for tonight, I want something for myself. I want Emma.

CHAPTER 7
Emma

My head is pounding. Wait. That's the door. I bolt upright in bed and my brain revolts. My attempt to peel open my eyelids is met with resistance, my mouth feels like somebody shoved a handful of cotton balls in it, and my lips are chafed and swollen. I try to wet my cracked lips with my tongue, but I come up empty, my mouth too dry to produce saliva.

I feel like hell. And I'm pretty much in need of every product Jennifer Aniston has ever done a commercial for. I look around for water and find a bottle beside the bed, along with two ibuprofen and my phone arranged neatly on the charging station. I guess between overloading my liver with alcohol and partying all night, drunk me managed the fore-sight to prepare for the mother of all hangovers.

There's another knock on the door. Ugh. Why is someone knocking on my door so early in the morning?

I glance at the clock on the bedside table. It's nine-thirty. Well, crap. I don't think I've slept this late since I was pulling all-nighters working on designs at NYFIT. Another knock.

"Room service," I hear a man's voice from the other side of the door.

Shit. I throw back the covers and force myself to stand,

60

which doesn't go well for my head. The too quick motion has my head spinning. I reach out for the wall to steady myself until my vision returns. My legs are sore, likely from trekking around Vegas in heels. And dancing. I remember a lot of dancing.

I'm in a tank top and sleep shorts so I reach for the neatly tied hotel robe on the hanger in the closet. I bundle myself up, tying it tight around my waist. The robe is a necessity for modesty but not a great option for my overheated body currently in the throes of metabolizing the gallons of alcohol I drank last night.

Another knock tells me it's too late for another option. I fan my heated skin, then finally, I open the door.

In the hallway I find the room service waiter with a food delivery cart.

"Good morning, miss. I apologize if I woke you."

I'm staring at the assortment of food, juice, coffee and flowers that his cart contains. Did I also have the foresight to order enough food for a basketball team last night?

I glance down the hallway, wondering if said basketball team is in sight. Maybe just fresh off the court from a morning scrimmage. Seriously, this guy must have the wrong room.

"We apologize for not having a larger suite available last night for your celebration, but we'd like to offer you complimentary in-room breakfast for your special occasion."

His words are confusing. What celebration? My bridal gown line launch? My birthday?

I'm sure the food is delicious being from a Michelin-star restaurant in a five-star hotel, but my stomach revolts at the idea of putting anything into it right now.

"I'm sorry. I think you have the wrong room." I take a step back, hoping he will agree with me so I can close the door and strip this robe off my boiling flesh. I desperately need to take that ibuprofen, chug some water and lie back down. I can honestly say I don't think I've ever been this hungover in my life.

He glances back at the number by the door.

"3019." He confirms my hotel room number. "Mr. and Mrs. Hart?"

"Now I know you have the wrong room." I sigh. "It's just me. All alone."

When I wave to the empty hotel room behind me, something on my left hand catches my eye. My ring finger is adorned with a simple gold band. It's nothing flashy, yet the sight of it sends my heart rate through the roof. The adrenaline dump that follows makes my stomach lurch.

What is this? my still foggy brain asks. And just like the song playing during my first dance with a boy in middle school, or the scent of my grandmother's decades old perfume, the sight of the gold band on my finger is like a key to the vault containing my memories from last night and they all come rushing back to me at once.

My fashion show. Alec's engagement. Penny slots with the little blue-haired woman. What was her name? Dottie. Then, Jess and I went to the male revue dance show. Griffin pulling me up on stage for my birthday. *Griffin.*

My lower belly clenches at the thought of him. His gorgeous smile, his strong arms flexing as he held himself above me onstage, the scent of his body wash when he leaned in close to whisper in my ear. I inhale. I can still smell it now. *Okay, focus.*

Drinks. Shots. Lots of lemon drop shots. And by lots, it might have been three. I'm a lightweight and it doesn't take much for me to become a limp noodle. That's what Jess calls me when I get tipsy and dance. She says I'm like one of those windsock advertising tubes. The ones that fill with air, then lose air and nearly collapse before filling with air again and moving back upright. I imagine I was in prime limp noodle form last night.

There was dancing at the club. Dancing with Griffin, his hands holding me close. Laughing and having fun. Kissing on the dance floor. I vaguely remember a car ride, which now doesn't make sense because the club we were at was inside the hotel. Then it gets fuzzy. Maybe the ring is one of those novelty toys out of a vending machine. A fun thing I decided to try on. Maybe it doesn't mean anything. Oh my God, what if it means something?

"Your picture package from the wedding chapel arrived as well." He hands me a manila envelope. I glance down the hallway, wondering if this is some elaborate prank that Jess set up. But she knows how badly I want to get married; like legitimately, not some drunken drive-thru quickie. There's no way she would do this after the whole Alec engagement thing. I flip open the top and yank out the pictures.

If this is a prank, it's good. Photoshop skills are on point. There, in the photographs, standing on the pink carpeted wedding stage are me and Griffin. I'm in my mother's wedding dress, the dress I had hoped to redesign and wear someday at my wedding, holding a bouquet of tasteful pink and white roses. I guess I can check that off my list.

With Griffin's black t-shirt and black wash denim, he looks like a casually cool groom, and my white slip dress is elegant, yet simple. We look like we could be on the cover of *Bride* magazine. 'Effortlessly Chic Wedding Attire' the caption would read. 'What to wear to your spontaneous Vegas wedding.'

My stomach clenches. I have to fight back the panic that is trying to rise out of it. Okay, but let's be real because people don't get married in Vegas and not remember it. That can't really be a thing. It happens in movies like the *Hangover* and television comedies like *Friends*, but not to bridal gown designers from New York who have been planning their elaborate wedding since childhood.

"No. Is this for real? It can't be for real," I ask the waiter.

Poor guy, he just came here to deliver food and he's now dealing with my existential crisis.

"This was also in the package." He reaches for something else on the cart.

I pull my hand from where I'm twisting the gold band around and around to accept the plastic-covered paper he hands me. It has the words Marriage Certificate scrawled across the top. There, clear as day, is my signature, along with what I would guess is Griffin's signature. I've never seen it before seeing as I met him last night, and between the revue show and our time at the club, I didn't bother to ask for a handwriting sample. There's a third signature, a witness, whose name I don't even recognize.

"Oh, God."

I stare back at the band. I've wanted to get married since I was a little girl attending celebrity weddings with my photographer father. His photos capturing the light and love in the couple's eyes on their wedding day. I've always wanted that kind of love. The weak knees, stomach twisting, can't live without that person kind of love.

I turn my attention back to the photo. Griffin's arms are wrapped around my lower back, pressing our bodies tightly together. I'm nearly tipping backwards, except I'm not because he's instructed his very competent arm muscles to hold me there.

I remember his strong, sculpted arms. What it felt like to be inside them.

My attention is on the camera, a huge smile on my face, while Griffin's mouth is smiling into my neck. Objectively we look like a happy couple in love.

"Don't worry," the waiter interrupts my thoughts. "That's just a copy. The wedding chapel will send the original to the county for recording. You should get the original mailed back to you in seven to ten business days."

I stare at him blankly.

"I only know that because my ex-girlfriend works in the county courthouse as a file clerk."

My gaze falls to the room service cart. I recognize the flower arrangement now as the bouquet from the wedding photo. "What is wrong with me?" I whisper.

"It happens to the best of us."

"So, you've drunkenly gotten married in Vegas?" I ask.

"No." He shakes his head. "I'm only nineteen. I thought you were talking about forgetting that you ordered room service."

That's right. He's still waiting in the hallway to deliver the food.

"Come in." I hold the door open wide and wave him in. If I thought my head was pounding before, somewhere in my skull a jackhammer has started operating.

He pushes the white table-clothed cart into the room, parks it, then moves to exit. He hesitates by the door and I finally realize he's waiting for a tip. I manage to find my clutch and a few dollars to offer him.

"Thank you and congratulations." He nods, then exits, the door clicking shut behind him.

I walk over to the cart and pick up the photo. My wedding photo. I drunkenly married a stranger in Vegas. How did this happen? I drop the photo back on the cart. I need to call Jess. I need to find Griffin and figure out what we can do about this. Vodka and stomach acid rises in my throat. A hand quickly moves up to cover my mouth. But first, I need to throw up.

Thirty minutes later, my stomach is empty and my mouth is still dry, but minty fresh. I also took a shower, hoping it would make me feel better. It didn't. Now, I've got a hangover from hell, but I'm clean. Wearing the hotel provided bathrobe, I exit the bathroom to look for some clothes.

"Hey," a deep, gravelly voice says from across the room and I scream.

"Shit!" I clutch my chest as my heart starts to race, then wince and grab my head. With the acceleration of my heart rate, my pulse begins pounding between my temples again.

My eyes seek out the source. Seated on a chair in the sitting area on the far side of the room is Griffin.

"You scared me," I say.

He must have a key. There's no way he came in through the thirtieth-floor window.

"Sorry about that." He rubs his hands against his black denim-clad thighs. "I heard the shower so I was waiting."

He stands. He's got the most adorable bedhead that makes his thick, wavy locks stick up on one side. *Husband*, my brain chimes from somewhere in the back.

I let my eyes roam over Griffin. Everything about him is familiar, yet I'd argue the dim lighting in the theater and club didn't do him justice. Seeing him in the daylight, even with the shades still drawn is overwhelming.

He's wearing the same clothes from last night.

His black t-shirt is stretched taut across his chest, planes of hard muscles encased by soft cotton. The definition of his forearms and the vein running along the side causes saliva to pool in my mouth, a difficult feat for my dehydrated state. I recall my fascination with Griffin's forearms when we met on the roof.

My greedy eyes take in the rest of him. Narrow waist and tight butt, which I can't see right now but I recall the way he moved his hips and ass during the show. The way we grinded our hips together on the dance floor.

Damn. He looks so good, it makes my chest ache and my skull feel too small for my brain.

Finally, my eyes find his again. He's watching me. I should be embarrassed that I blatantly checked him out, but my brain can't even muster up a flush. It's got other priorities right now. Like figuring out what the hell happened last night.

Griffin runs a hand through his hair.

That's when I see the gold band on his left hand.

Despite the mounting evidence provided by the teenage food service worker, it's the final confirmation I needed to know that last night was real.

Seeing that ring on Griffin's finger does a funny thing to my chest. It suddenly feels like someone is blowing up a balloon underneath my sternum. Because the only thing sexier than a wedding band on a man's finger is knowing that man, even if by accident, belongs to you.

Wait. *What am I thinking?* It's not sexy that I'm married to a stranger. That I hardly know anything about this man yet I vowed to be with him until death do us part. That's foolish. Insane. Impractical. All the other synonyms for downright stupid.

"I got you a coffee," he says.

I reach out to accept the paper cup. Our fingers briefly touch, yet the contact sends a buzz of electricity through my body.

"Cream and one sugar, right?"

I nod, dazed at the situation. It's as if I blinked and suddenly have a husband that knows my coffee order overnight. Actually, it's exactly that.

"Thank you."

"Last night…" he starts.

I lift my hand, showing him the matching gold band there. Not bothering to analyze why I didn't take it off when I showered. "We got married." I try to laugh, but it falls flat. What have we done?

He's my husband. My *husband.*

I think we know alcohol is to blame. Also, my roaming hands in the dance club might have urged me in that direction. The sensory input that his muscular body was giving me was enough to prevent my brain from making rational decisions.

"Yeah." He drops his gaze to his finger and rotates the band there before meeting my eyes again. "We did."

"Like how did this even happen?!" I exclaim.

Griffin opens his mouth to respond, but I cut him off. I'm overwhelmed and anxious and confused and it all comes spilling out.

"People don't get married to strangers." I wave my hands in his direction. "No offense. It's not you personally that is upsetting. I mean, you're you," I motion toward him again. "You look like that and you're a really good kisser, but I think we both know that this isn't normal. There are procedures for this kind of thing. Marriage, that is. Like getting to know someone. Dating. An actual proposal."

He clears his throat. "You did propose." He grips the back of his neck and presses his lips together. "On the rollercoaster."

"What?!" I blink, confused. That doesn't sound like something I would do. But then there's that nagging feeling again. That I do remember, and Griffin's mentioning it brings the memory to the forefront of my mind.

Oh my God. He's right.

We were at the rollercoaster, talking to a couple in line. They had just gotten married at a little chapel north of The Strip. They loved rollercoasters and said they took every opportunity to ride one when they could. That a rollercoaster is like a relationship, there are ups and downs, turns you don't see coming, but if you have someone you love and trust beside you to hold your hand through it all, someone to laugh and cry and scream with, then you can get through anything. I thought it was terribly romantic.

The rollercoaster was a blast. Wind in my hair, screaming and laughing so hard I had tears running down my cheeks, and gripping Griffin's arm as we flew along the track at nearly seventy miles an hour. I remember feeling it in those moments. I knew what they had been talking about. So, it made perfect sense when we pulled back into the loading zone and I turned toward Griffin—he had a huge smile on his face as he lifted his thumb to wipe the tear from the corner of my eye.

Marry me.

The words had fallen out so easily.

He'd cradled my face and kissed me breathless until the coaster operator had asked us to get out. We stumbled off the ride and onto the street to find a taxi. No, it was an Uber. The driver's name was Felix or Felipe or Felicity. Heck, Britney Spears could have been driving the car and I wouldn't have noticed. At that point, I couldn't see anyone but Griffin.

I did this. I proposed to a man I'd known for a mere handful of hours.

"And you said *yes*?" I attempt to hold back a screech, but it fails.

"Yeah." His green eyes rake over the length of me and I swear my bathrobe just caught on fire. "I did."

Beneath my ribcage, my heart flutters.

It's stupid, because Griffin didn't say yes to me, the alcohol and wild night we were having just prevented him from saying no. There's a big difference.

The juxtaposition of spending years with Alec, the man I desperately wanted a proposal from, and Griffin, a stranger I had a fun night with, saying yes to my marriage proposal, is baffling.

What am I even saying? We were drunk. And horny.

I rack my brain for memories of sweaty, passionate sex but I come up empty. My eyes drift over to the unmade bed. The sheets and duvet are pulled back from my exit, but nowhere near messy enough to have been subjected to a wild night of hot sex. Nothing in the room is broken, or even out of place. Even the pillows on the sofa are still resting in their respective corners, housekeeping's signature indent on the top from fluffing them yesterday while I was out.

"We didn't…?"

Somehow Griffin understands my non-question.

He shakes his head. "No."

"Oh." Huh. It's hard to pinpoint my feelings about it. Disappointment? Regret? Relief that I don't remember sex with Griffin because it didn't happen, not because I was barely coherent?

I married a gorgeous stranger last night and we didn't even have sex. Based on the way my personal life has been going lately, that checks out.

"We kissed," he says.

I nod. "I've seen the photo."

"At the ceremony and later."

He picks up a baseball hat off the couch and fits it onto his head, covering his rumpled hair.

The hat reads 'I rode the rollercoaster at NY-NY.' Griffin's quiet confidence and the way his wavy hair peeks out from under the edges makes it look trendy. Like Justin Bieber wearing Crocs, except it's a cheesy souvenir hat.

My fingertips find the tender flesh of my swollen lips.

Somewhere in the foggy depths of my mind, another memory resurfaces. He's right. We didn't have sex, but we kissed for hours. And the tenderness between my legs is from Griffin's raging hard on that never made it out of his pants. My cheeks flush. Why does that feel more awkward than if we had drunk, messy sex?

"Did we want to?" I don't know why I say 'we.' I wanted it. What I really mean is *why didn't we?* Is something wrong with me?

"Have sex?"

I fidget with the ends of my robe. Why is this conversation making me flush? I was groping him on the dance floor last night and now I feel like giggling when he says the word *sex*.

He smiles, his lips doing this adorable twitching, like he's fighting back a laugh.

His hands move from his pockets to the bill of the hat, where he uses his fingers to shape the stiff bill.

His movements put me at ease because I realize I'm not the only one feeling self-conscious this morning.

If we weren't married, would we close the feet between us and pick up where we left off last night? Is it the weight of marrying a stranger that has chased the wild abandon from our veins? Or the lack of alcohol?

"How did we manage to get married but not have sex?" The octave of my voice is rising again.

I want to drop my head into my hands when I realize that I married a man I barely know and then dry humped him like a horny teenager.

With each new memory, my head feels like it's tightening around my brain.

"I can't believe we did this. I fly back to New York tomorrow. We can't stay married. We have to fix this!"

I wince, my head reminding me that my brain is basically a vodka-soaked sponge right now.

"Why aren't you freaking out?" I ask.

"I'm processing."

"Can you process out loud? I feel like I'm going crazy here."

I drop to the edge of the bed and sigh.

Griffin walks over to where I'm sitting.

"You're right. We'll fix it."

"An annulment?" I suggest. That's the solution in every cinematic version of this story I've seen.

"Yeah." He nods.

"Sorry. It's not you. I can't even think straight right now." I press my fingertips into my temples. "My head is pounding."

Griffin drops down beside me. His weight on the bed

shifts me toward him, and our hips press together. I'd expect after a night of drinking and dancing for him to smell like liquor or sweat, but he smells like…reassurance. That's not really a scent, but for some reason Griffin's combination of fresh linen detergent, body wash and hint of sandalwood makes me feel calm.

His hand comes to rest on my thigh in a comforting gesture. There's a good inch of thick cotton robe between us, but feeling the weight of him there suddenly makes me aware that I'm not wearing anything underneath.

Beneath my robe, my belly clenches and I can feel my heartbeat in my clit.

"Did you take the ibuprofen I left?" he asks.

"Yes, thank you. And drank a bottle of water. I probably need to sleep it off, but my brain is having a hard time relaxing." Also, my brain is now working hard to remember every detail of last night. The exact feel of Griffin's hard, muscled body against mine as he hovered above me. The stubble on his jaw scraping against the sensitive skin of my neck. My leg is now on fire where his palm still rests. The ache in my head is suddenly contending with the one between my thighs. I'm struggling to keep up my end of the conversation.

"Are you hungover?" I ask.

"A little. Not too bad."

"How is that possible? You had way more shots than I did."

"And I'm twice your size," he teases, and his arm brushing against mine causes another wave of lust to head southward.

"Good point." I laugh, but end up wincing at the sound. "I'm thirty. You'd think I would've learned that champagne gives me the worst hangovers by now. And those shots…not a great idea on my part."

"Yeah." A chuckle reverberates in his throat. He's quiet a moment before he speaks again.

"I don't know if it works, but the guys have a hangover cure they swear by."

"Oh, yeah? What is it?" I ask. I'll try anything if I can avoid feeling like this all day. I stand up, ready to take on the challenge, whatever it might be. God, I hope it's not drinking raw eggs. I saw that on a video once and I nearly threw up. I don't think I could stomach it right now, even if it would help in the long run.

Griffin stares at the knot on my robe, then lifts his gaze to mine.

"An orgasm."

CHAPTER 8

Griffin

"I'm sorry, what?" Emma's eyes widen at my suggestion and immediately I regret my words. Maybe I am hungover. Or still drunk. Or I'm sober and my attraction to Emma is making me say things that are completely out of character.

Being near Emma appears to be my kryptonite. That's the only way I can explain what happened last night. How badly I fucked everything up by letting this woman, her infectious spirit and our explosive chemistry, obliterate my plans to see her safely—and with no regrets—to her hotel room.

Safety was never a question...the matter of no regrets...a complete failure.

Emma is my *wife* now. My *wife*.

That word carries enough weight to make my shoulders instantly twenty pounds heavier. I'm not ready to be anyone's husband. And, before last night, I'd never thought I would be. There's so much I need to achieve for myself before I can be good for someone else. And Emma deserves someone ready to be her everything. Right now, I'm not that guy.

Marriage and a family were never things I saw for myself. I've raised Sophie. Dedicated my twenties to the stress of being a good role model and making sure she had everything she needed. I'd learned from my mom that love was fleeting, my dad, then Sophie's, as well as the multiple boyfriends she had in between.

Last night I wanted Emma. I let myself give in to the idea of having something, someone, for myself. A fun night. It's what we both wanted. But instead of falling into Emma's hotel room when Jess walked us to the door, Emma wasn't ready for the night to end.

I followed her lead, letting her pull me across the street to the rollercoaster.

As we flew around the turns and loops, even with the weight of the g-force the rollercoaster put on my body, I felt the lightest I had in my entire life. Emma's laughter, her hair whipping around her face. We pulled back into the loading zone and she turned to me with a sparkle in her eye and the question on her lips.

In that moment, I knew what my answer should be. *No.* I'd used that word so many times over the years, but for once, it wouldn't leave my mouth. It felt like I was standing at a cross section, the convergence of two different lives, the one I've been living and the one I've been waiting for. Leaving the revue, starting a new career, anticipating Sophie's graduation and the freedom that all these changes will allow me. All of that coupled with my overwhelming attraction to Emma had me enthusiastically agreeing.

That's how I got into this situation. And while I still want Emma, still feel that intense connection, I have nothing to offer her.

That was the first thought I had when I woke up next to her this morning. I watched her sleep for a moment, her dark hair strewn across the white pillowcase, her lips parted slightly taking in air with each breath, and the gold wedding band on her finger that told me she was mine. It was both thrilling and terrifying. Then, convincing myself that coffee, not pulling Emma into my arms, was the right choice, I rolled out of bed and away from her warmth.

In the light of day, it's clear we made a mistake. Getting married to someone you just met is not normal behavior, no matter how attracted to them you are.

But I can't deny the way my heart squeezed when she walked in the room. Her dark, wet hair piled on her head; her entire body enveloped by the hotel's one-size-fits-all robe. Plush, pink lips that I had memorized every detail of in the early hours of the morning.

Now, staring up into her huge brown eyes, watching her fingers fidget with the tie of her robe, I try to tamp down the desire that led us here in the first place.

I didn't touch her last night, not like I wanted to. There was a point when I had her beneath me, the teeth of my zipper nearly imprinted on my dick just from kissing her, that I knew I couldn't take it any further. I wanted her bad, but she was a mixture of very drunk and exhausted; that had me tucking her beneath the sheets instead of sliding between her legs.

And now I'm talking about orgasms as headache cures. Clearly, this woman has the capacity to short circuit my brain.

Fuck.

I might as well explain it now that I've put it out there.

"The chemical release from an orgasm is supposed to help with a headache."

"Oh." Her teeth capture her bottom lip. "I had no idea."

I'm determined to do my part to help us undo last night's mistake. I'm confident I can make it right. Right now, all I want to do is make Emma feel better, and if touching her, *tasting* her is part of that, then it's a win-win for both of us.

"Do you want it?" My voice is low, and there's almost a growl to it. It's not my usual tone, but reminds me of the way I talked to her last night when we were dancing. The way I murmured praise in her ear when she followed my lead.

Good girl.

That's it.

Just like that.

And how I could tell she liked it when her body quivered against mine. I watch the tremble move through her now, her shoulders, then hips shaking as it moves down her spine.

"Yes," she whispers and I have to restrain myself from immediately yanking on the belt of her robe to pull her closer.

But then, Emma reaches for the knot of her belt and unties it.

The ties fall to her sides and the robe parts slightly, exposing a sliver of Emma's nakedness. I can see there's nothing under her robe but smooth, taut skin. Slowly, I lift my hands to hold each side of her robe, then I move the thick cotton aside to expose her.

At the sight of her, my pulse starts pounding against my neck and every muscle in my body tenses. I feast on her nakedness with the starving eyes of a celibate man.

I haven't been with a woman like this in years. Six to be exact. And Emma? She's perfection. Small breasts with tight rosy nipples, curvy, luscious hips and neatly-trimmed patch of dark hair at the apex of her thighs. Saliva pools in my mouth just thinking about licking her there.

With my heart pulsing in my ears, I can't decide what to do first.

My hand moves to her belly where my eyes snag on the gold band around my finger. For a brief moment, my breath catches at the sight. The wedding band Emma placed on my finger last night now pressing against her naked skin. *Mine.* That would be the caption of the photo of this moment.

But she's not mine. Not really. She'll get on a plane tomorrow and after a few exchanged texts and emails about the annulment, I'll never see her again. This is all we'll have.

The thought makes me feel desperation and relief at the same time. Emma's exactly the kind of woman I could see myself with, but I'm not ready for her. This is all I have to give right now.

I shake the thought loose, and sink back into the moment.

With my finger pads grazing over her skin, her stomach quivers. My dick responds by swelling against my zipper. There's no doubt I'll be taking care of myself later to the memory of Emma.

My hands slide up her ribcage while my nose finds the nook of her neck. Her skin feels like silk under my rough palms. And fuck, she smells good. A light perfume, something floral with a hint of sweetness.

My thumb sweeps over her hardened peak, and Emma's body jolts forward, her knees knocking into mine. She lets out an audible gasp that has me pulling back.

"Is this okay?" I ask, pressing my thumb pad against her tight nipple. "I want to lick you here."

She gives an affirming nod, so I spread my legs and pull her closer.

With me sitting on the bed, her height makes it easy to lower my head and kiss the swell of her breast. My hands grip her ribcage, holding her where I want her. Then, moving one hand to cradle the underside of her breast, my tongue swirls around her nipple before closing around the distended peak.

Another breathy gasp crosses her lips, and she steadies herself with hands on my shoulders.

"They're so sensitive." She says it like it's a revelation. "I didn't realize."

"That you like your nipples played with?" I ask.

"Mmm." Her hands move along my neck until they're cradling the back of my head, holding me to her. "No one's given them much attention before. They're pretty small."

"Your breasts are perfect," I say, sucking one nipple into my mouth while squeezing the other nipple between my fingers. It feels so good to touch her, to know I'm making her feel good.

I play with her there until her skin is slick and pink from the stubble on my jaw before giving the same attention to her other breast.

"Do you like this, Emma?" I ask, still teasing her nipples while lowering my hands to her ass. I wasn't lying last night when I said it was like a juicy peach. My fingers grip the firm flesh there and squeeze. "Could you come just from me sucking your tight nipples?"

"Ahh." Her entire body shakes.

I love the way she responds, the tremble in her legs, telling me she's so fucking turned on. Before she collapses, I stand and scoop her up, then place her on the bed. Standing over her, seeing all of her now, I can't help but discreetly run a hand over my crotch to adjust the aching bulge there.

The skin of her chest is glistening from my mouth, and that's nothing compared to the slickness between her thighs.

Moving over her, I place gentle kisses on her collarbone, then give each nipple one more tweak. Emma's pelvis rocks against me in response.

"I bet you could." I release her nipple and start a slow descent, kissing every inch of her skin along the way. My tongue dips into the shallow of her belly button before I reach my destination. "But then I wouldn't get to taste this sweet pussy."

Emma's legs have pressed together, likely trying to find friction in her aroused state. I want to see what I've done to her.

"Spread your legs wider, Emma," I demand.

CHAPTER 9

Emma

On Griffin's command, I let my knees fall open. With the warm flesh of my legs parted, the cool air of the room makes me aware of the slickness gathered there. The pool of wetness that started the moment Griffin offered an orgasm to help with my headache.

At this point, a marching band could come through the room and I wouldn't even flinch. I'm solely focused on Griffin. I'm so turned on I'll burst into a million pieces if he doesn't touch me soon. No, I'll probably burst into a million pieces when he does.

I see how this is an effective hangover remedy.

I lay quietly, trying to stay confident while I watch him indulge in my nakedness, his gaze on the space between my thighs. He lets out a low growl and my pussy clenches in response.

"Good girl," he says.

Oh, God. Those words do something to me. Or maybe it's the way Griffin says them, like I'm pleasing him. I love the thought that spreading my legs gives him pleasure. My eyes are on him as he takes in my body. The evidence of *his* arousal pressed against his zipper makes me ache for him. I'm fighting against the urge to rock my hips when he climbs back over me. He presses a kiss against the corner of my mouth, his soft lips a contrast to the rough stubble of his cheek. Griffin is in no hurry as he leisurely peppers kisses along my jaw, down the column of my neck and across my collar bone.

It's turning me on to the point that I'm now involuntarily grinding my pelvis against his core. He's still fully clothed, which should make me feel exposed, but it's the opposite. I feel worshipped.

The way my nipples drag against the soft cotton of his t-shirt reminds me how thoroughly he tended to them.

My small breasts have typically been overlooked during sex. Yes, men have groped them, kissed them, but the amount of attention that Griffin gave them is unheard of. I had no idea how sensitive my nipples could be.

His hand snakes down my front, his touch is feather light, but I feel it everywhere. He drags a single finger down my wet center.

"You're dripping, Emma."

I'm squirming now, dying for more friction, but Griffin hooks an arm under one of my legs and holds my hip to the mattress while he uses the thumb of his other hand to spread me. When his tongue swipes up my center, I nearly scream. A strangled moan that I've never made before escapes my throat.

"You taste incredible. So sweet."

He sucks my clit hard, then circles it with his tongue. When he presses a finger inside me, I see stars. He pumps his finger in and out, then adds a second. The feeling of his thick fingers filling me is heaven, but I'm greedy and begin rocking my hips to meet each thrust of his fingers.

"That's it, sweetheart. Fuck yourself with my fingers."

No one has ever talked to me like that. It's an added layer

of seduction I didn't know I would like. My heels dig into the mattress, my hands fist into the duvet. When he thrusts his fingers deep inside me and sucks my clit, I come undone.

"Griffin!" I call out as my orgasm hits me with unrelenting pleasure. I ride the wave, my muscles clenching around his fingers repeatedly until my body starts to shake. The aftereffects of my orgasm make my skin tingle. My fingers release the duvet, my limbs now impossibly heavy.

I'm vaguely aware of Griffin withdrawing his fingers, and placing one last kiss on my stomach before he pulls the sides of my robe back together.

"How's your head?" he whispers.

My palm lifts to my forehead to make sure I still have one. A head that is, because I can't feel anything. I'm boneless and my brain is mush. So basically, it worked.

"So good," I tell him, a euphoric giggle escaping from my lips.

One corner of his mouth pulls up revealing that dimple of his. "Good."

I manage to prop myself up on my elbows.

He leans forward. I think he's going to kiss me, but a loud knock at the door stops his forward progress. Our eyes dart toward the door.

Another knock. It's less of a knock and more of a banging.

He retreats and I scramble off the bed, retying my robe as I make my way toward the door.

"God, if I ordered more room service…" I mumble, then yank the door open to find Jess.

Her honey-brown hair is gathered in a messy bun on top of her head, mascara is smudged around her eyes, evidence that she didn't take her make-up off last night and she's still in her pajamas, black shorts and matching Peter Pan collared shirt with white piping on the edges. I don't think I've ever seen Jess look quite so disheveled.

"What the hell happened last night?" She pushes past me and into the room.

"Um, do you want the long version or the short?" I ask.

"I can't believe this is happening." She starts breathing heavy. I share a look with Griffin. Although it feels odd to go from Griffin's head between my thighs to Jess rushing into the room in the span of two minutes, I'm grateful that I no longer have a headache and can focus on making sure Jess doesn't hyperventilate.

"What is happening?" I steady myself for the crisis Jess believes is so important that she couldn't get dressed before coming over. There's no way I'm going to tell her about marrying Griffin right now, she'll have a coronary.

She shoves the tablet in her hands at me.

"What am I looking at?" I ask, scrolling up and down the screen.

She hits the back button and scrolls down until I see the article she's upset about.

'Bridal Gown Designer Says 'I Do' in Vegas' I read, my pulse immediately quickening. I'm trying to run the stats on the chances that another bridal gown designer got married in Vegas last night but the numbers get all jumbled in my head. I'm hoping the odds are high.

"What is this?"

"*Page Six!*" Jess screeches.

"Oh, shit." My stomach bottoms out. "How would they know? It happened ten hours ago."

"News travels fast," Jess takes a sharp breath, "especially when you post a video and it goes viral."

"Nooo." I shake my head slowly, but just like everything else about last night, the simple suggestion that something happened and my brain loads the memory. It's fuzzy, but the imagery is unmistakable. Me in the chapel bathroom, drunkenly recording my thoughts about my new husband.

Jess taps the screen again and the voice in my head syncs up with the sound coming out of her tablet.

I'm married.

Yup, that's me squealing as I flash my left hand, complete with gold wedding band, at the camera.

We did it! It's the best night and I'm having so much fun. Listen, ladies, a bit of advice, if you want something you have to go for it. Don't wait around for a guy to propose to you. Take charge of your life and go after what you want. That's what I did and I'm the happiest I've ever been.

I cringe. Apparently, also the drunkest.

The screen jolts as the phone falls to the side, but then I straighten it and continue talking as I pull out a lipstick and begin to apply it.

Griffin is so hot. I don't know why I'm applying this; he's going to kiss it right off me. God, he's such a good kisser. I can't wait to see what else he's good at. And how big—

I slam my finger down on the pause button.

"I think we get the picture." The tips of my ears are burning and I can't look at Griffin. The video has over a million views, yet it's the guy standing a few feet away hearing my words that has me feeling flustered by humiliation. I try to tell myself I shouldn't be embarrassed. We got married, of course we were—are—attracted to each other. But to have him hear me drunkenly discuss my musings about his dick is probably not necessary.

"My phone is blowing up." Jess waves her phone. "Everyone has seen this and wants a comment."

I walk across the room to my phone that hasn't made a sound all morning. It's silenced, but there are over a hundred text messages and seventy-three missed calls. I don't bother to open my email or social media.

Griffin's phone buzzes.

Jess throws her arm out in his direction. "Don't answer that. Nobody responds until we have this under control."

"It's my sister." Griffin holds up his phone. "I need to respond."

"Don't say anything about you two getting married."

"Yeah, I got it."

"Both of you sit. I need to think."

I rejoin Griffin on the end of the bed.

While he types out a text, Jess starts pacing in front of us.

"I walked you to the room." I assume she's talking to me but she's not looking at me as she continues to pace. "I said goodnight." She suddenly turns toward us. "You two were supposed to have drunk, sweaty stranger sex, not get married!" She motions dramatically, her arms waving above her head. "How did this happen?"

Griffin and I are teenagers being scolded for missing curfew.

"Change of plans?" I say weakly, but then remember Griffin and I already have a plan. "I know you think this is a crisis, but I think we'll be okay. Griffin and I know it was a mistake. Impulsive. We've already talked about getting it annulled."

Beside me, Griffin clears his throat.

"Right?" I turn to find him squeezing the brim of his hat between his hands.

Jess shakes her head, not bothering to wait for his affirming answer. "Emma, Kandi Kline knows. She emailed me this morning."

"What?" My stomach fills with dread.

"That's why I'm freaking out. She wants to include your love story," she air quotes love story, "in her feature of you."

My legs go numb. If I wasn't already sitting, they would have given out.

"If we tell her your marriage is a sham, a drunken night in Vegas gone too far, this could impact the article, your brand, hell, even the pending contract with Bergman's. Do you think people want to get married in a gown designed by a woman who thinks marriage is something you flippantly enter into and can undo after twelve hours?"

Shit. Jess is right. Now that everyone knows about my marriage to Griffin, it won't be as easy to undo as we first thought.

"I mean why don't you just design a replica of your mom's dress and call it 'The Mistake.'" Jess scowls. If she's resorting to sarcasm, she's really stressed.

I gasp. "Oh, no, my mom's dress."

Griffin nods toward the door. "I hung it in the closet."

Relief washes over me. "Oh, thank you."

I'm starting to process how sweet it is that he hung up my dress when he speaks.

"Who is Kandi Kline?" he asks.

"Editor-in-chief of *The Dress*, an elite bridal magazine," I offer.

"I'm sure if you told her what happened, she'd understand."

Jess takes in his suggestion, then starts to laugh. It's more of a cackle, and I know why.

"Kandi Kline is the most influential person in the bridal gown world. Her opinion about anyone in the industry holds weight. She can make or break your career. For better or for worse," she says dramatically. I can practically hear the *duh, duh, duh* sound effect in the background.

"She makes Anna Wintour look like a golden retriever," I offer.

Griffin shakes his head, a quizzical look on his face. "Who's Anna Wintour?"

I turn to meet Jess's gaze. With her hands on her hips and her lips quirked to the side, I can tell the wheels in her brain are cranking. Jess is a fixer. She knows Griffin is out of his element, and what is at stake for my brand. She'll come up with a genius plan and everything will work out. It's what she does.

"Okay. I've got a solution," she announces.

"So, what do you suggest we do?" I ask, hopeful.

"It's simple really." She looks between us, her lips pulled into a tight smile. "You two need to stay married."

CHAPTER 10

Griffin

In the hallway of my apartment building, I run into my neighbor, Mrs. Moskiwitz. She's a retired nurse who watched Sophie while I was working when she was too young to stay home alone. She's a bit meddlesome with her attempts to set me up with women she knows, but the peace of mind she's given me with her medical advice and help with Sophie over the years has made it worth it.

She's originally from Boston. And while she's lived in Nevada for over a decade, her accent is still very much intact.

"Griffin," her face lights up, "so glad I ran into you, I was talking to my hairdresser the other day and she's got a niece that just graduated from veterinarian school.

"She's a doctor, Griffin. You're going to be a lawyer and she's an animal doctor. I think it's a perfect match."

"Good morning, Mrs. Moskowitz," I do my best to sound friendly, but of all the mornings for her setups, today is not the day. "It's nice of you to think of me, but I'm not dating right now." It's the answer I've always given her, but today it has the added complication that I'm married.

"You've got to get out there. You're a handsome young

88

man with so much to offer. It can be scary, but you have to take the leap at some point."

She has no idea what kind of leap I took last night.

"Soon," I tell her, hoping it's enough to placate her and end the conversation. "I've got to help Sophie." I motion to my apartment door and start to unlock it. "She's going to LA for a student conference and final project submission."

My change of topic does nothing to dissuade her mission to find me a girlfriend. Too late, Mrs. Moskowitz, I've already got a wife.

"I'll give her your number." She waves me on, yet keeps talking. "Did you know women call men these days? It's a thing."

I nod, thinking of Emma. *They also propose marriage.*

"Okay. Bye, Mrs. Moskowitz."

I shut the door behind me and for a moment relish in the quiet of my apartment.

A second later, Sophie comes racing into the living room. She's lugging a suitcase in one hand and wielding a spatula in the other.

"Hey." I toe off my shoes and arrange them neatly by the front door.

She stops suddenly, looks me up and down, then, with a huge smile on her face, pulls her phone from her back pocket and holds it up. *Click.*

"It's your first walk of shame." She holds the phone in my direction to show the picture. I look disheveled and stunned. "Had to capture the moment."

"Really, Sophie?"

"Someday you'll look back on it fondly." She tucks the phone into her back pocket. "Okay, time to spill the deets."

"I sent you a text. I was out with the guys." I drop my wallet and keys on the table by the door. The table Sophie insisted I get when she moved back in after her freshman year in the dorms. Apparently, my life was in complete disorder without an entry table.

She eyes me suspiciously.

"Yeah, but you never go out."

I shrug. "It was the last night at the revue so I decided to change it up."

"Where did you go? What did you do?" Her eyes are filled with curiosity as she rapid fires questions at me. "And where did you sleep last night?"

On my drive home from The Strip, I'd thought about what I was going to tell Sophie, my brain still working through what Emma and Jess had proposed. Me going to New York for the next three weeks to pose as Emma's husband. Technically, I am Emma's husband, so the posing would be to show the world—specifically this Kandi Kline woman—that we intentionally got married and are living our happily ever after.

Initially, I thought it was a ridiculous idea, but seeing the chaos her viral video and the announcement of our marriage has caused for Emma and her brand, I don't know that there's any other way to protect her image. Seeing the look of desperation on Emma's face, I've determined it's what I need to do to make things right.

Before I left Emma's hotel room, she and Jess offered me compensation. Jess wrote me a check, assigned a number value to my participation in this scheme, but I don't plan on cashing it. I don't think Emma should pay me thousands of dollars for a mistake we made together. To satisfy Jess, I folded the check and put it in my wallet.

While I always make it a point to be honest with Sophie, I'm having a hard time informing her I got drunk and married a stranger. Everything I've done for the last twelve years is to set a good example for Sophie and I hate that this could change how she sees me. I know everyone is allowed mistakes, but I've held myself to a higher standard and one night of poor decision making could undo it all.

Also, I know that Sophie harbors guilt about me raising her and giving up things in my twenties, like dating and partying—which was always my choice—but if she knew I had found a woman that I was interested in, let alone *married* her, she'd never let me blow it off as a wild night. She'd have some romantic notion about it. Tell me it's meant to be.

Sophie is a romantic. She's never had a serious boyfriend, that I know of, probably because I've done my best to keep her focus on school and her future career, but she wants to plan weddings for a living. The union of two people and the romance of that event makes her gush with happiness. From the early days when she was planning Barbie and Ken's wedding to her high school junior prom where she headed the committee that coordinated a rustic romance themed prom complete with wooden doors and archways and thousands of twinkle lights. She talked a local florist into donating greenery so she could make vine-like chandeliers to hang from the ceiling. Then she entered a prom theme contest and her school was featured in *Seventeen* magazine. It gave her the confidence to seek out a part-time job assisting a wedding planner at one of the hotels on The Strip. And now she's weeks away from graduating and starting her career.

I'm searching for the best response when I sniff the air. "Is something burning?"

"Oh, shit. Pancakes!" Her blonde ponytail whips the air as she abandons the suitcase and rushes into the kitchen.

I quickly follow.

"Oh no!" she wails when she flips the pancake and finds it overdone.

"You're making pancakes?" I ask.

"I thought we'd do happy face pancakes." She sighs at the charred surface of the pancake. "We haven't done them in forever, but I got distracted with packing, and interrogating you. Now they're burnt."

Happy face chocolate chip pancakes are a Sunday tradition. I started it when Sophie was ten, shortly after we lost our mom. The social worker who was in charge of our case said it would be good for us to establish some routines together. It would give us both a sense of order and stability, something we hadn't been given by any of our parents. Now that we're older, it doesn't happen every Sunday, but we try to do it once a month. We've been busy the last few months. Sophie approaching graduation and preparing for her final project, while I had been studying for the bar exam during the day and working for the revue at night.

I reach out my hand to indicate for her to hand me the spatula. "You finish packing, I'll take care of the pancakes."

She hands me the spatula. I lift the burnt pancakes from the griddle and drop them into the compost bin, then reach for the batter to start a fresh batch.

While I cook, Sophie moves around the kitchen collecting items for her trip.

"Are you ready for this?" I ask.

"God, yes. Three weeks and I'm graduating! I can't wait to be done."

"Have you heard from your summer internship applications?"

"A few."

I watch the batter bubble, then carefully flip it over.

"I'm waiting to make a decision."

I nod, then watch as she pulls a mixing bowl out of the cabinet and puts it in her tote bag.

"Why are you taking that mixing bowl?" I ask.

"You know how I hate to eat popcorn out of the bag."

"It's two weeks."

She gives me a look that tells me two weeks is clearly a lifetime and how could I possibly suggest she eat microwave popcorn out of the bag for that duration. I lift my hands in surrender.

"What time are you leaving?" I ask, placing the golden-brown pancakes on our plates.

Sophie peeks out from behind the refrigerator door where she has loaded her arms with cases of bubbly water and diet soda. She glances at the clock on the counter.

"Piper is picking me up in ten minutes."

I take the drink boxes out of her hands, giving her a questioning look as I set them on the counter.

"Necessities," she says.

"They have Diet Coke in LA."

"Sure, they do. But if I already have it then that's one less thing to worry about."

I refrain from teasing her more. Being prepared and having everything she needs is Sophie's anchor. It stems from a childhood of chaos and uncertainty which we've coped with in our own ways. Hers is to be prepared, mine is to avoid those situations altogether. A situation exactly like flying to New York to pose as Emma's husband which has more question marks than Jim Carrey's The Riddler costume.

The microwave dings.

"Bacon's done!" Sophie grabs out the tray.

I reach into the fridge for the berries and whipped cream.

At the table, we work together to assemble our happy face pancakes. Sophie placing on the bacon mouth, blueberry nose and strawberry eyes, while I use the can of whipped cream to spray on the hair.

We sit down to eat. Sophie digs in, stabbing her pancake's blueberry nose. Then, she looks up at me.

"So, last night..." She takes a bite of bacon, then prompts me to answer by waving the crispy breakfast meat in my direction.

She wants the details.

"We went to Vibe."

She looks thoughtful, her interest piqued.

"That's not your scene at all."

"I don't have a scene," I reply.

"I know. And if you did, it wouldn't be there."

"Reggie and Mike wanted to go." I don't bother mentioning Dallas. He's the last person I would want to spend time with outside of work. "What did you do last night?" I ask, looking to pull the attention off me.

"I waited until it wasn't a million degrees, then I went for a run."

"Alone? In the dark?" The displeasure is clear in my voice.

"No. Geez. I went with Coco."

My mind draws up the visual of Sophie's petite friend.

"That doesn't make me feel better. I could fit her in my pocket."

"Relax. We ran the track outside the campus rec center. There were like a gazillion people there."

"Hmm." I know I'm overprotective at times, but I can't help it. The moment Sophie became my responsibility, it became ingrained in my brain. I know she's an adult now, about to graduate college, but I'm still having a hard time letting go.

I take another bite of pancake. The chocolate chips and whipped cream are sweeter than what I regularly eat for breakfast, but I know Sophie still loves them and there's no way I'd ever say anything about it.

"Then, we watched a movie with her boyfriend. It was some serious third wheel action."

"Good."

"That I was the third wheel?" She lifts her brows.

I shrug. "Safety in numbers."

She rolls her eyes at me. "What's your plan for the day?"

Before I can answer, there's a knock on the door, followed by the entrance of Sophie's friend, Piper.

"I know I'm late!" she calls as she slams the front door. "We'll do ninety on the highway and make up for time."

"Hi, Piper." I announce my presence.

She stops when she sees me.

"Griffin," a look of surprise on her face, "lovely to see you this morning. What I meant to say was, let's drive five under the speed limit and take our time. There's really no rush."

I've known Piper since the girls were in high school. She's Sophie's loud friend who has no filter. She's also been pulled over for speeding a handful of times, yet somehow is always let go with a warning.

"That sounds good. Let me help you load the car."

I stand, leaving my half-eaten pancake at the table. Sophie woofs down her last bite, then takes her plate to the kitchen.

"Thanks."

"How was last night?" Piper asks.

"Sophie told you I went out?" I ask, putting on my shoes.

"Of course, she did. For the rare occasion that it was, it should have been on the news."

I think about the *Page Six* article following Emma's viral video. It was news. Only I have the benefit of not having my face be on camera. And no one knowing who I am.

Piper grins flirtatiously. "And you should have called me."

"Gross!" Sophie calls from where she's collecting the rest of her things in the kitchen. "Stop hitting on my brother."

I give Piper a kind smile. I have zero interest in her, but I'm not going to be a jerk about it. I grab Sophie's suitcase and move toward the door.

"What's that?" Piper asks.

I turn to find her staring at me.

"What?" I wipe at my face, wondering if I've got whipped cream caught in my stubble. But, when the cool metal of my wedding band hits my cheek and Piper's eyes go wide, I know exactly what she's talking about.

"Is that..." Piper's brows pinch together as she points toward my hand.

Fuck. How had I forgotten to take it off? Did Sophie see it? If she had, she would have said something.

"Okay, I'm ready." Sophie hikes her tote bag onto her shoulder as she enters the room.

Piper's doing some kind of calculation in her head. Her face moving through the stages of questioning to understanding as her brows lift and her jaw drops.

"Oh my God, Griffin, did you get married last night?"

After twenty minutes of questioning from Sophie, she and Piper finally got on their way to LA. Piper promised me she wouldn't speed even though they were definitely going to be late for their three o'clock check-in time.

I've received ten text messages from Sophie since she left. Mostly all variations of questioning how her boring, predictably routine brother could have accidentally gotten married to a stranger last night.

Sophie: *Were you drugged? Held at gunpoint? The details aren't adding up. Text me our secret code if you need help. Also, were you going to tell me if Piper hadn't seen your ring?*

Griffin: *I'm okay. No drugs or guns. I wanted to tell you, but I didn't want you to be disappointed in me.*

I exhale forcefully. The words are easier to type than to say.

Sophie: *I could never be disappointed in you. You're my hero. Even Superman had kryptonite to contend with.*

As I read her text, Sophie's words ease the tightness in my chest a little. And I have to smile at her use of the kryptonite analogy. It's exactly what I thought about this morning when I woke up next to Emma. That the universe had found my Achilles' heel; a spirited, extremely sexy, yet vulnerable woman that I couldn't resist wanting to protect.

I need to talk to someone other than Sophie. A guy that can understand the situation. Someone who has ended up in a similar situation before.

I tap his name and the line rings twice before he picks up.

"So how does it feel?" Chad asks in lieu of a greeting.

"How did you find out?" I respond.

"Find out about what?" he asks.

I pause. "What are you talking about?"

"How it feels to be done with the revue. Your last night. How does it feel?"

"Oh, right. Good."

"Kenny said you went out last night. That's different."

"It was the last night."

"I'd say I'm sorry I missed it, but I haven't missed Vegas clubs in years."

Chad has been sober for three years, and while he attests that he can still have fun without drinking, like me, he prefers a quiet night in. Chad's a few years older than me, and he's seen and done everything you can imagine, including drunkenly marrying a woman after a club appearance five years ago. This makes him the perfect person to talk to about the situation with Emma.

"We went to Vibe," I say.

"Not the worst place to go."

"Emma, the woman that I did my hot seat dance for, was with us."

"No kidding?" he asks.

"Dallas was pursuing her hard and I wanted to watch out for her."

"I don't condone violence, but please tell me this story ends with you punching Dallas in the face. His black eye will heal in a few weeks, but the legend of you knocking him out will live on forever."

Chad likes Dallas as much, if not less, than I do.

"I didn't punch Dallas. With me there, he lost interest in Emma and took a redhead home instead."

"Damn. Missed opportunity."

"I got married," I mumble, finding it harder to tell him than I thought it would be.

The line is silent and then Chad is snort laughing into the phone. His laughter is so loud, I have to lower the volume on my phone.

"That's a good one. I'm surprised you didn't wait to deliver that in person so you could see the tears of laughter rolling down my face." Between howls of laughter, he takes in a breath. "Whew." I can imagine him pausing to wipe a tear. "That one got me good."

"I'm serious. I married Emma, the woman I danced for."

"Fuck. You're serious?"

"We were having fun. She proposed and I couldn't say no. It was the strangest thing. I'd had some drinks but I wasn't that drunk. I should have known better. But, being near her, I wasn't in control of myself."

"Fuck, man. That's insane." He pauses. "You know why this happened, right? You're so backed up. You need to have sex. It's affecting your brain and your decision making."

"I'm not backed up," I argue. I'm not a monk. I've had plenty of self-love.

"It's like that Ashton Kutcher movie where he doesn't have sex for forty days and by the end of it, he's hallucinating and has to be tied to a bed for his own safety. Multiply that by how long it's been since you touched a woman and it's no wonder you're making impulsive decisions."

"I didn't call you so you could tell me I need to get laid."

"You got married. Didn't you already get laid?"

I'm silent, my mind returning to Emma. Last night, her body beneath mine. And this morning, when she came against my tongue. That visual will be enough to sustain me for another six years. Not that I plan to be celibate for that long. It was never a plan, only a result of my situation. Now, my situation has changed, but that doesn't mean I want to go out and fuck every woman who is willing. Even before I made the decision to be celibate, that wasn't the kind of guy I was.

"Fuck, man, this is worse than I thought. As a friend, I am concerned for your wellbeing. I can have one of my lady friends over there in minutes. There's an entire lineup that would be glad to rid you of this burden."

"I'm not having sex with your friends. And, I'm married now, remember?"

"That's an easy fix. You can even do the paperwork yourself. Unless she's like Glenn Close in *Fatal Attraction* and she becomes obsessed with you. I guess you can be thankful that you don't have any pets for her to boil."

I'm really starting to question why I called him.

"She's not obsessed with me, but it's not an easy fix. She needs me to go to New York and pretend to be her husband."

"You are her husband."

"It's an image thing. She's a wedding gown designer and she's got an important interview with a magazine."

"And you're going to do it." It's not really a question.

"Yeah, I am."

"What about your job?" Chad asks.

I'm supposed to start as an associate at Terrence's firm, McGregor & Lange, next week. I had given myself a week to transition between jobs, but with Emma needing me in New York right away, I'll need to talk to Terrence about postponing my start date.

"I'll have to postpone it a few weeks."

"So you go to New York, for how long?" he asks.

"Three weeks," I reply.

"Then you get an annulment and come home?"

"Yeah, that's the plan."

Chad starts laughing again.

I groan. "Really? Why is that funny?"

"I'm sorry. It's not funny." He chuckles again. "But there is no fucking way you're going to make it three weeks without completely falling for this woman. You couldn't make it a handful of hours without marrying her. As your friend, I mean it in the nicest way when I say…you're fucked."

I consider Chad's assessment. He's not wrong. When I'm around Emma, I'm not thinking clearly. I told myself I wouldn't touch her, then minutes later, I'm offering her an orgasm to cure her headache with the knowledge that even if her head didn't get relief, I was desperate to taste her. To feel her pussy clench around my fingers. Even thinking about her now has my heart hammering in my chest. The crotch of my jeans tightening.

Orgasms aside, Emma is in a situation that my actions helped put her in and I can't abandon her.

"She needs me. I already told her I'd go. I can't back out now."

"Since I don't have the time or psychology degree to dive into what I believe to be your superhero complex, I'm going to offer you a piece of advice."

"Yeah?" I ask, warily. "What is it?"

"Do not, under any circumstances, have sex with your wife."

CHAPTER 11

Emma

"I feel nauseous," I announce, biting into another gummy bear.

"Then stop eating those things." Jess scrunches her nose at me. "I highly doubt artificially flavored, high fructose corn syrup laden gummy bears are going to make your stomach feel better."

She's right, but they were preventing me from biting my nails, so I thought it was a win.

After a smooth flight from Las Vegas, we're now standing at baggage claim at La Guardia.

She looks at her watch. "Griffin should have landed by now."

Our flight was sold out, so Jess booked Griffin on another airline. My stomach squeezes at the mention of him. I've been anxious since he left my hotel room yesterday, wondering if he's going to show up. I wouldn't blame him if he didn't. It was my video that announced our wedding to the world; that put me in this mess with not only the Kandi Kline interview but with my family and friends.

"He'll be in the same terminal so you'll meet him on Level

2 where I've arranged a car service to take you both to your parents' apartment."

At the mention of my parents, my stomach drops out. My phone still has hundreds of unanswered text messages and voicemails, but the hurt in my mom's voice in the message she left me yesterday morning had me calling her back as soon as Griffin left. We all determined that the fewer people who know that mine and Griffin's marriage was a mistake, and will ultimately be annulled, the better, but it was hardest to lie to her and my dad. To let them think that I purposely didn't invite them to my wedding to a man they've never met. But Jolyn Warner's lips are looser than a garter belt with no elastic. She wouldn't do it maliciously, but I can't risk her letting it slip to one of her friends. A single word to one of the ladies in her Upper East Side society circle and my plot to conceal mine and Griffin's drunken nuptials would fold.

"I'm kind of freaking out here."

Jess moves to pull her suitcase off the carousel, and I join in to help her muscle the oversized bag.

"About which part?" she asks.

"Um, marrying a stranger, then flying that stranger to New York to pose as my husband even though he is technically my husband on paper, but it's not real, but we're going to pretend it is and try to convince a magazine editor, as well as everyone I care about, that we're legitimately in love."

"Oh, that."

"Yes, *that*."

I spot my bag and move to reach for it, giving Jess an incredulous look as we heave it over the side of the carousel.

"You and Griffin have chemistry. I saw it Saturday night. You two will need to lay low for the next day or so to work on your back story, learn as much about each other as you can, and then everything else will fall into place."

Jess is right, Griffin and I do have chemistry. That's how we got into this situation in the first place.

Last night, I lay awake most of the night thinking about him. His hands on me, his mouth between my legs. His deep voice rough in my ear telling me I'm a good girl. Also, the way he had hung my mom's wedding dress—now, mine—with care and precision in the closet after I had left it in a heap on the floor.

Jess grips my shoulders and turns me so we're face to face.

"Emma," she takes a deep breath, "as your friend, I have to say this to you. You have an amazing heart. Its capacity to love and give itself to others is huge, but in this particular situation," she points a finger toward the ground between us and motions in a circle, "you need to lock that shit up tight."

I nod slowly, taking in her advice.

"I know you're still recovering from heartbreak with Alec and it would be so easy to fall into another guy. But now isn't the time and Griffin isn't the guy."

I open my mouth to argue, or at least question why Griffin wouldn't be the guy, when Jess cuts me off.

"He's a rebound. And sometimes when rebounds don't work out, they hurt even more than the original heartbreak. You need time to heal and be on your own. So, I think the best thing for you right now is to focus on getting the Bergman's contract signed and nail the interview with Kandi Kline, without putting your heart in the mix."

Jess is right. She's been beside me from the beginning. She knows the effort that has gone into getting to this point and how much I want to prove that it's my designs that deserve the attention, not the fact that my parents are well-known with connections. There's too much at stake right now to be anything but one hundred percent focused on my business. Griffin was a fun distraction when I was feeling down about Alec's engagement, but I'm not ready to put myself out there again. And even if I was, Griffin lives in Las Vegas. How would that even work?

It wouldn't.

I think about how lonely my relationship with Alec was. How with us living in the same city, and under the same roof, we still felt distant.

No, Griffin is posing as my husband, and I won't let my heart get involved. I need to stay focused and diligent or this whole thing could blow up in my face.

"I got this." I nod, giving her a reassuring smile. I signal a locking motion in front of my heart and then I throw away the imaginary key.

Jess nods. "Yes, you do."

I give her a hug, then square my shoulders and march toward the exit where I'm supposed to meet Griffin and our driver. I'm only a few strides in when I catch sight of Griffin walking toward me. When I stop short at the sight of him, momentum carries my oversized suitcase, clipping my heel and nearly running me over from behind.

Griffin's head is down looking at his phone in one hand, and he's pulling his suitcase with the other. He's wearing a backpack over his broad shoulders, causing the fabric of his t-shirt to pull taut across his chest. The weight of his suitcase in his hand activates those glorious muscles of his, giving me an eyeful of forearm porn.

My brain registers every last detail of him as I grip my suitcase handle and start walking again.

I curse my genetics for perfect eyesight. If I wore contacts, I could rip them out right now and be oblivious to the gorgeous man walking toward me. If I could make him a blurry blob that would definitely make these next few weeks easier.

He taps on his phone, slides it into his back pocket, then looks up.

The moment those green eyes land on me, my heart stutters and my mouth goes dry.

"Hey." He lifts a hand in greeting, then closes the last few feet between us.

"Hi." I try to play it cool, but my body is reacting to his proximity, an uncontrollable inconvenience. "How was—"

"You look—"

We start talking at the same time.

Griffin smiles. "You go ahead."

"I was just going to ask how your flight was."

"Uneventful."

"That's nice." I nod robotically. I know we have chemistry, but if my attraction to Griffin gets in the way of me acting like a normal person, this isn't going to work. I have to find a way to not want to melt into a puddle in his presence.

"You look nice."

I drop my gaze to the blush-colored dress I'm wearing.

"Thanks. I guess you've only seen me in a hand-me-down wedding dress and a bathrobe. Surprise!" I wave my hand along the front of my body. "I do own clothes."

"Yeah, you do." He's smiling again. The dimple popping in his left cheek is making my palms sweat.

I rub my hands together and focus on getting us out of here.

"There should be a driver picking us up." I motion toward the door Jess mentioned.

"Okay."

Before I know what's happening, Griffin reaches for the handle of my suitcase and starts pulling it alongside him. Apparently, two muscular forearms working hard are better than one.

"Thank you."

"You bet." He offers a small smile.

The giddiness I'm feeling at the simple gesture of him pulling my suitcase is ridiculous. Having a man to help me with my luggage is not a reason to swoon. I tamp down the butterflies swirling in my belly.

We move through the sliding doors and toward the curb where a driver holding a sign with my name is waiting.

The driver loads our suitcases into the black sedan, then holds the door for us to enter.

I'm not usually an awkward person, but in the back seat of this car with Griffin, I can't seem to find my footing.

Griffin seems at ease. He's like that. I think.

It's like flying to the largest city in the country to convince a magazine editor, not to mention my family and friends, that we've had a whirlwind romance and our marriage was not just a drunken mistake in Vegas is not fazing him at all. Or maybe I'm projecting the chaotic feelings I'm having onto Griffin. A sense of panic enveloped me the moment we touched down in New York. Everything since Saturday night has been happening in hyper-speed and only in this moment of calm on the drive to my parents' apartment am I finally realizing the magnitude of what course I have set in motion.

Griffin's in New York. He's here to be my husband. There's no going back.

He's silently staring out the window, taking in the city. His hands are resting on his legs, his fingers curved over the outside of his thighs in a relaxed pose. My fingernail finds my mouth.

I should have a million things to say to him. We have so much to talk about before we meet with Kandi Kline...before we meet with anyone, but when I look over at him, my throat goes dry. I settle for pointing out landmarks and tourist attractions along the route.

"My cousin, Barrett, and his fiancée, Chloe, live on 72nd Street." I point down the street as we pass. "They're getting married in two weeks from Saturday. We'll need to get you a suit."

He nods.

"Thank you, again, for doing this. I know it's a lot to ask."

"I want to make things right. You didn't get into this alone."

"But I'm the one who made the video that outed us. You had nothing to do with that."

"If I'd tucked you into bed like I promised myself I would, then you wouldn't have been at that chapel making the video."

"And if I hadn't proposed to you on the rollercoaster, we wouldn't have been at the chapel."

His lips twitch, considering my theory.

"I guess I'm a bad influence, huh?" I laugh.

"The worst." His smile tells me something different.

For the moment, my nerves subside.

"This is it." I motion out the window to the apartment building we've pulled up to. "Home sweet home. Well, my parents' place. I moved back a few months ago after Alec and I broke up. I'm still looking for a new place."

The driver sets our bags on the curb while we exit.

"Welcome back, Miss Warner." Scott, the doorman, opens the glass door for us. "Sir." He nods at Griffin.

"Scott, this is Griffin. My...husband." My brain trips over the word husband. This is the first time I'm introducing Griffin to someone in my life. Even though the media post is out there confirming our marriage, this is me confirming it. The first of many introductions. It feels like a pivotal moment.

Scott smiles warmly and extends a hand to Griffin. "Pleasure to meet you, Mr..." He prompts for Griffin's last name and I draw a blank. Oh my God...what is Griffin's last name?

It's a huge detail that was lost among the fuzziness of Saturday night. I know I saw it on the marriage certificate.

"Hart," Griffin informs him. And me.

I thread my arm through Griffin's, and hope my beaming smile makes up for my lack of memory.

He nods at both of us. "Congratulations. You make a stunning couple."

"Thank you, Scott," I say.

"I'll have your bags brought up."

He motions us inside.

"You couldn't remember my last name?" His tone isn't admonishing, it's more playful, but my own shame makes me feel defensive.

"When I introduced you, it was weird to call you my husband. I got tripped up on that, then couldn't remember anything. If he would have asked my own name I would have struggled."

From behind the concierge desk, Mariella smiles and nods. "Good evening, Miss Warner."

"Then it's a good thing everyone here knows you." Griffin's lips quirk, and I know he's teasing me.

"Good evening, Mariella. This is Griffin Hart, my husband." I give emphasis to the word this time, letting it sink in.

"It's a pleasure." She smiles, her professional mask dropping for a moment when her eyes scan the length of him. I can't blame her. "And congratulations."

A minute later, the elevator doors close behind us and I sigh with relief at having almost made it safely to the apartment.

"We'll need to talk about our relationship, when we started dating, how we met, the basics," I tell Griffin as we step off the elevator. "It's still a whirlwind relationship because we wouldn't have started dating until after Alec and I broke up, but it's plausible that we fell head over heels in love and wanted to elope."

At the door, I pull out my key and unlock it.

"My parents are traveling for work; they won't be home until Wednesday so we have—"

My words drop off when I open the door to find a crowd of people in my parents' apartment.

CHAPTER 12

Griffin

At first, I think we've arrived at the wrong apartment, but the initial shock on Emma's face morphs into wary cheerfulness when a woman notices our arrival and rushes toward us.

"They're here!" she calls, moving to wrap Emma in an affectionate hug. "Happy birthday, sweetie!" The woman kisses her on both cheeks before holding her at arm's length. "And congratulations! You look radiant, what a blushing bride." The woman turns to me, extending her hand. "I'm Sally Foreman, Emma's piano instructor, well, former piano instructor. She decided fashion was her passion so we gave up the Julliard dream, but Emma was one of my best students. Such a delight." She turns my hand in her smaller one, examining my fingers. "Do you play? You've got the fingers for it."

"Sally, I don't think—" Emma's cut off by the next person in line, because there is a line forming now. A receiving line, like at a wedding. Judging from the ten-foot-high balloon arch and accompanying banner that reads 'Congratulations, Emma & Griffin,' we've arrived at some sort of post wedding celebration.

As we move through the crowd, I can't even take in Emma's

parents' apartment because all I see are faces staring back at me, eager to meet and greet. My brain switches into revue dancer Griffin—not that I'm going to start offering lap dances—but it's easier to pretend I'm at a show, that this attention is due to the part that I'm playing, not because people are genuinely excited to meet *me*, Emma's accidental husband. The guy that will disappear in three weeks, never to be heard from again.

That's my way of coping, but from the anxious look on Emma's face, I can tell she doesn't have the same ability to put on a mask. I don't know any of these people, but for her, it's a room filled with family and friends, relationships that she's collected over the course of her thirty years, and I can tell facing them all at once under the circumstances is over-whelming.

When she looks up at me, her eyes wide with alarm, that squeeze in my chest is back. All I want to do is comfort her, protect her. In the short time I've known her, it's become a reflex.

My arm slides around Emma's waist, pulling her into my side. I lean down to press a gentle kiss against her temple. The softness of her skin under my lips and the already familiar lavender scent of her hair pulls me out of my head. Almost makes me forget what I'm doing here.

Play the part.

"We got this," I whisper against the shell of her ear. Emma's body quivers against mine. The sensation pulls me back to the hotel room yesterday morning when I parted her robe. The same tremble of her legs when my tongue licked between her thighs. I pull back from her, knowing if I don't get control of these thoughts this situation is going to take an embarrassing turn.

Soon enough, her body relaxes into mine and the satisfac-tion of knowing that she's feeling better inflates my chest, making it easier to breathe.

When my gaze lifts, I find the crowd parting to let a couple pass through.

A tall, lithe woman in a mid-length red dress. The man, shorter than her, but with broad shoulders and a salt and pepper beard. They are a striking couple.

Without a word, the woman embraces Emma. Up close, the similarities between Emma and this woman are obvious. They share the same silky brown hair, though this woman's is shorter than Emma's, and with more layers, the same eyes and heart-shaped face. They could be sisters, but I know Emma is an only child, so she must be Emma's mom. And that would make this man...

Before I can say anything, he grips my hand tightly, using leverage to pull me down toward his face.

"You're not a father yet, or maybe you are, I know absolutely nothing about you...but if you don't have children, you can't understand how a man feels about meeting the man who married his daughter for the first time *after* their wedding."

While his grip is tight, it's nothing I can't handle, but I don't want to insult him anymore than he already believes I have, so I pull my features tight, hoping it gives the illusion of pain.

He's right, I'm not a father, but raising Sophie has given me enough perspective to know that if she showed up married to some random guy, I'd feel the same way. I'd be hurt. Wondering what I'd done wrong to be excluded from such an important part of her life. I want to reassure him it isn't what he thinks—a secret whirlwind relationship punctuated by a quickie marriage. That even though getting married was a mistake, I do care about Emma. I wouldn't be here if I didn't.

"I—" I begin, but he silences me with a squeeze.

"I'm a professional photographer. I find people's angles

for a living. If you have one, I'm going to find it." His voice goes even lower. "And everybody has an angle."

With my lack of relationships, I've never had to meet a woman's parents before. Never been set up to be judged if I was worthy of someone's daughter. The feeling is new and even knowing I'm here to pretend, so is the desire to pass the test. Ultimately, it doesn't matter if Emma's parents like me, but that doesn't stop me from wanting to try.

"Understood, sir." I nod, deciding this isn't the moment to try to build trust with Emma's dad. Trust that will ultimately be broken when we part ways. The thought makes my chest feel hollow. In Emma's Vegas hotel room, the idea of coming here to pretend we're together was an abstract idea. Now standing in front of Emma's parents, family and friends, I'm realizing this will be a more difficult task than I thought.

"Dad," Emma admonishes, placing her hands over our joined ones. His grip slowly loosens until I can pull my hand back. "Griffin, this is my dad, Philip, and my mom, Jolyn."

"Griffin, so nice to meet you." Emma's mom embraces me. I'm waiting for a whispered threat, a mother's vow to seek revenge on the man who deprived her of mother/daughter wedding errands, but it doesn't come. Clearly, she's taking the news easier than Philip. "Welcome to our home." Jolyn motions around us. The crowd of fifty-plus has dispersed to give us a moment, but is still milling about, sipping on champagne, while cater waiters pass hors d'oeuvres.

"Thank you," I say, feeling slightly more at ease with Jolyn's kindness.

"What is happening here?" Emma whispers to her parents.

"Your father and I felt bad that we missed your birthday and your fashion show, which I know you told us a million times it was okay we didn't come, so we planned a birthday gathering for your return and under the circumstances, it is now doubling as a wedding shower."

She motions to a table in the foyer that is overflowing with gifts.

"I don't think we're up for this. We just got off the plane. We're not dressed for a party." Emma motions to our clothes.

"You both look great," her mom counters, raising a hand to flag down one of the waiters. "Let's get you something to drink."

Emma pinches my elbow between her fingers. When my eyes meet hers, she's giving me some sort of eyelash batting morse code distress signal.

"Um, maybe we should freshen up," I suggest.

My effort to escape is shut down just as quick.

"Later." Jolyn smiles as a waiter appears beside us. She moves to hand both of us a glass of champagne, only pulling Emma's back at the last second. "Wait, are you pregnant?"

"Jesus, Mom!" Emma's mouth gapes open in horror. She looks around to see if anyone's attention is on us, then whispers, "No."

"What?" Jolyn asks innocently. "It would explain the elopement. And it wouldn't be the worst thing in the world, would it?"

I can see the twinkle in Jolyn's eyes, the vision of grandbabies dancing in her head.

"I'm not pregnant." Emma's face flushes. She doesn't meet my eyes. Not only did we just meet, but we've yet to consummate our marriage. Another image of Emma on the bed, her thighs spread open, her pussy slick and swollen, waiting for my tongue. Fuck. I'm going to need to figure out how to keep that image from popping into my head every five seconds whenever Emma is next to me.

Jolyn hands her the champagne glass, then motions us toward the windows on the far side of the living room. "Your father and I would like to make a toast."

"Give us just a minute." Emma skirts past a group of

guests to pull me into a quiet space off the living area where she promptly tosses back her entire champagne flute.

"Easy, tiger," I say.

"You don't know how bad you're going to need that." She motions to my full glass. "Is this not stressing you out in the slightest?"

I glance around the room. "I'm processing."

"Well, I've already processed and this party has catastrophe written all over it. What are we going to tell people? How did we meet? How did you propose?" She looks at me pointedly. Apparently, a drunken rollercoaster proposal is off the table.

"How would you have wanted me to propose?" I ask.

A waiter walks out of the kitchen behind us and Emma snags a bacon-wrapped scallop off the tray. I grab one, too, and we chew in silence for a moment, Emma still contemplating my question.

"Something timeless and romantic. Nothing cliché like a jumbotron at a sporting event."

I nod. "I didn't take you for a jumbotron proposal type of woman, so we're on the same page there."

She wipes the corners of her mouth with the napkin. When she pulls it away from her lips, I notice they're monogrammed *Griffin & Emma* in an elegant font.

Emma notices them, too.

"Should I save it for the scrapbook?" I ask, trying to make light of this bizarre situation.

Emma sighs. "No need. There are probably a thousand more where that one came from."

We still have no plan in place when the clinking of a spoon on the side of a champagne glass draws our attention across the room. Emma's mom's eyes find us on the edge of the crowd and she motions us forward.

Upon on our arrival, the crowd quiets and Emma's mom starts talking.

"Thank you, everyone, for being here to celebrate Emma's milestone birthday and to congratulate Emma and Griffin on their nuptials. Emma, it's been such an honor to be your mom, to watch you grow into the hard working, compassionate, spirited woman that you are. There were many bumps along the way, but even through the difficult times, your father and I always knew you'd find your happiness. In life, in your career, and now with a loving partner." She motions to me. "Griffin, we are overjoyed to welcome you into our family. Everyone, please join me in toasting to the happy couple."

I turn to find Emma's eyes brimming with tears and a wobbly smile on her face. Again, my instinct is to pull her into me, and press a kiss to the side of her head.

"You okay?" I ask.

She gives me a quick nod, then clinks her glass to mine and swallows back the bubbly liquid, her empty glass having been refilled by a passing waiter.

Philip steps forward like he's going to speak, but Jolyn cuts him off. From his greeting earlier, she's likely afraid of what he might say. The 'if you have nothing nice to say, don't say anything at all' concept in effect.

"We're going to cut the cake, then we'll let Emma and Griffin make the rounds," Jolyn announces.

Our attention moves to the corner of the room, where the floor-to-ceiling windows adjoin, and to the small fabric-covered table there where a five-tier wedding cake sits on top.

"Holy shit." Emma's eyes bulge. "It's my dream wedding cake."

As we're ushered toward the cake, another woman approaches Emma. Her features are identical to Emma's mom, the difference being her hair is lighter in color.

"Hi, doll," she says to Emma.

"Aunt Jo." Emma lunges toward her, hugging her tight.

"Sorry I'm late, it was a hectic Monday."

"This is Griffin." Emma introduces us.

"Wonderful to meet you." She hugs me. "Congratulations." She hands Emma a large pink bag. "This is from Chloe and Barrett, mostly Chloe. They're sorry they couldn't be here; they're flying back from Seattle tonight."

"Oh, that's so nice." Emma takes the bag from her. "I'll see Chloe tomorrow. She's coming in for her dress fitting."

"I'll let you two proceed to the cake cutting."

We move along, finally making our way over to the behemoth cake. Upon our arrival, it is discovered that the Waterford cake cutting knife and server set Jolyn has gifted to us for this occasion has been misplaced and is currently being searched for by the catering staff. While the search ensues, Emma and I are left standing on display in front of the monstrous cake.

The people at the front of the crowd move in closer.

"You make an attractive couple. Plans for starting a family?" a woman asks.

"Um—" Emma starts, but is cut off by a woman pushing her way toward the front.

"Let me see the ring." The woman holds her hand out.

Emma extends her hand.

When the woman's eyes drop to Emma's simple gold band, I see surprise register on her face. She pats Emma's hand and gives her a small smile. "Simple. Elegant. And you won't have a huge rock getting in the way. Just a thin, modest band. Great for everyday wear." I think she means to be reassuring, but she should have stopped at simple and elegant.

Emma forces a smile. "Thank you."

It's the first time I'm thinking about the ring in terms of what other people think about it. From the appearance of this apartment, the way everyone here is dressed, the pile of meticulously wrapped gifts that have been procured with under twenty-four hours' notice of our wedding, it's clear that Emma's family has wealth and status.

A woman like Emma is expected to have a large shiny diamond on her finger. I can see the disappointment in the women's faces. The flush of discomfort creeping up Emma's neck.

"How did he propose?" another woman calls out.

"Oh, yes. Let's all hear the story while we wait on the cutlery." Emma's mom tucks in beside her.

"Um, well—" Emma starts, but I can see the panic in her eyes, hear the tremble of her voice. I squeeze her hand and she looks up at me.

"It was on a rooftop in Vegas." I'm referencing how we met, drawing from the moment I first laid eyes on Emma. "I —" A loud clatter pulls everyone's attention to the other side of the room where the caterer has collided with one of the cater waiters on her way to bring us a long, narrow black box.

"Found it!" The caterer rushes toward us, leaving the cater waiter scrambling to pick up the dropped tray with hors d'oeuvres. She's nearly out of breath as she presents the box to Emma, who in turn visibly sags with relief.

"And he said 'will you marry me?' and I said 'yes,'" Emma tosses out quickly before taking the cutlery box from the caterer. "Thank you." Only I know she's thanking her for the cutlery and for the interruption.

With custom cutlery in hand, we move behind the cake.

Emma's mom smiles brightly while Emma's dad grumpily holds his camera up to take our picture.

"I can't do this anymore," Emma whispers from beside me. "I know my mom wants to be a part of all this stuff, I feel bad, but we have to get out of here. Can you fake an injury or something?"

With Emma's back pressed against my front, our arms aligned and our hands joined over the knife, we press into the smooth buttercream. Another cut, and a triangle is removed from the tier. Emma gingerly places it on the plate then cuts it in half, the intention that we feed each other a piece.

They're big pieces. More than what can fit in anyone's mouth. Emma lifts hers, and I lift mine. As I'm moving the cake toward her mouth, the idea hits me. A way to escape. That's what Emma asked for.

Right before the cake meets Emma's lips, my fingers relax their grip, letting the cake fall back into the palm of my hand. And then I press my hand firmly into Emma's face. I aim for her mouth, but the large piece of cake conveniently spans across her nose and cheeks. With smeared buttercream around her lips, I watch as her mouth drops open in shock. The remainder of the cake crumbles down the front of her dress, then falls to the wood floor. She's staring back at me with confusion and annoyance, but then her eyes light with understanding, and her lips twitch knowingly. With the cake in her hand, she doesn't hesitate as she moves toward me, winding up her arm and smacking the slice of cake square against my jaw. She rotates her hand for good measure, really smashing it in good. Bits of cake crumbs fall down the neck of my t-shirt and a large glop of buttercream drops onto my shoe.

To this room full of elegantly dressed people, we probably look uncivilized, but Emma's smiling up at me now, and that's all that matters.

Kiss!

I can't tell if the sound came from someone in the room or my brain, but I listen. It's part of the show after all.

My clean hand wraps around Emma's waist, loving the way it fits perfectly in the space between the fitted bodice of her dress and the curve of her hips beneath its skirt. I pull her to me and drop my mouth to hers. Her hands grip my arms. The buttercream on her hand is sticky against my skin, but my main focus is the feeling of her soft body pressed against mine.

My tongue dips between her lips. She tastes incredible. The cake is nice, too.

The room cheers and there's a repetition of clicks from Emma's dad.

As we pull apart, somebody hands us towels to wipe our faces, but Emma grabs my hand, quickly leading me out of the room and down a quiet hallway.

We spill into a room, laughing, our faces still dripping with frosting.

"That was genius," Emma says, now wiping at tears, as well as frosting. "I'll admit, at first, I was annoyed, but when I realized your plan, it made so much sense."

"I'm glad you were quick to understand."

"Thank you for helping us escape." Emma reaches up, swipes a finger through the frosting on my cheek, then places it in her mouth. "Mmm. It is good cake, though."

She swipes again, but before she can lick her finger, I grab her hand and sink it into my mouth.

The cake is good. I tasted it on her lips a minute ago, but being playful with Emma is even better.

Her eyes widen as my tongue swirls around her finger. "It's good, right?" she asks.

"It's delicious."

"Well looking at the size of it, we might be eating it for the next three weeks."

"Your parents went all out. When I saw the size of that cake, I thought for sure someone was going to jump out of it."

"That's the burden of being an only child. All the focus is on you. Good or bad. Whether you want it or not."

I know Emma was feeling overwhelmed out there, surrounded by friends and family, but she's lucky to have them. If the situation were reversed, there wouldn't be a room full of people for me to celebrate with. Only a handful of people I've learned to trust over the years.

She must see the look on my face.

"I'm sorry. I know you and Sophie have been on your own

for a long time. I'm grateful for my family. I just didn't expect everyone to be here tonight."

"I get it. Your dad is pretty intense."

"He's an artist. He feels everything. My mom's a ray of sunshine. She balances out his moodiness."

"Yeah, I could tell."

I take in the room we've entered. It's dark, except the glow from the lamp on the bedside table. She guides me past a four-poster bed with pink bedding, and an insane number of pillows, all in various shapes, sizes and colors. There doesn't appear to be a theme.

It could be a guest room, but there's a desk on the far wall, between two large windows framed in gauzy pink curtains that has a bulletin board filled with pictures. Shelves above the desk have trophies and plaques on it, ribbons hanging from hooks under the shelf. I move in for a closer look, but Emma pulls me toward a door.

"Bathroom is in here," she says, kicking off her heels as she moves us into the ensuite bathroom.

She flips on the light, revealing a white marble bathroom with gold accents. When I take in the double vanity, I think about Sophie and her constant complaint about our lack of bathroom counter space at home.

Using the cotton hand towel I was given, I lean toward the mirror to wipe a clump of buttercream off my cheek.

I watch as Emma dabs at the remnants of frosting and cake crumbs. She rinses her face and pats it dry before hopping up on the counter between the two sinks, her dress inching up her thighs while her legs dangle over the counter.

"Do you think they expect us back?" I ask.

"We're newlyweds. They probably think we're sucking each other's faces off."

"In this case, it would be licking."

"Exactly," she says. "So, let's get our story straight. What should we tell everyone?"

She reaches for a bottle on the counter and pumps it against her hand before rubbing her palms together, then patting down her face.

"The truth," I say, solemnly, knowing that the only way to get Emma to relax is to show her I'm relaxed. And to tease her a little.

Her eyes bug out. "If I wanted to tell them the truth, you wouldn't be here."

"Okay, let me think."

"Here, let me," she says, pulling on the towel to move me closer. Positioning myself in front of her, I let her wet a corner of the towel, then start wiping it along my jaw.

"I got it. We met online, have been dating long-distance for two months, per your requested timeline, and you begged me to marry you while you were visiting Vegas."

"Begged?" She scoffs.

I shrug, enjoying messing with her.

"I was on the fence. Convincing was required."

"Very funny. I didn't realize I married a comedian."

"Isn't that the problem? You don't know who you married?" I mean it to be teasing, but the second my words land, I can tell by Emma's weak smile that it wasn't funny.

"Hey. I was trying to make light of the situation. I'm sorry. I didn't mean—"

"No, you're right. We don't know each other. And we only have ten days until the interview with Kandi Kline. We'll have to be better prepared than we were tonight." She continues talking as she wipes.

With resolute concentration, Emma inches closer, her focus on the left side of my face where she's working hard to clean frosting out of my ear.

Her proximity is intoxicating. With no makeup on now, I can see the freckles on her nose, the mole above her lip. She's beautiful. My hands find her wrists, encircling the smooth, sensitive skin there before pressing in closer to her. Her gaze shifts to mine and her work with the towel slows.

I watch as the column of her neck bobs as she swallows.

Right now, I'm dying to close the inches between us. To take my time kissing her. Touch every inch of her. Taste her again. My head between her thighs in Vegas was merely an appetizer. I want the main dish. Every. Last. Bite.

Emma's head tilts, her eyelids flutter closed. Her body readying itself for my descent.

I'm almost there, ready to capture her full lips, but I stop myself.

I have to be careful with Emma. It's dangerous how easily she draws me in. How being near her makes me quickly forget the reason I'm here. That regardless of what our marriage license says, we don't really belong to each other. Being here with her is a detour. A bump in the steady path that I've been on, and once I've done what she needs, I'll be going home.

It's one thing to fall into the role of husband when we're in front of her family and friends. We'll need to touch each other, to kiss, like a real couple would. But, when we're alone, I need to keep my distance. For her sake and for mine. When this charade is over, I'll be walking away. Returning to Las Vegas to do what I've been waiting years to do—watch Sophie graduate college and move forward with *my* life.

There's no question, I have to set boundaries.

"Griffin?" Emma's lids lift, her eyes searching mine.

I lower her arms, setting them in her lap as I back up. Her brows furrow with my retreat.

"I think we should keep things between us platonic."

"Oh." Her lips twitch like she's thinking seriously before she nods in agreement. "No, you're right. That's probably best."

"Good. We'll kiss or touch if we need to in public, but otherwise we'll be friends."

"Friends," she echoes. I watch as Emma processes our agreement. Her eyes drop to my lips for the briefest of seconds before returning to mine. The question behind her brown eyes is as obvious as the sexual tension between us right now. How do we forget about my head between her thighs? I think about our night together, how palpable the chemistry was between us. How caught off guard I was that I couldn't fight my attraction to her. She was like a wave crashing over me, pulling me under, with no hope for escape. It's like I had been walking around in a world filled with repelling magnets, and Emma comes out of nowhere with her attracting magnetic force. I can't tell her that simply looking at her knocks the wind out of me. None of these confessions will be helpful to our situation, but I don't want to lie to her. I search for something in between.

"Yesterday morning, I wanted to make you feel better. I didn't think I was going to see you again," I say.

They are both true statements, only omitting the fact that the reason why I licked her pussy was because I thought it would be my only opportunity. That before it was discovered that our marriage was a headline in *Page Six*, the thought of walking out of that hotel room without tasting her, without watching her come apart under my tongue, was unbearable. At the time, I was desperate to collect the memory. Now, it's going to haunt me for the next three weeks. More likely, forever.

"Wow." She blinks. "Okay." Emma pushes off the counter and past me.

I'm playing my words back and realize I sound like an asshole. Fuck.

I don't want to hurt her, but selfishly I need to make sure she thinks I'm not interested. That our attraction to each other Saturday night was fueled by alcohol and loneliness, the desire to have a fun night, nothing more.

I try again.

"That's not how I meant it."

"No, I get it. You're right. Let's focus on the task at hand and not confuse anything. Let's be friends."

Her tone is anything but friendly, but I decide it's best to end the conversation before I get myself in more trouble.

I shove my hands into my pockets and nod. "Good. We're on the same page."

I watch as Emma starts moving the large assortment of pillows from her bed to a bench beside it.

"What's with all the pillows?" I ask.

Before I even get the question out, Emma's flinging one of the pillows in my direction. I catch it right before it smacks me in the face.

"I collect them," she says. "Collected. I haven't gotten a new one in a long time. They're from different milestones in my life. Family trips. Special holidays. As a child, I wasn't big on stuffed animals but I loved getting new pillows. My parents kept it going through my teens and twenties."

"My first time skiing." She nods to the mountain scene on the one in my hand. *Swiss Alps* it reads. "Piano recital." She moves the piano key pillow off the bed.

"My cat, Abby," there's a pillow shaped like a cat with an orange Tabby stitched on the front. "She was with us for nearly twenty years.

"Graduating fashion design school." She indicates the one with a pink sewing machine on it. "They're kind of childish, huh?"

"That's not what I was thinking at all."

Even with the pillows removed, the bed looks small.

It's a queen-sized bed. Not a king where you could roll to your side and barely notice if someone else is there.

"I can sleep on the floor," I offer.

Her features soften. "No, it's fine. We can share the bed."

I clear my throat. "I'd prefer to sleep on the floor."

For the briefest of seconds, her face goes slack. If I wasn't staring at her, I'd miss the change, because in the next moment she's smiling.

"Fine," Emma says sharply.

She walks over to the closet, yanks a pillow and blanket out, then dumps them into my arms on her way into the bathroom.

"Suit yourself," she says before slamming the door behind her.

Emma's my fake wife, but I think I might really be in the doghouse.

CHAPTER 13

Emma

A knock on the door pulls me out of a deep sleep. A sense of déjà vu washes over me from the wild night in Las Vegas. But this time when my eyes fly open, I find familiar surroundings. My bed. My room. New York. A momentary sigh of relief before the knock happens again followed by my mom's voice muffled behind the door.

"Emma? Griffin? I've got a tray of breakfast for you here," she calls.

I spring upright to peek over the bed. Griffin's there on his back, shirtless, one hand rests on his chest while his other arm is bent with his hand tucked under his head. The blanket covering him has slipped below his belly button. If it weren't for the waistband of his underwear peeking out, I'd think he was naked.

Don't think about him naked, Emma.

My eyes zero in on his face. The sharp angle of his jaw and the two-day beard covering it. The visual has me recalling the feeling of his stubble scratching the sensitive skin of my inner thighs when he eagerly dove between them in Vegas.

Another thing I shouldn't be thinking about.

I continue to stare until the knock comes again.

"Just a minute," I call with false cheeriness before whisper-hissing in his direction. *"Griffin."*

He shifts slightly, but doesn't wake. It would be easier to smack him in the face with a pillow, but I try to remain polite and move closer to him. *"Griffin."*

He shifts again and mumbles something, but his eyes are still closed. Ugh.

I hop off the bed and kneel down beside him, placing my hands on his shoulders. "Griffin, *wake up.*"

That does it. Except it's not a slow blinking realization, no, Griffin flings his body upright in a sudden motion, knocking me backwards. His reflexes to reach out and grab me are just as quick and a moment later, I'm securely in his lap.

He holds me there while the heel of his hand presses into his eye. "What's going on?"

"My mom's at the door," I whisper urgently.

"Your eggs are getting cold," my mom calls from the hallway. Our gazes move to the door, then back to each other.

Instead of dumping me off his lap so we can both scramble into the bed, Griffin wraps his arm around my back and lifts me up. A moment later we're under the covers, the tops of Griffin's muscular thighs pressing against the back of my legs.

"Come in," I call.

My mom, who appears to have been a millisecond away from barging in, pushes open the door carrying a breakfast tray.

"Good morning!" She's a beaming ray of sunshine as she carries the tray over and places it above my lap. "It's a few days late but I figured since you're here now, I'd bring you your birthday breakfast in bed."

"Gee, thanks, Mom." For our family, breakfast in bed on your birthday is a long-standing tradition. I'm thirty now, so while it would be easy to poo-poo this yearly ritual, I know it's important to her.

"It's a family tradition to get breakfast in bed on your birthday," she explains to Griffin. "Griffin, when is your birthday?"

"September twenty-second," he answers.

"A Virgo." She smiles at me. "That's a nice pairing for you. You're both Earth signs. Very compatible, especially sexually." My mom is into astrology and will drop little tidbits like this into everyday conversation.

"Mom." I shift, trying not to look as uncomfortable as I feel talking to my mom while pressed against Griffin's naked chest.

"What?" She looks innocent as a lamb. "We're all adults here. I'm sure you two have already discovered this."

I want to dive under the blankets and suffocate so I don't have to be a part of this conversation anymore. Beside me, Griffin is quiet. He must realize there's really nothing to add to this highly inappropriate conversation.

"I didn't forget about you, Griffin. There's an extra plate of eggs and bacon. I'm sure Emma will share her donut with you."

"Thank you, Mrs.—" Griffin starts.

"Call me Jolyn."

"Thank you, Jolyn."

My eyes lock on the glazed donut with pink sprinkles. Ha! There's no way I'm sharing with him. Husband or not, our current friend status doesn't even earn him a lick. Maybe I'm being petty, but the sting of rejection from his words last night is still fresh in my mind.

"Okay, we're going to eat now." I move to pick up a fork.

"Let me get a real quick picture." She stands to move toward the foot of the bed.

"We're in our pajamas." Griffin is only in his underwear. I try to not think about it.

She waves me off. "That's part of the tradition. Smile."

She takes the requisite picture. I can't wait to look back on that gem. Hair a mess, face covered with pillow creases and my shirtless fake husband by my side. Ahh, welcome to my thirties.

Just when I think this awkward moment is going to end, my dad walks in.

"I was on the phone and your mother was insistent that she deliver you warm eggs."

"Nobody likes cold eggs," my mom confirms.

My dad comes over to kiss me on the forehead. "Happy birthday, sweetheart."

"Thanks, Dad. Now, I think—"

"Oh, I almost forgot," my mom rushes out of the room only to return with a gift bag in her hands. "We wanted to give this to you last night but then you snuck off." She winks at us. "I get it. I was a newlywed once, too."

After my mom's sexual compatibility comment, I'm terrified of what might be in the bag. Griffin makes no move to reach in either so I bite the bullet and pull out the tissue paper. Wrapped inside the tissue is a novelty pillow like the rest of my collection. I turn it over. Our names—Griffin and Emma—are sewn on the front with a heart between them, the date we got married stitched beneath.

"I rushed to get it made," my mom says. "It's been a while since you added to the collection. Do you like it?"

I stare down at the pillow, then back up to my mom's beaming face. It's only a pillow but for some reason seeing our names on it, stitched meticulously together, joined in the middle with a small heart is making me feel unsettled. Getting married is a huge milestone, one I have dreamt about since I was little.

"Emma, I know you like the colorful pillows but I went neutral because I wanted to make sure it will work with your décor. Whatever you choose to pick out once you two find a place. Of course, there's no rush to move out. You're welcome here as long as you need."

Words fail me and staring down at the pillow, it starts to blur.

"It's great." Griffin takes it from my hands and sets it on the bed. "Thank you."

"Griffin, we didn't have a chance to talk much last night." My dad crosses his arms over his chest. "Tell me more about yourself. What do you do for a living?"

"I don't think now—"

I try to interject, but Griffin is already responding.

"I'm between jobs right now."

My dad smirks. "And what field of work are you in?"

"I've been a professional dancer for the last eight years while attending college and then law school. I'm awaiting my bar exam results, but plan to practice business and commercial law."

Law school? Bar exam? My head whips in Griffin's direction. I'm about to open my mouth but realize it will be odd if I admit I don't know any of this.

"A lawyer." My dad nods. "Well, Em, I guess you have a type."

"Philip," my mom scolds. She knows how hard the breakup with Alec was. How much I invested in the relationship while Alec focused on his career.

"Enjoy your breakfast!" she calls before ushering my dad out the door and shutting it behind them.

I immediately turn to Griffin. "Did you make that up?"

"What? Law school?" He shakes his head. "No."

"So, you're really a lawyer?"

"Pending my passing of the bar."

I stare at him.

"What about the revue?"

He shrugs. "Saturday night was my last night."

I move the tray off my lap and get out of bed. This has got to be some kind of joke the universe is playing on me.

Never in a million years would I have thought that the sexy male revue dancer I married is a *lawyer*.

It may be ridiculous to think that a person's career could place them firmly in someone's undatable category, but for me, after the heartbreaking experience I had with Alec, lawyers are a no for me. Been there, done that, refuse to do it again.

"You're upset."

"You bet I'm upset. After Alec, I vowed never to date another lawyer again. Now, I find out I'm *married* to one? What the hell?" I start pacing. "And you knew how I felt. I told you all about Alec and how awful playing second fiddle to his career was."

"We were having fun; I didn't think it would be an issue." He frowns. "And we're getting an annulment, remember? You won't have to play second fiddle to anything."

He's right. It doesn't really matter. Griffin's career is none of my concern. We're not in this for the long haul. Three weeks, the Kandi Kline interview, finalize the contract with Bergman's, then Chloe and Barrett's wedding. We'll pretend to be a happy couple in love, then Griffin will return to Las Vegas. Time will pass and we'll break up quietly. No one the wiser that our wedding was a drunken mistake.

"You're right." I nod my head slowly. "I was caught off guard, that's all."

Trying not to stare at Griffin's naked torso, I shift my eyes to the other side of the bed where the monogrammed pillow glares back at me. It's only a pillow, but for the way my stomach fills with guilt, it might as well be a slab of granite that someone has chiseled our names into.

I drop back onto the side of the bed and gather my knees into my chest.

"I'm wondering if we can do this. We can't shove cake in each other's faces every time we want to avoid someone's question. And I'm not a great liar. I feel like I'm moments away from screaming the truth just to get some relief from the anxiety I'm having."

Crunch.

I turn around to find Griffin biting down on a piece of bacon.

"You're eating right now?"

"I'm starving. We didn't eat dinner last night and believe it or not, this body can't function on a few licks of frosting. If you want my thinking power, I need to eat."

He shovels in the plate of scrambled eggs and devours the remaining bacon. When he reaches for my donut, I swat his hand away then scoop it up to take a big bite.

"Sprinkles, huh?"

"They're my favorite," I say around another huge bite. Normally, I might eat more delicately, take my time and use a napkin, but there's something about this revue dancer turned lawyer lying half-naked in my bed that has me out of sorts. Or maybe it's the fact that I don't care if Griffin thinks I'm a messy eater, I don't need to impress my fake husband.

"I'm stressing out because this is real now. And I didn't think everything would be so in my face. The party last night." I motion to the pillow my parents just gave us. "An embroidered pillow commemorating our marriage."

"It's been an interesting twenty-four hours, that's for sure." His phone buzzes next to mine and he reaches for it. "Sophie," he says, typing out a quick reply.

I sigh, realizing I'm complaining about a pillow when Griffin has left his life in Las Vegas for three weeks to be here for me. "I'm sorry. I know this is not what you want to be dealing with either."

I break off half of my remaining donut and extend it to him as a peace offering. Lawyer or not, I need him. He takes the donut and pops it in his mouth.

"Thanks."

He tosses back the covers and stands. "So, what's the plan for today?"

I try ignoring the fact that Griffin is standing there in his boxer briefs. But my attempt at taking a calming breath results in sucking in too much air and a donut crumb goes down the wrong pipe, causing me to cough uncontrollably.

Griffin pats me on the back, his face filled with concern. "You okay?"

I nod and take the glass of orange juice he hands me. The liquid helps, but so does turning away to take my eyes off Griffin's perfectly sculpted body. Able to breathe again, I set the juice down and move toward the bathroom. I need to focus on something other than the deep Vs of muscle on either side of my husband's pelvis.

"I've got some meetings this morning," I say, turning to reach for my robe. "We'll meet up this afternoon, sound good?"

When I turn back, Griffin diverts his gaze away from me, his hand casually running through his wavy hair. It's almost like he was checking me out, but I chase that thought away. That's not what I need to be thinking about at all.

"You said there's a gym in the building?"

"Yes. Top of the line equipment."

"Cool. I'll check that out later."

"Great! If you need anything, call me." I shut the door.

Doing my best to block out the memory of Griffin's nearly naked body, I get in the shower. Unfortunately, I get distracted and can't remember if I shampooed my hair, so I do it again, or maybe it was only once, not knowing is the issue. It's going to be a long three weeks.

The office for Emma Belle Bridal is located in an old Civil War Era warehouse building in Brooklyn. Ten years ago, it was renovated into a multi-use office space, and last year I leased the top floor of it for my growing business. Its brick walls and large windows make it both homey and modern. The multi-functional space is great for my bridal boutique, with a design and office space in the back half, and a consultation and try-on area set up in the front.

Because Emma Belle Bridal is a small team of five, we're a close-knit group. That's why I beam with excitement when Kiara, Leo and Josie appear at my office door with flowers, a tray of coffees and a brown bag from Northside Bakery, the Polish bakery I love.

Their cherry kolaches are sinful. It's only been an hour since I ate, but my stomach growls at the thought of them.

"Are those for me?" I ask.

"No. These are for the bitch that invited us to her wedding in Vegas," Kiara says pointedly. "You know, the one you failed to mention was happening Saturday night after the show."

Oh shit. Another group of people I've disappointed.

Their eyebrows lift simultaneously, giving me over-the-top attitude. I think they're joking, or at least attempting to, but I do feel bad because if I would have wanted them at my wedding, if it hadn't been unplanned.

"I'm sorry, but no one was invited." Jess appears behind the trio. "Not even Jess," I say, to prove my point that there should be no hard feelings. "Not even my parents. It was last minute and just the two of us."

"Ahh, that's so fucking romantic." Leo sighs, then moves to set the coffee and pastry bag on my desk. "Okay, it's impossible to be mad at you, but we fully expect to be at your second wedding."

Before I even attempt an answer, Josie cuts in.

"He's kidding," she says, moving around the desk to give me a hug. "But seriously, when do we get to meet him?"

"Soon," I assure them. Soon being sometime in the next

three weeks. And after Griffin and I learn everything we possibly can about each other.

"Oh, I see what you're doing." Leo grabs a vase from the collection off the bottom shelf of my bookcase and starts arranging the flowers in it. "You're keeping it low-key, like a celebrity wedding. It creates more buzz that way. If people know all the details, they get bored. Mystery is what keeps people interested."

Jess moves between the group, "All right, I need a moment with Emma. We'll huddle up at ten."

They grumble but start moving toward their desks in the open office space. Leo rips off a piece of kolache on his way out.

Jess drops into the chair next to my desk, while I grab the mangled kolache and take a bite.

"I can tell by the way you're devouring that pastry, you're in emotional turmoil. What's wrong?"

"I think this thing with Griffin was a horrible idea," I say around another bite of kolache. The cherry filling oozes out the corner of my mouth.

"Because?" she prompts.

"We know nothing about each other. And last night we walked into a surprise party that my parents were throwing for us. A birthday party slash wedding shower that was the most insane experience of my life. I don't think I'm cut out for this kind of deception."

"Yes, that does sound pretty awful. But," Jess pulls a paper from her lap and places it on my desk, "here's the official offer from Bergman's. They want the exclusive production rights to six of your dresses." She points at the bottom line. "And this is what they want to pay you."

I nearly choke on my kolache at the sight of all those zeros.

I wash down the clogged kolache with a sip of coffee, then clear my throat to speak. "That's insane."

"No, it's what you deserve."

"But also, a little insane."

"So, look at this thing with Griffin as part of your business plan."

"That will be easy. He thinks we should just be friends. I've officially been friend-zoned by my husband."

"Good." Jess smiles. "One less thing to worry about."

It's confusing because of the morning in Vegas. His head between my thighs was not exactly a friend move. But he said he wanted to make me feel better. So, now I'm thinking it was a pity orgasm? And he thought he'd never see me again. The words every girl wants to hear.

Had I been imagining the chemistry between us? Was it the alcohol and my need to escape from reality for a night? To block out the beaming smiles of Alec and Brecken's engagement post?

It still feels like there is something between us, like last night when he kissed me at the cake cutting. But maybe there's not. He is a performer. I saw how different he was up on that stage than the guy I had enjoyed a quiet moment with on the roof.

"And you know what they say…the best fake relationships are built on friendship."

"I don't think that's how the saying goes."

I have to forget about Griffin's rejection and focus on how we can get to know each other as quickly as possible. We need memories, inside jokes, all the things a real couple would have.

"Well, it applies here." She gives me a small smile. "It's only three weeks. You can do it."

"Thanks." I groan.

"Griffin's suit fitting is at three. You've got a custom consult with a new client at one. Looking at the schedule, you can get out of here by two-thirty to meet him there. Oh, and I emailed you a list of personality tests and questionnaires for you both to fill out. They'll be a quick way to get to know each other. There's also a list of date ideas for new couples I thought would be helpful."

"Perfect." I scroll through her email, glancing at the questions. Occupation is the second question. It reminds me of my startled discovery that Griffin is a lawyer. Or soon to be. Information that I was unaware of until my mom and dad sneak attacked us with their breakfast in bed ritual this morning. Which also reminds me that I need to find a new place to live. After the breakup with Alec, I focused on work, getting ready for the fashion show in Vegas, and now that it's over, I need to move on with my post-breakup life and move out of my parents' place. "Can you get in touch with Paulina about speeding up my condo search?"

"Your parents' Park Avenue penthouse getting a little cramped?"

"Yeah, my fake marriage is taking up too much space."

"I'll have her send you some options by the end of the day."

"Thanks."

After Jess leaves, I spend a few minutes filling out the questionnaire.

I enter the front display room and find Chloe sitting in the waiting area. She's dressed adorably in a high-waisted red skirt and cream short-sleeve sweater with cherries on it.

Before I can say anything, she rushes toward me, screaming with excitement. "Ahh! You're married!"

I laugh as she wraps her arms around me and squeezes me tightly.

"I need all the details." She throws her hands up in the air. "I didn't even know you were seeing anyone."

"It's been a whirlwind."

"I'm sad that we couldn't share in the moment with you two, but respect that you and Griffin wanted something different for your wedding." She rolls her eyes playfully.

"Barrett would invite the entire world to our wedding if he could, just to put everyone on notice that I'm his."

With everything happening so quickly, this is the first time I'm realizing that me and Griffin getting married might feel like we're trying to steal the spotlight from Chloe and Barrett's upcoming nuptials.

"Oh God, I haven't even stopped to think how this is making you feel with your wedding in two weeks. I'm so sorry. I hope you don't think that I was trying to take attention away from you and Barrett." I swallow thickly. "That was never my intention." *Because I never intended to get married at all.*

"Of course not. I don't care about that. You're in love and happy." Chloe beams. "That's what I care about."

"Right." I nod. "Okay, let's get you into this dress."

I motion her toward the fitting room, deciding it's best if we talk while I work.

"It's your final fitting. I'm excited for you to see your dress on." I attempt to drum up enthusiasm for why Chloe is really here, but she doesn't take the bait.

From behind the closed curtain, she continues the conversation.

"Tell me everything. How you met. What he's like. Do you have a picture?" She laughs. "Of course, you do. We'll have to do a double date. Barrett is excited to meet him."

"I'm sure he is." I think about the unanswered texts and voicemails I have from Barrett. How I've been avoiding calling him back. If there's anyone besides my parents who would be concerned about my sudden nuptials, it would be Barrett.

"I've assured him that if you *married* the guy, he's got to be great."

"Griffin's the best. Everyone will love him." I nibble on my nail. The uncertainty behind my words causing my anxiety to spike. What else can I say? I have no clue who my

138

husband is. At this point, all I can do is mold Griffin into the man my friends and family will approve of and hope for the best.

Chloe pulls back the curtain, and turns so I can zip her up.

I help her out to the three-sided mirror and alteration box. I kneel to help her put on her heels. She was adamant about wearing four-inch heels to help offset the height difference between her and Barrett.

When she turns to face me, I take in a deep inhale. Everything else moves to the background, it's just this moment with Chloe, a beautiful friend and soon-to-be bride, trying on her wedding gown.

For Chloe's dress, we chose an A-line design, the front with a plunging neckline and one inch gathered straps attach at the waist for an open back. The sides and front are connected by sheer tulle. The dress is gauze with a under layer of tulle, with a cascade of small, three-dimensional flowers on the bust and skirt.

Chloe spins to get the full effect of the flowy, yet structured skirt.

"It's perfect. I'm biased of course because I designed it, but it's absolutely gorgeous on you."

She's glowing. A sense of pride rushes over me that the dress I designed for her is bringing her that much joy. That she'll walk down the aisle toward Barrett in this dress and the moment he sees her, the moment their eyes meet, it will be everything.

I attempt to replay that moment at my wedding to Griffin, but it's fuzzy. Fragments of a wild night that I don't remember clearly, but as evidenced by the man sleeping on my bedroom floor now, also one I can't forget.

"Everything happened so fast," I say, more to myself than to her.

Chloe sighs. "It sounds like a fairy tale. Or the plot of a romance novel."

"Something like that." I give her a small smile.

"And there are pockets!" Her face lights up when she finds the discreet pockets I had sewn in.

After Chloe's fitting, I return to my office to catch up on emails I missed while in Las Vegas last week. As I work through my inbox, it feels like business as usual.

While I'm going over a client's design notes, Leo brings in a large arrangement of flowers.

"Oh, wow."

"Aren't they gorgeous?"

I pluck the card out of the holder and open it.

"Who are they from?" Leo prompts.

Congratulations on your elopement. We are hopeful to be working with Emma Belle Bridal on a Bergman's exclusive collection.

"It's from the Bergman execs." I ignore the dip of disappointment my belly. There was a moment right before I opened the card that I wondered if they were from Griffin. It's so silly. Why would my accidental husband be sending me flowers? There's nothing between us but a wild night and one headache relieving orgasm. Now, we're just friends.

"Oh, honey." Leo drops his nose into the extravagant bouquet. "They are courting you something fierce."

After Leo leaves, I arrange the flowers on my desk. I know Jess is right. This thing with Griffin should be treated like a business transaction. I even offered to pay him for his time, but he insisted he didn't need anything from me, only his roundtrip ticket. I need to remember that whenever I start to think about him. Three weeks of pretending, then he's on a plane back to Las Vegas.

CHAPTER 14

Griffin

After using the building's gym, I took a hot shower, trying to ease the tension in my neck and shoulders. The stiffness there not from my workout, but from sleeping on the floor. I can't be mad at anyone but myself, it was voluntary, but after snuggling up next to Emma when her mom brought breakfast in this morning, it was confirmed to be one hundred percent necessary.

I roll my shoulders out. I'm going to need a chiropractor when I get back to Vegas.

I get dressed, then check my emails. Exam results are supposed to be posted on May first. That's still two weeks away, but I'm anxious to hear. There are two emails from Emma's assistant, Jess. One with a calendar invite for a suit fitting this afternoon. Another with a questionnaire attached to it that I'm supposed to fill out and return. I'm about to open the questionnaire when my phone rings.

"Hey, Soph," I answer.

"What are you doing right now? Times Square? Top of the Rock? Oh, I hope you're strolling the High Line with a gelato from L'Arte del Gelato."

Even though she's never been, Sophie is obsessed with

141

New York City. She loves the romance of it. That's a direct quote.

"It's ten thirty."

"So, what?" she argues. "It's never too early for gelato."

"I'm not strolling with gelato. How is your conference going?"

"It hasn't officially started. It's only seven thirty," she answers then quickly diverts the conversation back to me. "There is so much more that you could be telling me right now. Where are you staying? What are you planning to do for the next three weeks? Oh, and Piper found the video of Emma talking about you. Let's just say it is nothing a sister should hear about her brother."

I scrub my hands over my face. I didn't bother looking for the video. There's no point in watching it. I know how the night ended.

"We're staying with Emma's parents. And as far as what I'll be doing, I'm here to help Emma. She's got an important interview next week that she needs me for. And a wedding to attend."

"No way. Whose wedding?"

"Emma's cousin and his fiancée."

"Is it going to be bougie?" she asks.

"He's the CEO of a major media company so yeah, probably." The discussion about Barrett and Chloe's wedding has me thinking about Emma's family, her parents' apartment and the type of life Emma is clearly used to living. That based off our short appearance at the wedding shower last night, the shock on everyone's faces at Emma's simple ring and her dad's dislike of me, I'm clearly not the guy anyone thought she would have married.

"Ugh, so jealous. Please tell me you're going to see some sights and eat some delicious food. And don't forget to send me photos that I'll drool over while I eat cafeteria food and be subjected to the dim lighting of this hotel and the stale air of the exhibition hall."

My chest lightens at Sophie's dramatics. "I'll do my best."

"I've gotta get in the shower now. Send me those pics!"

"Love you, Soph."

"Love you," she says before ending the call.

My phone rings again. I expect it to be Sophie calling back, having forgot something she wanted to tell me, but it's not Sophie, the caller ID says McGregor & Lange, Ltd.

"Hello?" I answer.

"May I speak with Griffin?"

"This is he."

"Hi, Griffin. This is Latrice with human resources at McGregor & Lange. How are you today?"

"I'm good. How are you?"

"It's only eight thirty and it's already hotter than Hades, but I'm hanging in there." I chuckle lightly. I've only talked with Latrice a few times over the years, but she's always been informative and easy to talk with.

"So, I shouldn't tell you it's cool and rainy here in New York?"

"That's why I'm calling. I got the message from Terrence that you are wanting to push back your start date."

I think back to the conversation I had with Terrence on Sunday evening before I confirmed with Emma that I'd be able to come to New York. He'd been understanding about my request to postpone my start date at his firm a couple weeks. He told me how proud he was of how hard I'd been working and that I should take a few weeks after the revue to take a breath before starting my new job. The way he went on and on about how proud he and Rita are, I couldn't tell him about Emma and New York. I figured it won't matter in the long run.

"Yes, that's correct."

"Okay, I'm going to resend you the paperwork with your

new start date. Please get that back to me by the end of next week so I have a week to process it and get you into our system. Also, I received the higher education tuition payback form from the State of Nevada and will fill that out and return it to them."

"Thank you, Latrice. I really appreciate it."

"No problem. You know, that is a great program they've started. I would say if I could have gotten my master's degree paid for by committing to work for three years in the State of Nevada, that would have been nice. I've already got thirteen under my belt."

Latrice is right. The higher education grant I received from the State of Nevada to cover my tuition, books and fees for law school was a huge factor in me being able to get my degree. While I had been assisted by financial aid with my undergraduate degree, once I discovered the cost of law school, I was certain I'd have to put it off until Sophie graduated. Terrence had clued me into the state's grant program for higher education. Besides showing my background, transcript and need for assistance, the other requirement was that I would commit to work for three years in the State of Nevada. The program targets lower income students and is designed to educate Nevada residents and keep them in the work force there. It was a no brainer for me to commit in exchange for getting part of my tuition covered by the state. Now that I've graduated, the program requires I show proof of my employment in the state.

"I'll get this paperwork over to you. You should receive it by the end of the day, if not, let me know. And then we'll be seeing you in a few weeks."

"Sounds good. Thanks, Latrice."

"Thank you. Have a good day."

"You, too."

After we hang up, I decide I should do what Sophie said and take advantage of being in the city. As I'm leaving the apartment, I run into Emma's dad. It appears he's headed out the door, too.

"Griffin." He gives me a curt nod.

"Sir."

We walk in silence to the elevator.

"Where are you headed?" he asks, taking in my jeans and sweatshirt. "Clearly not to a job interview."

"Not today. No." I try my best to not let his dig get under my skin. I've worked my ass off to get where I am and I refuse to let his opinion of me based off what little he knows get to me.

When the elevator opens at the lobby, Emma's dad steps off and continues walking toward the front door.

"Have a good day," I call.

He lifts his hand but doesn't bother to look back.

"Okay, then. Good talk," I say, but Philip is long gone. I take a moment to appreciate that he won't be in my life permanently.

Out on the sidewalk, I try to orient myself, but I have no idea where I'm going.

"Do you need a car, sir?" the doorman asks. He's not the same man that was here when we arrived yesterday.

"No, thanks," I tell him, knowing I have no idea where I want to go. "I'm going to walk."

New York City and The Strip have similarities, crowded sidewalks, people busking on the corners, and lots of street traffic, but where Sophie and I live in Henderson, a suburb sixteen miles southeast of The Strip, New York City is another world entirely. I spend most of the morning trying to find places that Sophie sent me to check out. A coffee shop in the West Village. I send her a picture of the gelato she recommended I try at Chelsea Marketplace. It's only been a few hours, but I'm starting to understand the appeal of this city. The energy it has. All the possibilities.

~

I've been fitted for clothing plenty of times for the revue, the seamstress making sure the pants fit just snug enough in the crotch for movement while also giving an eyeful, but walking into the store that Emma's assistant, Jess, sent me to is an entirely different experience.

The walls are covered with dark mahogany cabinetry. The lighted display windows showcasing shirts, dress shoes and ties. It's something out of the *Kingsman* movies.

"May I help you?" the woman at the front counter asks.

"I need a suit."

"I'm sorry, we're completely booked up," she scrolls on her tablet, "until September. But I'd be happy to put you on the waitlist."

"Actually, I have an appointment. Griffin Hart."

"Oh, you're Emma's husband!" she exclaims. "Of course, we were delighted to fit you in today." She motions for me to follow her deeper into the shop. "Right this way. I'm Bridget," she motions to herself, "Ernesto is just finishing up with another client. May I get you a drink while you wait? Coffee, tea, wine, beer, San Pellegrino?" She rattles off an entire menu of items.

"Water is fine."

"Still, sparkling or seltzer?"

"Just water."

"Okay." She smiles brightly, opening a door and motioning me inside. "This is your dressing room for the duration of your experience." I look inside to find what appears to be an entire living room set up. The only thing missing is a television. "Get comfy and I'll be back with your water in a moment."

Bridget comes back a minute later with a bottle of water and a short Hispanic man follows behind her.

"Ernesto, this is Griffin, Emma's husband."

"Ahh. We've been expecting you. Emma is the best, is she not?"

My mouth opens to respond, but he waves off my reply.

"I don't need to tell you that, you're her husband. Okay, let's have a look at you." He motions for me to follow him out to the three-way mirror.

An hour later, after a multitude of measurements and alterations, Ernesto holds the suit jacket up for me to try on.

I push my arms through the jacket and adjust it over my shoulders then turn toward the mirror to check out his work. Ernesto is a magician; the suit fits me perfectly.

"Looks good." I nod at Ernesto. "Nice work."

"Let's see what the lady thinks," he says, turning toward the fitting room's seating area where Emma is seated.

CHAPTER 15

Emma

Gulp. My throat works to swallow but all the usual lubrication there has abandoned its post and gathered between my legs.

The sight of Griffin in a suit is lethal.

I want to grab Ernesto by the lapels and curse him for doing his job too well. Beg him to make it ill-fitting, a little looser around his ass, sloppy in the shoulders, saggy in the crotch. Something that will reset the balance of the universe.

He's a lawyer, I remind myself.

Ugh, that should do it.

"Emma?" Griffin interrupts my thoughts.

"Hmm?"

"What do you think?" He spreads his arms out to the sides.

"Oh. It's nice."

"Nice." He lifts his brows. "So, you approve?"

I take him in again, allowing myself one last perusal in the name of discernment. Noticing how every inch of fabric hugs his body to perfection. Not to mention how incredibly sexy the flash of his gold wedding band is when he buttons his jacket. That's not Ernesto's fault. That one is on me.

I nod. "Yes, it'll do." It'll more than do. It'll make menopausal women start ovulating again.

"Do you have a preference for the tie?" Ernesto asks, a collection of fabric swatches in his hands.

Maybe an ugly tie will tone down his devastatingly handsome appearance. But when I hold up the fabric swatch with avocado halves on it, it only brings out the green in his eyes. And makes me hungry. For avocados…and other things.

"We'll stick with black," I tell Ernesto. He looks to Griffin for confirmation.

"What my wife wants," he says. And damn it if that doesn't make the ache between my thighs worse.

While Ernesto retrieves the black silk tie, Griffin continues to stand there assaulting my eyes with his potent combination of sex appeal and compliance. Now's a good time to catch up on emails. But I don't get far when Griffin drops down beside me on the leather couch.

"How was your morning?" he asks, one arm stretching out along the back rest.

I look up to find him staring at me with apt attention. Like he asked the question and is sincerely interested in the answer.

I set my phone down.

"Busy. I had two fittings and three consultations. Chloe, my cousin Barrett's fiancée, came in for her final dress fitting. That's the wedding we'll be attending in a few weeks." He nods. "You'll meet Chloe and Barrett before then. There's a party on Saturday night we need to attend."

I don't bother to mention that Chloe wants us to have dinner with her and Barrett. Our fledgling relationship isn't yet ready for an intimate setting like that.

Ernesto arrives with the various style options of black ties. Four-in-Hand, Skinny, or Seven-Fold. I make my selection, the classic Four-in-Hand, and signal Griffin to stand so I can tie it.

"I know how to tie a tie," he says.

"Good," I say, looping the tie around his neck. "So do I."

His lips twitch, but he makes no move to take over.

"Consultations?" Griffin asks as I begin my work. "Those are with women interested in you designing their dress?"

"Yes. It's my favorite part. The beginning, where I'm getting to know a bride, understanding her personality while also taking into account her style preferences and body type. Things like wedding location and time of year. It's like gathering all the ingredients for a recipe, but you don't know what you're making yet. Finding out how it's all going to come together is the most fun. And with the designing process, sometimes it takes more than one attempt." I feed the tie end through the front loop, then slide the knot up and adjust it.

"Sounds like you love what you do."

"I do."

My fingers run down the length of Griffin's tie. The feel of the smooth silk beneath my fingers, and the contrast of his hard, muscled body beneath has my mind racing.

Going places it shouldn't.

Now, I'm imagining his hard cock would feel the same. Smooth and silky on the outside, hard steel beneath. I imagine wrapping my fingers around it, pumping him from root to tip, then licking my way along the smooth, yet rigid shaft. Just imagining the weight of him on my tongue has a pool of saliva gathering in my mouth.

When the image of me on my knees, one of Griffin's large hands tangled in my hair, his hips thrusting as he fucks my mouth surfaces, I nearly choke.

Jesus, Emma. What the hell?

I don't normally go around imagining sucking guys' dicks. Griffin's technically my husband, but even when I've dated guys, I've never felt that strong of a desire.

When I look up, he's watching me again. Those pools of

green intent on making me squirm. God, I hope my thoughts aren't written on my face.

I draw in a shaky breath.

"Green is the rarest eye color. It's a genetic mutation." I spout a random fact I found on Google this afternoon when I was between clients. It was purely research about my new husband, completely necessary, and had nothing to do with the fact that over the few days since I've known Griffin, his striking green eyes are constantly at the forefront of my mind.

"With my brown eyes and your green eyes, our children would have a fifty percent chance of having brown eyes, but only thirty-seven-point five percent of having green." When I realize how ridiculous I sound telling him stats on eye color of the children we don't plan to have together, I add, "Hypothetically speaking."

"Good to know." It's that small smile he gives me when he wants to be reassuring, but not overly so. The same one he gave me in Vegas when I was panicking about our marriage.

He adjusts the neck of his tie and turns to look in the mirror.

"Do I look like I could be your husband?"

I stand beside him, taking in the full effect. It's too good.

"You look like you belong in a Dolce & Gabbana cologne commercial with a black and white filter and smooth jazz playing the background."

"Is that a good thing?"

I sigh. "Unfortunately, yes."

Griffin's reflection smirks at me, then he disappears into the dressing room.

I need to refocus the energy with which I'm lusting after my fake husband to something more productive. Like getting to know him so we can convince Kandi Kline we're madly in love.

"Did you fill out the questionnaire?" I ask, trying not to

appear flustered by the sound of his zipper lowering on the other side of the door.

"Yeah, I emailed it to you."

I pull my phone out, find his email in my inbox and start to read it.

"You graduated law school last May. You took the bar in February and you're awaiting your results; we went over that this morning."

I keep scanning the document.

"Contract law. That's your area of expertise? Why?"

When he answers, his voice is low.

"My mom wanted me to be a lawyer. She thought there was nothing more powerful and important than knowing the legal system. When she died, I had Sophie to worry about and college seemed like a pipe dream. But then I started making decent money at the revue and with that safety net, I began to think about what I would want to do. I met my mentor, Terrence, through the revue's choreographer, Rita. They're married, and he's a commercial contract lawyer in Vegas. He encouraged me to pursue law school and I'm planning to be an associate at his firm when I get back to Vegas. Commercial contract law isn't exactly curing cancer, but I like reading and negotiating contracts. I think I'm pretty good at it."

I appreciate that Griffin is passionate about his career path, and I could be overgeneralizing the profession based off my experience with Alec, but none of that matters. Once Griffin and I are done with this charade, I'll stay firmly in the no dating lawyers camp.

"I suppose I'm in my lawyer era."

The door swings open. Griffin has changed back into his t-shirt and jeans. His wardrobe change does nothing to calm the fluttering sensation in my belly. Maybe it wasn't the suit after all.

"I could never treat you like that."

I liked having the door between us. Now, with Griffin's

eyes on me, that wobbly knees feeling is back. I'm transported back to Vegas. To the feeling of Griffin's arms bracketing me at the bar, keeping me close and protected.

"Like what?" I ask.

Griffin's eyes drop to my lips. "If you were really mine, I'd never stop making you feel wanted."

While I'm embarrassed recalling all the things I told Griffin in Vegas about mine and Alec's relationship, my brain chooses to focus in on his sweet words. If I was really Griffin's, he'd never stop making me feel wanted.

Griffin's intent stare is enough to make good on his promise right now.

The moment feels electric. Too intense.

But we're friends. *Just friends.*

I don't know how to respond, so I say the first thing that comes to mind.

"Thank you."

One corner of Griffin's mouth pulls up. "You're welcome." Now, there's humor in his tone. His response almost a question. Maybe I misread his body language. He's just trying to be nice and I think he's about to press me into the wall in this tuxedo shop.

Okay. Time to go.

Griffin follows me to the front of the store.

"We'd like the suit delivered," I tell Ernesto.

He nods. "Of course."

Then we get into an argument about who is paying for the suit. After a few minutes, I relent to Griffin paying. His argument being that the discount he gets due to my close relationship with Ernesto is my contribution.

"You're married." Ernesto motions between us. "It comes from the same place, no?"

"He's right." Griffin smiles. "What's yours is mine, what's mine is yours."

It's funny for a second, until an alarm goes off in my brain, and I realize that I don't know anything about marriage laws and how marrying Griffin in Vegas could affect my business. We didn't discuss a prenup. We didn't discuss anything.

As we walk out of the store, my mind is reeling. This could be worse than I thought. Everything I know about Griffin as a person tells me he's not the kind of guy who would try to stake a claim on my business when we split, but I didn't prepare for this at all. The interview with Kandi Kline means nothing if my business is in jeopardy.

"You really don't think much of lawyers, do you?" he says.

"What do you mean?" I ask, trying to get my bearings.

"My comment in there. About what's yours is mine. I was joking. But the horror was written all over your face."

"You saw that?" I swallow. What else has he observed? Are my furtive glances obvious? My covert ogling of him completely transparent? "I hadn't even thought about what our marriage could mean legally for Emma Belle Bridal. If you were to—"

"I would never stake a claim on your business, Emma." He says it sincerely, but there's an edge to his voice. He's definitely annoyed.

I think back to my talk with Jess this morning. Her mentioning that Griffin had declined the additional compensation she had offered him for his time here.

"We can have a postnuptial agreement drafted if it would make you feel better." He takes my silence to mean I don't know what it is, but I'm really going over the worst-case scenarios in my head. "It's a marriage agreement covering all the aspects of a prenup, but after a couple is legally married. With our short marriage timeline, it's not necessary, but with your business it's a good idea."

"Yeah, I know what it is. We should do that."

"I'll have it drafted and your lawyer can look it over. I'm sure you have one helping you with your business affairs."

"Yes." I nod, feeling better about the situation.

Griffin looks around. "Are you hungry?"

"Starving. There's a popular bistro a few blocks this way." I point in the direction of the restaurant.

"Sounds good."

We start walking, but a few steps in, Griffin shifts around me. I'm about to ask what he's doing, when it becomes clear that he wanted to walk on the street side. I glance at his profile as we walk, but then the sidewalk narrows and the crowds of pedestrians force us into single file. Griffin's hand reaches back to grip mine, so he can keep me close in the crowd. I'm used to the city's chaos, but what I'm not used to is a man being so protective of me.

He holds my hand until we arrive at the restaurant and separate to sit across from each other in the booth.

"Any allergies?" the waiter asks as we browse the menu.

"No," I say, and Griffin shakes his head to confirm he's good, too.

While the waiter rattles off the specials, I stare at the menu. It's a bit overwhelming, so I gravitate toward my usual, a salad with grilled chicken and a glass of wine. Griffin orders a pastrami sandwich that sounds mouthwatering and a beer.

When the waiter leaves with our orders, Griffin takes a sip of his water.

"Are you changing your name?" he asks. "Hypothetically, would you?"

"I don't know. Would you want me to? Hypothetically speaking?"

"It would be your decision. For business it might make sense to not change it or hyphenate. But it wouldn't matter to me, as long as I could call you Mrs. Hart in private." His words make me tremble. "Hypothetically speaking," he adds to continue this game we're playing.

We're talking in hypotheticals, but that doesn't prevent

Griffin's words from igniting a fire in my lower belly. I grab my water glass and chug, because dumping it over my head would be overly dramatic.

These are all discussions that a couple would typically have had long before they got married, but for us, it's a crash course. But responses like that make me lose focus of what we're doing here.

I pull out my phone and scroll through the questionnaire again, until I notice a blank section. The question pertains to past relationships. I know that Griffin prioritized raising Sophie in his twenties, but it seems impossible that he has nothing to report.

"You missed this question," I say, showing him my phone and the blank space.

"It's supposed to be blank."

"But the question says, past relationships or partners in the last five years. Even if it wasn't serious, surely there's been *someone*."

He shakes his head. "No."

Now, I'm even more curious.

"What about sex?" I whisper. I don't really want a list of Griffin's past sexual partners, but it's probably wise to cover our bases. To understand who the person was before we got married. No more surprises. I know that Griffin isn't a partier, our night out together was unusual for him, but I would expect he was having his needs met somehow.

His green eyes meet mine. "I'm celibate."

I sit back, taking this information in.

"You mean like right now, we're not having sex, and you're not planning to sleep with other women until our marriage is annulled?"

"No, I haven't had sex in years."

Years, as in, multiple. At least two years. He says it so matter of fact, maybe we're not talking about the same thing.

"Like, you mean no penetration? But other stuff, right?" I

ask, trying not to burst into flames at using the word penetration.

"No," he shakes his head, "nothing."

"How long?" I ask, aware that my hand is gripping my water glass unbelievably tight.

He tilts his head to the side, like he's mentally calculating. "Six years."

Six years. I'm officially the exploding brain emoji; stunned by his confession.

The waiter brings our drinks, so I release my grip on my water glass and take a large gulp of wine.

I can't wrap my head around this. Not because I think sex is the most important thing in the world or a relationship— it's not. Sex with Alec was mediocre at best. Again, it was him putting his needs before mine ninety-nine percent of the time.

But Griffin exudes sexuality. Even if I didn't see him perform at the revue show and I met him on the street, he has a presence, a look, an appeal. I saw it firsthand in the club with the women approaching him. It obviously hasn't been due to a lack of willing partners.

I'm fascinated by this revelation.

"Why?" I ask.

If Griffin is uncomfortable with my questioning, he doesn't show it.

"I had a high school girlfriend, we'd been together for two years, both planning to go to Texas for college. I had a full ride for football and she was going for dance team. I'd been hesitant to even dream that I could go out of state to school, but my mom was doing better. She'd been doing well for six months and had a steady job cleaning houses. When I lost my mom and became Sophie's guardian, I knew I had to stay in Vegas. She went to Texas and we broke up."

"That must have been hard."

"We were young. I couldn't expect her to change her life for me.

"Eventually, Sophie and I found our new normal, but money was always tight. I dated but nothing was ever serious. I was exhausted from working multiple jobs and there was no extra cash to hire a sitter to take a woman out even if I'd had the energy. It was like being a single dad at twenty-one. Trying to figure out my life while keeping Sophie's as normal as possible. It got to the point where I didn't have time for a relationship, so instead of seeking out meaningless sex, I went without. Eventually, it became my norm. Then, when I started at the revue, I made a point of not socializing with the women at the show." He takes a drink of his beer, his eyes glued to mine. I hear his unspoken words. *Until you.*

"But you masturbate, right?" The minute the words are out of my mouth, I want to yank them back in. Why did I ask that?

"Yes." He laughs quietly, his smile genuine and completely at ease. "I'm well acquainted with my hand."

"I bet." I can't help it; the wine is already making my lips loose.

Griffin's confession makes me feel better about us not having sex in Vegas, but it also makes me wonder what it would take for him to break his celibacy. With his sister grown up now, what is he waiting for?

"It's clear you're not waiting for marriage," I wiggle my left hand, "so what would a lady have to do to be the lucky recipient of your pleasure sword?"

He nearly chokes. "My pleasure sword?"

This conversation is starting to go off the rails. I'd normally never be this intrusive or bold when getting to know a guy, but time is of the essence here, so I'm trying a new approach. Also, I'm beyond curious. And hearing the words 'pleasure sword' come out of Griffin's mouth is a fun bonus.

I wait patiently for his laughter to subside. My eyebrows lift to indicate I'm waiting for his response.

"That's a serious question?" he asks.

My lips press together. "You heard me."

"Okay, let me think."

He runs his palm along his jaw, his fingers sliding over the two-day beard there. I can hear the bristle of his hair against his hand and it has me recalling what it felt like to have his face between my thighs. The delicious scrape of that jaw against the sensitive skin of my inner thighs while his tongue licked up my center. My core clenches at the recollection.

That was only two days ago, yet it feels like a lifetime. I do my best to shake the memory and focus on what Griffin is saying.

"At this point in my life, it would have to be a woman who knocks the wind out of me. Someone I can't imagine going a day without seeing. That makes my heart thud against my ribs and my palms sweat because I'm both nervous and excited to be in her presence." He pauses for a moment, eyes trained on the table before he looks back up at me. "It needs to be more than just lust and attraction, a real connection."

My lungs are suddenly devoid of air, as if I'm experiencing firsthand the magic Griffin is talking about. Meeting someone who knocks you back on your heels, makes you open your eyes and take notice.

I nod silently, then take another sip of my wine to clear the lump in my throat. To soothe the sinking feeling that I'm not that woman for him.

"I'm sure she's out there. And once you're freed of your fake husband duties, you'll find her."

He gives me a small smile.

Emotions threaten to bubble up, so I look back to my phone. "Okay. Back to the questionnaire."

"Hold on. What about you?"

"I answered the question." I point to the notes. "You know

about Alec. And before him I was with Stephen, and a year before him, it was Will."

"Yeah, I know all about you and the Baldwin brothers." Griffin shifts forward. "How do you take care of yourself, Emma?"

I glance around, this conversation far more alarming in a public place now that it's directed at me.

"Like specifically?" I whisper. "I don't think this is going to be something Kandi will ask."

"I shared with you."

"You said you were well acquainted with your hand. That's pretty vague. And for guys, pretty much a given."

"Okay, I prefer to fist myself in the shower, easy clean up, but sometimes I'll change it up and watch porn."

He lifts his brows to indicate it's my turn now.

"Fine. Yes, I have a dildo with a vibrating head. It's multi-functional, if you know what I mean."

"What color is it?"

"Bright pink," I tell him, wondering if my face is starting to turn the same color.

"Where do you keep it?" he asks.

"Top drawer of my bedside table."

Griffin is quiet for a moment, his eyes drifting from where his fingers are rotating his beer bottle to my face. I could be wrong, but I swear he's imagining me on my bed, legs spread open, with my neon pink dildo dipping into my center. It's suddenly unfair that he's seen me naked, touched me, licked me. When I think about him fisting himself, I have to really use my imagination to bring the visual of his cock to life.

Our food arrives and I try to put Griffin's dick out of my mind. The waiter places the salad in front of me. It's what I ordered, what I thought I wanted, but now it looks depressing. Nowhere near the orgasmic salad Meg Ryan had in *When Harry Met Sally.* I look over at Griffin's sandwich and I immediately know I made the biggest mistake not ordering the pastrami on rye. It looks so good.

It's only a food order, but it registers a familiar pang. Me not listening to myself. Going against my gut because I think it's what I *should* do, not what I actually want. It's remnants of my relationship with Alec where I felt like I had to be a certain person in order to be with him. For him to love me. Turns out none of that mattered anyways.

I grab my fork and start eating, determined to do better next time. Delicately chewing around a piece of arugula, I watch Griffin cut through his meaty sandwich. The dressing oozes out and I nearly combust. If it's not the man across from me making me sweat, it's his sandwich.

After a minute of silent eating, Griffin reaches across the table and places half his sandwich on my plate.

"It's delicious. You should try it."

I don't hesitate. I pick up the sandwich and take a bite, when the flavors hit my tongue, I'm unable to control my moan of satisfaction. So good. I will myself not to take another bite and hand the sandwich back to him.

He shakes his head. "It's yours."

My eyes narrow at him. "You're giving me half your sandwich?"

"Yup, but you have to give me some of your salad."

He makes it sound like that's going to be a hardship for me.

"Done," I say, reaching across to fork half of my lifeless salad onto his plate. I also snag a few of his fries. He chuckles and puts a large handful on my plate.

It's a simple thing, sharing food. Yet, it feels intimate.

In the two years Alec and I dated, he never once offered me a bite of his food. Until now, it never occurred to me that it was odd he didn't. His food was his, my food was mine.

My eyes move back to Griffin, studying him as he chews, then takes a sip of his beer.

He catches me staring. "You good?"

"Yeah." I nod, then pick up my phone and scroll to the next section of the questionnaire.

As I listen to him talk about his childhood and family, I realize this thing with Griffin is far more dangerous than I anticipated. I've been concerned that my attraction to him was going to be my biggest problem. That his muscular torso glistening with sweat post workout, or the recently discovered fact that he wears the hell out of a tuxedo would be the greatest challenges to overcome. Now, I'm becoming aware that there is a far more distressing phenomenon to be concerned about. That Griffin is a man who is kind, protective, genuine *and* has a body made for sin. And that getting to know him over the course of the next few weeks might only intensify my attraction to him.

I remind myself of Jess's pep talk at the airport. While the goal is to convince everyone around us that we're a real couple in love, I can't let myself get swept into the mix.

Keep your heart out of it.

And Griffin's insistence last night that we keep things platonic, friendly.

Evidently, those reminders aren't enough to keep me from swooning around Griffin.

I'm ill-equipped to be around this man. I need to unearth Griffin's flaws. Make a list and remind myself of them whenever I feel this undeniable attraction to him. I'll get started on it right away.

I open a new note in my phone and begin to type.

But, since not wanting to be my fake husband with benefits isn't necessarily a character flaw, all I have so far is that he's a lawyer. It's a short list, but I'm sure in time, I'll be able to add more to it.

Later, when our dinner plates are empty, our waiter returns.

"Would you like to see the dessert menu?" he asks, looking between me and Griffin.

The D-word alone makes my eyes light with excitement, but I do my best to hold back.

I'm poised, ready to grab my phone and like every man who has come before him, add 'dessert denier' to the list.

Without hesitation, Griffin nods. "Definitely."

Damn it. I'm so screwed.

CHAPTER 16

Griffin

"We dated for two months mostly long-distance. Where was our first date?" Emma asks, stabbing the last bite of triple fudge brownie sundae on the dish between us. She ate nearly the entire thing, but I don't mind. I ordered it because I could tell she wanted it.

Before I can respond, she's answering her own question.

"Oh, I know! You surprised me with a weekend away for Valentine's Day. Somewhere cozy and romantic...like Vermont! Stowe is gorgeous in February. Do you ski?" She waves, indicating she doesn't need an answer. "It doesn't matter. They have luxury chalets that we wouldn't have wanted to leave anyways."

She continues down her list.

"You live in Vegas, but are planning to move to New York. We're condo shopping. Preferably Gramercy or the Lower East Side. Not our forever home, but a good starter place before we have kids. Do you want kids? I want two, so you'll have to say you do. Close in age so they can play together. That was the hardest thing about being an only child, no built-in playmates."

"Emma."

"Yeah?" She looks up from her phone.

I motion to my phone and the questionnaire I filled out. "Do you want to know my answers?"

"Of course." She scrolls through it again. "Hobbies: reading, rock climbing and playing pool." She looks up, scrunching her nose. "You know what would be good to add?" She smiles brightly. "Sailing. Have you been?"

My eyebrows lift. "In Nevada?"

"Right." She makes a face as she scrolls through the questionnaire. "Tattoos?"

"None."

"I have a butterfly on the inside of my right ankle. I'd wanted a tattoo for a long time and finally decided to get it a few years ago."

She kicks her leg out to the side, lifting her foot in my direction. I reach out to catch her heeled foot in my hand, holding it there so she can relax her leg. There, beside her ankle is a simple outline of a butterfly. It's the size of a quarter, and only an outline with no color.

"I was supposed to get it colored in, but I couldn't decide on the color, so I never went back, just left it blank."

My thumb traces over the ink next to Emma's ankle. I don't even realize I'm doing it until I feel the gooseflesh break out on Emma's leg. Touching her like this shouldn't feel second-nature.

My eyes lift to find her staring intently at my thumb on her ankle. Her lips are parted, her breathing heavier than it was a moment ago. How badly I want to slide my hand farther up her leg, part her thighs, and run a knuckle over her center.

Then, I remember I have to fight against my instincts when I'm near her. Every moment in Emma's presence is a battle against my body's desire to explore hers.

Our conversation over the course of dinner was a perfect example of best intentions gone awry. I told her last night we should be friends, but the moment we started talking about sex, I couldn't stop myself from asking her how she pleasures herself. Now with the details she's given me, I can imagine her spread out on her bed, a fuchsia vibrating dildo sliding between her legs. I wonder how often she uses it. If she'll play with it while I'm here. I already know that fisting myself in the shower will be a daily occurrence over the next three weeks.

I set her foot down, and she straightens back into her seat. The moment is gone and she's back to the questionnaire. That's been the focus of this dinner. I know it's the main focus of why I'm here, to prepare for the interview with the bridal magazine editor, but this questionnaire thing feels clinical. I haven't been on a date in forever, but this isn't how you get to know someone.

"What do we have in common? If our marriage wasn't a mistake, what would have made us click and know that we wanted to be together forever?"

"Sometimes you just know?" I offer.

"Favorite board game." She reads my response. "Yahtzee. Oh, I love Yahtzee!" Emma shouts like she's won the lottery.

I snap and point at her. "There it is. The connection."

"We're basing the foundation of our marriage on Yahtzee? It's a dice game."

"The best dice game EVER."

"True."

"And no, we're not basing the foundation of our marriage on it. That is based on my inability to be near you and make rational decisions."

She smiles.

"You make me sound like a lot of fun."

"Oh, you are." I pocket my phone. "But this," I point at the questionnaire on the screen of her phone, "is not. I may be out of practice, but I know a relationship isn't a test you can study for. We need to experience it. Go on a date. Like this." I motion to our table setup.

"Is this our first date?" Emma asks.

"It's not Vermont, but it's a good start."

"What should we do then?" she asks.

"I'm not sure yet, but let's get out of here."

Emma stands, and with my hand on her lower back, I guide her out of the restaurant.

There's a crispness to the air that wasn't there before. On the sidewalk, I reach for Emma's hand before we start walking down the street. She looks down at our joined hands.

"Practice," I say.

She gives me a small smile and nods.

I don't know the city at all, but as we walk, the neighborhood we're in feels somewhat easy to navigate. Lots of quaint shops and restaurants. It's a side of New York I didn't know existed. Less chaotic. I get an idea. A Google search helps me find what I'm looking for, and we arrive at our destination after a ten-minute walk.

"Amsterdam Billiards Club." Emma reads the sign. "I've never been here before."

"See, we're making memories together." I hold the door open for her and she cautiously steps in.

While Emma's eyes move around the space, I pay for a table. We grab drinks at the bar, a beer for me, and a vodka soda for Emma, then find our assigned table. There are a few other tables in use, but it's not crowded.

At the table, I hand her a cue stick. She pinches it between two fingers.

"You know how to play, right?" I ask, Emma's demeanor makes me feel like she's a second away from asking what she's supposed to do with the stick I gave her.

"Yes, I've played before."

I move to start racking the balls.

"Do you want to break?" I ask.

"No, I'll let you do that."

I take off the triangle and set up the break.

"The solid seven and three fell in, so I'm solids, and you're stripes," I tell her. I line up my next shot, sinking the four ball, then my next shot is a miss.

I instruct Emma to move around the table to look for her best shot and when she finds it, I help her line it up. With my body arched over the back of hers, I show her how to tent her fingers on the felt and position the stick underneath.

"Like this?" She turns her head back toward mine. Her scent washes over me.

"Just like that. Now, slide it between your fingers, nice and smooth. Do it a few times to get a feel for it, then one long stroke."

Emma's head drops and her shoulders start to shake. She's laughing.

"Oh my God. I had no idea there would be this much dirty talk in pool."

At her reaction, I play my words back. Maybe we should have gone bowling. Though I have no doubt Emma would manage to make bowling shoes look sexy.

When I'd searched out this activity, I hadn't thought about how sexy Emma would look holding a cue stick, or the fact that when she leans over the table, her short dress would ride up the back of her thighs. Now I not only have the image of Emma pleasuring herself with her dildo in my head, but the visual of bending her over this table and sliding my hands under her dress is at the top of the list of images I won't be able to get out of my head.

Emma's shot isn't successful, but I can tell she's determined to do better. After my turn, where I sink two more balls, she spends a few minutes walking around the table, analyzing her options.

"There are so many, I can't decide."

"Do you need help?" I ask.

"No, I think I can manage." Finally, she settles into position. It's not the easiest shot on the table, not the one I would have gone for, but she sinks two of her balls in the corner pocket.

"Nice work." I notice her form has improved greatly from her first attempt.

"Thanks." She smiles.

She moves into position and sinks another ball, while banking one off the side and setting herself up for her next shot. Emma makes the shot easily, then sinks another ball in the side pocket. I watch confused at her sudden skill and honestly, I'm turned on by the way she closes one eye and bites her lip in concentration before each shot.

Another ball falls in the corner pocket. It's clear she's played before, and didn't need any pointers on setting up a shot.

"You're a ringer."

"Maybe you're just a superior teacher." She smirks. "I'm sure it was that one long stroke technique you were mentioning earlier."

"I'm sure." She lines up for another shot. "How did you learn?"

"My dad was a pool shark in his twenties, before he got into photography. He bought his first camera with profits from his pool playing. He taught me how to play, but it's been a long time since I played."

A few minutes later, Emma has cleared the table, and I'm officially hard beneath my zipper. Watching her beat me at pool is doing nothing to keep my attraction for her at bay.

"Should we play again?" she asks. "I can shoot with my left hand."

I laugh at her offer to give herself a handicap. "No, I think we should call it a night."

She nods, but I can see the disappointment in her eyes. That look makes my stomach drop and my chest tighten.

While I'm used to giving one hundred percent to everything I do, I can't do that with Emma. I need to stay on the surface, not dive too deep. It's the reason why we shouldn't play another game. It's self-preservation.

Later, as I lay on the floor beside Emma's bed, I think about what is to come in the weeks ahead. And for the first time, I'm nervous. Not because I'll be meeting Emma's friends, or we'll be trying to pass as a real couple in front of a famed magazine editor. It's because I'm realizing that spending time with Emma, getting to know her better is far riskier than I anticipated. I *like* her.

It feels too early to admit that, but I married the woman hours after I met her, so it's fair to say everything with Emma is moving at hyper speed. And admitting that to myself will only make me more vigilant in my interactions with her. More aware of my need to stay indifferent.

I roll over and adjust the pillow under my head, hoping the image of Emma leaning over the pool table, her heart shaped ass pressing backward as the hem of her dress crept up the back of her legs, won't haunt my dreams tonight.

The next morning, after I finish my workout at the building's gym, I find Emma standing in front of the pile of gifts still stacked in her parents' living room. I ignore the way my body responds to seeing her there in her white pajama set with tiny pink flowers on it. How my eyes immediately drop to take in the way the soft cotton hugs the curve of her ass.

"Good morning," I say, while mentally chastising myself for checking her out.

"Oh, hey." She turns, her eyes giving my sweaty shirt and shorts a once over before turning back toward the gifts.

"What are you doing?" I ask.

"I'm imagining all the wonderful things in these boxes."

"Did you want to stop imagining and open them?"

"No. We can't possibly keep them. It feels wrong." Her usually upbeat tone missing. She picks up a light blue box with a white ribbon tied around it. "If I know this is the Elsa Peretti thumbprint bowl, I won't be able to part with it." She shakes her head. "No, it's best that we don't open them."

"How did people know what to get us? We weren't registered."

Emma's silent, but when I catch her eyes, I see the guilt there.

"You were registered with Alec?" I ask. They were never engaged, but I know they were close to it. It's what Emma said she wanted.

I look back to the gifts wondering if they were meant for her and Alec.

"Not exactly. It wasn't an official registry. Just a few items I put on a wish list. It didn't even have Alec's name on it. Only mine."

I can see now that the guilt on Emma's face isn't because they were meant for a different couple—not for us—but because they weren't meant for a couple at all.

"When I was with Alec, I was more focused on the idea of my wedding than the man who would be standing at the end of the aisle." She looks up at me. "Isn't that awful?"

I was the guy at the end of the aisle in Vegas. But other than her mom's wedding dress and the bouquet of flowers we picked out beforehand, there were no extravagant details at our wedding.

I shake my head. "That doesn't make you a bad person. Sometimes people's priorities get mixed up."

"Yeah, well, I seem to have thrown all my plans out the window in Vegas. I went from overplanning my nonexistent wedding to marrying a guy I just met in a detail-less wedding."

"Come with me." I motion toward the kitchen.

She looks longingly at the gifts one last time before following me into the kitchen.

"You're awfully comfortable around here already."

I shrug. "I'm comfortable in most kitchens."

I start pulling out the ingredients I got at the grocery store yesterday.

"What are you making?" Emma asks.

"You mean, what are we making?"

"Right."

I walk Emma through the process of whisking together the dry ingredients, cutting the butter into the flour, then mixing in the wet ingredients.

"This is a lot of work. You know they have these at the coffee shop down the street, right?"

"Baking is something Sophie and I would do a lot when she was younger. It was a cheap activity we could do together. We have a Sunday tradition of making chocolate chip pancakes with fruit and bacon faces and whipped cream for hair. Happy face pancakes are what she calls them."

"That's sweet. I love that." Emma watches me shape the dough into a circle on the counter. "You're an amazing big brother. She's lucky to have you."

I nod. "Yeah, we're lucky to have each other."

I move in behind Emma to show her how to cut the circle of dough into wedges. Her messy bun tickles my nose when I lean over her. Fuck, she smells good.

"What did she think about you getting married?" Emma asks as she uses the dough cutter to shape the scones.

"She was shocked. Like I told you yesterday, I haven't dated in a long time. So naturally, she wanted to know everything about you."

I help her move the wedges to the pan, then we sprinkle sugar on top of the scones.

"And what did you tell her?" Emma asks, turning to watch me place them in the preheated oven and set the timer.

"The basics. You're a bridal gown designer who loves lemon drop shots and rollercoasters."

"That pretty much sums me up." She laughs, moving the mixing bowl to the sink.

"And you look cute with flour on your cheeks."

"Do I—" she reaches up to wipe at her cheek, but realizes too late her doughy hands only make it worse.

"You've got flour on your nose." She reaches up to swipe a finger over my nose.

I can feel the texture of the flour on her fingers.

"Something tells me I was fine until you wiped your finger on me." I grab her hand to keep it from swiping at me again.

Emma smiles innocently. "I guess we'll never know, will we?"

I lean over her, enjoying the feel of her hips pressed against mine. I grab a pinch of flour from the open bag on the counter and sprinkle it over her head.

Emma gasps. I can tell she's trying to appear angry, but she can't keep a straight face. She reaches for a handful of flour and pelts my chest with it. I hold her with one arm so she can't escape, while I sprinkle more flour over her head.

"It's in my bra! It's in my bra!" She dances around, trying to shake it out of her shirt.

We should stop chasing each other around the kitchen with flour and act like adults, but baking with Emma is the most fun I've had in a long time.

"What's that lovely smell?" Emma's mom enters the kitchen to find us in a full-on flour war. "Oh, my." She takes in our flour-covered appearance. "I haven't seen a mess this big since Emma's wedding cake bake attempt when she was eight."

"Sorry, we got a little carried away," I say.

"That's okay. As long as you clean up after yourselves."

Emma's dad walks in with his coffee mug in hand.

"What the hell is going on in here?" he barks.

"We made scones?" Emma presses her lips together, trying to hold in her laughter.

"You know where the cleaning supplies are," her dad grumbles before stalking out.

When he's gone, Emma turns to me with wide eyes.

"Sorry. You probably weren't expecting grumpy in-laws as part of the deal."

I shrug. "It's okay. It's only a few weeks."

We clean up the kitchen, then Emma excuses herself to shower for work, while I wait for the scones to finish baking.

When they're fresh out of the oven, I spread butter on top of one and take it to Emma on a plate. She's in her bathroom, wrapped in her robe, putting on makeup.

I realize too late that everything about the moment is an exercise in restraint. The way her robe gapes slightly at her collarbone, revealing the smooth, touchable skin there.

Don't look.

I focus my eyes on her face, but the visual of Emma placing the buttered scone between her lips, watching her eyes widen with satisfaction as she bites into the warm, buttery pastry isn't any less enticing.

When she hums her approval, my cock stirs to life. It's the same breathy moan she made when she came on my tongue in Vegas.

Fuck.

"It's so good. The blueberries are warm and sweet. I love how they burst open on my tongue." She licks her lips and wipes the sugar from the corner of her mouth, then she sets the rest of the scone back on the plate. "I'm almost finished. I'll get dressed and meet you in the kitchen so we can eat together."

"No." It comes out harsher than I mean it to. "I mean, I've got some stuff to do."

"Oh, okay." She nods, giving me a small smile. "Thanks for making these, they're delicious."

I nod. "You helped."

"I guess I did." Her smile turns up a notch. "I'll see you later?"

"Yeah." I back out of the bathroom and head to the kitchen to pack up most of the scones for Emma to take to work for her staff. I don't need any moan-inducing scones lying around here. I keep a few for Jolyn and Philip. When I'm done, I realize I have nothing to do, but hoping to avoid Emma, I decide to go for a walk. I throw on a sweatshirt and grab the book I'm currently reading.

On my way out, I pass Philip's office. He's nibbling on a scone, but when his eyes meet mine over his glasses, they narrow in disapproval. I try to not let Emma's dad's clear dislike for me bother me. If Emma and I were really together, then I'd be concerned, but I'm only here for a few weeks. Ten minutes later, I stumble on a coffee shop with a reading area. I order a coffee, then work to push my thoughts of Emma's dad and my escalating attraction to Emma aside so I can enjoy my time in the city.

CHAPTER 17
Emma

By Thursday, my search for Griffin's flaws has stalled out. But, with yesterday morning's discovery that he possesses superior baking skills and looks adorable covered in flour, I'm confident there is something lurking beneath the shadows. No man can look like he does, act like he does, *and* make a mean blueberry scone. It's not possible.

Griffin doesn't have to look hard to find one of my flaws. Currently, they're piled up in the corner of my parents' living room. When I told Griffin about registering for wedding gifts even though I wasn't engaged and I admitted that the idea of a wedding had more of my attention than my relationship with Alec, he didn't judge me. Ugh. Why didn't he judge me? If he had, that would have been a good one to add to my list.

With my parents out of town, Griffin and I have spent the last few evenings ordering in food and preparing for tomorrow night's party. It's our first test as a couple since the impromptu wedding shower my parents threw us Monday evening and it'll be the first time Griffin meets my friends.

Everyone has been voicing their excitement to meet Griffin. I know we need to make an appearance, to put our efforts these past few days to the test, but part of me wants to stay in this bubble with Griffin, hide in the safety of my parents' apartment with take-out and Yahtzee!

"How was your day?" I ask, dropping a spoonful of rice on my plate.

"It was good. I've never had this kind of free time before. I went to a coffee shop this morning and read. Then I filled out paperwork for my job at McGregor & Lange."

"That's Terrence's firm?" I ask.

"Yeah."

The vision of Griffin in a suit looking ridiculously sexy behind a desk as he discusses contract stipulations is easy to conjure.

"Did you always plan to work there once you graduated?" I ask.

Griffin chews a bite of beef lo-mein with his mouth closed before answering. He also doesn't snore, leave wet towels on the floor or forget to close the toilet seat. His obnoxiousness knows no bounds.

"I owe Terrence a lot. He's been in my corner from day one, him and Rita, pushing me to apply to college, then law school. It was a dream I let go of those first few years after my mom died and I was working any job I could find to support us. So yeah, it's always been part of the plan."

"For the sake of our story, you'll need to express interest in finding work here. Or maybe you can work remotely? I don't know the logistics, so we'll leave that question open-ended."

Griffin's phone starts ringing. He reaches across the counter to check it.

"It's Sophie. I can call her back."

"You should answer it."

"You sure?"

"Yeah."

He stands with his phone and walks across the room. I can't hear their conversation, but I can see his face.

Add loves his sister and prioritizes his family to the list.

The evidence is piling up and none of it is helpful in my quest to not develop a crush on my husband.

After dinner, we play Yahtzee!

I do my best to ignore the way my skin tingles every time our fingers touch when we pass the dice cup back and forth. And when I win and do my hilariously awkward but completely necessary celebration dance, I don't analyze the reason why Griffin's eyes linger on my bare legs. At bedtime, I pull out my tablet and studiously work on the preliminary sketch for one of my new bridal clients and disregard how sexy he looks in his glasses as he reads in the chair across the room.

Behind closed doors, we seem to have found our groove. But tomorrow night, our relationship will be put to the test by my friends. We'll need to touch. As I drift off to sleep, I wrestle with the fact that I'm way more excited at the thought of Griffin putting his hands on me than I should be.

The irony of tonight's party, a lavish affair hosted by Premier Real Estate, the largest real estate development firm in Manhattan, is that instead of using one of its many luxury building locations throughout the city, it's being held on a boat. A fifty-foot yacht, so it's nothing to turn your nose up at.

Hunter Cartwright, CEO of Premier Real Estate, knows how to throw a fabulous party. He's a good friend of Barrett's and his party tonight will be the perfect place for Griffin and me to put all of our practice into action. Except there are certain things we haven't practiced.

As we approach the boat, Griffin reaches for my hand, his strong grip a steadying presence as we walk along the unstable dock. I try not to jolt with the sudden contact. The way his warm, slightly rough skin feels against mine. You could super glue our hands together and I don't think I'd ever get used to the sensation of his palm on mine.

I sneak a glance at his profile. My pulse skyrockets. It's the same reaction I had when I saw him dressed and waiting for me in my parents' living room. I should have been prepared for it, I saw him in it at the tux shop, but paired with a smooth jaw and his thick waves, effortlessly styled, it was a solid punch to the ovaries.

We're welcomed aboard and offered a signature cocktail before being shown to the upper deck. With glasses in hand, we make our way through the crowd. On the far side of the deck, we find Chloe and Barrett, chatting with Carl and Lindsay. Carl is Barrett's friend and the in-house attorney for St. Clair Media, Barrett's company. Lindsay and Carl have been dating for a few years.

As we approach, there's a nervous pit in my stomach. Griffin squeezes my hand as if he knows that's the exact moment I need support. I realize then, my nerves aren't because I'm afraid we won't be able to pull off this charade. Griffin and I have been inseparable this week, working to learn everything about each other and to define who we are as a couple. And now I *like* Griffin. It feels good to admit it. It doesn't really mean anything, other than its good news my husband isn't an asshole. It would be horrifying to find out I don't even like the guy. What it really means is I care whether he fits in with my friends. I want them to like him, but most of all I want him to like them.

The moment we step up to the group, all eyes are on us.

"Hi! Everyone, this is Griffin." With one arm around his back, I pat his chest lovingly with my hand. "My husband."

Even in my nervous state, my body registers the feel of his muscular body beneath my palm. And when Griffin's left arm brackets around my lower back, tucking me into his side, his hand splayed out over my hip and ass, a zing of awareness settles between my thighs.

The guys shake hands, and individual introductions are made.

"You look stunning." Chloe embraces me. "I love your dress."

"Thank you. You look gorgeous. You're glowing."

"Oh, I just tried out a spray tan. Does it look okay?" she asks.

"Yes, you look great."

"I want to have a little color for the wedding so there's enough contrast with the dress." She holds out her arms to examine the skin there. "Barrett's not a fan."

Barrett shrugs. "I like your natural skin color. The way it flushes when you get embarrassed," he lowers his voice to Chloe's ear, but his deep baritone makes it possible to still hear him when he whispers, "or turned on."

I watch Chloe's cheeks flush pink.

"Don't worry, she's still got it," Lindsay points out, making it clear that the entire group just heard him.

Carl addresses Griffin. "I heard you're a fellow lawyer."

"I graduated UNLV last year, and I'm waiting for my bar results. I took it in February."

"That's cool. UNLV is a tough program," Carl says. "Lots of complexities with the Nevada laws. But I guess you won't be dealing with those here in New York."

Carl's assumption that Griffin will be moving to the city now that we're married is expected, but as planned, we don't elaborate on what exactly he plans to do for a job.

"You are planning to move here, right?" Chloe looks to me. "You're not moving to Las Vegas, are you?"

I shake my head. "No plans for me to move."

Hunter joins our group and introduces everyone to his date, Natasha.

I've known Hunter for years and have yet to see the same woman on his arm more than once, but I always give my best effort to get to know them in case he changes his bachelor ways and decides to settle down. It just takes the right one. Like Chloe was the one to pull my grumpy cousin out of his workaholic ways.

With introductions over, and the group appearing to welcome Griffin whole heartedly, I start to relax.

An hour later, I'm feeling at ease chatting with the ladies while Griffin talks with the guys. The only disappointment is that the pink fruity cocktail I was drinking is gone.

I lift my empty glass to my friends. "I'm going to grab another drink. Anyone want anything?"

"I'll take a refresher." Chloe nods to her champagne glass. "Do you want me to go with you?"

She's in the middle of talking about wedding details with Lindsay and Natasha, so I wave her off.

"I've got it."

I excuse myself and make my way through the doors to the bar just inside the main salon. There are a few people gathered there waiting for their drinks. While I'm waiting in line, a couple that are friends with my parents stops to congratulate me on my wedding.

"Is your husband here tonight?" Anita asks.

"Yes. He's over there," I point. "Tall, wavy brown hair, talking to Hunter Cartwright."

As Anita's eyes follow my finger, mine stay glued on Griffin. He looks exactly like I want him to. The picture-perfect husband.

When Anita's eyes land on Griffin, they light with approval. "Oh, very handsome. How did you two meet?"

"Online. A dating service." It's the story we agreed to, but as I say the words, my enthusiasm for the lie diminishes.

Anita must pick up on my weak reply.

"Oh, that's okay. I think that's how a lot of modern couples meet. That's how my niece met her husband."

"And what does he do?" Victor, Anita's husband, asks me.

"He's a lawyer, specializing in business and commercial law."

Victor nods. "Good career. Plenty of stability."

As we talk about Griffin's appearance and his career, I realize it doesn't even scratch the surface of who he is. I want to tell them about his kind heart and how protective he is, how he puts others before himself, how he took guardianship over his sister when he was just eighteen and has been working every day since to give them a good life. And how he came here to help me, no questions asked. He didn't even take the money that I offered. But I don't say any of that, I smile and nod when Anita tells me about the Mediterranean cruise they just got back from. She highly suggests it for the honeymoon that we haven't taken yet.

After a few more minutes of small talk, they move on.

As I turn toward the now open bar, I let my plastered-on smile slip and release a heavy breath. Pretending to be over the moon about my newly married status is exhausting. I think about what it will be like when Griffin and I eventually break up. If there's something people like talking about more than a surprise wedding, it's a divorce...an annulment in our case. Talking about our breakup will be even more draining. I'm hoping Jess can spin it somehow. Or that there will be a million more interesting things than the end of mine and Griffin's short marriage.

I place my drink order. When I turn to scan the crowd, I find myself face to face with Alec.

"Hi," I say, trying to hide my shock. With the exception of perusing his social media account, I haven't seen Alec since we broke up. My parents had sent movers to retrieve my things and I'm still questioning if my Le Creuset round oven was really lost in the move or if it's still neatly tucked into his kitchen cabinet.

"Emma," he leans forward and kisses me on the cheek. "Nice to see you."

The formality in his voice is grating. It's always fascinating to me how one moment, someone can be in your daily life, sleeping in bed next to you, kissing you goodnight, then poof! They're gone. How does one retrain their brain to not see that person as their other half? At the very least a good friend. I've always struggled with that part of breakups. Right now, staring at Alec's slender frame in the navy Prada suit I bought him for this birthday last year, with his black hair parted and slicked over to the side, all the feelings I once had about this man, the way he was threaded into the fabric of who I was, come rushing back.

But then I glance over his shoulder at Griffin. I watch as my husband nods at something Carl is saying, but in the next second, like he can feel my stare, his eyes lift to meet mine. His intense pools of green are a calming force, yet the way they darken as he takes me in has my stomach tingling with nerves. I shift my attention back to Alec, hoping to wrap up our conversation.

"Good to see you," I say, giving him a small smile. "You look well."

"Thanks," he says, smoothing the lapels of his jacket. "I've been working out more. My fiancée has me on a new weight training regimen. One of the companies she works with."

"That's great." It feels like we have as much to talk about now as we did when we were together. I'm looking for a quick exit from the conversation, but then Brecken appears by his side.

"Hey, gorgeous." Alec kisses her. "This is Emma." He introduces me like I'm a random person he just met at the bar.

"Nice to meet you." She extends her left hand. Emily Post would be shaking her head in disapproval right now. Everyone knows that even if you're left-handed you shake with your right, so now I'm awkwardly fondling the giant rock on her hand. I try to not look at it, but it's a large, glittery beacon pulling my eyes downward. I can't help myself. I rotate her hand in mine and take it all in. Cut, emerald. Carats, over three. Clarity, magnificent.

I've already seen her ring on social media, but that's nothing compared to real life.

"It's beautiful," I say, nearly breathless from its presence.

"Thanks." She pulls her hand from mine.

The bartender sets my drink on the bar. I reach for it, hoping it will wash down some of the jealousy I feel. Even if I'm over the idea of Alec and me, that doesn't mean I'm immune to watching him with another woman, her finger weighed down by an engagement ring that I hoped would be mine.

"Congratulations on your engagement," I tell them.

"And congratulations on your wedding." Alec holds his lowball glass toward me in salute.

"Thanks," I say tightly.

"I thought Brecken and I were moving fast, but then I saw your wedding announcement in *Page Six*. To be honest, I was shocked. You'd been bombarding me with all those wedding details, the cake, the flowers, a spring wedding at the Plaza or a fall wedding at the Botanical Gardens. It was overwhelming. And then you ended up eloping."

He chuckles and takes a long pull of his drink.

If I thought this moment was uncomfortable before, now that Alec is explaining in detail my plans for our wedding before he broke up with me, in front of his fiancée, the humiliation factor has leveled up.

And while it makes sense that exes can move on, find new love and congratulate each other on finding happiness, that's not what is happening here. Griffin and I aren't real. The happiness that Alec is congratulating me on isn't real. He doesn't know that, but I do and that makes this conversation feel like salt in an open wound.

"Everyone is entitled to change their mind, right?" I say, channeling lighthearted, determined to exit this conversation gracefully, when in reality my heart is hammering in my chest, the fruity drink I'd enjoyed so much before now turning to acid in my stomach.

"Yeah, but you were pretty insistent there at the end. You could say you were begging me to get married."

"Alec—" Brecken tries to interject.

"Now you're married to another guy. It's a bit suspicious, that's what I'm saying."

For a moment I thought he actually cared, but now I get where he's going with this. His ego is bruised. He was perfectly happy moving on with Brecken, but I should be alone and miserable? Walking around with sad puppy dog eyes, mourning our relationship for months, maybe even years.

I'm about to walk away, be done with this ridiculous conversation, when a strong arm encircles my waist.

"There you are." Griffin pulls me to him and before I have a chance to react, his palm cups my jaw and he crushes his lips to mine. It's confusing how his lips feel both familiar yet completely uncharted. I get lost in the feeling of rediscovering how Griffin tastes, the slide of his tongue against the seam of my mouth, the way he grips me to him so tight, like he's afraid I'll slip out of his grasp.

When he pulls back, I'm not even half done with him, but I'm forced to open my eyes and remember where we are. Who we're standing in front of. My eyes widen, and Griffin's lips quirk in a sexy knowing smile.

"Hi," I tell him, still breathless.

"Hey, gorgeous. Did you get your drink?"

I nod, still trying to reconnect the pathways in my brain that Griffin's kiss dismantled. All the work I've been doing all week to keep my brain from going to this place with Griffin is annihilated with one kiss.

Alert! Alert! My brain sounds the alarm. *We've been breached.*

He turns to Alec and Brecken, whose jaws are hanging slightly and extends his hand to Alec.

"Griffin Hart."

Alec seems as dazed as I do and he wasn't on the receiving end of Griffin's kiss.

"Alec Mitchell," he says, then introduces Brecken and Griffin politely shakes her hand.

Griffin smiles confidently, if not a little cocky. "And how do you know my wife?"

CHAPTER 18

Griffin

"God, Alec's face." Emma laughs, turning on the barstool. "It was too good."

"What do you mean?" I ask.

I set a glass of water down in front of her, then turn back to flip the grilled cheese I'm making us.

After we finished our conversation with Alec and Brecken, we spent the rest of the night talking with Emma's friends. Now, we're back at her parents' apartment, rustling up some late-night snacks and water to rehydrate from the cocktails we consumed.

"How do you know my wife?" She repeats my words. "If you knew anything about Alec, he hates when people don't know who he is. So, the fact that you swooped in with such confidence and raw sex appeal, and then acted like you didn't know he was my ex." She laughs, the airy sound making it impossible to take my eyes off her. "It was the best line of the night."

I set the grilled cheese on a plate, then cut it in half.

Alec hasn't entered my mind since Emma and I left him and his fiancée at the bar. My brain has been too focused on replaying every second of our kiss. And wondering how soon I can make it happen again.

With water glass and plate in hand, I join Emma at the counter.

"The guys really liked you. Barrett can take a while to warm up to, but he told me he thought you were a good guy."

"He asked if I would join him, Carl and Hunter for tennis tomorrow morning."

"Do you play tennis?" she asks.

"Not since high school, but I think I'll be able to handle it."

"Oh my gosh, Barrett is really good. He's been the club singles champ a gazillion times in a row. I'm kind of nervous for you now. A good wife would drag her butt out of bed to come watch and make sure you aren't injured too badly."

"I'm meeting them there at six thirty."

"Well, I'm glad I never claimed to be a good wife."

I chuckle as she snags half of the grilled cheese and takes a huge bite.

"Mmm. It's so good." Her eyes close and her head falls back in pleasure. She looked gorgeous tonight. I'll have dreams about the way that green dress hugged her curves. Even now after she's pulled her hair back into a clip, taken off all her makeup and changed into sleep shorts and a tank top, I can't take my eyes off her.

There's always been an awareness my body has when I'm around Emma. From the first moment I saw her on the rooftop in Vegas, it was there buzzing under the surface.

Being near Emma all night, playing the part of her devoted husband, touching her, *kissing* her, that awareness has increased to a steady thrumming in my blood. And it's becoming harder to silence.

Despite my valiant efforts to ignore my body's automatic responses to Emma over the last few days, I'm starting to realize it's all been in vain. The intensity of my desire for her has only magnified to the point of frustration.

I pull my eyes away from her lips and focus on eating my half of the sandwich.

"So how do you think tonight went?" she asks. "On a scale from one to ten? One being not convincing at all and ten being we nailed it."

I chew slowly, taking a moment to think about my answer. While I'm doing a full analysis of the evening, an idea starts to form. It's introduced by the version of me that married Emma in Vegas. The man that has desires and wants; the longing to take something for himself, escape from the responsibilities he's shouldered all his life. I should know not to listen. That's exactly the thinking that landed me here in the first place, but just like my awareness of Emma, that man, the one with wants and desires of his own, is becoming harder to ignore. Looking at Emma propped up on the bar stool, her tiny shorts revealing smooth, toned legs, the hardened peaks of her nipples are just visible as they graze against the soft cotton of her thin tank top, my resolve weakens.

Fuck it.

"A seven," I practically growl.

Emma takes a drink of water. "What? I was thinking a solid nine. Where do you see room for improvement?"

"When I touch you, you either jump in shock, or you giggle."

Her lips pinch together. "Perfectly normal reactions under the circumstances, I think."

"Under the circumstances that we don't have a physical relationship?"

"Exactly."

"I think that's something we need to work on."

To prove my point, I let my knuckles trail along the inside of Emma's knee. Her knees snap together, sandwiching my hand between them and she starts to laugh.

She releases my hand and I pull back reluctantly.

"That's not fair. My knees are ticklish."

"And when I kissed you on the boat, I could tell you were surprised. It took a good five seconds for you to relax."

"Well, I was surprised. I was talking to my ex and then you came out of nowhere to lay one on me."

I shrug. "A married couple would be comfortable with each other that way, don't you think?"

"Yes, well, I'm trying." I can hear the defensiveness in her tone, the twinge of hurt that I'm critiquing her. I want to reassure her that she's perfect, but then I won't get what I want. Emma's mouth.

"And it's not just me," she continues. "You're in this, too. And we haven't practiced touching or kissing at all this week. We've been focused on getting to know each other. Our 'just friends' status hasn't exactly leant itself to experimental make-out sessions."

I want to take an axe to our 'just friends' standing. Send it through the woodchipper. But I can't. I need to keep some semblance of restraint here.

"You're right. We've been neglecting that part of our relationship. I think we need to practice."

The lie falls out easily. We don't need to practice kissing. I memorized her mouth in Vegas, by the time I kissed her at our wedding, I knew the curve of her lips, every inch of her tongue and the throaty moans she makes when I dive deep into her mouth.

"Kissing?" she asks, her nose wrinkling in confusion. Fuck, she's adorable. "Kandi Kline isn't going to sit us down and analyze how we kiss, is she?"

"I don't think we should take the chance."

Emma ponders that for a moment. She presses her lips together, and the crease that forms between her brows when she's worried appears. Part of me wants to comfort her, tell her it won't happen, but my greedy mouth, dying to capture hers, stays shut.

She nods. "Okay. How do you want to do this?"

She doesn't realize how dangerous of a question that is. How easily I could come unraveled with her permission. That the crotch of my sweatpants is already tightening just thinking about my mouth on hers.

"I'm going to touch you. Kiss you. And you do your best to not react. To pretend like it's the most natural thing in the world. Then, you do the same to me."

In one swift motion, I stand and lift her up onto the counter.

Emma yelps, then her eyes widen. "That doesn't count. The counter is cold."

She steadies herself with her hands on my shoulders, then dips her head side to side like she's warming up.

"Okay. I'm ready."

"Think about how natural it should feel when I touch you." I let my gaze fall to where my knuckles start their slow, agonizing ascent on the inside of Emma's knee. When I reach her inner thigh, I rotate my hand and let my palm glide over her skin, letting my fingertips explore the hem of her shorts. The skin there is so smooth, I let myself indulge in the feeling of it beneath my hand. "Your husband's hand stroking your thigh."

She shivers and a puff of air leaves her lips, bringing my eyes back up to her face.

"You good?"

Her eyes are closed, her lips pressed together. I start to pull my hand back, but Emma's eyes pop open, a look of determination now filling them.

She nods. "Yeah, keep going."

I let my hands move to her hips, feeling the soft cotton of her shorts. My fingers splay to grip the flesh of her ass while my lips press a featherlight kiss to the column of her neck. I can feel her pulse racing beneath my lips. It matches the tempo of my own and urges me to increase my pace. Crush my mouth to hers and put us out of our misery. But I force myself to take it slow.

"A kiss for when I want to whisper something in your ear." I press my lips against the delicate spot below her ear. "Good girl."

Emma's fingers curl around my shoulders, digging into the muscle there, but a moment later, they relax and she leans into me to copy the kiss I gave her.

Her lips find that same sensitive place below my ear.

"I'm wet," she whispers.

Her words hum against the shell of my ear and when my brain registers them I almost growl. I pull back to meet Emma's eyes. She must see the surprise in mine, because I can see the satisfaction in hers. She lifts her shoulder as if to say 'what else do you got?'

I thought I had this under control, but now Emma's messing with me.

And now I'm trying to not think about how wet she is beneath her sleep shorts. Or was she just teasing? My fingers itch to slide between her legs and find out, but I need to stay focused.

"A kiss to greet you at a dinner party."

I let my lips ghost along her jaw, then press a kiss to her cheek.

"My beautiful wife."

Emma nods. Her hands move along my neck, her fingers teasing in the hair at the base before she presses her soft lips against my cheek.

"My handsome husband."

She moves to pull back, but my hands quickly find her jaw, keeping her in place.

"A kiss before you leave for work."

Slowly, I lower my lips to hers. The feeling of her soft,

pliable lips against mine makes me lightheaded. It's that head rush, the feeling of being out of control when all I've done my entire life is keep my shit together, put everyone's needs before mine. It's what I've been craving since I kissed her on the boat tonight, and at the cake cutting before that. Every moment since that dance floor in Vegas.

My tongue teases the seam of her lips and they part for me, inviting me in so I can taste her sweetness.

All too soon, Emma pulls back.

More. I fight back a growl. I chase her but her hands press against my chest, and I have to retreat. She's resetting our position, letting me know it's her turn.

"A goodnight kiss," she says before her hands move to my jaw. I lean into her touch, loving the way it feels to have her hands on my skin.

Her lips drop to mine. The kiss is agonizingly gentle. My desire to take control, to devour her mouth is overwhelming. I channel that energy into my hands, letting them roam. Over her ass, up her back, beneath her tank top until my thumbs are teasing the undersides of her breasts.

When Emma's tongue dips into my mouth, I lose it. I forget all the rules and kiss the fuck out of her. One hand grips her ass, pulling her farther into me, aligning her center with the bulge beneath my sweatpants. The pad of my thumb teases over her hardened nipple.

A breathy moan attempts to escape her lips but I swallow I down.

Emma matches my urgency. Our tongues swirl, our mouths open wider. We dive deeper, we can't get enough. I'm a second away from yanking off her shirt, sucking her nipple into my mouth, when a voice registers behind me.

"Oh, goodness. I'm sorry!" It's Emma's mom.

We pull back, both trying to pretend that we're not out of breath as Jolyn rushes toward the cabinet to grab a glass. Emma hops off the counter.

"I'll be gone in just a moment," she says, opening the refrigerator to fill her glass with filtered water.

My eyes connect with Emma's. Her lips are wet and swollen from my bruising kisses. The guy that started this game, urged me in this direction, is gone, leaving responsible Griffin to deal with the consequences.

I should thank Jolyn for the interruption. For stepping in before I took things too far, before I let myself forget what I'm doing here.

"Did you two have fun tonight?" she asks, taking a sip of her water, now she appears to be in no hurry to leave.

Emma clears her throat. "It was a nice party. Good to see everyone."

"That's nice. Glad you had fun. I've got to get to bed, our flight to Miami is early. We'll be back on the Monday before Chloe and Barrett's wedding."

"Sounds good," Emma says, giving her mom a quick hug.

"Goodnight, you two."

"Goodnight, Mom."

"Goodnight." I nod. When Jolyn is gone, I turn to Emma. "I thought they just got back."

Emma shrugs. "They're always on the move."

"How did I do? Do you think that was enough practice?" she asks.

My eyes drop to her lips. *Fuck, no. It will never be enough.*

"Yeah. That was good."

Emma slips around me, moving to start collecting our dishes.

"I got this," I tell her. "Why don't you go ahead."

"Okay. I'm not going to argue with you." She stifles a yawn. "I'm exhausted."

"I'll see you in there." I drop a kiss to her forehead, every cell in my body restraining myself from giving her the good-night kiss I really want. To pick up where we were before her mom walked in.

I watch Emma exit the kitchen, then I start to put the dishes in the dishwasher and tidy up. I linger there, giving Emma enough time to get ready for bed, crawl beneath the sheets and fall asleep. It's necessary because my resolve to keep things platonic between us has already started to waver. While I still have the desire to protect Emma, to push forward with this charade so she can keep her business's reputation intact, and nail the interview with the bridal magazine editor, there's something else starting to wriggle its way out from under that obligation.

Something I don't dare put a name to.

Besides Chad, I haven't made much of an effort to have friends. My priorities have always been Sophie and school. While I've gotten to know the guys from the revue and a few peers at law school, the time constraints that doing both put on my life, as well as keeping up with Sophie, made it difficult for me to spend time with friends. I never went out with the guys from the revue because I had reading and case file studies to prep for class the next day. It was nearly impossible to meet up with classmates for study groups or social events the law school put on because I had to work at the revue in the evenings.

I didn't mind at the time because I knew what I was working toward. But playing tennis with Barrett, Carl and Hunter has made me realize that spending time with guy friends is something I want to put more energy into. It's another aspect of my life that being here with Emma has highlighted as lacking.

And it appears I'm not a horrible tennis player.

We're playing doubles, Carl and Barrett versus me and Hunter.

I volley the ball back across the net to Carl. He shuffles his feet to reach for the wide shot, but his racquet comes up empty, ending the third set.

Carl places his hands on his knees and huffs out a breath. "I thought you didn't play." He directs his comment toward me.

Barrett smirks. "Yeah, when did you say you last played?"

"High school gym class," I say, answering honestly even though I doubt it's what the guys want to hear.

Hunter claps me on the shoulder. "Clearly a natural athlete." Then to Barrett and Carl, "Don't be sore losers."

We gather at the sideline for a break. We're all wearing the requisite white polos and shorts of the NYC Racquet Club. I'm used to wearing coordinating outfits at the revue, but the wealth and status this club exudes makes this experience completely different. These guys are only a few years older than me, but their careers are light years ahead of mine. Barrett and Hunter are CEOs of major companies. Carl has nearly a decade of experience in corporate law.

And their lifestyle? The guys don't flaunt their wealth, it's just a fact. From the way they dress to the lavish parties they attend, their membership at this club, it all seems to be a natural part of their lives. Something that has always been there. These are the kind of guys that Emma associates with. The kind of guy she's used to dating. Like Alec, her ex.

"Last night is catching up with me." Carl drops onto the bench and wraps his towel around his neck, then reaches for his water.

"How did things work out with Natasha?" Carl asks Hunter.

"She's nice."

"But?" Barrett prods.

"She wants more than I am able to give," Hunter responds. "With the Las Vegas project on the horizon, I have nothing to give a relationship."

"When do you ever?" Carl says. "Watch out, man, because

someday, a woman is going to knock you back on your heels. Have you desperate to see her more. That's when you know it's all over for you."

"Is that how it happened for you, Griffin?" Barrett asks. "With Emma?"

The question is a way for Barrett to engage me in the conversation, but I can also tell he's protective over his cousin. He's been welcoming, but not overly so. I can appreciate his wariness and don't fault him for it. Emma says he takes a while to warm up to people. I've only got two more weeks in New York, so the chances of us being best buddies before I leave are not great. But I can appreciate his efforts in trying to get to know me.

"Yeah. It was something like that."

"And now you've moved across the country and are living with your in-laws. The things we do for love." Carl chuckles.

"Are you and Emma looking to buy or rent?" Barrett asks. "Hunter's company has a new development in Gramercy. I'm sure he'd get you a first look before it hits the market."

"What was that?" Hunter looks up from his phone, having not heard a single word of our conversation.

Barrett motions to me. "You could get Emma and Griffin a first look at the condos at Gramercy Square."

"Yeah, of course. Easy." Hunter's attention is still on his phone when his expression turns grim. "Fuck. Well, there goes my good mood."

"What's up?" Barrett asks.

"I told you Walt Barrows is looking to retire in a few years, so we're interviewing associates that will work alongside him, so he can bring them up to speed on all our projects. With our expansion, there were two positions open."

"I remember. Tanya Ellis was my recommendation," Carl says.

"Tanya's been great. But the other candidate we offered it to didn't work out, so we're looking again." Hunter looks to me. "Walt is Premier's in-house attorney. Finding his replacements has been an effort."

"I can only imagine," I say.

Carl nods toward me. "Griffin, what are your job plans? I've got plenty of connections, so let me know if you need any help in that regard."

I don't know how to respond. I'm not looking for a job here, I'll be back home in a few weeks, but I can't say that so I nod. "Thanks. I'll let you know."

Barrett motions to me. "Hunter, don't you need someone with knowledge of Nevada law for the Las Vegas project you're starting?"

Carl chimes in. "You'll eventually get your New York accreditation and, in the meantime, with Premier's new development in Las Vegas, it'd be beneficial to have an attorney familiar with Nevada laws."

Hunter looks to me. "I want it to be equitable for the other candidates, but you should apply for the position." He pulls out his wallet and hands me a business card. "Send your resumé over to me. I'll get it in the hands of the hiring manager."

I take the card. "Thanks."

These guys don't know me that well, but they know and love Emma. They'd do anything to help her, and it seems by association, me. Having that kind of network, a safety net to fall into in times of struggle or change is new to me. It took me years to get comfortable with Rita and Terrence offering any kind of help. I never wanted to take advantage and honestly, having no experience being able to rely on others, it felt like slowly walking out onto a frozen lake. One small step at a time, holding your breath as your weight settles, for fear that the ice would crack underneath you.

For a moment, I let myself imagine a life here with Emma. An apartment of our own. Date night at the pool hall, or cuddling up on the couch to watch one of the black and white movies Emma loves. Hanging out with other couples. Saturday morning playing tennis with the guys. But then the guilt settles in. I've already committed to working at Terrence's firm. And the thought of leaving Sophie on her own doesn't sit well with me.

No, I need to remember what the goal is here. To play my part as Emma's husband, then leave.

Barrett tosses his towel on the bench. "All right. Let's go best of five."

∿

Back at Emma's parents' apartment, I find Emma in her closet. The way she jumps when she sees me, you'd think I interrupted a private moment. She was asleep when I left earlier, now she's still dressed in her pajamas on the floor of her closet with a large box and several three-ring binders scattered around her.

"How was tennis?" she asks, snapping the binder in her hand closed.

"Good. Hunter and I won. Carl said he wasn't playing his best. Barrett wasn't pleased."

"Ouch. If Barrett celebrates when we break up, I guess I'll know why."

She drops another binder into the storage box.

"What are these?" I point at the collection of binders scattered on the floor around her.

"Nothing. Just some old stuff." She reaches for the one closest to my foot, but before she can grab it, I snatch it up. *My Wedding* is scrawled across the front.

"*Griffin,*" Emma looks up at me, her big brown eyes wide with panic, but in the next moment, she sighs and drops back to the carpet. "Fine, go ahead and look. It's completely embarrassing but you already know about the registry so what's the point in hiding it?"

I open the binder to find a collection of sketches, magazine clippings and diagrams. Wedding venues, dresses and floral arrangements. It's clear from the vintage of some of these clippings that Emma's been collecting them for a while.

"Is that Cindy Crawford?" I ask, staring at the photo of a couple on a beach, the leggy supermodel in a short white dress.

"Yes. She married Rande Gerber on Paradise Island in a short wedding dress by John Galliano, and it set off the beach bride trend of the late nineties and early two-thousands."

I flip through a few more pages. "So, what's the plan for all this?"

"Nothing now. I should toss them out."

"Don't get rid of it. You can still have the wedding of your dreams."

The unspoken words left between us: *After we get an annulment.*

"I don't know. It all seems silly now."

Her eyes find mine and my chest tightens. I wish I could give her all the things she wants. The things she deserves.

"Going after what you want isn't silly." The words are for Emma, but hearing them out loud, they hit a weak spot of mine. Most of my life, I've put others first. Until the night I met Emma, I'd never let myself consider wants or desires, let alone pursue them. Up until the moment I married Emma, everything in my life had been based on necessity, what I needed to do for others.

"Yeah, I guess." She takes the binder out of my hands and studies my face. "What about you? Do you always go after what you want?"

The second her words fall between us; the air in the closet crackles with electricity. The weight of her stare threatens to push me to my knees. I'd happily be there, eager to slide my hands up her legs and tug down her shorts. Lick between her thighs and feel her against my tongue again. Go after what I so desperately want. *Her.*

"No." It's my response to Emma, but it's also a warning to myself. "I haven't had that luxury."

"Sorry, I didn't mean..." She turns to put the binder back in the storage box.

"It's fine." I turn away, letting the distance between us relieve some of the tension.

For a moment it's quiet. I can tell we're both searching for a change of topic. Emma's the first to break the silence.

"Oh, Jess told me I need to post some photos on social media. I figured we could do that today. Grab lunch, walk in the park, that sort of thing if you're up for it."

"You bet. I'm completely at your service." Truer words were never spoken.

"Thanks." She smiles. "Oh, and thanks for practicing with me last night. You're right. The more at ease we are with each other physically, the more convincing it's going to be at the interview with Kandi Kline."

"Happy to help." When she lifts up on her tip toes to grab a pair of sandals off the shelf, I allow myself a moment to stare at her ass before she turns and I have to pretend that I'm stretching my neck. "The interview is on Thursday, right?"

To distract myself, I pull open one of the drawers with my clothes in it.

Emma's walk-in closet is huge and her stuff takes up most of it, but upon my arrival, she cleaned out a few drawers for me to put my things in. I peel off my sweaty shirt, the white athletic polo that Barrett's tennis club required I wear today, then start pulling out clothes to change into after my shower. I toss a pair of underwear and a t-shirt onto the center counter, then grab a pair of jeans off a nearby hanger.

I look up just in time to catch Emma staring at my naked torso.

She blinks twice, clears her throat and looks away.

"Yes. The interview is Thursday. Oh, and there's a photo-shoot, too. I forgot to mention that. It will follow the inter-view. The editor's feature always has some unique shoot, a well-known photographer, that kind of thing." She reaches for her phone. "And Jess sent me some more suggestions for dates and activities we could do this week. I think the more prepared we are, the less stressful it's going to be."

I move to put my sweaty shirt in the laundry hamper, it just so happens that Emma is standing right in front of it. I lean over her, reaching around her side to open it. My nose brushes against her hair, taking in her feminine scent. Fuck, she smells good. Her eyes drop to my chest again, and I can see her throat bob when she swallows. I'm tempting us both now.

I take her phone out of her hand and set it back on the closet shelf.

"So, we should keep practicing. Really commit to it. It's the most important interview of your career, we'll need to give it one hundred percent."

She looks up and nods.

"Yeah, you're right."

My hand lifts to her chest, my thumb stroking the front of her neck before I lower my lips to hers. It's a searing kiss that awakens every cell in my body. My tongue slides between the seam of her lips, then I dive deeper. Emma's fingers tease into my hair. The soft cotton of her shirt tickles my chest. The overwhelming desire to lay her down right here and sink into her warm, tight slickness is enough to make me pull back.

After last night, I should know better. I should know that when I put my hands on Emma, press my lips against hers, there's nothing fake about it. I can't let myself take it that far with her. If I know what it feels like to claim Emma as mine, I'll never be able to walk away.

"Okay. I'm going to shower." I press a gentle kiss to the corner of her mouth.

I leave Emma standing there in her closet, still working to catch her breath. Then I fuck my hand in the shower, hoping the release will take the edge off my desire for her.

It doesn't work.

Later while we're out having lunch, then sharing an ice cream cone and walking hand in hand through Central Park, I find every opportunity to touch her. Wrap my arms around her and claim her mouth. It's under the guise of taking photos to post to Emma's social media, but I'm starting to care less and less about having an excuse to kiss my wife.

I hope I can hold out long enough to keep from ruining us both.

CHAPTER 19
Emma

"Is today 'bring your hot husband to work day'?" Leo asks, his gaze fixed over my shoulder as a wicked smile spreads across his face.

I turn to find Griffin walking toward us. My breath catches at the sight of him. He's in dark jeans and a button-down. As he moves closer, his eyes rake over me and when they reach my face, his smile expands, making his dimple pop. He's carrying a small bouquet of flowers.

He stops right in front of me. I only have a second to wonder how he's going to greet me, because then he's greeting me. His large hands encircling my waist and pulling me flush against him. His lips pressing to mine in a gentle, yet exploratory kiss. By the time he releases me, I've forgotten where I am and what the capital of Delaware is. That one was always tricky.

He looks around, taking in the space. "I hope you don't mind I stopped by."

Leo speaks for me. "Honey, we don't mind. Not at all. In fact, we've been dying to meet you."

"This is Leo," I tell Griffin. "He's our social media manager and marketing extraordinaire."

"At your service." Leo shakes Griffin's hand and simultaneously takes a bow.

"Nice to meet you, Leo."

"I thought we were meeting at the restaurant?" I say.

He shrugs. "I thought I'd pick you up. And I wanted to see your office."

My heart flutters at Griffin's interest in my business. He made good on the post nuptial agreement. My lawyer, who received it on Monday, has already approved the financials and given me the green light to sign it.

Now, with every touch, every kiss, my quest to uncover Griffin's flaws is waning. The reality is, I want to spend time with him and I'm finally starting to allow myself to enjoy our time together. While the upcoming interview with Kandi has put pressure on us to get to know each other, this week feels different. When I'm at work, I think about him constantly. I can't wait to get home and see him. To tell him about my day and hear about his. To make him laugh so I can get a glimpse of the dimple that pops when he smiles. To cuddle up next to him and watch a movie or tease each other while we play Yahtzee! And all the practicing we've been doing? The touching and kissing are great, but I'm dying for more. I know that's not part of the plan. That Griffin doesn't want to go there with me. He's waiting for someone special. Someone he didn't mistakenly marry.

It feels impossible to think that twelve days ago, I didn't know Griffin existed. And that in another ten days, he'll be gone.

I push the thought out of my head and bring my attention back to Griffin.

"Well, would you like a tour?" I ask.

"Yeah," he nods, "show me."

As I walk Griffin through the space, he asks questions about my process and the business itself. I introduce him to

Kiara and Josie who are hunched over a computer working on updating the website.

Behind Griffin's back Josie fans herself.

"Damn, Emma, your husband is a snack. Mmm, mmm, mmm." Unlike Josie, Kiara doesn't bother to hide her stare.

"Okay. Thanks, Kiara, for that keen observation." I feed my arm through Griffin's to guide him along. "Jess is out of the office at a meeting." I motion to her workspace just outside my office door. "And this is my office."

He looks around at the shelves filled with design books, swatches of fabric and a few photos. The mannequin busts I have set up in the corner, so I can affix fabric to them while I'm working on a design. He runs his hand along the dining table I originally bought for mine and Alec's place, but am now using as a design table.

"You have a photo of us?" He picks up the framed photo that Leo gave me. It's the photo from our wedding night. Leo was horrified to find it still in the manila envelope from the wedding chapel so he bought me a frame to put it in.

"It was a gift. Leo said it was criminal that I didn't have a photo of you in my office."

He smiles at that. "He's right. After all I'm a...what did your colleague call me...a snack?"

"You'll have to excuse Kiara; she says exactly what is on her mind. Usually, it's more eloquent than that."

Griffin places the photo back on the shelf, leaving his hand to casually rest against the frame of the bookcase. As he leans closer to me, I find my body gravitating toward his.

"What they don't know is you're so much more than a pretty face," I tease.

"Ahh, babe, you think I'm pretty?"

A laugh escapes me at the goofy look on Griffin's face.

Through the window of my office, I can see all three of my employees not so stealthily watching us. For how far they are leaning to get a glimpse, their faces might as well be plastered to the glass window.

"Oh God. They're looking right now."

"Yeah?"

Griffin closes the inches between us. The fingers of his free hand tease into my hair, then he's gripping the back of my neck and pulling me to him.

"We better give the people what they want," he says before capturing my lips with his.

When he pulls back, his eyes are filled with adoration. It takes my breath away.

My stomach rumbles.

Griffin chuckles. "It sounds like you're ready for dinner. Should we go?"

"Yeah, let me grab my stuff." At my desk I grab my phone and purse, then the print outs for tonight's activity.

"Are you going to tell me what we're doing tonight?" he asks.

"Nope, you'll have to wait and see."

It's the moment of truth. Everything in the last week and a half has been preparing us for this moment. The Kandi Kline interview is tomorrow, but tonight, our final relationship test…Target Date Night Challenge.

It was one of the many items on Jess's list that we've been working to check off this week.

Across the island, Griffin sets his bag on the counter. My pulse races with anticipation.

"All right," I say. "Favorite color. Go."

He reaches into his bag.

"Pink, because, of course." Griffin shrugs. "Fuzzy socks because your feet are always cold."

My lips twitch with his assessment.

"Nailed it," I tell him, then reveal my findings. "Yours is black so I got you this."

I set the travel thermos on the counter.

"Because you might need one for work, when you start your new job. I didn't know if you already had one, but even if you do, you could keep one at home and one at the office."

He picks it up and examines it. At first, I think he's not impressed, but then he catches my gaze and smiles. "Thank you."

I clear my throat. "Okay, favorite snack or drink. This one was challenging because I feel like you will eat anything."

Griffin nods. "True."

"But I settled on this." I pull out the packet of wasabi flavored organic beef jerky. "You like spicy food and I feel like protein is something you need lots of to maintain this." I wave a hand at his body.

"Excellent choice. One of my favorites."

I beam with pride and clap my hands together. It feels like a test that I'm passing.

"Your turn," I say.

He pulls out a pack of Haribo gummy bears and a bottle of Diet Coke.

"You have achieved husband level status," I tell him as I reach for the gummy bears and soda. I pull the bag open, but hesitate. "As everyone knows not all gummy bear flavors are created equal. Which color is my favorite?"

"Red."

"Lucky guess."

"Luck has nothing to do with it." He smirks, then reaches in the bag to snag a bear and toss it in his mouth.

I pop a few in my mouth, then set the gummy bears aside.

"Something you need," I announce the next category.

Griffin pulls his selection for me out. "I got you a gel pen set."

"I do love a good gel pen. They're very satisfying to write with," I say reassuringly.

"It's so you can color in your butterfly tattoo and decide which colors you like best before you get it officially filled in."

I stare down at the pen set, then back up at Griffin.

"Oh," is all I can manage, because it's so thoughtful. I recall Alec's response to my tattoo—he hated it—and thought it was even more ridiculous that I didn't get it finished. Like Alec being indecisive about our relationship wasn't an issue, but if I wanted to take more time to think about what colors of ink I wanted to tattoo on my body, that was a character flaw.

Griffin must read my silence as displeasure.

"You don't have to use them for that. It was a thought I had."

"No, that's a great idea. It's so thoughtful, I was just surprised."

"Surprised that I was thinking of you when I made my selection?"

"No, I mean that's the point of all this, but it's more effort than I'm used to. And that you remembered my tattoo and wanted to help me with it."

He picks up the pen set and opens the case, then pats the counter next to him.

"Come here."

I hop up on the counter and cross my right ankle over my left thigh to give him access.

"What colors do you want to try first?"

"Pink and purple," I point to a bright pink and a pretty lilac color.

"Solid choices." He uncaps the lilac pen and with my foot in his hand starts to shade in one of the butterfly wings. "Your significant other putting in effort should be mandatory. You deserve someone who will put in the effort every day for you. If this was real, I'd do that for you."

His words fall out gently but are spoken with conviction. My ears carry them straight to my heart, wishing he didn't preface them with 'if this was real.'

He's so close now, leaning into my space as he picks up the pink pen and starts coloring the inner parts of the butterfly, shading together the pink with the lilac. He smells amazing. It's not a manufactured scent like cologne or aftershave, but a simple, yet intoxicating combination of soap and natural male scent. It's a comforting smell that I'm starting to associate with him.

He finishes his coloring on my butterfly. I stare down at his handiwork and it makes my heart happy to see color there.

"I can do another color tomorrow, after you shower."

I nod. "Thank you."

"What did you get me?" he asks.

I reach over and pull out the box for the handheld massager. "For your neck and shoulders."

Sleeping on the floor has to be hard on his body. Even though we've been practicing our touching and kissing, Griffin hasn't made a move toward my bed. He's still determined to sleep on the floor, so I thought a massager might be a necessity at this point.

Griffin laughs. "You're right. That's exactly what I need."

"Last one," I say. "An item that triggers a memory of us. We go on three."

"One."

"Two."

"Three," we say in unison, then set our items on the counter.

At first, I'm confused by what Griffin has purchased, so I watch as he picks up the keychain with a single dice dangling from it.

"The dice hanging from the door at the wedding chapel," I tell him.

"Yeah, I remember," he says, palming it with a thoughtful smile.

I look back down at Griffin's item for me. A tube of lip balm.

"Lemon lip balm. It reminded me of the shots we took that night. The way you tasted when I first kissed you."

I open the tube and twist the bottom until the balm appears at the top, then apply it to my lips. It's soft and buttery, and the scent is sweet, like lemon candy.

Without hesitation, I lift onto my toes and press my lips to Griffin's. The moment his tongue teases into my mouth, I pull back.

"What do you think?" I ask.

He leans forward to kiss me again. This time his hand grips the back of my neck to keep me in place. He lets his tongue lick the seam of my lips before dipping inside. When he pulls back a minute later, I'm breathless and so turned on I've forgotten what we're doing here.

"Yeah, that's it." He nods, his eyes lingering on my lips.

Trying to pretend I'm not about to combust right now, I reach in my bag and pull out my final items.

"Something we can do on our next date night was the other item." I place the Twister game box on the counter between us. Then place the package of Double Stuf Oreos next to it.

"Twister and Oreos," he announces.

Twister was on Jess's list of ice breaker games for new couples. And the Oreo personality test is something I've always been intrigued by. I'd almost forgotten about it until Jess mentioned it today while we were having lunch.

"And since we're limited on time, our next date starts," I glance at the clock on the counter, "right now."

Griffin chuckles, his green eyes staring intently at mine. "You're the boss."

His words are one hundred percent sincere, but over the

last few days, Griffin's demanding kisses have taught me that while I'm in charge of running our crash course in dating, I wouldn't be the boss in other areas. Not by a long shot.

Before my panties burst into flames, I focus on getting my mind back on track.

"Oh, but first," I move toward the refrigerator and grab out the container of milk I bought. I pull a short glass from the cabinet and fill it with milk, then set it in front of Griffin. Placing the package of Oreos next to the milk, I pull back the tab to reveal the rows of cookies inside. "I need to know how you eat an Oreo."

He glances at the cookies and milk, then back up to me.

"You want me to eat an Oreo?" he asks, sounding somewhat unsure, but also intrigued.

"Yes, but don't mind me. Pretend I'm not even here. That you stumbled upon a glass of milk and a package of Oreos. What would you do?"

With his hands braced on the counter, he stares down at the cookies and milk, then back up at me.

"Remember, I'm not here," I remind him.

"Right." He laughs, knowing I'm watching his every move.

With bated breath, I watch as he reaches for a cookie. I let my sigh of relief out slowly. Alec never made it this far. He told me I was being odd, that he wasn't a child and therefore didn't eat Oreos.

Griffin twists the cookie apart and starts licking the frosting inside. Okay, damn, maybe this exercise wasn't such a good idea. I was using it to reveal something about Griffin's personality, but now I have to stand here and watch his tongue circle the inside of a cookie.

It's torture knowing what that tongue feels like on my clit. Knowing how thorough Griffin is, how he'll take his time licking every last bit of frosting off that cookie.

I make a strangled noise and Griffin shifts his eyes to me.

"Am I doing it wrong?" he asks.

"No, no. There's no wrong way," I assure him, while trying to discreetly fan myself.

That's a lie. There is a wrong way, but Griffin is passing this test with flying colors. He's also making my panties wet.

When the frosting is gone, Griffin places the two cookie pieces back together, then dips them into the milk. He lifts the soggy cookies out of the milk and devours them in one bite before chasing it down with the remainder of the milk. I watch his throat bob with every swallow.

Jesus. This was the worst idea ever.

He sets the glass down, wipes his mouth with the back of his arm and looks at me.

"So?"

"Yeah, okay. Thanks for that."

"Wait. You're not going to tell me what it was for?"

"It was just a little 'get to know you' exercise."

"And what did you learn?" he asks.

I pull out my phone and the Oreo personality test results. Griffin falls into multiple categories. He's slow and meticulous, the licker and the dipper.

"You're a hybrid. You follow the rules, meticulous and detailed. You're curious in nature and generally upbeat."

He nods toward the cookies. "What about you?"

"I already know what I am."

"Show me." His words are low and just a bit rough.

"Fine."

I pour more milk into the glass, then select a cookie. I dunk one end, letting it soak in the milk before I place it in my mouth and use my teeth to pull the soft cookie off the frosting. I return to the milk, dipping the remaining cookie, then repeat the process, leaving the circle of frosting. I place the frosting in my mouth, loving the way the sweetness hits my tongue. I swallow, then take a sip of milk to wash it all down.

"There," I say, setting down the glass and looking over at Griffin.

One hand is braced on the edge of the counter, his knuckles white from the force with which he's holding on. His green eyes are settled on my mouth, but they're not the shade they normally are. No, they're nearly black with only a hint of moss around the edges. His lips are parted, like he's about to say something, but then he blinks, breaking the intense moment.

He clears his throat. "And what does that tell me about you?"

"That I'm perfectly imperfect and don't play by the rules."

"I'd say that hits the nail on the head."

I dust off my hands and seal up the Oreo package because I may not play by the rules, but I refuse to let these cookies go stale.

"It's Twister time."

~

I'm spreading out the Twister mat in the living room when Griffin appears in a t-shirt and athletic shorts. I'd tease him for changing out of his clothes but I did the same, swapping out my skirt and tank top for a sports bra and leggings.

I lunge back and forth, warming up my hamstrings. They're tight and not in a good way, and something tells me I'm going to need to get limber for this.

"This looks serious," he says, eyeing me.

"Twister is a serious game," I tease, releasing my quad stretch. "Help me move the sofa."

Griffin doesn't help, he does it himself, his biceps bulging against the sleeves of his shirt as he lifts, then places my parents' sofa a few feet away.

"With two players, one calls out the body part, the other

one picks the color, then we switch. We're supposed to start with one foot on yellow, one foot on blue," I read out.

Griffin moves to the opposite end of the mat and does as I've instructed. But then he reaches for the hem of his shirt and pulls it up over his head.

I can only stand there and gape at him and all the glorious muscle he just revealed.

I've seen him without a shirt before, most recently this past weekend in my closet. Now, under the optimal lighting of my parents' living room, every muscle is defined, every shadow and contour evident. The weight of his hands on his hips pulls at the waistband of his shorts, exposing more smooth skin and those deep Vs of muscle, I feel like he's messing with me.

Or this is retribution for me beating him at Yahtzee, multiple times.

As we start, Griffin calling out the body part, right foot, while I choose the color, red, it's clear by the grin on his face that he's got a strategy.

It only takes a couple of minutes for us to get completely tangled up. And that's when I learn that Griffin is the worst person to play Twister with. His long legs can easily stretch across the mat, and his broad shoulders make it difficult to reach around him, making the circles I need to access hard to reach.

"I take it you weren't a gymnast," he comments.

I look under my armpit to find Griffin smirking at the way I'm positioned. Despite the yoga outfit I'm in, my body is not known for its ability to bend. My hips and hamstrings are tight from sitting while I work, and while I've kept in shape with walking and tennis, after a match, I have a propensity for hitting the snack bar instead of the stretching mats.

"You're not exactly Gumby yourself," I retort.

He chuckles. "I forgot about that show."

"It's a classic. And speaking of classics, right now, I need a go-go-gadget arm to reach around your butt."

I had no idea Twister was an actual work out. I'm sweating. I can feel the bead of perspiration rolling between my boobs. My arms are shaking and I don't know how much longer I can hold myself up, let alone change positions.

"Left hand," Griffin announces.

I look around, analyzing my best option for color choice.

"Blue," I say. "Oh, thank God." My hands are now closer together, giving me a reprieve from the wide-armed position I had been in. I try to ignore the fact that Griffin is right behind me, his face only inches from my butt. "Sorry my butt is in your face."

"I don't mind. I like your ass."

I like the way he says ass. A bit rough, and a lot sexy.

"Yeah?" I gulp, his words causing a ripple of lust to shake my core.

"I love everything about your body," he growls near my ear.

He's messing with me. I just know it. Trying to throw me off my game so he can win.

I shouldn't let him affect me that way, I need to focus on my next move.

From what I can tell, Griffin is purposely choosing the dots close to me so he can crowd me out. Make it more difficult for me to continue playing.

If I could change directions, that would be my best bet.

"Right hand," I call out.

Griffin is quick with his response. "Green."

Ugh. That's the worst option for me. Instead of going under my body to reach it, I twist my body in half to where my upper body is now facing upward, while my hips and lower body are toward the floor.

"Right foot," Griffin says from behind me.

I scan the mat; my best option is to swing my right leg over and have my entire body facing the ceiling.

"Green," I puff out, then shift my leg around.

When I settle into my new position, I find that while my body is less fatigued in this position, there are other issues with it. Like the fact that Griffin is smiling down at me now.

With the transition, my hair has landed in my face. I shake my head trying to move it, but the sweat on my forehead is making it stick. It would be fine if it wasn't tickling my nose. I puff out a breath in hopes of blowing it off to relieve the itch, but that doesn't work either. I scrunch my nose, trying to fight the urge to lift my hand and scratch it.

"How's it going?" Griffin's lips twitch. His casual comment is the equivalent of 'I could do this all day.'

"I'm great." I force a smile. "How are you?"

My left hand is struggling. If I could move it one dot closer to the rest of my body I'd be fine.

"Left hand," I whisper.

Griffin eyes the mat, then me.

"Red," he whispers back.

It's the opposite direction I wanted to go. My hand starts to inch toward the red dot, but it's too far. My muscles are aching, crying out for relief. I know I'm not going to make it. I've accepted my fate. I'm prepared to land in a heap on the mat when Griffin's arm catches me.

"I win." It's an echo of what I said when I won our Yahtzee game, except it's spoken so softly. His eye contact so intense that he looks pained.

His arm bands around my lower back, then he slowly pulls me upward, his solid mass of a thigh sliding between my legs. I know his intention was to help me, to not let me fall, but this new position is far more dangerous than me collapsing onto the floor. With the seam of my leggings and the way his thick thigh is positioned, there's now a delicious pressure against my clit. It's a quick message to my nervous system—party's down here—then there's a flood of wetness and the tiniest heartbeat pulsing between my legs. My core feels heavy, like a weight has been dropped between my thighs, anchoring me to Griffin.

The pressure is so good. *So good.*

My body urges me to rock my pelvis, to move against him.

My brain responds. *Don't you dare.*

I'm internally fighting a battle of my hormones when Griffin's hand presses against my lower back, pushing me farther up his thigh. Caught off guard, I'm not able to hold in the breathy moan that his movement and added pressure on my clit causes.

With the sound of my whimper hanging between us in the otherwise quiet room, my eyes widen and my neck flushes, embarrassment claiming me. As he stares down at me, Griffin's eyes are dark and moody, but the tender smile on his face remains. He's like that. Equal parts dangerous and sweet. It's so sexy that it's infuriating. Also, how obnoxious is it that he is currently holding up his body weight and mine? Like what human being is designed to do that? And do it so casually. His arm muscles contracting with their use, but no evidence on his face that he's strained in the slightest.

And why does he really have no shirt on right now? His perfectly sculpted shoulders and chest are looming over me to show me what I definitely can't have. What I'm not supposed to want because we're only pretending. And honestly, it's a little embarrassing how much I've been lusting after my own husband lately.

"Excuse me," I push on Griffin's shoulders in order to put space between us so I can dismount his leg, "If you'll let go…I can…get off."

But he doesn't move an inch.

"You want to get off?" His voice is low, and if I'm not mistaken, laced with hunger. And when he slides me against his leg again, a shudder of pleasure racks my body. He does it again, this time not only sliding me against his leg, but applying a downward pressure that intensifies the sensation between my legs.

Oh, my God.

I could easily fall apart beneath him. Knowing that I'm starting to have feelings for him makes the idea of coming apart with Griffin even more intense. I'm suddenly feeling vulnerable. And I wouldn't be able to stand it if he started down this path, then pulled away.

"Griffin, don't tease me." My voice is barely above a whisper.

"I don't want to tease you, sweetheart. I want to make you come. Do you want that?" he asks, this time perfectly clear about his intentions.

I guess we're doing this.

So, I decide to be entirely clear about mine.

I rock my pelvis forward, letting my clit pulse against his thigh. I nod urgently before whispering, "Yes."

CHAPTER 20

Griffin

Somewhere between Emma's sexy moan and the incredible feeling of her warm pussy on my leg, I lost my willpower to hold back from her. And when she told me not to tease her, when I saw the vulnerability in her eyes, it made me want her even more. The only thing I want to tease is Emma's orgasm out of her.

While I wouldn't mind holding this position, I want to feel her body beneath mine, her soft curves reaching up to meet me, so I lift her up, abandoning the Twister mat for the comfort of the couch.

I lower her down on the cushions, then climb over her, letting my eyes travel the length of her body. When I saw her in these leggings, I knew I was in trouble. The material clings tightly to her thighs and ass, showing every curve, accentuating the contrast between the supple curve of her hips and the dip of her waist. My hands trail along the sides of her body, and over her ribcage, until I'm gathering her arms over her head.

Emma's cheeks are pink, her dark, silky hair feathered out in every direction on the white linen beneath. Her eyes are alert, filled with hunger and excitement as I gather her wrists and press them to the pillow behind her.

"Keep these here," I tell her, knowing her hands on me would be a threat to my sanity. We're already crossing the line that I've drawn.

We've been touching and kissing all week, but nothing like this.

Do not have sex with your wife. Chad's words echo in my mind.

We'll keep it safe. Dry humping like teenagers.

I lower down over her, placing my thigh between her legs, giving her the widest part of me to grind against.

"Use me, Emma." I press a kiss to her neck, trailing my lips to her jaw, before allowing more of my weight to settle on top of her. "Make yourself feel good."

She rocks her hips up to meet me, and I press down, giving her the friction she needs.

"Ahh," she gasps.

"That's it." I nip at her neck, encouraging her, loving the feel of her writhing beneath me.

She squeezes my leg between her thighs, inching her center higher on my thigh.

I tuck my face into her neck, teasing her there with feather-light kisses. My erection is sandwiched between us, swelling against her hip as I imagine what it would feel like to have her hand wrapped around me, her sweet mouth, the snug warmth of her slick pussy closing in around me.

I wanted her to take control, but the images I've conjured, along with the feel of her beneath me are too much.

My body takes over, deciding it's going to do whatever the fuck it wants. And it has a primal urge to fuck. To thrust against Emma's center, to let her feel every inch of my hard cock until she's coming apart beneath me.

I pin her down with my hips, and roll my hard cock into her center. Through her leggings and my shorts, I can feel the warmth of her again. *Fuck.* I squeeze my eyes shut, hoping that blocking one of my senses will help, but it doesn't, it only makes every slide against her center more intense.

The feel of her body, her scent and those breathy sounds she's making surround me. Her hands are still overhead where I put them, but it feels like she's wrapped herself around me and is pulling me in deeper.

Our faces are inches apart. Emma grinds against me at the same time I rock into her. We're two bodies, desperately trying to fuse into one, held back only by the barrier of our clothing.

She gasps, her throaty moan splitting her lips apart in unrestrained pleasure.

My hand moves to her face, my thumb tracing along her full bottom lip. I dip the pad of my thumb inside and roll her lip down.

"You like that?" I ask.

She nods, so I give it to her again.

Then, before I can change my mind, my mouth descends on hers. Our kisses are rough and dirty, matching the rhythm of our hips.

I dive in deeper. Loving the feel of Emma beneath me, chasing her orgasm. Mine so close I'm nearly blinded.

I can tell she's close and it spurs me on. I'm careful to not change anything. Giving her exactly what she needs to get there.

Then, she's arching into me, her thighs clamping tight around my leg.

"*Griffin.*" Her breathy moan is soft. "Oh, fuck…yesss." She sighs, clinging to me so fucking tight as her orgasm rocks through her body. I let myself go then, groaning against her neck as I rock into her one last time before spilling into my shorts.

Slowly, she lowers her hips back to the couch and opens her eyes.

"Wow." She giggles. "That was—"

"Incredible," I finish for her.

"Yeah," she agrees, her face slack with pleasure.

"You did so good." I kiss her forehead, then pull back. I reach for the tissue box behind the couch and clean myself up.

Emma sighs in contentment. "I can't move, I'm so tired."

"You'll sleep well tonight. A good thing with the interview tomorrow."

"Is that why? You wanted me to relax?"

There are plenty of reasons, the feel of her against me, the pleasure I get from watching her pleasure. My true feelings on the subject are complicated, so I let her believe it.

"It worked, right?" I give her a small smile.

"Yeah, it did." She smiles back.

She lies there for a moment watching me as I fold up the Twister mat and put it back in the box. Then, I help her up and to her bedroom.

Emma changes in the closet then meets me in the bathroom where I'm brushing my teeth.

"My whole body is shaky. I used muscles tonight that I haven't used in a long time," she says, loading her toothbrush with paste. "I can barely hold my toothbrush up."

"Do you need me to brush your teeth for you?"

"I'd take you up on that offer, but you've done so much already." She smiles around her toothbrush.

Biting back a grin, I rinse out my mouth and dry my hands.

"Tonight was fun." Talking around her toothbrush causes a dribble of toothpaste to run down her chin. I reach out and wipe it with my thumb.

"Yeah. It was."

"Not just the orgasm, I mean that was *a lot* of fun, but I meant the Date Night Challenge and Twister."

"I knew what you meant."

She nods, then rinses her mouth.

When she's done, I follow her out of the bathroom and shut off the light. As she moves toward her bed and I get ready to settle onto my place on the floor, Emma hooks her pinky with mine and looks up at me.

"Will you lay with me?" she asks.

My lungs take in a deep breath.

No. My brain's knee-jerk reaction is what I should be listening to, but my sore neck, my aching back, they're louder.

"For a little while."

She climbs in, and I follow. I reach for the lamp and turn off the light. At first, my body is on high alert, aware of Emma's every move. My brain still pleading its case for why this is a terrible idea.

"Griffin?"

"Yeah?" I respond.

"Are you nervous about tomorrow?" she asks.

"Yeah," I answer honestly.

"Really?"

"I want it to go well for you."

I can hear her smiling in the dark. "That's sweet."

"It's the truth."

"I'm nervous, too, but knowing you'll be with me helps."

It's quiet for a moment, and I finally let my body relax into the cloud-like mattress. I'm going to regret this when I move to the floor in a few minutes. *Add it to the list.* My brain smirks.

"Thank you for doing this with me. You didn't have to." She shifts closer. I can feel the warmth of her body, smell the combination of her shampoo and face wash. Her hand finds mine; her fingers skim along my palm until they intersect with mine. "I appreciate it."

My fingers collapse around her hand, holding her there.

"Yeah, of course." I swallow. Suddenly, I'm bone tired. And it has nothing to do with the fact that I've slept like shit on Emma's bedroom floor for nearly two weeks. No, it's the emotional drain of being near her, trying to fight our attraction and not let feelings get involved. The effort it takes to hold back from her is making me weary. Tonight, I let myself get caught up in her, but there was still restraint. I'm not sure how I'll handle it if the situation happens again.

And now I'm lying in her bed, letting my eyelids close and listening to her breath even out beside me. My thumb skims over the smooth metal of Emma's wedding band.

Emma's wrong when she said that I didn't have to come to New York to help her. I didn't have a choice. From the moment I saw her on the roof, I knew she was mine.

∾

Emma's eyes scan my naked chest, then lift to my face.

"Why are you half naked and sweaty?" she says, panicked. "The interview with Kandi is in an hour."

"I just finished up tennis with the guys." My lips twitch. "It only takes me a few minutes to get ready."

"Lucky you." She paces across the room again, stops short, then backtracks to grab her phone off the dresser.

This morning when I woke up next to her, our fingers still intertwined, and my dick hard as a rock, my brain waged war against the thought of pushing her onto her back and teasing another orgasm out of her.

She's not dressed yet; she's in a pale pink silk robe. Her wet hair is in a messy bun on her head and her face is free of makeup. "You look beautiful."

She laughs like I'm telling a funny joke. "I'm so stressed out, I could cry."

I step in front of her and put my hands on her upper arms, trying to give her comfort in this clearly stressful moment. "Take a deep breath."

She closes her eyes, takes in a deep breath, then exhales before opening her eyes again.

"Better?"

"A little."

I follow her to the closet.

"Let's focus on right now. What are you most worried about?"

She pulls one of the dresses off the rack and examines it. "Last night, I felt prepared, but then I woke up this morning and," her eyes meet mine, "I felt unsure."

If she's talking about my absence, I want to reassure her it has nothing to do with her.

"What can I do to make you feel better?" My eyes fall on the knot of her robe, the silky material and how a flick of the wrist could have it parting in no time. Every cell in my body is begging to touch her, to help her find peace in this stressful moment.

Her hands move to her face.

"If you shower and get dressed, that will make me feel better."

I nod, and follow her directions. In twenty minutes, I've showered, shaved and dressed in the clothes she picked out for me. Tailored pants and a button-down shirt.

Emma is now dressed in a sleeveless knit dress. It hugs every curve and the cream color contrasts with her dark locks and red lips.

She lifts her phone to take a selfie, but I step in behind her. Flipping her camera so that the picture is a reflection of us in the mirror, I place one hand against her hip and let the other slip around her neck. I duck my head, and kiss her jaw.

Her breath hitches, but then I hear the click of the camera.

She turns her face up toward me and smiles.

"You're getting scary good at this."

She has no fucking clue how easy it is to pretend she's really mine.

In the car, Emma lifts a finger to her mouth, a delicate nail poised to be crushed between her teeth, so I take her hand and hold it in mine.

"We've got this," I tell her.

She bites down on her lip and shakes her head. "I don't know. I don't think we're ready."

"At this point, we have to be. Besides, this woman is not the be all and end all of your career. You are moments away from signing a deal with Bergman's and you've got a waiting list a mile long. Do we really care what Kandi Kline thinks?"

"She once told Atlas Villamor his designs were 'too simple.'"

I shake my head. "I don't know who that is."

"Exactly." She stabs her finger in the air to emphasize her point. "He was a designer on the rise and then, poof, just disappeared."

"I don't think me not knowing that bridal gown designer is an indication of his career success."

"What I'm trying to say is we have to be flawless today." She tucks her hair behind her ear and bites her lip. "Can we do that?"

"Yeah, we can."

CHAPTER 21

Emma

While *The Dress*'s headquarters are located at One World Trade Center, Kandi's assistant, Nakita, indicated that we were to meet at a more intimate location in Hell's Kitchen. The word intimate has my body breaking out into a cold sweat.

Recalling memories from last night with Griffin on the sofa sends a surge of heat across my skin. Now, I'm really a mess.

Thinking about Griffin's body on top of mine, the way he pinned me down, like he was in control, but then he let me use him to find my release makes my heart hammer in my chest. I don't know what changed last night. We'd been ramping up our touching and kissing this week in preparation for this interview, but nothing like last night has happened since Vegas. Since Griffin told me he thought we should keep things platonic. Now, I don't know where we stand. I don't know what it means or if it was a one-time thing. All I know is I liked it. Aside from Vegas, it was the most erotic experience of my life and he didn't even touch me.

I try to steady the rhythm of my pulse, but it's near impossible. Not when Griffin's sitting next to me, holding my hand so I don't chew off my manicure.

That's the thing about him, one minute my panties are wet, and the next my ribcage is tightening at his sweet gestures. It's all so confusing.

When we arrive at the warehouse building, Nakita greets us at the main entrance, then takes us up to the third floor.

"Coffee? Tea? Champagne?"

"I'll have tea," I say. There's no way I can do champagne on an unsettled stomach.

"Water, please," Griffin adds.

Nakita disappears behind a door on the far side of the small space.

Not a minute later, the elevator door opens and Kandi Kline exits.

I've seen pictures of her, so I know it's her, but she is even more intimidating in person. Short, jet-black hair, flawless skin with rosy cheeks and fine arching eyebrows. She's dressed in wide-leg trousers and a fitted blazer, the soft lavender a stark contrast to her sharp features. Her dark eyes focus in on us.

"Bonjour, ravi de vous rencontrer."

Oh, shit. Was I supposed to learn French?

I'm frozen to the spot, uncertain of how to respond when Griffin steps forward to extend his hand.

"Vous aussi, Madame," he says confidently.

She looks between us.

All I can do is smile. Yes, my husband speaks French. I totally knew that.

"Vous êtes tous les deux assez beaux ensemble," she directs at Griffin.

"Merci. Nous sommes heureux d'être ici." While I can tell he's not fluent, hearing Griffin speak French is making me flustered.

A smile spreads across Kandi's face. "Charmed. I just

returned from Paris. That city gives me life." She extends her hand to him and he kisses it, then she turns her attention on me.

"Emma Warner. Pleasure."

"The pleasure is mine," I tell her, taking her hand. It's unnaturally smooth. I wonder what moisturizer she uses.

Nakita appears with our drinks, then leaves again to get Kandi a cappuccino.

"Take a seat, I'm going to grab my notes." Kandi indicates for us to sit in the chairs.

"You know French?" I whisper to Griffin, when she's out of earshot.

"I studied it in undergrad for my language credits. I don't remember most of it. Mostly short everyday phrases."

"Say something else."

He looks toward the ceiling, clearly thinking about it.

"Tu es á moi," he says, finally.

"Tu es á what?" I ask, reaching into my purse to grab my phone so I can write the phrase down and Google translate it later.

Griffin smiles, looking down at his hands. "Don't worry about it."

Kandi returns and takes a seat across from us, a pair of dark-rimmed glasses on her nose as she looks down at her notes.

With her cappuccino in hand, she takes a sip, then sets it down on the table between us. If she's trying to make me more nervous, she's succeeding. I think she might have been an interrogator in a previous life. Her practiced patience is making me squirm. Is this how Harry and Meghan felt sitting down with Oprah? Griffin's hand finds mine, and he gives it a subtle squeeze. Kandi glances at her notepad again, sets the recorder on the table and presses play. Then, she slides off her glasses, and pinching one leg between her fingers, twists them to the side.

I'm expecting a hard-hitting question, something that will make me flustered or derail our meticulous preparation for this interview, but instead Kandi leans forward with a giddy smile on her face.

"Full disclosure, Griffin, I've been to your show five times." Kandi undoes her blazer to reveal a Rainin' Men shirt with Griffin's face on it. My jaw drops. I don't know what I'm more caught off guard by, the Rainin' Men fan merch with Griffin's face on it or the fact that Kandi is wearing it. "I'm your biggest fan."

"Wow." I blink.

"Thanks for your support." Is all Griffin can manage as we process this news.

In a matter of thirty seconds, I've watched Kandi Kline, hard-nosed editor of *The Dress* magazine, transform from a poised interviewer into a puddle of mush. She's fangirling hard right now. There are legitimate hearts in her eyes right now as she gushes over Griffin.

"Emma, I can't wait to discuss the detail and design that have made your bridal gowns a hit with the modern bride, but first, I'm dying to know how a male revue dancer from Las Vegas and a bridal gown designer from New York City fell in love."

I'm prepared for the question. It's the foundation of the whole relationship we've been building from the ground up for the last week, but I'm still processing Kandi's crush on Griffin, and words escape me.

"Um, well…that's a good question…you see, it's a funny story…"

"We met on a rooftop." My heart stops at Griffin's words. What is he doing? That's not part of our story. Okay, it's exactly how we met, but it's not what we planned to tell Kandi. "That's the first time I saw her. I was on a rooftop in Las Vegas, she appeared and it was like the whole world stopped.

"She was getting some fresh air, the same reason I was there and we started talking. I felt an immediate connection to her. Something in her eyes." He looks over at me, and my heart trips over itself. "A vulnerability that made me want to protect her, but also a lighthearted warmth that I was drawn to. It was something I saw in her that made me think about what I had been missing in my own life."

Griffin's words are certain and clear, compared to my fumbling attempt. At this point I can't argue with him, tell Kandi that's not really how it happened. When I glance at Kandi, she's enraptured with Griffin's account of our meeting. She's on the edge of her seat.

"And then?" she asks.

"And then we got married," he says.

I wave my hands. "What Griffin is trying to say is that we fell so quickly, it felt like it happened right away. But there was stuff in between."

Kandi ignores me, her dark eyes staring intently at Griffin.

"Maybe it was too quick, but I couldn't help myself," he continues. "I knew there would be nothing better in this world than to have Emma by my side every day. And I wanted her to be mine."

"Wow." Kandi's thin lips pull into a beaming smile. She plucks a tissue out of the box on the table and dabs at her eyes. "That's beautiful."

I'm still stunned by Griffin's deviation from the plan. Clearly it worked, Kandi is eating out of the palm of his hand, but now I'm left feeling off-balanced. Not sure where to go from here. Unsure of what page we are on in the script we rehearsed. If we're even using the same script anymore. I'm also left wondering if Griffin actually meant anything he said. The details on our first meeting were correct, but everything he told Kandi about how he was thinking and feeling that night, are they true? Or embellished to give her a good story?

"Emma, what was your reaction? The first time you met Griffin?"

I think back to that night on the roof, how upset I was about Alec's engagement, my body felt like it was buzzing with every emotion. My mind reeling with the shocking news. I needed fresh air. I needed calm. And while I think that stepping out on the roof in the night air was helpful, it was Griffin who gave it to me. Not because he was attractive and I felt a spark when our fingers touched, but the way he made me feel protected, safe, like I could be open and honest and he wouldn't judge me.

"Honestly, I was overwhelmed by him. It was like his presence was suddenly taking up all the space around me, and filling up the emptiness inside. I didn't think I was ready to put myself out there again so soon, but I knew there was something special between us from the very first moment."

As the words fall out, I realize they're all true. My face flushes with panic. I cling to the hope that Griffin doesn't realize I'm being honest, just like I have no idea if he was speaking the truth about his feelings.

Internally, I breathe a sigh of relief when she moves on from how we met to our life together in New York.

"Will you be making your home here in the city?" Kandi asks.

"Yes," I answer quickly, because my brain has finally started working again. "That's the plan."

"What do you plan to do in New York, Griffin?" she asks.

"I'm awaiting my bar exam results; I'll be pursuing a career in business and commercial law."

"Handsome and smart?" Kandi beams. "Emma, you've got the whole package here."

She has no idea. Handsome and smart doesn't even scratch the surface. But I can't explain to her how selfless he has been during this entire process. That he put his life on hold to come to New York and help me. That he spent the last week getting to know me, preparing for today so I don't put my business at risk. He likely has a million better things to do but is sitting next to me right now because he's protective and loyal and kind.

And then there's the way he made me come last night. The way he plucked an explosive, all-consuming orgasm out of me, without even touching me. I won't mention that, but it's definitely worth noting.

Since Griffin arrived in the city, I've been concerned about making him fit into the mold that I thought the perfect husband would be, but he doesn't need to fit. He is the mold.

All I can do is smile and try to push the emotion I'm feeling back down.

"That's why I married him."

Jess sent over samples of my gowns, which are now hanging on brass busts in the open space behind the sitting area. I walk Kandi through the dresses in my line. She asks about my design process, favorite projects I've worked on and upcoming trends I see with bridal fashion.

I expect Griffin to be sitting in one of the comfy chairs checking his phone, maybe secretly watching a game online, like a man waiting on his significant other to finish shopping. But he stands with Kandi and me, listening to our discussion and giving me encouraging smiles.

"Which one is your favorite?" Kandi asks Griffin.

He takes his time answering, walking around each gown, like he wants to make sure he answers the question thoughtfully. His interest, or at least the appearance that he's interested, in my work is surprising. Maybe I'm skeptical from the years of Alec's disinterest, but to have Griffin actively participate and seem to enjoy it is warming my heart. It's also making my belly flutter with anticipation.

"This one." He points to the lace-covered dress. "It's the most similar to how I see Emma. The cut of it is delicate and sweet, the lace makes it romantic, and the strap detailing on the back is sexy. All those details together show her passion for what she does."

My heart pounds in response to Griffin's words. Why does my husband have to be so adorable?

I can see the effect he has on Kandi. His reserved nature and humble charm have reduced what I thought to be a no-nonsense, severe magazine editor to a mushy pile of love.

"Meeting you two was a pure delight. You have such a special relationship." She looks between us, "And Emma, your designs are everything I imagined and more. I'm going to be watching you and look forward to what you have in store for us in the future."

"Thank you, Ms. Kline."

"I'm going to have Nakita see you to hair and makeup for the photoshoot."

Nakita appears and motions us down the hallway, toward a small room. Inside, a makeup artist is setting out brushes and compacts. Next to her, a man is pulling out styling products.

I drop into the seat Nakita indicates and Griffin takes the chair beside me. After introducing themselves, Bobbi gets to work on my makeup and Luis starts to style Griffin's hair.

With the interview behind us, I can feel my body relaxing. The hardest part is over. Now, it's the fun part of getting pampered with hair and makeup, smiling for the camera. With a photographer father, all of this is second nature to me.

"Somebody has a crush," I tease Griffin.

"Who?" he asks.

"Kandi does. On you. She's smitten. She loves you. She's your biggest fan, remember?"

"What's not to love?" He wiggles his eyebrows, which makes me laugh. "I guess it's a good thing you locked me down when you did," he teases back, "or you'd have competition."

I roll my eyes.

"Don't get a big head or I'll be forced to dominate you again in Yahtzee."

"Then I'll be forced to pull out the Twister mat."

The tone of his voice is joking, but when I look across the mirror at him, his eyes are the same intense pools of green that they were last night when he told me to come against his leg. So much for relaxing.

"Kandi wants your makeup natural and your hair up," Bobbi informs me as she applies a tinted moisturizer.

"Sounds great."

It's customary for the editorial feature to have some over-the-top photoshoot, so the fact that we're in this random building and Kandi wants minimal makeup and hair has me wondering what she has in store for us. There was the notable May 2018 Grand Central Station photoshoot featuring Maggie Kwan, and a personal favorite, designer Vivienne Castillo's dress floating in Central Park Lake. The last week and a half, the priority has been getting to know Griffin, so I haven't had much time to dwell on what the photoshoot might be.

Fifteen minutes later, Griffin and I are done with hair and makeup. Nakita leads us back down the short hallway, past the sitting area where Kandi interviewed us, and toward another room on the opposite side of the space.

Kandi is there waiting for us with another woman. She has short, salt and pepper hair and dark freckles across her nose and cheeks. She looks familiar.

"Emma, Griffin," Kandi motions toward the woman beside her, "this is world renowned photographer Shonda Picard."

The name registers instantly. As Kandi mentioned, Shonda Picard is known worldwide in the photography industry. She's the Anne Geddes of adult, intimate photography.

My stomach drops. My mind races with all the possible scenarios. I remind myself *The Dress* is a national magazine; we're not going to be posing nude.

Nakita opens the door behind Kandi and Shonda. "Everything is ready."

Kandi smiles warmly. "This is going to be a moment you'll treasure forever. The photos of you two are going to be utterly breathtaking, I can feel it." She clenches her fist in passion.

God, I hope she's right.

Nakita motions us in the door. Kandi and Shonda follow.

Inside, the room is small. The walls are made of brick and there are three large ornate windows on the far wall letting in natural light. The window frames are black and rustic looking, likely preserved from the time this building was constructed. There, positioned below the middle window is a large claw foot bathtub with gold accents.

Nakita is busy hanging one of my dresses from a hook on the wall between two of the windows. It's the dress from my collection that Griffin had said he liked the best.

Flanking the tub are two large photo lights on tripods.

I know what's happening, but Griffin hasn't caught on.

"What is this?" he asks.

"The photoshoot set," I tell him, before swallowing thickly.

His brows furrow. "A bathtub?"

"Intimate photoshoots are Shonda's specialty."

I see the moment he gets it.

"That's a thing?"

"A very popular thing, actually."

"So, we have to get—"

"Naked," I finish for him, my heart pounding against my ribs.

While Shonda prepares her camera and Kandi settles in near the digital playback monitor, Nakita ushers us toward a table on the side of the room.

"We have refreshments available." She motions to the large assortment of food. My stomach twists with anxiety. There's no way I'm eating anything right now.

"No thanks." I shake my head.

"I'm good." Griffin holds up a hand.

"It's here if you change your mind." She walks us over to a door on the left side of the room.

"Your wardrobe is in here." She motions inside the room. It's a tiny bathroom complete with water closet, walk-in shower and a vanity. On the vanity is a variety of skin tone underwear. "Emma, you'll wear a thong and Griffin, there are briefs for you. Robes are hanging behind the door. I'll let you two get changed while I draw the bath."

She closes the door behind her and that's when I start to lose it.

"Oh, my God." My hands tent over my nose and mouth. "How are we going to do this?" I start pacing. "We can't do this. There's no way. We didn't practice. We've never," I motion between us, "you know, touched body parts. They'll know. We can't fake it, Griffin. They'll *know*." As panic starts to set in, I can feel my neck and face starting to heat. The mirror over the vanity reveals splotchy red spots on my neck. Luckily, my face is faring better with the makeup they put on. I fan myself, trying not to overheat.

"Hey," Griffin comes up behind me and turns me to face him, "I get it, but it's going to be okay."

I grab a tissue off the vanity and dab at my eyes. "Everything was going so well, and now I don't know how we're going to do this. The photos are going to be so awkward."

"We'll figure it out together. And listen, even if we'd been together for years, photoshoots can be intimidating, especially for people who aren't used to being in front of the camera. My first set of photos for the revue were horrible. The photographer was directing me to be sexy and mysterious. I ended up looking like I was trying to do a *Zoolander* impression."

The image he paints has a laugh bursting out of me.

"Nothing can be worse than that," he assures me. "Besides, we've come this far, we can't give up now."

Griffin's encouragement means so much to me. The fact that he doesn't have to do this, he could walk away right now and leave me here, but instead he's making me feel better about this stressful situation.

"You're right." I reach up to kiss him on the cheek, my hands gripping his biceps for balance. "Thank you for making me feel better."

Griffin's hands wrap around my hips to hold me close. Memories from last night immediately emerge, chasing away the calm I was starting to enjoy. That doesn't bode well for the fact that we'll be mostly naked sitting in a bathtub together in a few minutes.

"I'm going to change." I pull out of his arms, grab a fistful of spandex and a robe from the back of the door, then shut myself in the water closet.

As I change, I work to keep my pulse from skyrocketing again. This photoshoot is the only thing standing in my way of a flawless interview with Kandi Kline, I need to be a professional about this. Not let a little thing like my attraction to Griffin mess with my head. I quickly change and pull on the robe. When I exit, Griffin is robe-clad, too, and waiting for me. Whether it's the robe I'm wearing or the look he's giving me, memories from Vegas pop in my head. Me on the bed, my legs spread with Griffin's head between them. And last night, the way he looked down at me, his eyes darkened with desire, yet eager and comforting at the same time, like he was enthusiastically taking in every move I made. The memory of that look and the intensity of my orgasm—like a bomb had been detonated—makes me shiver.

But, I can't think about any of that right now.

"Are you ready?" he asks.

I exhale, my breath leaving my lungs in a whoosh. "Yeah, let's do it."

CHAPTER 22

Emma

I wonder if this is how a heavyweight boxer feels walking down the tunnel toward the ring. I'm so laser-focused on getting to the bathtub so I can toss off my robe and dive in, that I almost trip on the cord for the lighting system.

Griffin catches me because he's smooth like that. No awkward, flailing limbs on that guy. Once I'm upright again, I discard my robe and lower myself into the water. I have no issues with my naked body. Yes, there are things I would tweak here and there, but in this moment it's not the naked-ness of *my* body that is causing heart palpitations. It's my husband's.

"Is the water temperature okay?" Nakita asks as she collects my robe.

"Yup," is all I can manage.

The water could be melting off my skin and I wouldn't even notice. All of my focus is on watching my husband disrobe. I take in every inch of his golden skin as he sinks into the water. There's the familiar view of his muscular chest and arms, the six-pack muscles that pull taut as he angles his body over the bathtub. Then, there are the solid muscles of his thighs that I became well acquainted with last night. And the

240

skin-tone briefs that are doing nothing to disguise the outline of Griffin's dick. I do my best to not look shocked by the bulge there. To pretend like this isn't the first time I'm seeing it.

With Griffin's lower half now hidden under the bubbles, I snap my focus to Shonda who is doing a few test shots.

Shonda looks through her camera. "The lighting is perfect. Let's get started."

My goal for this photoshoot is to listen to Shonda's voice, take her directions and ignore the warm, muscular body sliding against mine in this bathtub. Professionals do this all the time; touch and rub themselves up against people they are not physically intimate with and make it look natural.

I've been instructed to position myself on top of Griffin, with my back to his chest. I'm trying to not put all my weight on him, to keep some distance, and it's one hell of an abdominal workout.

"Emma, you look stiff. Relax into him," Shonda calls from behind her camera.

Under Shonda's instruction, I let my full weight settle on Griffin. Between our bodies the warm, soapy water sluices out, leaving nothing but the friction of our skin. My abs are grateful.

"Now, Emma, raise your left arm up and place your hand behind Griffin's neck."

I reach my warm, wet fingers up to grip his neck.

The action makes my left breast break the surface of the water. My nipple is still encased in the surrounding bubbles, but the exposure to the cool air has it tightening.

"Emma, chin up." Click. "Beautiful."

There's movement to our side, Shonda adjusting her angle, but we keep our gazes forward.

"Now, Griffin, cradle Emma's left breast in your palm."

Even though I know it's coming, and I tell my body not to react, the moment Griffin follows her direction I can't help arching my body into his touch. His hand on me feels so good, I can't stop the low moan that escapes my lips.

I'm dying. I will not survive this.

"That's perfect, Emma," Shonda praises me, and thankfully doesn't draw attention to the fact I just moaned loudly. "Now, Griffin, tease her a little. Whatever feels natural. Your hand on her leg, kiss her neck."

Griffin doesn't hesitate. He moves to draw my right leg up, bending it at the knee until it emerges from the water. His hand splays over the inside of my thigh, his fingertips teasing just beneath the water. It feels just like the night we practiced touching and kissing in the kitchen after the Premier Real Estate party.

"That's beautiful. Griffin, very natural. Emma, soften your mouth."

The shoot continues like that, Shonda directing us, which makes it feel less awkward about touching Griffin because when she tells me to grip his neck I can point to Shonda and say *she told me to!* Plus, this falls under the category of touching each other for public appearances. I never thought we'd need to apply it to a bubble bath photoshoot, but here we are.

I'm also aware of Kandi sitting next to the monitor, her dark-rimmed glasses pinched between her fingers as she assesses what she sees on the screen.

The steady click of Shonda's camera pauses and I turn my head to see Kandi murmuring to Shonda.

Shonda nods. "We're going to take a short break."

"Should we get out?" I ask. I don't really want to get out but I'm not sure what we should be doing.

"Please wait in the tub so we can continue the session shortly." Kandi says.

I nod. There's nothing to do but wait. I shift my body forward, so I'm no longer leaning on Griffin.

Behind me Griffin moves, extending his bent legs on either side of me.

"I have to stretch; my legs are cramping."

"That's okay." I bend my knees and hug them to my chest to allow more space for him. "Do you think we're taking a break because the photos aren't turning out well? Do you think Kandi is upset? I knew this was going to be a disaster."

Griffin doesn't answer any of my questions, but instead reaches for the fresh bar of soap perched on the soap dish.

"What are you doing?" I ask.

"When I was little, before Sophie was born, my mom would cover my entire back with soap, then she'd draw pictures or write words and I'd guess what she was drawing." I can hear his hands lathering the soap between them. "I thought we could try it while we wait."

"Oh."

"It's very relaxing."

"Is that your way of telling me I need to relax?"

"It couldn't hurt."

A second later, Griffin's hands sweep across the top of my back. They move over me, the tips of his fingers tickling my ribs as they curve around my side. I try to ignore my anxiety about the photoshoot and focus on what Griffin just told me.

"That's a nice memory of your mom." I whisper, aware that Kandi and Shonda are not far away.

"It's something simple. Me in the bathtub playing with a plastic boat while she wrote in soap on my back. It's one of the few times I felt taken care of. That she was the adult and I could just be the kid. I think I was four."

I can't see his face, but I can hear the hint of nostalgia in his voice.

"I'm sorry." I want to turn around and give him a big hug. Make him feel taken care of like he didn't in his childhood, but Griffin's finger starts moving against my back.

243

"Thank you," he whispers, and a puff of air hits my wet back, causing a shiver to slip down my spine.

"Wait. I'm not ready." I straighten, ready to focus on his finger's movement, what he's spelling out on my back. Griffin's fingertip glides over my back, on one side of my spine, then the other.

"Was that 'hi'? That was pretty easy."

"You're a novice, so I'm starting off easy," he teases.

He lathers more soap and smooths it across my back.

"I'll make this one more challenging."

He's right. It is. Not only do I have to identify each letter, but then I have to remember what they are so I can guess the word.

"Emma," I say when he's done. "That was pretty easy."

"I'm not done," he says, drawing a shape around my spine.

I think it's a heart. His fingertip drops to my mid-back to the space that hasn't been written on yet.

"G-R-I-F-F-I," I call out the letters as he makes them.

I'm so focused on Griffin's fingertip, the shape of the letters he's making, that the click of the camera from behind us startles me.

We both turn to find Shonda there with her camera.

"I didn't mean to sneak up on you, but that's one of the best shots so far." She smiles. "Clever use of the props."

Before I turn back around, I catch Griffin's eye.

"Emma heart Griffin?" I have to know that I got it right.

He winks at me. That single movement has my heart rate soaring.

Shonda moves to the table by the monitor and switches her camera. Kandi is back in her seat by the playback monitor.

"I'm going to let you two take the lead on the second half of our session. I might offer adjustments if the shot is blocked, but I really want to capture your intimacy as a couple. So as best as you can, pretend I'm not here."

My stomach drops at Shonda's advice to be ourselves. I think it was safer when she was directing us. But then a moment ago when I thought she wasn't here and Griffin was tracing letters on my back, it was easy. Just me and Griffin.

I remember my parents' surprise wedding shower and how smooshing cake in each other's faces created levity for the stressful situation. I cup my hand and scoop bubbles from atop the water, then tap them onto Griffin's nose, complete with a *boop* sound effect.

Griffin smiles up at me, his dimple in full effect. *Click.*

I gather more soap on the palm of my hand, this time shaping a pile on his head into a hat. It's not my best bubble work, but I'm out of practice. Also, I should get an Oscar for portraying a woman who looks like she's having an adorably romantic bubble bath with her husband, while doing everything in her power to ignore the feel of his muscular thighs beneath her ass. And the fact that leaning ever so slightly forward would align our centers. Viscerally aware that one tiny movement would allow me to feel the pressure of him against my clit.

I force myself to ignore the building sensation between my legs.

We laugh, we tease. *Look how cute we are!*

But with every click of Shonda's camera, my thighs are losing the battle with trying to hover over Griffin's lap. I need to rest, just for a second. In that moment, Griffin's eyes find mine. There are bubbles on the side of his head. The ends of his hair at the nape of his neck are damp. He looks adorable.

I let myself relax. My knees spreading as far as they can go, allowing myself a moment where Griffin's thighs cradle my ass.

The second I make contact I discover that the wet material between us disguises nothing.

Griffin's erection presses into my clit. I stifle a whimper. And then I freeze.

But Griffin doesn't freeze up. One large hand supports my neck while his other arm brackets around my lower back, holding my body to him. Tilting my head back, he kisses along the front of my neck. At my center, I can feel his hard length nudge against me. To keep from gasping, I focus on my breathing. Taking in controlled breaths as Griffin's warm mouth works its way across my collar bone. God, his mouth is everything. Warm, firm lips mapping every inch of my skin. My hands move to the back of his neck, my fingertips teasing the damp edges of his hair, holding him close to me. I've finally found my groove.

"That's a wrap," Shonda calls. Griffin's lips pull back, but he keeps his arms banded around me. My hands drop to his shoulders, trying to orient myself after the sudden end to our intimate moment.

"She got some great shots. Sweet, playful and steamy. There are so many to choose from, it will be a difficult decision," Kandi says.

"That's great," I finally find my voice.

"It was wonderful meeting you two." Shonda hands her camera to Nakita.

"You as well," I say. "Thank you."

"I'll be in touch." Kandi follows Shonda toward the door.

Nakita brings our robes over and lays them over the stool. She places a mat down in front of the bathtub for us to step out onto. "There's a shower in the bathroom for you to rinse off and I put fresh towels on the vanity. Take your time getting dressed and I'll be out front when you're ready."

The door closes behind her with a click.

I lift my hands up to examine my wrinkled fingers. "I'm turning into a prune."

Griffin presses his fingertips into mine. "Me, too."

Our fingers interconnect, palms pressing together.

I'm still turned on, but now that we're alone, I'm even more cautious. There's no one here to stop us from touching. From getting caught up in the feel of our wet skin sliding against each other's.

"Thank you. Again. This," I nod my head toward the photoshoot equipment around us, "was a lot to ask."

Griffin squeezes my hands. "Taking a bubble bath with my beautiful wife? Not exactly a hardship."

I laugh. "You know what I mean."

"Yeah, I know."

Maybe it's the stillness of the water, or the fact that the adrenaline from the photoshoot has worn off, but suddenly, I'm freezing. Griffin must be sharing the same feeling, his lips are tinged purple, his skin suddenly rough with gooseflesh.

"We should get out." He nods.

"Yeah, we should."

When I stand up, the bubbles cling to my skin, giving me coverage. Somewhere between me straddling him, and his hands all over my body, I've decided being half clothed around him is normal. I decide not to use the robe. I'd rather keep it dry and enjoy the soft, plush material when I'm rinsed off, so I opt to quickly dry my feet on the mat, then grab the robe and race for the shower. Griffin follows behind me.

"You go first," he tells me when we're in the bathroom.

I nod, my teeth chattering as I hang up the robe on the hook outside the shower stall.

"Aren't you freezing?" I ask, doing my best to not drop my gaze to the wet skin-tone briefs clinging to his front.

"I'll be fine." He nods for me to go ahead.

I'm dying to crank the hot water to full blast and plant myself under the piping hot stream, but I stop short. The only reason today went as well as it did was because of Griffin. He can't take credit for my designs or the hard work I've done to get my gowns and my business this opportunity, but he played his part perfectly, and just having him beside me gave me a sense of calm.

I know he came to New York because he felt regretful that he didn't stop us from getting married in Vegas, but getting to know him, I've discovered that's who he is. He's selfless. Always looking out for others. He's been taking care of his family his whole life, whether it was his mom when she was drinking, or Sophie when he became her guardian.

Griffin is always taking care of others, always putting other people first, and for once, I want to take care of him. To let him know that I appreciate him and everything he has done.

My fingers wrap around his wrist and I give him a tug in the direction of the shower.

"You first," I tell him. His eyes drop down to my hand, then slowly back up to meet mine.

The bubbles giving me coverage are quickly evaporating, causing a fizzy sensation against my skin. I try to ignore the tingle of my skin as I wait for his response.

He nods. "Okay."

While I know it was the right thing to do, my body is not happy with the decision. It lets out a fierce shudder as I reach for my robe, but then, Griffin catches my wrist.

"Only if you're in here with me." He pulls me toward the shower with him.

I shake my head and smirk. "I'm trying to do something nice for you."

"I can't relax in here if I know you're out there shivering. If you want to do something nice for me, get in here."

He doesn't have to tell me twice. I nod eagerly, desperate for the relief I know the hot water will bring.

The shower stall is tiny, and instead of a fixed shower head, there is a moveable shower wand. It's similar to the one in my bathroom at my parents' apartment. The same one I've placed between my legs multiple times while thinking about Griffin.

Griffin lifts the shower handle and water starts spraying out. He slides the temperature handle to the warmest setting. It's like he knows scalding hot showers are my love language. I'd propose right here on the spot if we weren't already married.

"Come here," he says, and I hurry under the now steaming spray.

When the hot water hits my skin, I close my eyes and sigh. The water runs over my back, washing away the soap. Next to me, Griffin edges closer, letting the spray hit his shoulders and back.

My body melts. My tight muscles relax, and my skin turns rosy.

"Better?" Griffin rumbles against my ear.

"Yes." I nod, trying to ignore the way his husky voice makes my core clench.

When my body was cold and desperate for warmth, it was easier to ignore the fact that we're nearly naked. After rubbing up against Griffin in the bathtub, I'd somehow gotten used to our naked bodies pressing together. In front of Shonda and Kandi, I'd done my best to focus on the photo-shoot, and tried to not think about how attracted I am to him. But now, there's no audience and as my body has warmed, I've become increasingly aware of all of Griffin.

He's beside me, slightly angled behind me, his torso and hip graze my side as he leans farther into the spray. We're still wearing our underwear. And where I'd tried to be discreet about ogling his crotch earlier, along with the bubbles from our bath, the warm water has washed away my restraint.

Without moving my head, I drop my gaze between his muscular legs. Where there had been a bulge before, now Griffin's cock is unmistakably hard. The briefs can barely contain him, his swollen crown only a centimeter from the waistband. The thin layer of wet material reveals every ridge and vein.

I think about dropping to my knees, tucking my fingers into the waistband of his underwear and pulling him free. How I want to feel the weight of him in my hand, to lick along the large vein on the underside, slip the crown between my lips and suck hard.

While my thoughts were running wild, I must have lost the ability to carry out this dick ogling mission covertly because when my eyes lift, Griffin is staring back down at me. His green eyes drop below my neck. I guess it's only fair he gets to check out my breasts, since I can now sketch his dick from memory.

He doesn't look long, though.

A moment later, he reaches up to take the wand out of the holder.

"You missed a spot. Turn around." I do as he says. He holds the wand to spray against my chest, letting the warm water cascade over my breasts.

I don't think I missed a spot, but the extra attention feels nice. The way the water hits my nipples sends another rush of arousal between my thighs.

Griffin doesn't stop at my breasts. He slowly lowers the wand, down my ribcage and over my stomach until it hits the waistband of my thong. He keeps it there. The pressure of the water causes a dull ache in my belly. My clit throbs with the anticipation of him moving the sprayer lower.

"Should I keep going?" he asks.

It's his same words from last night, asking me if I want what he's offering.

"Yes." The word is barely audible over the rush of water, but I know he hears me because he lowers the wand between my thighs.

My breath comes out in a rush, my hands move to Griffin's arms to steady myself. The sensation of the sprayer is even better with him holding it against me.

My hands move over his chest, running my fingers over his tight nipples and then trailing lower toward his waistband, but when I get close to dipping beneath, Griffin gathers my wrists and lifts them above my head. He presses me backwards until my ass bumps against the tile. I'm pinned to the shower wall. His hold is firm, but not painful. It's like he knows how to assert his strength without overwhelming me.

"Is this—"

Even before the words leave his mouth, I know what he's going to ask. I can see the concern in his eyes. The question if I'm comfortable with what we're doing.

"Yes." I nod. "I want it."

I can see the effect my words have on him. How his erection jolts between his legs. I lick my lips, the need to have him in my mouth is overwhelming, but I know that's not happening with my hands pinned above my head. Griffin is in charge right now, and I like it.

The stream of water pulsing against my clit disappears. I moan in frustration, but then, the water is back, at the waistband of my thong. Griffin slides the sprayer beneath it, pushing it down into my panties.

The full force of the spray hits my clit. The overwhelming sensation has me rocking my hips forward and crying out.

"Is this what you like, Emma?"

He releases the grip on my wrists, and brings my right hand down to the sprayer.

"Show me how you make yourself come."

The way he's looking at me right now, like he'll burn up from desire if he doesn't watch me come, there's no way I'm going to stop. He steps back a few inches. His eyes follow my movements intently while he gives himself a long stroke with the heel of his hand.

I want to keep watching him, but the building pleasure between my legs forces my eyes closed. I rock my hips as the water beats against my clit. My left hand cups my breast, rolling my hardened peak between my thumb and index finger.

"Good girl. Keep going." His growl has me rocking my hips faster. "You look fucking perfect like that."

"I want to see you." The words fall from my lips so easily. I've never been good at voicing what I want, what I need, especially in the bedroom. But the reverence in Griffin's voice when he praises me and tells me to keep going, the hunger in his eyes, unleashes the desire in me. "Stroke yourself."

"Yeah?" He doesn't hesitate.

That's something I don't want to miss, so I force my eyes open. I watch entranced as his cock springs free from the wet material and he begins to stroke himself from crown to base.

The sight of him makes me suck in a sharp breath. With every thrust of his cock into his hands, Griffin's abdominal muscles contract, and his chest and arm muscles bulge with the effort.

While the water beating against my clit feels good, there's still an ache between my thighs. An emptiness and a desire to be filled. I dip my free hand into my panties so I can press two fingers inside.

"How does it feel, baby?"

"I wish it was you." I rock my hips, finding a rhythm.

"I'd fill you up. Stretch you so good."

His hair, darker now from the water, hangs seductively across his forehead. That's nothing compared to the way his hungry eyes eat up every inch of my body. And when he licks his bottom lip…oh my goodness, *that* is my favorite sight ever. The visual of Griffin pumping his thick cock to the sight of me pleasuring myself with the shower wand sends me over the edge.

"*Griffin.*" I gasp as my orgasm pulses through my body, my muscles tightening around my fingers.

"Emma. *Fuck.*" His face turns upward, the muscles in his neck tightening as he groans his release.

As my orgasm subsides, the water still rushing against my sensitive skin makes me shudder, so I pull the shower wand out of my underwear.

Griffin takes the shower wand from my hand and rinses himself off, then his release down the drain. I want to sag against the wall, my body boneless from the exhausting day and from my orgasm. Griffin pulls me to him and kisses me on the forehead.

I let my body sink into him. I'm too tired to care right now how confusing things are becoming between us. All I want to do is soak in the feeling of his strong arms around me. Enjoy the calming sensation of his finger pads massaging the shampoo into my scalp, him rinsing me, then wrapping me in a fluffy towel. So that's what I do.

At home, we pull on lounge clothes, for Griffin it's his gray sweatpants that I threatened to burn and a t-shirt while I throw on a knit long-sleeve shirt and matching shorts. We order in dinner. Griffin's favorite Chinese place. I already know his favorites. Beef lo-mein and cashew chicken. We eat side by side at the kitchen counter, me picking the mushrooms that Griffin doesn't want off his plate, while he takes the water chestnuts I refuse to eat off mine. He pushes the last Crab Rangoon toward me. After dinner, we snuggle up in my bed, Griffin reading his book, while I binge watch *Love Is Blind*.

At some point, my eyes fall closed and Griffin shuts off the television.

I curl into him and he kisses the top of my head. It's in that moment that I know I could do this with him every night for the rest of my life. That's what makes falling asleep in Griffin's arms, however comforting they may be, absolutely terrifying.

CHAPTER 23

Griffin

I take the bottle of water that the receptionist offers me, then sit down in the waiting area. I check my phone. Another text from Sophie.

Sophie: *Nailed my presentation! Piper and I are headed home tomorrow. One more week and then graduation!*

I text back.

So proud of you.

She immediately responds.

Sophie: *How's New York? How's your WIFE?*

I hesitate with my response. *How's my wife?*

Emma's fucking perfect.

I look around the modern, minimalist waiting area of Premier Real Estate. Isn't that why I'm here? Seeing if there is a future for me in New York, with Emma?

When I played tennis with Barrett, Carl and Hunter again yesterday morning, Hunter suggested I stop by today to check out the office. To meet the other members of the legal team. It would be casual, not an actual interview. I thought, why not? There's no harm in having a meeting. But sitting here now, I'm starting to feel guilty. I've already committed to Terrence and his firm.

Over the last week, my email has been filled with new hire paperwork from McGregor & Lange. It's a commitment I've already made, before I even met Emma. That's the issue right there. I've known Terrence for eight years. He and Rita have been in my corner since day one. They're like family. Sophie is my family. How would I tell her that I'm abandoning her to go to New York? She's an adult now, but we are the only family we have. I can't up and leave her.

I'm about to reply to Sophie when a text from Emma appears.

It's a picture of her.

She's lounging in a pink satin robe, her hair in a messy bun, with a dark gray substance painted on her face.

Seeing her, even in a picture, makes my heart skip a beat. She was still asleep when I left for the gym this morning, and when I got back, she was already gone to meet the other ladies for Chloe's bachelorette party. It's a whole day thing. Spa, dinner and dancing. I hate that I won't see her for the rest of the day.

Memories of yesterday have been at the forefront of my mind all morning. I almost let out a chuckle when I think of the photoshoot in the bathtub. It was an odd situation, but with Emma it didn't feel awkward. It's easy to be near her. To talk to her. To touch her. To want more with her.

Being in the bathtub with her allowed me to touch Emma the way I've been dying to. The weight of her breast in my hand, the curve of her hips and the smooth flesh of her ass under my fingertips. Sitting in that soapy water with Emma in my lap was pure bliss. And then there was the shower. Stroking myself while she pleasured herself with the shower wand. It was completely unexpected, but so fucking hot.

And more than finding our releases together, it was Emma offering for me to go first in the shower that had my heart pounding, my chest tightening. It was in that moment, with that small gesture that I felt like she saw me. The guy that takes care of others, puts their needs ahead of his own. That's what I've been doing my whole life. With my mom, then Sophie, and now, even with Emma. Jumping on a plane to help her was never a question. It was what I wanted to do. It's what I do for the people I love.

Love. I repeat the word, letting my mind turn it over as I process.

I think back to my relationship with Lainey. It was high school, we were young, but I cared about her a lot. I told her I loved her, but what I felt for Lainey is nothing compared to how I feel about Emma.

My throat is thick as I swallow another drink of water.

It doesn't feel possible. I've only known her for two weeks. And I'm not the guy that rushes into things. My childhood taught me to be flexible, how to adapt when things go off the rails, but in my adulthood, I'm more methodical. I make plans. It's my way of maintaining control.

But that's not what happened with Emma. Marrying her in Vegas. Flying to New York to help her. Falling for her.

My desire to protect her, comfort her, and while I've tried to maintain a friends only status and be on my best behavior, in the four corners of my mind, I've imagined devouring every inch of Emma, claiming her in every way possible.

Love.

As this revelation hits me full force, Hunter appears.

"Hey, Griffin. Thanks for coming."

I stand and shake his hand.

"Thanks for having me."

"I know I said it was casual, but when I told Walt about you and your knowledge of Nevada law, he got excited."

"He knows I'm still waiting on my bar results, right?"

"Yeah, I told him your status. He likes the idea of an unseasoned attorney that he can mentor, pass on the torch, that kind of thing. Before I was CEO, my dad ran the business. He and Walt have known each other for decades, so I trust Walt's judgment implicitly."

He motions for me to follow him down the hallway.

"You'll be at Barrett's party tonight, right?" I ask.

"I wouldn't miss it. I've known Barrett for years and still can't believe he's getting married." He chuckles. "You can be the angel on his shoulder, telling him how marriage is great and I'll be the devil urging him not to do it."

"Not a fan of marriage?" I ask.

"It's not for me. I'm old. Set in my ways. And I'm tired of women trying to lock me down. It feels like a game."

I nod. I could see that a single guy with a lucrative business would be a target for some women for reasons other than love and companionship.

"I never gave much thought to marriage or having a family either," I tell him, realizing as I say it that I can now see having it all with Emma. "Until Emma."

"Someone's got to keep the population count up. It's not going to be me."

Hunter leads me back to a conference room where I'm introduced to Walt and Tanya. We talk casually, about my background and my time at law school. Walt reviews my transcript.

"A 4.0 at UNLV. Graduated with honors. And a member of the Nevada Law Journal. Very impressive."

"Thank you."

"Tanya, did you have any more questions?" Walt asks.

"No, I think we've covered everything."

"The position would involve travel. Your focus would be on the Las Vegas properties and contract negotiations. Most of the work can be done via video conferencing but every once and awhile it will be necessary to make the trip."

"I understand," I say, thinking that maybe this could be a good fit. I would be traveling to Las Vegas somewhat on a regular basis and that would allow me to see Sophie more often.

As Walt is talking, it's easy to get wrapped up in the idea of this job. Of staying here with Emma. I can't get ahead of myself. There's still so much unknown. But in order to see if this life is even a possibility, I need to go down this path. Explore what my options are.

After the meeting, Hunter walks me back out to the reception area.

"We'll be in touch about the job. And I'll see you later at Barrett's bachelor party."

"Sounds good."

On the cab ride back to Emma's parents' apartment, another text from Emma pops up.

Emma: *We're teasing all the guys with sexy photos of ourselves. I'm playing along, so here it is.*

I click on the photo. It's angled down the front of Emma's robe. The robe is loose at the top, showing the top of her breasts, the silky material cuts right across the middle of her breasts, just covering her nipples. Then, the robe parts high on her thighs, where her legs are crossed exposing her smooth, toned legs.

Griffin: *You look so fucking good. I wish I was seeing you tonight.*

Emma: *What would you do if you saw me?*

What wouldn't I do? I let myself indulge in her game, and allow myself to respond honestly.

Griffin: *I'd spread your smooth thighs open and lick that sweet pussy of yours.*

Emma: *I'm sweating now. I was supposed to be teasing you, not the other way around.*

I smile, imagining Emma fanning herself.

Griffin: *Don't worry, baby, you've got me so worked up. I'll be thinking about you in the shower later.*

Emma: *Say 'hi' to the pleasure sword for me*

I chuckle as I tuck my phone away. Maybe it's best I won't be seeing Emma tonight. It's one thing to tease over a text message, but the desire I have to act on that text is over-whelming. To track her down at the ladies' spa day and slide my hand underneath her robe. I want Emma badly and it's only a matter of time before my restraint snaps.

CHAPTER 24

Emma

"Heels are a helpful tool to help you sink low." Lydia, the dance instructor, bends her knees to drop her butt to the floor, then straightens her legs to lift it back up. Her legs are spread on either side of the chair she is using to demonstrate her lap dance technique. She looks up at us from her bent position and motions between her butt and the mannequin that is perched on the chair behind her. "You want your ass in their line of vision." She points to the mannequin's eyes then her butt. "And then you twerk."

With a pelvic motion that has me questioning human anatomy, Lydia bounces her butt in the mannequin's face.

We're gathered in a small dance instruction studio at Studio Y in Uptown. While I made arrangements for dinner and our late-night activities, Jules, Chloe's co-worker and friend, scheduled this fun, yet personally challenging activity.

"Good thing I just got waxed," Jules announces to the group.

A wax job isn't going to be my biggest issue here.

"When you said dance class, I was thinking something more along the lines of Zumba," I whisper to Chloe.

She just laughs and threads her arm through mine. "It's fun, right?"

It's fun because this is Chloe's bachelorette party and she's having fun. That's what matters.

We take turns having Lydia instruct us on our twerk, the final step in the lap dance routine she's teaching us. When it's my turn, I do my best but it's basically me gyrating against the mannequin's knees. We all have a good laugh. Lydia attempts to work with me on my moves, only because she doesn't realize it's hopeless.

While Lindsay, Carl's girlfriend, gets her instruction, I join Chloe, Jules, and Chloe's friends, Lauren, Amelie and Sloane, on the plush sofa positioned against the wall of the small studio room we're in.

This girls' day for Chloe's bachelorette party has been exactly what I needed after the generally hectic week and yesterday's Kandi Kline interview. A relaxing morning at the spa where we got our nails done, facials, body scrub and massage, and blow-outs. I feel polished from head to toe. And now, an evening with these ladies, laughing and dancing to celebrate Chloe, is what I'm looking forward to.

And a night away from Griffin. Not because I don't want to see him, but because I need a moment to catch my breath. To sort out if these feelings I'm having are because he's pretending to be my husband or if they're real. And if my feelings for him are real, can I trust them? I've known him for two weeks. I dated Alec for two years and was blindsided by our breakup. How can I put my heart on the line for a man I've known for such a short amount of time?

And while I'd been insulted at first by being friend-zoned by Griffin, now that we've ventured into the physical realm, I can see why he insisted. It was safer there. Less complicated.

While his actions at the Kandi Kline interview and the bathtub photoshoot were for appearances, there was nothing fake about Griffin stroking his cock while he watched me masturbate with the shower wand yesterday. But maybe that was just pent-up sexual frustration. He hasn't had sex in six years. It could be the same reason for the Twister night hook-up, too.

I want to chalk it up to that, but that's the thing, I don't think Griffin would do that.

Today, my brain has been working overtime imagining all sorts of scenarios with Griffin. And, peppered in amongst the fantasies of him taking me roughly against a wall or telling me I'm a good girl while I choke on his dick, there are others.

Earlier, when the realtor I'm working with sent me a new listing to look at, I immediately imagined what it would be like if me *and Griffin* lived in the apartment. His clothes hanging in the closet, his toothbrush and razor by the sink, his tennis shoes by the door and his sweaty gym shorts in the laundry hamper. We'd be snuggled up on the couch—an oversized, mustard masterpiece to be specific—watching an old black and white movie. He'll make blueberry scones on the weekend and I'll do my part by picking up lattes at the corner coffee shop.

Then I look at the calendar and the looming countdown to Griffin's departure. Ten days.

Griffin will leave New York the Monday after Barrett and Chloe's wedding. I've been looking forward to their wedding for months, since they got engaged in December, but now that it's the marker for Griffin's departure, I'm begging time to slow down.

Every event leading up to their wedding is only a reminder of how much time is left. Nine days until Griffin returns to Las Vegas. I don't even want to think about it.

Once everyone has had their personal instruction on twerking, we run through the routine Lydia taught us. By the end of the song, we're all laughing and a bit sweaty. No wonder Griffin is in such good shape, dancing and making it look good is no easy task.

I'm having so much fun with Chloe and the other ladies that I don't realize the end goal of this tutorial until it's too late.

Lydia motions for us to gather around. "Okay, ladies, time to put everything into practice. We're going to test out your new skills."

This is intense. I didn't realize there was going to be a test. Even after an hour of instruction, I'm still the least coordinated one here, so I'm hoping it's more of a written test than practical.

I lock eyes with Chloe. She's pressing her lips together, like she's got a secret and it's about to burst out.

"The guys are here!" Chloe announces. "We're going to have them escorted to private rooms where we can show off our new moves." She bounces on her toes with excitement.

What?! That's the worst idea in the history of ideas. The lap dance skills I acquired in the last hour were never meant to be seen by anyone! Now, she's telling me that I'm supposed to give Griffin, my fake husband and a professional male revue dancer, a lap dance? Uh-uh. Nope.

"This will be fun," Chloe says, patting my shoulder in encouragement.

I smile weakly. It's her bachelorette party and I'm here to appease the bride, but dancing for Griffin doesn't sound like fun to me.

Memories of the time I attempted a lap dance for Alec resurface. The humiliation I felt when he rebuffed me. Griffin isn't Alec, I remind myself, but that doesn't stop my hands from shaking, my chest tightening from the anxiety that memory triggers. Then, I remember how supportive Griffin has been. How sweet and encouraging he was on the dance floor in Vegas, and my body relaxes slightly. But there's still no part of me that thinks this is going to go well.

The room is a flurry of chaos as everyone starts prepping. Lipstick is reapplied, hair is tousled, heels adjusted.

"Oh, and there's one more thing to make it a little more interesting." Chloe holds up a set of cards. "Everyone has to draw a card and add whatever it says into your lap dance. Some are songs you have to dance to; others are moves you need to perform. And then there are a few naughty challenges mixed in."

I'm one of the last to draw a card.

"What did you get, Emma?" Lindsay asks, peeking over my shoulder.

I read the card in my hand, my belly clenching anxiously.

Remove your underwear.

Lydia guides us down the hallway of the VIP section. With every step I take, awareness hits that I'm not wearing any underwear. Yes, I took the challenge. Not because I really wanted to but because all the ladies dutifully carried out their card's demands. It's all in good fun, right? I mean why would I have an issue with taking off my underwear and giving my husband a lap dance?

I shouldn't be turned on right now. But there's something freeing about being naked under my dress. Until I remember what it is that we're doing here.

"The guys are already inside so you can make your grand entrance. When you're ready to start your music, there's a black button on the wall on the left side of the door to press."

As we walk, she indicates who has each room and the women disappear until I'm the last one standing. It's like the pods on *Love Is Blind*, except I've already married the man and we're not even a real couple. Though I would say the way the spicy texts we exchanged this afternoon turned me on made it feel very real. Maybe that's why I'm suddenly nervous to see him.

"And Emma," she motions to door number seven. "Your husband, Griffin, is waiting for you."

"Thanks." I smile tightly.

I'm hoping Lydia will leave so I can follow her out, but she continues to stand there waiting for me to enter like she's not sure I know how to work a door handle.

To prove my point, she reaches forward, but I intercept her.

"I got it," I say. "Thank you."

"Have fun!" She beams at me while I reach for the door.

As I crack the door, my heart is in my throat. I'm moments away from passing out while also planning to tell Griffin this is a silly idea and we can just sit in silence while the others complete their routines.

"Hey, I—" I stop short when I see that no one is in the room. I do another scan. It's not a big room, but the lighting is dim so maybe I've somehow glossed over him. It would be impossible to do that with Griffin, because even if my eyes were playing tricks on me, my body is always aware of him. And right now, it knows he's not present.

Sitting in the otherwise empty room is a plum-colored velvet loveseat and a small wooden side table. The walls are dark, with two sconce lights, pointing toward the floor, on each of the side walls.

I could stay in here and wait, or I could leave.

Decision made; I move back toward the door.

I'm reaching for the handle when I feel the stir of electricity against my back.

"Emma?"

Griffin's voice registers behind me. I turn around to see him standing there, one hand tucked into the front pocket of his slacks, the other gripping a low-ball glass of amber liquid. His white button-down shirt is open at the top, giving him a dressed down casual look.

Damn, he looks good.

"Hey." He smiles, his eyes consuming me.

A wave of lust slams into me, causing an ache between my thighs. It's a completely different sensation with no underwear on. I'll admit that I like it. It feels like someone could find out at any moment that I'm bare underneath my dress.

And now that Griffin's here, the full effect of no panties is at play.

"They had us come through the back doors and I got turned around." He motions to the door behind him.

I wave him off. "No problem. I'm just in here killing time until this whole thing is over."

He looks around the room. "Until what thing is over? The woman outside said something about a surprise?"

Damn it, Lydia. She's like a warden, making it impossible to escape this ordeal at every turn. I could lie and escape my fate of humiliation, but the way he's looking at me right now, like he's so damn happy to see me, makes the truth come out.

"All the ladies took lap dance lessons before you got here," I tell him.

"You took a lap dance lesson?" He chuckles. Either the idea as a whole or the fact that he knows I'm not a good dancer is amusing.

"Yeah, and I'm no better at dancing than I was before." I want him to know that no miracles have occurred. I'm still the rhythmless dancer I was prior to this evening's festivities.

"You must not have had a good teacher." He smirks.

His words remind me of our night in Vegas. His Bad Teacher routine at the revue and then his hands on me at the club as he instructed my moves.

"She was pretty good. Way more flexible than any person should be, but that's my tight hamstrings talking."

At my joke, Griffin's smile expands, his dimple now winking at me.

My chest struggles to expand. Oh, and it feels like someone just threw a bucket of water up my dress.

"We don't have to do it. It's kind of ridiculous. Besides, no one will know if we just sit and talk." I set my clutch on the table, drop onto the loveseat and cross my legs. The motion, adding pressure where I desperately need it, makes my pulse pound. I do my best to sound unaffected. "So, how's your night going?"

Griffin moves toward the loveseat.

"It's better now." His eyes scan me from head to toe. I swear they linger on the spot where my dress hem meets my thighs. There's no way he can know I have no underwear on, but the thought of it makes me squeeze my legs tighter. Makes me think of his text from earlier.

I'd spread your smooth thighs and lick that sweet pussy of yours.

I think he's going to take a seat but then he extends his hand for me to take. I stare at his hand for a beat, then lift to meet his gaze. As always, it's warm and assuring, but tonight there's an edge to it.

Using his hand for support, I stand.

"I want to see you dance."

Griffin guides me in front of him, then takes a seat.

I swallow thickly, my nerves creeping back in.

He reaches forward, his fingers brushing the back of my thigh as his thumb caresses my knee.

"Please."

Manners are so sexy. So is the way he's looking up at me. Like he wants it. Badly. It reminds me of how he looked at me in the shower yesterday. I'm becoming addicted to that look. It's my favorite, especially when no one is around. No one watching to observe that he's an attentive, loving husband. It's just me and him in this tiny room.

I roll my shoulders back. Fine. If Griffin wants a lap dance, he's going to get one. Nobody said it was going to be good. But I don't think that's what he's expecting anyway.

I reach down and pluck the tumbler from his hand, then

lift it to my lips. I recognize the scent. Barrett's favorite scotch. Macallan. I toss it back, then wipe my mouth as the liquid burns its way down my throat.

"Feel better?" Griffin asks when I set the glass down on the table.

"I don't know. I guess we'll find out."

With a renewed sense of purpose, mainly to knock Griffin's socks off, or any other loose clothing items, I march toward the wall by the door and press the black button.

It takes me a few beats to recognize the song as "Maneater" by Nelly Furtado. It's not the song we practiced to but there's no way I'm going to call Lydia in here to fix it.

As I make my way back over to Griffin, my limbs feel warm and tingly, the scotch having already made its way into my bloodstream.

Griffin watches my every move. Because he's entranced by my presence or because he's concerned he'll need to catch me, I'm not certain. His hands rest next to his hips and when he sees me approach, he spreads his long legs wider, creating a space for me.

My body feels looser from the scotch, but my brain is struggling to remember the moves I practiced.

Get low. That's what Lydia preached. It's all about the legs and ass and hips.

With as much confidence as I can muster given the situation, I place my hands just above his knees and do my best to lower myself seductively between his legs, before coming back up.

The material of his pants is soft, in contrast to the hardness of the muscular legs they are concealing. My heart is racing. I hope he can't feel how sweaty my palms are through the material of his pants. Being this close to him gives me a head rush, and I nearly stumble on my heels and go face first into his crotch. Thinking back to the club in Vegas, it wouldn't be the first time.

My first move is a little jerky and I have to stifle a giggle at how ridiculous I feel. When I'm upright again, I shake out my hands and give myself a mental pep talk. I can do this. Think sexy. Don't be awkward.

I tell myself to focus and try again. I lower down again, this time sliding my hands up Griffin's thighs as I drop. Beneath his slacks, I can feel his thigh muscles flex under my hands. I slowly pull back and lift up. Once I'm upright again, I roll my hips to the music and run my hands through my hair, gathering it off my neck. That was another tip from Lydia, your hair is a tool, use it.

I repeat this movement a few times, gaining confidence as I get more comfortable.

Griffin's eyes never leave mine. He watches every move-ment. His eyes are narrowed, his lips slightly parted, like he's really focused. I dance and sway until my back is to him, then perform the same slow lowering maneuver I did before. This time with my back to his front, arching my back so I can extend my ass toward him, just like Lydia taught me. With my hands on his knees, I lower until I can feel his thighs just under my ass. I arch my back and grind into him, circling my hips. His belt buckle digs into my lower back, a sharp reminder of how close my body is to his. It only makes me want to press further into him. I'm so turned on right now, the dance is becoming less about seducing Griffin and more about how I can rub my body against his to get some friction where friction is desperately needed.

My thighs are getting a killer workout. One they have not been conditioned for, and I can feel my muscles starting to quiver. For a minute, I let my weight rest on Griffin's lap. My back is flush against his chest, and I can feel his warm breath against my hair, the heat of his body against my back. It's the same position we were in yesterday during the photoshoot. I continue to rotate my hips, grinding into his lap, as I reach my hands up behind his neck and snake my fingers into his hair. Then I tug.

Griffin's response is a growl and a press of his hips up into my ass. In this position, I can feel his hard length rubbing into me.

"Do you like teasing me with your sweet little ass?" His lips are right next to my ear.

I respond by grinding my ass down into his erection. His words make me feel sexy, and desirable. Somewhere along the way, instinct has taken over, or maybe it's the scotch, but I find myself letting go.

Griffin's hands are resting at his sides. I want to get closer. Put my hands all over him. And feel his hands on me. I'm desperate for him to touch me.

I lift up and turn to face him again. Moving closer, I slide my left knee between his legs, and place my hands on the back of the sofa, on either side of his head. I lean in close, letting my breasts press into his chest as I move. Our lips are inches apart. His emerald eyes appear almost black now. He would only need to lean forward an inch and our lips would meet. We're so close I can feel the warmth of his breath on my face. There's a hint of scotch but mostly I'm surrounded by his familiar manly scent. Griffin still doesn't make a move. My eyes lower to stare at his lips. They're full and soft, a stark contrast to the surrounding skin sporting a two-day beard.

With one leg on the sofa, I'm feeling a bit off balanced. I think Griffin can tell because he brings his legs closer together, so I can straddle him. As my dress inches up my thighs, I'm highly aware of the fact that I have no underwear on. And that this lap dance has done nothing to soothe the ache between my thighs. My dress isn't obscenely short, so there's still plenty of material covering me, but the shameless urge to flex my hips and grind my pelvis onto Griffin's crotch is overwhelming.

My hands slide over his shoulders, and behind his neck,

finally making contact with his skin. It's smooth and warm, and I have the desire to bury my face there.

A moment later, the song fades out, and the only sound in the room is our heavy breathing.

I'm overcome with a surge of pride. I did it! Now I'm not sure what to do. Take a victory lap? Ask Griffin to take off his pants?

I'm contemplating my options when Griffin slides a large hand behind my neck and presses his lips to mine.

CHAPTER 25

Griffin

With Emma in my arms, I feel like I can breathe again. I hold her to me, devouring her mouth. Letting myself have this moment of unrestraint where I don't question what I should be doing, and give into what I want.

It's our night together in Vegas all over again, yet unmatched by the fact that knowing Emma, if only for two weeks, has made me even more attracted to her. My desire to be near her, protect her, hear her every waking thought is so potent, it makes me weak.

"That was incredible," I tell her, stroking her thigh while I kiss her jaw.

I capture her lips again, letting my hands explore under her dress. I knead her ass, loving the feeling of her smooth skin beneath my palms. My fingers move up along her lower back. And that's when I realize something is missing. I pull back.

"No underwear?"

"I had them on, but taking them off was on the challenge card I pulled before I came in here."

"Challenge card?" I ask.

"Some of them had specific songs to dance to. Chloe had

to do her lap dance with Barrett to the *Ghostbusters* theme song." She laughs. "Lindsay and I had to take off our underwear."

She shifts in my lap, her fingers trail along my collarbone, and come to a rest at my chest.

If I'm going to stop things between us, right now would be the time. I could help her off my lap, pull her dress back down and let her rejoin the other ladies ready to continue their evening. That's what the old Griffin would do. Keep the lines clear. But I haven't been doing that very well. Making her come on my thigh during our game of Twister. Using the shower wand to get her off after the bathtub photoshoot yesterday. Technically, I haven't touched her since that morning in Vegas, but every moment with her these last two weeks has brought me to the edge and now I'm beyond desperate for her.

Love.

That word keeps popping up.

Emma looks incredible sitting on my lap. Her smooth dark hair laying over her shoulders, her pink lips parted, breathing hard from her efforts. So fucking beautiful.

My fingers curve around her trim waist, pressing into the soft flesh of her hips. I could lift her up and off, or I could give in and pull her farther down onto me, make good on the texts we exchanged earlier.

My hands make the decision for me, the feel of Emma beneath them making it impossible to turn back now.

"Are you wet, Emma?" I ask, my dick already swelling at the thought of her slick pussy only inches away. How I ache to bury myself inside her.

I ignore the warning bells in the back of my mind telling me I'm already too far gone for this woman. That she's already seeped so far into my bones that I'm prepared to turn my life upside down for her. But I don't want to think right now, I only want to feel. To be here with Emma in this moment, taking what we both desperately need.

She bites her lip and nods.

My voice is gravel when I reply, "Show me."

She hesitates for a moment, like she's not sure how to proceed. Not sure if we're really going to do this.

I take one of her hands from my chest and start moving it toward the hem of her dress. Her eyes follow the motion of our hands, then look back up to mine. I release her hand and lift my chin in encouragement.

The visual of Emma's hand disappearing underneath her dress makes my cock twitch against my zipper. Slowly, she dips her hand between her legs, then lifts two slick fingers to my lips. With our eyes locked, I open my mouth and welcome her fingers. My tongue curls around her knuckles, then I pull my lips tight against her fingers and suck. I lick them clean, my eyes instinctively closing with the indulgence of how fucking good she tastes on my tongue.

"Good girl," I growl before pulling her mouth to mine. This time we dive deeper, our tongues swirling, exploring, lapping each other up. It's too fucking good. I can't stop.

"I need more, Emma. I need to make you come. Do you want that?"

She nods eagerly. "I want you to touch me." She pants between kisses.

I'm more than happy to oblige. I slide my hand up her inner thigh, searching for her silky center. Upon contact, Emma gasps, her fingers digging into my hair.

My fingers run the length of her, letting her soak my knuckles.

I tease her. Slipping my finger barely inside before withdrawing to circle her clit.

"Dancing for me made you so fucking wet, sweetheart."

"It wasn't the dancing. I'm wet whenever you're around," she admits.

I lean back to look at her. This beautiful woman sitting on my lap, her legs straddling me. Her pussy wet and needy for me. And she's my *wife*. It feels like a dream.

She leans forward, her lips moving along my jaw.

"I want to touch you," she says, pulling back. I nod for her to go ahead.

She reaches for my belt, a second later her hand is inside my briefs, encircling my shaft. My hips buck in response to the long-awaited sensation. A guttural moan escapes my lips.

Emma strokes me good, her thumb circling my head, spreading the precum gathering there. With her hands on me, my vision goes black. She's barely touched me, but I can already feel the orgasm building. The pressure starting to build at the base of my spine.

"Fuck. Emma. It's—"

"Too much?" Her hand goes slack, almost releasing me.

I grab her wrist to keep her there, where the briefest touch from her is making me see stars.

"It's perfect."

"I want you in my mouth," she says, rocking her hips against my hand, my fingers easily diving farther into her wetness.

I want that, too, but I'm too greedy for the taste of her, and we don't have much time before the rest of the group will be finished. Likely, they're already done and waiting on us. But I don't care, because there's no way I'm leaving this room without Emma coming on my tongue.

"I want to lick you while you suck me. Do you want that?"

"Yes." She nods eagerly.

Leaning back onto the arm rest of the loveseat, I help Emma move to straddle me backwards. Once she's in position, I push her dress up over her ass to give me access. Massaging the soft flesh there, I pull her ass back toward me.

"Your ass fits perfectly in my hands." I kiss one cheek, then the other. "And your skin is so soft."

Then, I spread her and lick down her center. Her pelvis bucks against me. A moment later her mouth descends on my cock and I groan against her pussy.

The only thing better than Emma sucking my cock is tasting her while she does it.

The suction of her mouth, the wet heat of her velvety tongue as she works my length, not to mention the scent of her pussy. That tingling sensation in my spine is back. Fuck. I'm not going to last long.

Trying to hold my orgasm at bay, I focus on making Emma come. I hold her hips firmly to keep her from squirming and fuck her with my tongue. I suck hard on her clit, then fill her with one, two, three fingers.

"Oh, my…*Griffin*." She moans.

"I know, sweetheart, it's tight, but you're taking it so well."

She continues pumping me with her fist, but I can tell she's close to coming. Her tongue now lazily circling the head of my cock as she clenches tighter around my fingers. Sucking her clit while I hook my fingers inside of her, Emma cries out my name, her pussy pulsing over and over. My tongue laps up the sweetness of her release.

When her orgasm subsides, Emma's mouth slides over me again. She sucks me down until I hit the back of her throat. I can feel the hum of her reflex against the head of my cock. I've never felt anything like Emma's mouth. I want to slow time, make this moment last forever, but I'm also desperate to give in to the pleasure she's giving me. To release all the tension that has built up between us starting the moment I saw her on the roof in Vegas.

"I'm going to come," I rasp.

Emma doesn't pull back, she keeps working me root to

tip, her hand fisting the base while her tongue swirls against my head.

"You want me to come in your mouth?" I ask.

She hums against me, her head bobbing faster and faster. Like a lightning strike, my orgasm shoots down my spine, then branches out in every direction, splintering my body.

A second later, I spill my release down the back of Emma's throat.

We lie there for a minute, Emma's hands splayed on my thighs, my palms caressing her ass.

We're less graceful in our dismount than we seemed to be in the heat of the moment. I lift Emma up to turn her while also trying to sit up and tuck my dick back in my pants. For a moment there are limbs everywhere. There's a close call with my face and the stiletto point of Emma's heel. Then, she nearly tips off the side of the loveseat, but I catch her. Finally, we arrive face to face, Emma in my lap giggling.

"I'm glad you're enjoying yourself," I say, teasing her as I brush her hair off her face.

She dabs at her eyes, her laughter subsiding. "The orgasm was a ten, the dismount a six and a half."

"Something to work on." I smile.

I take the monogrammed handkerchief Barrett gave me earlier and wipe between Emma's thighs. This probably isn't the scenario he had in mind, but it's useful nonetheless.

"Thanks," she whispers.

"Thank you."

"For what?"

"The dance, the orgasm, letting me lick you."

She laughs again, like she thinks it's funny I'm thanking her for letting me taste her. She has no idea that's the real highlight of the night. That I'd stay here all night with my head between her legs if she'd let me.

I tuck a loose hair behind her ear, then run my thumb over her lips, loving this post orgasm moment with her.

There's a knock on the door followed by voices in the hallway.

"We should go," Emma says, attempting to move off me.

"Mmm." I tighten my arms around her waist, not ready to let her go yet. I want her here, near me, even if we're holding up the rest of the group. "What are the ladies doing the rest of the night?"

"We're going dancing." She smirks. "I guess I haven't put in my quota for the night yet."

My hand traces up her inner thigh, letting the tip of my index finger tease against her wetness again. She shivers.

"You're going to put your underwear back on, right?"

Emma looks up at me, her brown eyes filled with mischief. "I don't know. Should I?" She's goading me.

"Where are they?" I ask.

She reaches for her clutch on the table and opens it, pulling out the scrap of black lace. I take them in my hand, then help her stand. On my knees, I guide her heels through each leg before pulling them over her thighs. Emma lets out a shuddering breath, her fingers gripping my shoulders for support.

With the black lace in position, I place a final kiss at the center of her thighs.

Mine, mine, mine, my heart pumps in a possessive rhythm. The need to claim her is becoming increasingly potent, but so is the fear of what it would mean. I know if I let myself have her, I'll bury myself so deep inside her, I'll never find my way out.

But here, right now, isn't the time.

I stand to kiss her jaw. Her lips.

Emma slides her tongue against mine and I groan into her mouth. I'm one kiss away from dragging her back to the loveseat when the door flies open. Chloe is standing there in a short, white dress with her hand over her eyes.

"Emma! We're leaving!" she calls. "Stop banging your husband and get out here."

We share amused smiles, then I steal one more kiss.

"I'll see you later," she says.

"Later." I release her. Watching Emma leave, it feels like part of me is walking out that door.

CHAPTER 26

Emma

After we leave Studio Y, we pile into the sprinter van that will take us to dinner. Playing hostess, I pop the bottle of prosecco, then pour into glasses and hand them out to the ladies. Lauren, Chloe's childhood friend, launches into the story of her bachelorette party. It's the origin of how Chloe and Barrett started fake dating. After a cancelled reservation Chloe moved Lauren's party to my aunt JoAnna's apartment, who is Chloe's boss, and when Barrett caught her there, he black-mailed her to play his girlfriend for a business deal. While they were fake dating, they fell in love.

With everyone sipping on their drink and contentedly listening to Lauren's story, I let my thoughts drift back to Griffin. The lap dance. His head between my thighs. The weight of his thick cock against my tongue. The warm, salty taste of his release sliding down the back of my throat. My body flushes and my panties dampen with the thought of it.

I smile to myself, the satisfaction of finally touching Griffin making me warm all over.

Griffin has the perfect cock. Big without being a monster, because who wants that? Thick, but not so much that I

280

couldn't get my mouth around him. I imagine how good it would feel to have him inside me, stretching me.

And the way he pulled my panties up and kissed me before I left. I close my eyes and replay the moment.

Griffin on his knees, his strong fingers pinching the delicate fabric of my underwear as he lifted them up my legs. The way he looked up at me as he placed a kiss against my center.

I might be able to orgasm again just thinking about it.

"What did all the guys think of the lap dances?" Jules asks.

"Barrett wanted to cancel the rest of the evening and take me home." Chloe laughs. "He said it wasn't nice of me to tease him like that."

"Definitely the hottest foreplay," Lindsay chimes in. "They won't be able to think about anything else tonight."

"Emma, how did it go?" Chloe asks.

"What?" I've caught the tail end of their conversation.

"The lap dance. What did Griffin think?" Jules asks.

"Oh, he liked it."

"Yeah, he did. You two were in there for a long time." Jules wiggles her eyebrows.

"Yeah, we were." I press my lips together in a conspiratorial smile.

As I come down from the high of being with Griffin, I start to wonder if this changes things between us. Was it simply hormones combusting after the lap dance? The fact that we've been in each other's personal space the past few days, the attraction between us building and it finally pushed us over the edge? What does it mean for the next week? After Griffin returns to Las Vegas? Is that still the plan? So many questions that I don't have the answers to.

With the conversation continuing around me, I decide to not focus on Griffin right now. Tonight is about Chloe, so I shake off the residual effects of my orgasm and when we arrive at the restaurant, I turn on hostess mode.

I'm elated that everything is set exactly how I'd planned. Table settings and décor in Chloe's cream and blush color palette. The food is delicious and the champagne flows easily. In the private lounge, Chloe opens her gifts, lingerie for her and Barrett's honeymoon as instructed by the invitation I sent. My stomach twists with each newly revealed teddy, lace bodysuit or panties set. At first, I'm wondering if the champagne is making my stomach hurt, but as a blushing Chloe holds up a garter belt and crotchless panty set, I realize it's envy.

Not for the lingerie she's receiving. I can buy my own lingerie. It's the look on her face. The love that she feels for Barrett and the excitement that their pending nuptials brings. The fact that they are truly in love, and while the parties and celebrations and gifts are nice, when everything is done, and Chloe and Barrett return to regular life, they'll have each other. That's what I'm jealous of.

"This one's from Emma," Chloe announces after reading the card taped to the rose gold box decorated with tissue flowers I made.

I smile, watching her open the box and pull out the delicate Italian white lace undergarments I made special to go under her wedding dress.

"They're beautiful," she exclaims, holding them up for everyone to see. "Did you make them?"

I nod. "They're one of a kind, so be sure to let Barrett know he shouldn't rip them off you if you want them as a keepsake."

She sets the box aside and embraces me. "I love them. You're the sweetest. Thank you, Emma." She squeezes me tight. "I'm so glad you found Griffin. It makes me so happy to know that you've found your guy and we're both happy and in love."

"Me, too." I force the smile to stick on my face.

Yes, I found Griffin, but that doesn't mean I get to keep

him. The ache in my stomach is back. I push it away, determined to celebrate Chloe and not let the mess I'm making of this thing with Griffin ruin her special night.

While the other ladies finish dessert, I settle the bill, and arrange for Chloe's new underthings to be delivered to her and Barrett's place.

We spend the rest of the night dancing at The Rumpus Room, an intimate dance club near the East Village.

When I finally get home, my feet ache and my head is fuzzy. My parents are still out of town, but I'm still trying to be quiet as I fill a glass of water before heading to my room.

I haven't heard from Griffin, so I'm not sure if he's home yet. If he's asleep, I don't want to wake him. In my attempt to turn on the flashlight on my phone, I tip my water glass and spill some on the carpet. I decide to give up on the flashlight and feel my way to my bed. I set the glass on the nightstand, then drop my shoes by the chair. I'm about to crawl into bed when big, strong hands reach out and pull me in.

I don't mean to scream, it's a reflex really. Like the urge to say 'ow' when I bump into something even if it doesn't hurt.

"It's me," Griffin says from his new position on top of me. "You know you could turn the light on."

"I didn't want to wake you up."

He chuckles. "I'm awake now."

"Oops. Sorry." I'm not sorry. I'm glad he's here in my bed, waiting for me.

"Don't be. I wanted to make sure you were home safe."

"I'm home safe." I run my hands all over him. His shirtless body is perfection.

"I see that." His hand smooths out the hem of my dress that has inched its way up my thighs.

"Are you going to take off your dress?" he asks.

I'm feeling sassy after some drinks tonight, and I wouldn't mind a repeat of what happened in the private dance room, minus the lap dance because I have no desire to be on my feet right now.

"Why don't you take it off," I say in my best phone sex operator voice, but a hiccup escapes my throat, ruining the vibe.

Griffin shifts on the bed. I'm hoping he's still going to strip me down, hiccups be damned, but he turns on the bedside lamp then climbs out of bed and walks over to the closet.

He comes back a minute later with a t-shirt.

"What's this?" I ask.

"A shirt to sleep in. You still have underwear on, right?"

"I don't know." I wiggle my brows. "Maybe you should check."

He doesn't check. Not the way I want him to. He pulls my dress up and over my head, then replaces it with the t-shirt. No fun.

"You want to brush your teeth?" he asks.

"Are you going to make out with me if I do?"

He shakes his head. "Not tonight."

"Huh." I don't like his answer, but maybe he's just playing hard to get. Maybe if I brush my teeth, he'll change his mind. I want to leave my options open, that being the option that Griffin changes his mind and I have minty fresh breath for him to taste.

He lifts me up, and I cling to him like a koala as he carries me into the bathroom.

"This is nice. You're nice." I sigh against his neck. "I like you."

It's not a deep confession, but it feels like I could easily say more. 'I like you' is the gateway to all the things I want to tell him, but know I shouldn't.

"I like you, too," he says softly.

Griffin sets me on the counter, then prepares my tooth-brush and hands it to me. I brush while I stare at his naked torso. He leans against the counter watching me. I watch him, ogling his crotch. I can see the outline of his cock in his boxer briefs. My mouth waters thinking about earlier when I had my lips wrapped around him. Then I realize I'm actually drooling toothpaste down the front of my—Griffin's—shirt. Oops.

When I'm done, he carries me back to bed then tucks in behind me. His body curves to mine, his warm skin heating my back.

"Did you have fun tonight?" he asks.

"I think I had just the right amount of fun. Not marry a stranger in Vegas fun, but dance until my feet hurt kind of fun."

He chuckles, then his voice turns husky. "You better not have had *that* kind of fun, you're mine, remember?"

His words make my belly swoop and a warm tingly feeling take over my body.

You're mine, remember?

How could I forget?

"What about you?" I ask.

"We played poker and drank scotch. It was a good time."

"Did you win?"

"A few rounds," he says. "I'm not much of a gambler."

"Me either. But I did enjoy penny slots in Vegas."

Griffin's arm is banded securely around my stomach, holding me to him.

I wiggle my ass into him.

"Aren't you going to touch me?" I ask.

"No."

"You did earlier." It comes out whinier than I intended. Then I whisper for no particular reason, "We did the sixty-nine. Remember?"

He chuckles, sending more warm puffs of air against my neck.

"Of course, I remember."

"It was hot, right?" I ask. I don't need his confirmation that it was hot. I thought it was so hot, but now I'm starting to wonder if I thought it was better than it was. Maybe he didn't think it was that good so he's not as desperate as I am to do it again.

He buries his face into my hair and sighs. "I haven't stopped thinking about you all night."

"So, we should do that again sometime." Sometime being right now.

"Emma, you've had a lot to drink. I'm not touching you tonight. Go to sleep."

In the middle of my pout, I stifle a yawn. I want to be annoyed that Griffin's not making a move but the more I lie here in his arms, the more content I feel. Finally, my eyelids close. Behind me, Griffin's breathing evens out.

"Griffin?"

"Yeah?" He tightens his grip on me.

"I don't hate that you're a lawyer. It was more about Alec and how he prioritized his work before me. How I felt invisible in our relationship." I swallow. "I don't feel invisible with you."

His large hand moves to rest on my hip, his fingers lightly gripping the t-shirt material gathered there. "You always have my attention, Emma. I don't know how to not look at you."

With Griffin's sweet words echoing in my ears and the contentment I feel with his warm, strong body holding me tight, I drift off to sleep.

It's still dark outside when I wake. I register two things, it's Saturday, so I don't have to get out of bed and Griffin's arm is locked over my stomach, our bodies still pressed firmly together, so there'd be no way to get out of bed even if I wanted to.

Our legs are tangled, my ass snug up against his crotch. I've just woken up, but from the dull throbbing between my thighs, I can tell my body has been awake for some time. Hoping to squeeze my thighs together to gain some friction, I start to slide my leg out from between Griffin's.

I'm almost free when his thick thigh wraps over the top of mine to pin my leg back into place.

"Good morning," his voice rumbles against the shell of my ear. "How did you sleep?" His nose nuzzles into my hair. He takes in a deep breath like he's starved for air and the scent of my shampoo.

"Good."

"I dreamed about you," he says.

"Yeah?"

His hand finds the hem of my sleep shirt twisted halfway up my torso, his fingers tickle along my ribcage on their way up to my breast. With his thumb, he circles around my hardened peak, then rolls it between his thumb and index finger.

God, I'm so turned on.

"You were disappointed with me last night."

"I was?"

"You were frustrated that I didn't touch you when you got home."

"Oh, yeah."

"I want to remedy that now."

Easiest answer ever. "Yes, we should do that."

I wiggle my ass against his crotch. I'm greeted by his hard cock nudging against my lower back.

His hand moves under the waistband of my panties. When his fingers reach my center, they dip between my legs and inside me.

I stifle a moan.

"So fucking wet." He growls against my shoulder. I can feel his erection jolt against my lower back.

I rock my hips, trying to pull his fingers in deeper.

"Griffin, I need…"

"What do you need, sweetheart? You want me to play with your tits? Fuck you with my fingers? Suck your swollen clit? Lick up every drop of your sweetness?"

If this is a multiple-choice question, the answer is E, all of the above.

"Yesss."

He withdraws his hand, and rolls me onto my back. Then, reaching over me, he opens the top drawer of my bedside table. A moment later, he returns, holding my bright pink dildo in his hand.

My eyes widen, and my lips part in anticipation.

"I want to fuck you with this," he says.

Griffin's words alone are enough to make my legs tremble. When he runs the smooth tip of the dildo across my center, over my panties, I let my legs fall open to give him better access.

"Good girl." He rewards me with another swipe down my center, firmer this time as the vibrating head of the dildo presses against my clit.

My hips buck.

Griffin drops the dildo by my hip and uses both hands to rid me of my t-shirt and underwear. I sit up to reach for him, desperate to stroke the large bulge beneath his briefs, when he gently pushes me backward.

"Not yet, sweetheart. You're going to come for me first." His deep voice is a little raspy, and a lot demanding. I like it.

His lips close around one nipple while his fingers tweak the other. It's just like Vegas, in a matter of minutes, he has me slick and writhing beneath him, desperate to come. My hands grip his hair, pulling him up to me.

His lips seal over mine, his tongue teasing into my mouth. I love the feel of his body on top of mine. The way the light smattering of hair on his chest brushes against my hard nipples.

"I'm going to make you come with my fingers first. Then, I'm going to taste you after your orgasm is dripping down your thighs."

Two fingers slip inside me while his thumb circles around my clit. Knowing exactly what I need, he finds that sensitive spot inside and has me pulsing around his fingers in two minutes flat.

"Ahh," I gasp when his tongue flattens against me a moment later.

"I love the way you taste." His mouth closes around my clit and sucks. "If joy had a taste, it would be this." A single finger skims down my center before he presses it inside, and his tongue starts to work its magic against my clit. A few minutes later, he draws another orgasm out of me.

I'm so content after my orgasm that I completely forgot about my dildo until Griffin plucks it from its place by my hip.

He trails it down the center of my body, its smooth tip gliding along the skin between my breasts, around my belly button and to the apex of my thighs. The contentment I felt a moment ago vanishes. I want more. And Griffin is going to give it to me.

His face is focused concentration as he teases the end of the dildo at my center, wetting it with my arousal. He flicks the power button and the head starts to vibrate.

"Show me what you like."

I take the dildo from him and press it against my clit. The familiar sensation of pleasure pulsing there has me sighing. I swirl it around. My orgasm is already close.

"God, you're beautiful." I'm expecting for his gaze to be between my thighs, but it's on my face. I can feel how flushed I am, how messy my hair is from sleep, but the sincerity in his eyes tells me it must be true.

Griffin's hand joins mine on the dildo, and we start to move it to my entrance. I think back to last night. How good it felt to be able to give each other pleasure at the same time.

I want him right there with me when I go over the edge.

"Wait." I sit up, an idea forming in my head. "I want to try something."

I crawl off the bed and reach for Griffin's hand for him to come with me.

I reach in to turn on the shower, then step out to pull his briefs down. His thick, hard cock springs out. I trail my fingertips up his silky-smooth skin, then back down, lightly grazing his balls.

His hand moves around the back of my neck before he kisses along my jaw. "What did you want to try, Emma?"

"Oh, right." I'm easily distracted by him.

Inside the shower, I suction the bottom of my dildo to the bench seat then turn on the vibrating head. Griffin has followed me inside and I turn to find him standing there, his eyes darkening as I angle myself over the dildo, then slowly, inch by inch, lower myself down on it.

"*Emma*," he growls, his eyes fixed on the base of the dildo, where it's splitting me open. I shift my hips up and down, loving the feel of him watching me fuck myself with it. "Look at you. Taking every inch like a good girl." He reaches for his cock and starts to fist himself.

"Come here," I say, licking my lips as he steps forward, his erection inches from my face.

My hands grip the base of him while I tease his crown with my tongue. His hands press into the tiled wall behind me and his eyes fall shut. A groan escapes his lips when I wrap my lips around him and suck.

"Look at my beautiful wife," one hand lowers to cup the back of my head, supporting my neck as my gaze lifts to his. His thumb traces the corner of my mouth where I'm stretched around him. "You suck my cock so well."

Griffin's large, powerful body is towering over me, yet I'm

the one in control, of his pleasure and of my own. And the desire I see in his eyes is intoxicating.

I find a rhythm, taking him deeper in my mouth while I continue to shift my hips up and down on my dildo. I thrust my hips down again and let the vibrating head tease that sensitive place deep inside me.

Griffin's hand drops to my breast. He grips me there, plucking and twisting, teasing my nipple before shifting his attention to the other one.

Then he presses me back, changing the angle of the dildo inside me and using his fingers to rub circles against my clit.

I'm so close, and so is he. I pick up my pace, sucking him farther back into my throat while Griffin increases the pressure on my clit. A minute later he pulses his release down the back of my throat, my orgasm only seconds behind.

"Come here." Griffin slowly lifts me up and into his arms. His lips are gentle against my swollen mouth, his hands exploring and caressing every inch of my body. He washes my hair then wraps me in a towel and we fall back into bed. We sleep again until I wake with Griffin's head between my thighs and we have to get clean all over again.

CHAPTER 27

Griffin

We spent the rest of the weekend exploring the city, with plenty of breaks in between to explore each other. I love tasting Emma, having her slick and writhing beneath me, I can't get enough. And the way she takes me into her mouth so reverently. Watches me with such desire and anticipation, for once I feel like I'm able to let go and enjoy letting someone take care of me. Take what I want without any guilt.

Sunday morning, we gathered ingredients at the corner market to make blueberry scones. Emma debated if we should actually make them because she wants her dress for Chloe and Barrett's wedding to fit perfectly. I told her to eat as many as she wants and assured her, while I think she's going to look beautiful, I would do my best to help her burn off the calories.

Now, it's Tuesday, and I'm routinely checking my email when I zero in on the message from the Nevada Bar Examination. My bar exam results are available. It's May first. The date has been on my calendar for months, yet I had completely blanked that it was today. I've been busy enjoying my time with Emma.

I click through and sign into the portal. I tell myself it's okay if I don't pass the first time. The State of Nevada has the fifth hardest bar exam in the nation, with an average pass rate of fifty-eight percent. I'll study harder and take it again. I've already got a plan in place when the screen appears.

I passed.

I fucking *passed*.

Relief floods through me. Another step closer to my goal. I take a screenshot, then exit the portal. My fingers navigate me to my recent contacts. I always thought my first call would be to Sophie or Terrence, but before I even question it, my thumb taps on Emma's name.

"Hi!" Her bright, bubbly voice comes through after one ring.

"Hey. I'm not interrupting, am I?"

"No, I was just answering emails. Is everything okay?"

I'm realizing this is the first time that I've called her. The first time I've talked to her on the phone. That seems strange. To be married to a person and have never talked to them on the phone. I like hearing her voice, even without seeing her. I make a vow to call her more often, then I remember why I was calling in the first place.

"I passed."

"You passed?" she questions, but in the next beat she exclaims, "You passed! Oh my God, congratulations! That's amazing. Wow, do you feel relieved? Of course, you're relieved, but I mean are you freaking out and so excited?! Oh, we need to celebrate!" There's a rustling, then a drawer slamming shut.

"Emma."

There's muffled whispering, then I think she drops the phone.

"Oh, sorry about that."

"You're good." I chuckle.

She sounds breathless. "I'm leaving now and I can meet you at the apartment. Are you there? Or we could go out.

Drinks to celebrate? We could go to Valerie, they have oysters. Or do you want to stay in? You're definitely getting a blow job for your efforts, but we can do both."

She's so fucking adorable. I put calling Emma every day at the top of my priority list.

"I didn't expect you to leave work. I wanted to tell you, that's all."

"You're too cute. Okay, I'm sending you the address of the bar. I'll see you there in thirty minutes."

Deciding I will call Sophie, and Terrence and Rita later, I quickly change into a button-down shirt and jeans, then grab my wallet and phone. I'm on my way out when I hear a rustling sound coming from Emma's dad's office. I could easily walk past and out of the apartment, but I hesitate. While Emma and I have been getting closer, her dad and I, not so much. He and Jolyn have been gone the past week. And while that has worked out in my favor with having time to spend with Emma alone, if things could work out between me and Emma, I know I need to make an effort with him. I poke my head in to find him there moving boxes around.

"Hey, Philip, I didn't realize you were here."

"It is my apartment," he says coolly.

I nod, trying to not let his response shut down my effort.

"I'm going out, to meet Emma." I gesture over my shoulder, but he doesn't bother looking up from the boxes he's moving. "I passed the bar exam and she wanted to meet up to celebrate."

His features soften and he nods. "Congratulations."

If we're going to be family, I know Emma and her dad are close, and I want him to like me enough to acknowledge when I walk in a room.

"Thank you." I take in the boxes and furniture that seems to be in a state of disarray. "Are you reorganizing?" Philip moves to place his hands under one end of the desk, so I move to the other end to help.

He doesn't say anything, but grunts and angles his head in the direction he wants to go. I somehow manage to follow his nonverbal commands and we set the desk down at the desired location by the window.

"Listen, I know I messed up. I know you and Jolyn were hurt that Emma and I got married without inviting you. It was never our intention to exclude you, it just happened."

He moves back to the boxes across the room, and starts carrying one over to the desk. I'm wondering if he heard anything I said. Or if he's ignoring me. It's frustrating.

"I want your blessing."

"It seems a bit late for that, don't you think?"

"I love your daughter." The words fall out easily, but there's also surprise because it's the first time I'm admitting it to anyone. I'm finally admitting it to myself. "I love her."

"You sound surprised." He arches a brow. "Is this a new realization?"

"Yes," I answer honestly.

"You didn't love her when you married her?"

"No, not like I do now. I mean I imagined I could, but I didn't expect it to get this far." I hesitate, not sure if I should tell him more about the situation. If Emma would want me to.

He studies me carefully. I can see him processing what I'm telling him, drawing his own conclusion.

"I see. So it was a mistake?"

I nod. "But also it wasn't. Everything I've done since the moment I put that ring on Emma's finger is because I cared about her, I wanted to protect her."

"Including coming here to pretend you were together."

"Yeah." I don't know if it changes anything between me and Philip, but I feel better that he knows my intentions. It's a weight off my chest. "And now, I just want her."

He clears his throat. "I didn't like the feeling that Emma would leave me and her mom out of such a big part of her life, but it seems she had her reasons that have nothing to do with us."

He rubs his hand along his jaw, still processing.

My phone buzzes. I look down to see it's a text from Emma.

"I've got to go meet Emma."

"Do you mind if I join you? To celebrate?"

I smile. "That would be great."

I wait by the door for him to gather his wallet and phone.

"Emma says you enjoy playing pool," Philip says on our way down in the elevator. "I'm not much of a player myself."

I chuckle. "Don't even try it. She already told me about you."

He claps me on the shoulder. "Well then when I beat you, it won't be a surprise."

When we get to the bar, it's packed. But as I look closer, I realize I know a lot of the people here. Hunter is at the corner of the bar talking to Tanya and another guy that works at Premier I met last Friday. Andrew, I think.

Hunter sees me and comes over to say hello.

"Congrats, man. I bet you're ready to celebrate." He motions to the bar. "What are you drinking?"

"You're here to celebrate?" I'm confused. I just told Emma I passed the bar thirty minutes ago.

"Emma texted," he says. "Shit. Was this a surprise? Did I ruin it?"

"I—"

Emma pops out from behind Hunter. "Congratulations!" She squeals before leaping into my arms. She looks gorgeous in a pale pink low-cut dress with tiny buttons down the front and strappy gold sandals. I hold her to me and kiss her deep. I get lost in our kiss, in her, until I remember that we're in a room full of people. It's amusing that before, we were trying to be affectionate enough to be believable as husband and wife, now I'm having to pull back because I'm having a hard time controlling myself when she's around.

"What is this?" I ask when I finally release her.

"Your 'I passed the bar exam' party."

"I didn't need a party," I say.

She shrugs. "I wanted you to feel special."

Emma releases me to say hi to her dad, then returns wrapping her arms around my waist.

My cheeks hurt from the huge grin on my face. "I do feel special. This is really nice."

"Yeah?" She bites her lip, trying to hold back her elated smile.

"Yeah, this is so much more than I expected."

"Oh, crap, I didn't get the banner hung up."

Emma grabs a gold letter banner from the bar and with the help of her dad, hangs it across the open space in the corner of the bar.

'Congratulations, Griffin' it reads.

"How did you find a banner that says 'Congratulations, Griffin' so quickly?" I ask.

"Oh, I had it already."

I blink at her. "Just lying around?"

"When you told me you were waiting for your bar results, I thought it would be good to have on hand."

"Because you knew I'd pass?"

"Yes."

"That's awfully thoughtful especially since you hate lawyers."

"We already discussed this. You're the exception." She grins. "And Carl," she motions to him across the bar, "when he's not being obnoxious."

She pecks me on the cheek. "Be right back, I'm going to grab my phone to take pictures."

As Emma leaves, Hunter hands me a beer and clinks his with mine. "To you."

"Thanks."

"It's only been a few days, but I'd like to know what you thought about our meeting on Friday."

"Honestly, after hearing more about the company, I was very impressed with the work that Premier does. I appreciate you considering me for the position. I know I don't have the experience that Walt and the company is looking for."

"Walt liked you a lot. He likes fresh blood. You're easier to mold, he said. And with his planned retirement in the next two years, he's hoping to be able to set up Tanya and whomever fills the second legal team position with an ideal succession plan." He takes a sip of his beer. "Your knowledge of Nevada laws would be an asset as we expand to the Las Vegas area. But listen, I'll let you enjoy the party and we'll circle back next week." Hunter walks off, and I let his words sink in. Next week I should be back in Vegas for Sophie's graduation, with no plans to return to New York. But that's not what I want.

As the idea of me and Emma together has started to take root, what our life would be like, the thought has crossed my mind to ask her to move to Vegas with me. But I know she's been working hard to build her business and being in New York would be ideal for her clients. She loves the city. Her family and friends are here. I've thought about her parents' packed apartment when we arrived at our surprise wedding shower. She has roots and a life here.

The reality is that it makes more sense for me to move here. I've got a mental laundry list of things I need to figure out in order for that to even be an option.

Emma's smiling face breaks through the crowd and I decide to not think about that right now. I want to enjoy this moment.

Emma and I make the rounds, greeting Carl and Lindsay,

Barrett and Chloe, and the rest of the group here from Premier Real Estate, Leo, Josie and Jess from Emma Belle Bridal, and a few more of Emma's friends that I met at the Premier party. Emma's mom shows up a few minutes later.

"Sorry, I'm late. Traffic downtown was horrendous," she says, pulling me in for a hug. "Congratulations, Griffin. We're proud of you."

The emotion that Jolyn's words bring up has my throat tightening.

"Thank you."

While Emma gets pulled into another conversation, Jolyn guides me to the bar where she orders a drink.

"Have you and Emma been looking at apartments? She mentioned she had a few viewings this week."

"Um—" This is news to me. Emma hasn't mentioned anything about apartments. But why would she? I'm supposed to be leaving on Monday. We haven't planned on moving in together, but I go along with it.

"Yeah, we're still narrowing it down."

"Philip and I love having you with us, but it will be nice when you're settled into your own place. Then you can open some of those gifts."

I smile. "Thank you for letting us stay with you."

"Of course. You're family."

Over the next hour, I mingle through the crowd, mostly with my arm wrapped around Emma's waist, but when she excuses herself to use the restroom, I set my beer on a table and take a moment to send Sophie a text. I've just hit send when Jess sets her drink on the table and drops down in the seat across from me.

"Congratulations," she says, lifting her wine glass toward me.

"Thank you." I clink my beer bottle against her glass.

"There's a lot to celebrate tonight. You passing the bar,

Emma signing the contract with Bergman's for her line. It's all very exciting."

"Wait. She signed the contract today?" I ask.

"Yeah, didn't she tell you?"

At that moment, Emma appears at our table.

"Do you want another round or should we go?" She tries to wink seductively, but she's tipsy and it turns out more goofy than sexy.

"Can we talk for a minute?" I try to keep the frustration out of my voice but Emma catches the edge in my tone.

"Ooh," she says it dramatically. "Am I in trouble?"

I take her hand and lead her down the hallway by the bathrooms. I pull her into a small alcove tucked back by the kitchen.

"Jess told me you finalized the contract with Bergman's today. That's huge. Congratulations!" I pull her into me and squeeze her tight.

"Thank you." Her laugh is pure joy.

I relax my hold on her, but keep her close, trying not to be too stern when I ask, "Why didn't you tell me?"

"I was going to tell you." Her fingers tease into the hair at the nape of my neck. Her tender touch eases my frustration at her omission. "I was about to call you but you called me first and told me about your exam and I wanted to celebrate you."

I shake my head. "We can celebrate both of us."

"I know, but I wanted to give you your moment. Not make it about me."

"You're my wife. All my moments are attached to you."

The second the words are out of my mouth; I realize what I've just said. What I've laid claim to. But Emma doesn't seem to notice.

She licks her lips and leans in for a kiss. "You're sweet."

"You know what else is sweet?" My hand slides under the hem of her dress, contacting the smooth skin of her thigh.

"Hmm?" Emma hums against my lips as I capture her mouth with mine.

My fingers are a fraction of an inch from her center when I pull back. I want to lay her out on the bed and take my time. Plus, I'm looking forward to the blow job she promised me, and I don't want her trying to do it in this cramped space with her parents and friends in the other room.

"Not here."

Her bottom lip juts out, pouting in frustration.

I kiss her jaw. "Let's go home."

That's what Emma and New York City are starting to feel like. Home.

I wake to a face full of Emma's hair. Her legs tangled with mine. Her perfect ass pressed against my quickly swelling dick. That's how I've woken up the past five days. It's this moment in my day that has confirmed what I already know. There's no way I'm letting her go, not if she feels the same as I do.

Emma rolls onto her back, her eyes are still closed, her lips slightly parted as she breathes softly. I move over her, pinning her hips with mine, and nuzzle her neck. Everything is perfect when she's beneath me.

"Are you still sleeping?" I ask.

She giggles, but replies, "Yes."

Beneath my briefs, my hard cock slides along her center.

I fucking ache to be inside her, to take that next step, but I'm trying to take things slow. It's a complete contrast to our quick marriage, but I've waited this long for Emma, I'm not going to rush it now.

I dip my head to capture her lips, but we're interrupted by the buzz of Emma's phone on the bedside table.

"Do you need to get that?" I ask.

"Um, what time is it?"

I pull back to glance at the clock on the nightstand. "Eight fifteen."

Emma jolts forward.

"Eight fifteen! You're kidding." She moves to look at the clock herself. "Shit! I have to be downtown by nine for a meeting with the Bergman's suppliers."

She pushes around me and flings herself off the bed. I collapse on the covers with a groan. So much for a relaxing morning in bed. I toss my feet over the side and join her in the bathroom. She's already in the shower, her leopard print shower cap covering her hair. I'd join her but I know I'd only slow her down. Instead, I enjoy the view. Unfortunately, it doesn't last long.

"Tell me about your meeting," I say, watching her naked body hungrily until her still damp, flushed skin disappears underneath her robe. She beelines for the vanity, so I lean against the counter to watch her.

I don't know what it is, but watching Emma get ready is captivating. Her routine is so efficient, I think she could do it in her sleep. I don't think she needs half of the stuff she uses, but what do I know? Sophie was pretty low maintenance with hair and makeup, learning from friends and online makeup tutorials, but never had a big interest in it.

After washing her face, she pulls off the shower cap, pins back her hair, then starts applying her makeup.

"The contract is signed, so now we have to work through the logistics of the gowns' production. The small manufacturer I've been using to produce the gowns for trunk shows won't be able to keep up with the production demand, at least that's the hope, so while I'll keep them to do all my custom designs, Bergman's is going to have their manufacturer make the gowns I've sold to them."

"And there are six gowns, right?"

"Yes, and they're going to have an Emma Belle Bridal

section at the entry of their bridal and evening wear department."

"That's so fucking cool, Emma."

She turns to look at me and smiles.

"It is, right?"

Once she's done with her makeup and hair, I follow her into the closet.

She pulls out underwear and a bra from the drawer and hurriedly puts them on.

"There's something I wanted to talk to you about," I say.

"Okay. What is it?" she asks, as she selects a dress and takes it off the hanger.

"I wanted to talk to you about our arrangement."

"Our arrangement?" Her voice is muffled as her head disappears into her dress. She manages to get her head and arms through without letting go of her phone. While she's slipping her feet into a pair of heels, her phone buzzes and she looks down to check the message.

"Sorry, Jess is texting me. What were you saying?"

While I'm eager to talk to Emma, to get on the same page with what has been going on between us the last few weeks, I can see that now is not the time. When I tell Emma that I want her to be my wife for real, that I want to stay in New York and build a life with her here, I don't want to be interrupted by a buzzing phone.

"You have to go. We can talk later."

"Okay. That sounds good." With the slightest hesitation, she adds, "I actually have something I want to discuss with you, too."

My hands reach up to cup her face and I press my lips to hers. It's a sweet kiss because I know she needs to leave.

"I'll be back after lunch. We'll talk then."

She's halfway through the door when she skitters to a stop and returns to me.

"One more for luck." Emma reaches up on her toes and

presses her lips to mine. My arms ache to wrap around her and keep her here with me.

"I l—I'll see you later." I catch myself before I let those three words escape.

When Emma's gone, I settle into the workspace that I've set up at her desk to check my email. I scan my inbox, zeroing in on the one that I've been waiting to hear back from. It's from the State of Nevada higher education grants division.

I scan through the email, the recap of the terms I agreed to when I signed it four years ago. If I fail to find employment in the State of Nevada by one year after my graduation date, then I must pay back the granted money from my first year, in full. I keep scanning. The due date is a week from today. My eyes land on the number in bold print. Ten thousand, five hundred dollars. The blood drains out of my face.

Fuck. I take a moment to process before I can start working on a solution.

The grant didn't cover my full tuition, but it was enough of an incentive to agree to the terms. And, when I agreed to the grant program, I had zero thoughts of leaving Nevada. Now, if I want to move to New York to be with Emma, I'll need to start paying back the grant money.

I immediately check my bank account. Paying it in full would wipe out my savings. And I know that Sophie has a final tuition payment due at the end of the semester. She'll need to pay off her balance in order to collect her diploma.

With my fingers linked behind my head, I lean back in the chair and think. I used the cash Rita and the guys pooled together to pay for my suit. Maybe I should have let Emma pay for it. That extra five hundred dollars would be helpful right now.

That's when I remember the check in my wallet. The check Jess wrote me in Vegas when Emma offered me compensation for coming to New York. I'd told her I didn't think it was necessary, but Jess insisted I keep the check. For incidentals.

The five-thousand-dollar check doesn't cover the amount I need, but it's a start. I should be able to cover the rest with my savings and with my last paycheck from the revue be able to cover Sophie's final tuition payment. I sign the back of the check and do a mobile deposit to my account. The check will process in time to make the payment and I'll be able to talk to Emma about everything later today.

The thought of revealing my feelings to Emma this afternoon makes my pulse quicken.

I decide a workout will help with my nervous energy; I change then head out to the gym, eagerly anticipating my conversation with Emma.

CHAPTER 28

Emma

After the meeting with Bergman's supplier, Jess and I share a black car back to the office.

"What are you—" I try to move my phone, but she sees the screen before I can lock it. "Are you looking at bedroom furniture right now?"

"Maybe," I say, trying to not sound as guilty as I feel. I should be paying attention to her notes from the meeting, but I'm scrolling through bedroom set options that would fit best in my top two condo choices. While Jess is discussing markup and gross profit, I'm imagining making a home with Griffin in our new condo. The furniture we would pick out together. Finally opening the gifts we were given at our wedding shower. Griffin, shirtless and sweaty from carrying boxes, dragging me into our new bedroom for the first time.

Sex. We haven't done that yet, but I already know it will be good. Better than good. Phenomenal. I'm trying to be patient because I know Griffin hasn't had sex in a long time. I'm waiting for him to be ready. I hope it's soon or I might spontaneously combust with need.

I take a deep breath, trying to not get carried away by the excitement of it all.

"So does that mean you've decided on one of the condos you viewed with Paulina?"

"I've looked at a few, but haven't made a final decision."

"You know how fast these things move. If you have your heart set on a place, you'll have to snap it up quick."

I set my phone in my lap and turn to her, my stomach churning with nerves. "Can I talk to friend Jess right now?"

She sets down her tablet and pulls off her glasses, tucking in the legs and setting them on the tablet. "What's up?"

"I haven't decided on a place yet because I'm waiting…to talk to Griffin."

I see her processing the information, the moment her eyes widen in understanding.

"Emma—" she starts, but I cut her off.

"I didn't tell you that he, that we, have become more than friends because I didn't want to hear that it wasn't a good idea. Griffin makes me feel so good about myself and our relationship. He cares about things I'm interested in. He shows up for me, like with the Kandi Kline interview. I've never felt as seen or as loved before like I do with him. I mean, he hasn't said he loves me, but I think he might. I didn't even realize love could feel this way. All my previous relationships I was so focused on the end goal, of getting married, that I wasn't present for the actual relationship. I know that sounds corny, but you know what I mean. With Griffin, that's never been an issue. We're already married. And now, I can't imagine him not in my life. I think I love him."

Jess places her hand over mine.

"For the record, friend Jess and work Jess want the same thing for you. To be happy." She presses her lips together. "That said, I don't want to see you hurt. Do you think Griffin feels the same way?"

I swallow. "I think so. But I know it would be a huge ask for him to uproot his life and move here. That's why I'm nervous. Even if he cares for me, it's only been a few weeks. An intense few weeks, but still, is that enough time for him to want to change his entire life? For the woman he accidentally married in Vegas?"

"I don't know." She shakes her head slowly. She takes a deep breath in, then releases it. "I wasn't going to say anything because I didn't think it mattered, but if you have feelings for him, I think you need to know this."

My heart thuds in my chest. "What is it?"

"You know how you offered Griffin compensation to come to New York, above the travel expenses you paid him for?"

"Yeah?" I prompt her to continue.

"And how he turned it down?"

I nod.

"The withdrawal went through. He cashed the check."

My stomach lurches. "Really? When?"

"This morning." She pulls up the account on the app. "The larger dollar amount initiated a notification. You might have gotten one, also."

I don't bother checking my phone. The evidence is right in front of me on Jess's screen.

"Okay." I take a breath, trying to process this information. Trying to not let it wash away all the good feelings I had a moment ago. "We offered him the money with the idea that he'd take it. That it would be compensation for his time and having to postpone the start of his job, an incentive to come to New York, and even if he originally turned it down, he still has a right to the money."

"That's true." Jess nods. "I don't know why he changed his mind. Maybe you can ask him about it?"

It sounds simple. Talk to him and find out. But what if I've let myself imagine a life with Griffin and he doesn't feel the same way? I try not to think about that outcome, but I already know the answer. I'll be devastated.

~

Griffin

After my workout, I showered, then continued my research on the process for a licensed attorney in Nevada to become licensed in New York. Nevada is one of the few states that New York doesn't have reciprocity with, so it's not an easy process, but it's one I'm willing to work through to be here with Emma.

Next to the grant repayment issue, having this process ironed out, knowing that there is a path forward for my career and my life here with Emma, releases the knot of tension in my stomach.

I call Sophie, and then Terrence to tell them about my bar exam results. Sophie is ecstatic, telling me we'll have to celebrate when I get home. *Home.* It's been a little over two weeks since I left our apartment in Henderson, but the thought of living there again feels foreign.

I don't mention anything to Sophie or Terrence about staying in New York. I need to have those conversations in person, and I haven't even talked to Emma yet. I'm counting down the minutes until she's back from her meeting. Thinking about what Emma's mom said yesterday, about Emma looking at apartments, I decide to check out the real estate options. When a two-bedroom, two-bath apartment in Gramercy appears for fifteen thousand dollars a month, I nearly choke on my water. Then, I have to rub at my eyes to make sure I'm not reading the numbers incorrectly. Nope, that's what it said. *Fifteen thousand dollars.*

The job with Premier Real Estate isn't officially mine, but their human resources department did send over an email with an estimated compensation package. I do the math and realize that with savings and Emma contributing, paying fifteen thousand dollars a month for an apartment isn't out of the budget.

While I'm trying to wrap my head around the insanity that is Manhattan's cost of living, Chad calls me.

"Did you do it?" he asks, not bothering to say hello.

"Did I do what?"

"Bang your wife."

"Do not say bang and my wife in the same sentence."

"You're testy, so I'd say that's a no."

"I'm not discussing it with you." That's what I say, but now I'm realizing Chad's the only person I can talk to about this besides Emma. "Did you call to ask me that?"

"Yes, but also, I got your text about passing the bar. That's fucking rad, man. Congrats."

"Thanks. It's a huge relief. How's everything going? How's the revue?"

"It's okay. Not the same without you, though. I'll catch you up on Dallas's latest shenanigans when you're back in town."

"Yeah, I'll be back next week for Sophie's graduation." I hesitate to tell him about the development between me and Emma, because do I really need Chad busting my balls about it? But then, I decide to tell him. His honesty is refreshing even if he's a little crass sometimes. "I'm thinking about moving here."

"What?"

"To be with Emma."

"Wait, so you haven't slept with her yet, but you're moving there to be with her?"

"Not everything is about sex."

"Fuck, dude. You're in deep."

"I know. I love her."

It's silent long enough for me to wonder if he's still on the line.

Then he says, "Fuck, this is crazy. But it sounds like you're happy, so I'm happy for you."

"Thanks."

"What does Sophie think about you moving?"

"I haven't told her yet."

He lets out a low whistle.

"I need to do it in person."

"Yeah, I get it."

"It's time for me to move on with my life. I don't want to hurt her, that's the last thing I want to do. It'll take some time and we'll have to sort everything out, but I'm hoping she'll understand that I need to do what's best for me. That maybe this is a fresh start for both of us."

"Sounds like you've got it all figured out."

My head turns toward the door where I thought I heard the sound of footsteps. I wonder if Emma is back.

"Listen, I've got to go, but I'll see you sometime next week."

"Cool, man. Take it easy."

"You, too."

I drop my phone in my pocket and take a deep breath. I'm ready to tell Emma how I feel.

CHAPTER 29

Emma

"Hey." Griffin walks into the kitchen. "How was your meeting?"

My hands grip the edge of the counter as I try to steady myself. If my confidence walking into my parents' apartment a few minutes ago wasn't already waning from my conversation with Jess about Griffin finally cashing the check I offered him, hearing him talking on the phone made it completely vanish.

I don't want to hurt her.

I need to do what's best for me.

A fresh start for both of us.

I know I shouldn't have been listening in on his conversation, but I'm glad that I did. It doesn't hurt less, but at least I'll save myself the humiliation of rejection. It will make these last few days together much easier to endure. Okay, who am I kidding? It's going to be absolute torture, but at least pretending like I'm not dying inside will be easier than having him look at me with sympathy when I tell him I love him and he says nothing back.

"Um, what?" I ask, still trying to get my bearings after my world has been knocked off its axis.

"Your meeting?" Griffin prompts.

"Right. It was good. Everything's good." I nod, but I know I'm trembling. My thoughts are racing.

Silly woman. It was a fun night in Vegas. And a few weeks pretending in New York. You're getting ahead of yourself again. He doesn't want to be your forever. This isn't going to work out.

"You okay?" His brows furrow with concern.

He reaches his hand out toward me, but I back away. If he touches me, I'll break. I need to find a way through this. Detach from the moment, so I can keep some semblance of composure.

"You wanted to talk?" I ask, hoping he'll rip it off quick like a bandage. I pick up a pen from the counter and start nervously tapping it against the granite.

"Yeah, I, uh," Griffin's eyes drop to the pen in my hand, "can you stop tapping that pen and look at me?"

"Sorry." I grip the pen in my hand and look up at him. He looks nervous. I swear there's a thin sheen of sweat on his forehead. He runs a hand over his mouth. I haven't seen him like this before.

"Emma, I—" he begins again, only for me to cut him off.

"Wait." I hold up my hand because I've changed my mind. I can't take his rejection, not right now. I'll never be ready for those words, but I need longer than five minutes to process this massive change in direction my life is taking. Is it really a change, or had I gotten ahead of myself again? Taking the fun we've been having together over the last two weeks and making it something it wasn't?

Griffin pauses and then we both stand there staring at each other in silence, until he breaks the quiet.

"Did you have something you wanted to say?" he asks. "Something you wanted to tell me?"

That's right, I did tell him I wanted to talk to him this morning. It was about the condos I've looked at, asking him to stay in New York and stay married, so clearly all of that is off the table now.

I scramble to come up with something else of importance. My brain latches on to the only thing I can think of in this moment.

"The annulment," I say. It's more of a shout as a lightbulb goes off in my head.

"The annulment," Griffin echoes less enthusiastically.

"I was thinking we should probably talk about when we're going to do that. You know, the timeline and everything."

I watch as Griffin's jaw visibly tightens. His eyes search my face. Sometimes I think he can read my mind so I do my best to hold in my emotion. Pretend like I wasn't about to throw myself at him and beg him to stay.

"We don't have to discuss it now. I just thought it would be easier to do it while you're still here. Face to face. And with the wedding this weekend, and you leaving on Monday..." my words trail off.

He sighs and looks down at the counter. I can't see his eyes now. Those pools of green have become a source of comfort over the past few weeks. I need them now, but when he looks back up at me, there's no comfort there. No emotion.

"No, you're right. We should discuss it."

My heart sinks again. Maybe I'd hoped that I was wrong. That he'd tell me he doesn't want the annulment. That there's so much to think about, but getting an annulment is the last thing on his mind.

"If you wouldn't mind waiting a few months. Until after *The Dress* article comes out and my line launches at Bergman's."

"Sure." He nods. "There's no rush. I'll have the paperwork drafted and you can sign it when you're ready."

And then because I'm already feeling miserable, I open my mouth and ask him the most inappropriate question.

"Will you start dating before it's finalized?"

"What?" If I thought there was no warmth in his gaze before, now it's cold as ice.

"I don't expect you to wait until the annulment is finalized, but if you could keep it quiet, not post anything on social media until I have a chance to tell my family and friends."

"Yeah, I'll make sure to keep all my hookups off social media."

"I just think it's best to keep it quiet, let the dust settle." I sound like a robot.

"Whatever you need me to do, Emma." He brushes past me to grab a water bottle out of the refrigerator. "I'm going for a walk."

"Okay," I squeak out.

My throat tightens as I watch him leave the kitchen. I'm completely numb as I make my way to my room. When I know he's left the apartment, I curl up in my bed and cry. Jess was right. Far more agonizing than Alec breaking up with me was watching the man I love walk away.

I'd hoped that Griffin and I would be on better terms when we headed to the Hamptons for Barrett and Chloe's wedding Thursday afternoon, but after our conversation yesterday about the annulment, he's been distant. I can't blame him. That's not how I wanted to have that conversation. I didn't want to have that conversation at all, but clearly I was right to second guess everything because Griffin didn't fight me on it at all.

When I came out of the bathroom last night, I found him already asleep on the floor. My stomach twisted at the sight of him there, wishing he was lying in my bed, ready to wrap his arms around me and kiss me goodnight. Now that I'm certain he's leaving, I know it's better that he doesn't. For the sake of my sanity and my heart.

We take a car service to the Hamptons, so Griffin reads and I work on design revisions for a client. Last night, as I tossed and turned, I put a mental list together of how to get over your fake husband. Sitting in a car with him for two hours while he firmly presses the spine of a paperback open with his large thumb all while looking devastatingly handsome and smelling like a sexy forest was not on that list.

But I make it through the car ride, and the wine tasting that evening and on Friday when Chloe asks me to help her run a few last-minute errands, I jump at the chance so I can leave our quaint and excessively romantic room at The Topping Rose House, the charming Bridgehampton mansion where Chloe and Barrett's wedding events are located.

We're at the bakery finalizing the food order for the Sunday morning brunch when Chloe pulls me to one of the small tables by the window. She pushes the plate with a chocolate croissant on it toward me. I hesitate. Even while being in emotional turmoil over the last few days, I've managed to steer clear of pastries.

"Are you okay?" she asks.

"What do you mean?" I ask, as I cave and start devouring the flaky pastry in front of me.

"Are you and Griffin good? You both seemed off last night at the winery."

"Really?" I do my best to sound surprised. "Um, no, maybe just a little tired. It's been a long week."

"Emma," Chloe scolds. She eyes me, then the empty croissant plate.

I sigh. "It's your wedding tomorrow. I don't want you to worry about anything."

Chloe gives me that look of hers, it's the one that tells me she's not buying what I'm selling and she really wants to know.

"You saying that only makes me worry more."

"That's the last thing I want to do. But I also don't want to dump my problems on you the day before your wedding."

"I know you're my designated big sister and all, but even big sisters need to talk sometimes."

I smile at the memory of meeting Chloe last summer at the Top Dog fundraiser event. I was so thrilled Barrett was seriously dating someone that I accosted her and declared we be friends. When we discussed our families, her being the oldest of five, and me being an only child, it was only fitting that I designated myself to be her big sister. Recalling the moment and all the ones we've shared since then gives me the assurance to tell her.

"Griffin and I aren't really married."

"What?" She shakes her head. "I don't understand."

"I mean we are technically, legally, but it was a mistake."

I tell her everything. At this point, there's no reason to hide it. She'll find out eventually, and it's a relief to share it all with someone. Someone other than Griffin who is leaving in three days.

"So, it was kind of like fake dating, but you're really married?"

"Yeah."

She looks thoughtful. "I know what you heard, but is there any chance you were wrong?"

"I don't know. Maybe. But at this point I'm too terrified to find out."

"Because you love him. And if he doesn't love you back, you'll be crushed."

I nod, because my throat is filled with emotion, making it impossible to speak.

"Love is scary. I know you were blindsided by the breakup with Alec. And your heart is still tender, afraid of being hurt again. But the fact that you were open to loving Griffin, that you did fall for him, means that you're resilient.

Maybe I'm just full of mushiness because I'm getting married tomorrow, but you need to talk to him. It doesn't have to be today, or even tomorrow, but promise me you'll tell him how you feel before he leaves."

My stomach churns thinking about telling Griffin, the thought of him rejecting me.

"What would be worse? Putting your heart on the line with the fear of him not feeling the same, or not telling him and always wondering what could have been?"

"Of course, I'll always wonder, but wouldn't Griffin have told me if he felt differently? He agreed to the annulment. He didn't argue against it at all."

"Maybe he's scared, too? You need to tell him what you want. That's the only way you'll know for sure."

I sigh. I know Chloe's right. Now I just need to work up the courage to talk to Griffin.

CHAPTER 30

Griffin

I can't pinpoint the exact moment that I fell for Emma, it's been a collection of moments over the last three weeks. While I thought she might be developing feelings for me as well, two days ago she asked me about our annulment. The plans for it, how it would be handled. If I could be discreet when I start dating other people. What the fuck?

It wouldn't have been such a shock if I hadn't been in the middle of completely rearranging my life to stay here in New York to be with her.

I was ready to tell her how I feel, and then she brought up our annulment out of the blue. It's what we agreed would happen after I returned home, but I thought things had changed between us.

That conversation pulled the rug out from under me, but my feelings haven't changed. They're the same as they were two days ago. But attending the events for Chloe and Barrett's wedding, pretending like we're happy and in love while I'm hopelessly in love with her, and she doesn't feel the same, has been fucking torture.

I know it's crazy to say after only three weeks, but I *know* Emma. I can read her body language, see it in her eyes. Something is off. She brought up the annulment, but even before she said it, there was this look in her eyes. She was scared. Maybe she sensed my nerves and it freaked her out. I don't know. Even though I was nervous to tell her how I felt, I never imagined our conversation would end the way it did. I left her in the kitchen to go for a walk, hoping moving my body would bring me some clarity. It didn't.

I think back to the real estate documents I found on her desk on Thursday before we left the city. Just like her mom mentioned, Emma's looking for a new place to live, making plans for the future. Apparently one that she doesn't see me in.

I'm trying to give her space. Which in our current situation is not easy. We're forced to play happy couple for her friends and family. I've embraced the role again, but now, nothing is fake. Not when I pulled out her chair at dinner, not when I brushed her hair off her neck and placed a kiss against that sensitive spot by her ear. It wasn't just for show when I put my jacket over her shoulders and wrapped my arms around her at the winery because she was cold.

I'd keep not pretending with her every day until she was convinced that our marriage is real. But I don't have that kind of time. On Monday, I need to fly back to Vegas for Sophie's graduation. I also need to make a decision about my job plans. Do I take the job at Premier? Let Terrence know my plans have changed? I've got less than forty-eight hours to convince my wife that we belong together.

My *wife*. There's still panic at those words, but now the fear isn't that I have one, it's that I'm afraid of losing her. That for how suddenly she came into my life, she could be gone. Fuck. How did this happen? How did I marry a woman I barely knew and now I can't imagine being anywhere that she isn't?

During the ceremony, while everyone else's attention was on the bride and groom, I couldn't take my eyes off Emma.

The way she smiled radiantly when she walked down the aisle, her silk champagne colored dress clinging to every curve. Or her dabbing at tears while she watched her cousin and friend exchange vows. Then when she meticulously adjusted the train of Chloe's dress for photos, and paused the photographer mid-session to help Chloe reapply her lipstick after Barrett had kissed it off.

And that's only in the last ten minutes.

Every moment I'm with her, I'm soaking in her smiles, her laugh, the way she makes the world brighter and my chest lighter.

Most of the guests have gone on to the cocktail hour that's preceding dinner while the wedding party finishes up with photos. I'm still seated in the audience watching the photo-shoot when Emma's dad sits down beside me.

"Beautiful wedding." He nods toward Chloe and Barrett locked in an embrace at the altar while the photographer snaps a photo.

"It is." I nod. We haven't spoken since Tuesday, since I confessed my love for Emma. Confirmed what he already knew had happened in Vegas.

"When Emma was little, she'd go to weddings with me. She wanted to be my assistant. She mostly just ended up eating cake under the table."

I smile thinking of a young Emma hiding under a white-clothed table eating wedding cake.

"She loved weddings, wanted to be a part of the magic. She started planning her own wedding when she was six. Cutting out clippings from magazines, making scrapbooks and poster boards. When Pinterest was developed, she went digital."

I swallow thickly, I know about the binders and clippings. Emma wanted a wedding like this. Our wedding in Vegas was nothing like she had imagined.

"Then she eloped with me in Vegas." I fill in what he's not saying.

"That's the beauty of growing up. Of discovering who you are as a person. Your dreams change."

But have Emma's dreams changed? Or does she want to undo our Vegas wedding so she can have a do over?

"I think Emma focused so much on the wedding she wanted because the guys she was with were never right for her. But with you, it was different. It wasn't about the wedding."

"Three days ago, she told me she wanted the annulment. That we should discuss it before I leave."

"If that's not what you want, then you need to tell her how you feel." Philip stands and passes in front of me to make his way to the aisle.

I know he's right. I know what I want. Emma.

But she wants the annulment.

Or does she?

When she left Wednesday morning she was rushing to her meeting, but she was so excited when she said she wanted to talk to me. I can't imagine that she would have been that thrilled to discuss getting an annulment. But when she came home, she was completely different. It's like she had shut down. Even when she played it off that nothing was wrong, I could tell something was. I was about to confess my feelings and she cut me off. It doesn't make sense.

My eyes lift to find her staring back at me. When our eyes connect, she quickly pushes a beaming smile onto her face. It's not her genuine smile. But it's not her smile I'm focusing on, it's her eyes. They tell a different story. Sadness. Hurt. Longing. Fear.

Everything clicks into place.

Emma's pushing me away because that's easier than the thought of me rejecting her. She must have thought I was breaking things off with her so she decided to beat me to it.

Clearly from the miserable look in her eyes, being the one to ask for the annulment has not relieved any of the pain.

I take in a deep breath; hope expands my chest.

Emma turns away, the group is moving locations for another round of photographs. Fuck. I want to run over to her, pull her away and make this right. Tell her how I feel, no interruptions this time.

But then I think about where we are. Emma's got a speech to give and there's all the bridesmaid duties she's a part of. While I'm anxious to fix things with her, I know I need to wait until after the reception.

"And Griffin?" Philip stops in the aisle and looks back at me.

"Yeah?"

"You have my blessing."

I nod. "Thank you, sir."

After the reception, I'll talk to her. I'll reassure her we didn't make a mistake that night. And that if given the chance, I will love her forever.

CHAPTER 31

Emma

I pick at the cake on my plate. It's delicious, but my stomach has felt unsettled all day. It's been a whirlwind of emotion, watching Chloe and Barrett exchange vows, seeing how in love they are, knowing I feel the same way about Griffin, but terrified to tell him how I feel.

He's beside me now, his arm draped casually across the back of my chair like any husband's would be. It's the third time in as many weeks that I've seen him in a suit, each time he's been more devastatingly handsome than the last. It physically hurts to look at him. My heart can't take the palpitations his stare causes, my stomach knotted like a pretzel, making it difficult to enjoy what is supposed to be a world class meal.

"Did you want a wedding like this?" Griffin breaks our silence, motioning to the large white tent we're under. The lights and flowers, the elaborate centerpieces on the tables. I immediately think of the binders filled with magazine clippings, the dozens of Pinterest boards I created, each dedicated to a different aspect of my dream wedding. I imagined something similar, grand and sophisticated, no expense spared. But in all that planning, I had no idea who I would marry. It wasn't about the guy. It was the wedding I was fixated on. The dress, the cake, the flowers I was meticulously picking out. Years before Alec. Even when Alec and I were together and I started thinking he could be 'the one,' nothing about my wedding plans changed. They weren't tailored to us as a couple, they were what I liked, what I wanted.

"I did," I answer honestly, *but that was before you.*

When I look around Chloe and Barrett's reception, I see that it's perfect for them. From the bookish themed centerpieces with Chloe's favorites books to the scotch sampling station Barrett requested. Their sweet dog, Baxter, in a bowtie, being led around the reception by Chloe's dad. They created this day together.

Getting married to Griffin in Vegas wasn't planned, but I wouldn't trade our wedding for anything else because it was us. It was *real.* Me in my mom's wedding dress, the pink bouquet Griffin picked out because he said the flowers matched my lips perfectly. Even the simple gold bands we exchanged. It had been ingrained in me to want a large diamond, that the ring my future husband would pick out, the cost of it would be equated with my value as a person. It's not about the ring, it's about the person who put it on my finger.

"How's the cake?" His fingers trail down the back column of my neck. The familiar quiver his touch elicits races down my spine. Even after the annulment talk this week, he hasn't stopped touching me. Light caresses, brushes of fingers, his lips against the shell of my ear when he leans in to tell me something.

"It's good, I'm just not that hungry." I set my fork down.

"You barely touched your dinner."

"I'm nervous for my speech." It's an easy excuse. One that allows me to pretend that I'm not losing control of this situation.

"That's understandable." His palm flattens against the

back of my neck, his thumb gently tracing the sensitive skin beneath my ear. It's possessive and sweet at the same time. And it feels like the most natural thing in the world. I can't handle the idea that it's just for show. That we're back to pretending.

I spring up out of my chair. "Excuse me. I need—" I'm about to say fresh air when it occurs to me that we're already outside. "—a moment."

Before he can respond, I drop my napkin on the table and rush toward the restrooms.

I have to keep it together, at least until after my speech. I take deep, calming breaths as I make my way across the lawn. Inside the restroom, I dab at my damp eyes and reapply my lipstick. A few minutes later I exit to the sound of Carl announcing the speeches. Announcing me. I hurry through the courtyard and back to the tent, weaving through the tables until I meet Carl on the dance floor to accept the microphone. For a moment, I'm breathless and my voice is shaky. So, I take a second to breathe and relax before proceeding.

"For those who don't know me, I'm Emma, Barrett's cousin. I've known him his entire life, minus those three years he has on me. We shared family vacations. I even rocked a pair of his old Osh Kosh overalls because I thought he was so cool. That means I knew him long before he met Chloe. I love you, Barrett, but most would agree with me that you're not the easiest person to get along with. I believe myself qualified to say that when Chloe and Barrett started dating, when I saw the way he was completely smitten with her, it was obvious that he'd found the person that made him a better version of himself.

"And Chloe, I've loved every minute of getting to know you. I'm your designated big sister from another mister and I love you so much." Chloe smiles back, tears forming in her eyes. "Together, you've found a love that challenges you, makes your heart sing, and makes you realize what is most important in this world. Your commitment to each other. It's a kind of love everyone strives for. A love that I—" My gaze snags on Griffin. He's now standing at the edge of the tent, his hands in his pockets, green eyes focused on my face. His lips slightly parted, like he's holding a breath.

"—that I wish for everyone." I shift my gaze away from Griffin so I can keep my emotions at bay. "Please raise your glasses and join me in congratulating the new Mr. and Mrs. St. Clair. To Chloe and Barrett."

The crowd lifts their glasses, some start to clink the side to indicate the couple should kiss. Barrett slides a hand over Chloe's jaw and pulls her close before capturing her mouth with his. My eyes scan the crowd, looking back over to where Griffin had been, but he's gone.

Carl takes the microphone from me, and I move to the side, fighting back the tears that are weighing heavy against my lower lids.

"And now Chloe and Barrett would like to take a moment to address the crowd."

Barrett and Chloe stand, and Barrett accepts the microphone from Carl.

"Thank you all for showing up to celebrate with us tonight. This day has been everything and more." Barrett's voice is heavy with emotion. "I want to thank my wife," everyone cheers and hollers as he pulls Chloe into him and kisses her. "It feels amazing to say that." He looks down at her with a huge grin on his face, "First, thank you for showing up today." The crowd laughs. "But most of all thank you for loving me completely."

Chloe reaches up to wrap her arms around his neck and pulls him down for a kiss. They're a perfect image of love and contentment. Normally, I would swoon at how adorable they are, but my own tangled up feelings for Griffin are clawing at my heart, making it harder for me to put on a happy face and celebrate.

With one arm wrapped possessively around Chloe's waist, Barrett continues.

"We're going to keep the party going, but first, we wanted to recognize another couple here that recently got married. My cousin, Emma, and her husband, Griffin." Barrett smiles warmly at me. "They eloped to Vegas a few weeks ago and while we respect their insistence on a private ceremony, we want to honor their union tonight with this next song."

Chloe pulls the microphone in her direction. "Emma and Griffin, please come out to the dance floor."

When I turn to search for Griffin, he's right beside me.

"Emma, may I have this dance?" I look down to find Griffin's extended palm.

The clapping quiets and the beginning chords of the song start to play. With over two hundred pairs of eyes on us now, there's nothing to do but honor Chloe and Barrett's request.

I drop my hand into his, and he closes his over mine before he turns to lead me onto the dance floor.

When the woman starts singing, I recognize the song as Kacey Musgrave's cover of "Can't Help Falling in Love." It's the song that was playing the night of our wedding. I remember Griffin's arms around me, her clear, airy voice carrying over the chapel's speaker when he slid the band on my finger.

Griffin's muscular arm encircles my waist, pulling me to him. His other hand holds one of mine against his chest. I can feel the soft *thud, thud, thud* of his heart beneath my palm. It's steady and strong, like the man himself. He holds me close as we start to sway.

"This song. It's from our wedding night. Did you tell them?"

He looks down at me, his eyes caressing my face.

"Chloe asked. She wanted to surprise you."

Out of all Chloe's surprises lately, this one is the best.

"You remember it?" he asks.

"Yeah." I smile. A song about a couple rushing into love, fools as they're described, but they can't help it. Likely the reason it was playing in a Vegas wedding chapel.

My gaze moves beyond Griffin, to the crowd of people surrounding the dance floor, watching us. Their faces are a reflection of what they're witnessing, two people in love. I close my eyes, blocking out everything else but the way it feels to be in his arms. What it would feel like if I could stay here forever. And God, it's perfect.

A camera flashes against our profiles.

It will look perfect from the outside. No one will know we were pretending.

Griffin's smooth cheek slides against mine, his head turning to press a gentle kiss against my temple. On the outside, it looks sweet and loving, but to me it feels like torture. This man, loyal, protector, secretly adventurous and up for my silliness, best friend, best cuddler, best everything of my life.

I'm suddenly exhausted. Tired of telling myself that I'll be okay when Griffin leaves. That telling him how I feel is more terrifying than the thought of him getting on that plane and never seeing him again.

As the song comes to an end, Griffin spins me away from him. At first, I'm caught off guard, a bit unstable on my heels, but when our arms reach their full extension, and my hand pulls tight against his, I feel the strength of his hold. The ease with which he pulls me back in and against his body.

He wraps his arms tight around my lower back, pressing his upper body against mine, nearly bending me backwards. The movement identical to the way we were posed in the photograph from our wedding night. When his mouth captures mine, it's the same explosion I remember, too, except magnified by a million now that I'm irrevocably in love with him.

The crowd claps and cheers. They're really eating it up.

Griffin pulls me back upright and slowly releases me. The warmth I felt in his arms dissipates and my body shivers as the cool evening air creeps in around me. The next song starts and the DJ announces for everyone to join us on the dance floor.

For a moment, Griffin is still, watching me with tender eyes. As the crowd forms around us, he reaches for my left hand again. His thumb smooths over the inside of my wrist, teasing the sensitive skin there before trailing a path down my palm to my ring finger. He pauses on my gold wedding band, rotating it between his thumb and middle finger.

My eyes lift from where I've been watching him stroke my finger to his green gaze.

His stare penetrates my skin, my mind, my heart. It's like he can see right through me. See my thoughts and my fears. My heart thumping wildly against my ribcage as I fight to keep my shit together. *Breathe,* I tell myself. But my lungs won't expand. The feelings I have for Griffin are gripping me so tight I can't breathe.

"I need to—" I motion over my shoulder, toward the main house.

"Emma—" He starts to reach for me, but I pull away.

"I'm fine. I'll be back," I tell him, a wobbly smile on my face.

I have to get out of here before I lose it.

As I speed walk away from the reception tent, I'm irrationally mad at Griffin right now. I know I'm being ridiculous. He's done everything I've asked. Played his part perfectly. The sweet, doting husband supporting his new wife. But it's because he was so good at his role that we're in this predicament. Dancing with him, his protective arms around me, holding me the way he does. And that penetrating gaze of his, the tenderness there. It's too much.

The real person I'm mad at is myself. For wanting him so badly it hurts. For doing exactly what I told myself I wouldn't do, fall for my husband.

"Emma, wait," Griffin calls from behind me. Of course, he would be concerned and come after me. He's a guy that knows the phrase 'I'm fine' means the exact opposite. The sweet gesture only adds fuel to the mounting fire of frustration that I'm feeling.

"Just stop!" I double back so quickly; Griffin struggles to stop his momentum and he nearly runs me over. His hands reach for my arms, but I maneuver out of his hold. Turning again, I continue walking in the direction of the house. "Please, stop," I say, more quietly this time. Because the anger is really fear. A realization that I've found the person who makes me feel everything and I'm terrified he doesn't feel the same.

His time in New York is coming to an end. He'll return to Vegas, fill out the annulment paperwork and move on with his life. It's the devastation I felt when my crush, Joey Milton, moved away in fourth grade, except it's a million times worse. These past three weeks have shown me what it would be like to be with Griffin. The man that he is and how it would feel to truly be his.

We walk in silence up the lush lawn and around the side of the estate.

In the shadows of the side yard, away from the reception tent and its twinkling lights, I pause.

"Talk to me, Emma. Please," Griffin says in the dark.

The old me, the me that didn't voice my needs in my relationship threatens to take over. To shut down and pretend like everything is fine. Keep things peaceful, everyone happy, except me. But Griffin has shown me I can be different. Telling someone my needs doesn't make me too much, it makes me human. And with Griffin, there are too many feelings to push down.

We could go inside, but right now, I need the cool breeze in my hair, the dim light cast by the torches along the stone path to shadow my face—all the emotion there I can't hide.

I turn around and find Griffin is right there. He doesn't crowd me, but he's close enough that his broad shoulders block out the moonlight, and I can see his full lips are pulled into a flat line. His freshly shaven jaw sharp and tense.

My bare back brushes against the stone retaining wall.

"I need you to stop being…" I wave my hand in his general direction, searching for the right words. The words to describe all the things that he is—sweet, kind, protective, thoughtful, romantic, funny, caring. That doesn't even cover the half of it. Attentive, selfless, patient. Those words could describe anyone. It's the special combination of them together with his quiet confidence and the way I feel when I'm in his arms that sets Griffin apart. Not to mention the fact that he's gorgeous and I love licking my way down his abs. I sigh. "You."

He's quiet, considering for a moment. He rubs the back of his neck before his hand returns to his pocket.

"Emma, I don't know what that means."

"It means…" I inhale. My heart is working overtime. It knows we're in trouble, on the verge of something dangerous. And right now, it's trying to claw its way out. The opposite of a pep talk is happening beneath my rib cage.

Not this time, lady.

Hell, no. We're not sticking around for this.

Haven't we been through enough?

Griffin's waiting patiently for me to find the words. He's not pushing me to answer. He's letting me take my time.

My only safety net is that I have a deep-seated feeling that Griffin is the kind of man who will let me down gently. He won't laugh or use my feelings against me. He'll tell me in the kindest way possible that it's too soon to feel this way. That he doesn't feel the same.

My eyes are set on Griffin's chest. It's a safe focal point. I study the buttons on his tuxedo shirt, hoping that one of them will open up a portal and pull me out of this terrifyingly vulnerable moment.

He takes a step closer, his body heat creating a cozy cocoon around me. He's a calming presence even as my heart rate ratchets up a notch with his proximity.

"It means…"

Don't do it.

If organs could brace for impact, my heart would be buckling a five-point harness right now. I take in a shuddering breath.

"It means, I love you, Griffin. I've fallen in love with you. It means I failed at not giving you my heart. And you're leaving on Monday. But I don't want you to. At least not forever. I want you to stay here. Move to New York to be with me. Please?" My eyes blink back tears. "Okay, that's all."

Griffin's thumb and index finger grip my chin to lift my gaze to his. I look into the green eyes of the man that has become my everything.

"I love you, too, Emma."

Like a reboot after a power failure, everything in my body comes back online. My chest lifts as my lungs expand and my heart that had nearly come to a halt starts beating again.

"You love me?" I ask, afraid my ears are playing tricks on me.

He nods. "For a while now."

"What about what you said on the phone? When you were talking about moving on and not wanting to hurt me when you left?"

His brows crease in confusion before relaxing again. "I was talking to a friend about Sophie, about leaving Nevada."

I'm so happy I could cry. Then I realize I am because

Griffin wipes a tear from my cheek, then replaces it with his lips.

"I've been wanting to tell you all day. All week in fact. Then when you brought up the annulment, I thought you didn't feel the same, but you do. You were just scared."

His hands lift to the stone behind me, bracketing either side of my head. Then he leans closer. His voice is as smooth as creamer being poured into a glass of cold brew. The way the cream gently seeps into the coffee, eventually dispersing to take over completely.

"Emma, I knew I wanted you the moment I saw you on the rooftop in Vegas. That hasn't changed. The whole friend thing was my attempt to keep you at a distance. To fight every urge I had to touch you, to kiss you, to claim you as mine. Waking up next to you has quickly become the best part of my day, even when I was sleeping on the floor. And after only a handful of days, I couldn't imagine my life without you in it." One hand moves to my chest, his long fingers splay out against my collarbone. His gentle touch tickles my skin as his fingers work their way up the front of my neck where they massage me there. The pressure of his fingers against my neck increases until he's got a firm grip. I can breathe, easily, but the way he's touching me, the intensity of his eyes, that's what steals my breath. "Before, I was skeptical because it seemed impossible that a wild night in Vegas could lead me to the woman I was meant to love and cherish for the rest of my life."

His words are unraveling me. All I want to do is touch him. And I want his hands all over me. I can feel his hard length pressing against my stomach.

My attempt to move forward, to lift my face up toward his is prevented by the possessive hold he has on my neck.

"Your turn, Emma." He caresses my collarbone with his thumb. "What did you want to tell me?"

It's a redo of the conversation we were supposed to have on Wednesday, but didn't.

"I found a couple of condos I wanted you to look at," I tell him.

He nods, his lips are flat, but I can see the warmth there in his eyes. "And why would you want me to do that?"

"Because I want you to move in with me."

"That's interesting." His lips pull into a small smile. "Tell me more."

"And I think we should stay married."

His lips twitch. "I like where this is going."

"Oh," I take a deep breath, "and I want you to fuck me right now."

"Good girl." He growls before taking my mouth with a searing kiss. His hands tangle in my hair, his tongue lashes against mine. But I want more.

My fingers encircle his other forearm where I guide it to my breast. But he doesn't grasp me like I want him to. His touch is featherlight and agonizingly gentle. I reach between us, palming him through his pants, then my hands reach for his belt, showing him how desperate I am for him. I think I'm going to die if he isn't inside me soon.

But he doesn't let me get it unbuckled, instead, he takes my hand and intertwines his fingers with mine, then hurries us up the path and toward our room. Shaking hands swipe the key card to open the door. The warmer air greets us as the door closes behind us with a loud click.

With our feelings out in the open, I feel relief, but I'm also a bundle of nerves. We're going to have sex! *Finally.*

Inside, Griffin's hand grips the back of my neck as he pulls me to him.

With my body flush against his, his erection presses into me through the thin fabric of my dress.

He holds me there, tracing his thumb slowly over my lips before lowering his mouth to gently brush against mine. It's unhurried and agonizing. After the weeks of buildup we've had, I expected this moment to be like lighting a stick of dynamite. The only possible outcome is an explosion.

My fingers rush to his shirt buttons. I'm dying to touch him, but Griffin's hands swiftly claim my wrists. In the next second I'm against the wall with my hands pinned above my head.

"I only get you for the first time once." He dips his head again, this time his mouth closes over my bottom lip, tugging the flesh between his teeth before he releases it and licks me there. "I want to savor this."

His muscular thigh pushes between my legs. When he shifts forward and presses into my center, I gasp with how good the friction feels.

"Are you going to be a good girl and let me give you what you need?" he asks.

The liquid heat those words cause to pool between my legs is my body's answer, but I voice it, too, to let him know that I want everything he's willing to give me.

"Yes."

My response prompts Griffin's hands to start a slow descent, his fingertips grazing over the sensitive skin on the underside of my arms. If I wasn't so turned on, I'd probably giggle, but my body has shut that part of my brain off. Its sole mission is to *feel* Griffin.

My pelvis rocks forward. The only thing between his leg and my clit is the tiny scrap of my silk underwear. God, it feels so good to press into him. It reminds me of our Twister game. How good it felt that night to feel him between my legs. It's even better now.

"I love the way you move your body against mine." He licks my clavicle. "The heat of your pussy against my thigh."

His hands continue their way down my ribcage and over my hips, until he reaches the hem of my dress. The moment he lifts it up and over my head, the coolness of the surrounding air rushes over my heated skin. He tosses my dress aside. I'm already braless due to the cut of the dress, so now I'm propped up against the wall, naked except for a thong and my beige heels which are conveniently giving me extra height.

"Look at you." Griffin leans back to take me in. One hand moves up to hold the weight of my breast. His thumb lazily circles my hardened nipple and my back arches into his touch. "You're perfect for me."

His head dips to my chest, his warm mouth closing around my nipple. When his teeth graze my sensitive peak, I cry out.

"I know how much you like it when I suck these." He uses his thumb to smooth over the wet peak while his mouth moves to my other breast and starts licking me there.

"More," I tell him, arching into him, loving the feeling of his mouth on me. I want it everywhere.

Instead of more, he pulls back.

He removes his thigh from between my legs, taking with him the friction that I was enjoying. But then, he hooks his fingers in my underwear and begins to slide it down my legs as he lowers in front of me. With his eyes on mine, he lifts my left leg over his shoulder, then kisses the inside of my thigh.

"Mine," he says, the word equal parts possessive and reverent. My heart trips over itself, my vision blurs with the emotion that this moment is conjuring.

But a second later, the friction is back. Now in the form of his tongue licking up my center.

"Fuck, I love how ready you are for me, Mrs. Hart. How sweet you are on my tongue."

Griffin's hands move up my thighs to grip my hips, pulling me against him. His fingers splay, digging into the flesh of my ass to hold me tightly against his mouth.

And then, he fucking *devours* me.

He worships my clit. His rhythm is perfection, the pressure, flawless. My husband knows what I like. What will have me coming on his face in a minute flat.

This position takes my breath away. The way he pulls back to look up at me with adoration, his lips coated in my wetness. His eyes briefly locking with mine as his hand dives between my legs. Then, with two fingers hooked inside me and a swirl of his tongue, I'm done for.

Boneless from my orgasm, Griffin lifts me into his arms and carries me to the bed, sliding my shoes off as he moves. My back hits the bed, then Griffin's pants hit the floor. A moment later his boxer briefs.

I rise to my knees, meeting him at the edge of the bed. Our previous interactions, while filled with pleasure, were quick, urgent. I've seen his body, touched him, but not like this. Every inch exposed.

Griffin's right. We should savor this. Make it last.

I reach out to fist his erection. Griffin dips his fingers between my legs, then guides his fingers, wet with me, down his length.

"Just like that." He groans, rocking his hips into my fist.

I look up to find him watching every stroke.

His eyes are hooded, but still watching as I glide my thumb around his tip, spreading the precum that has accumulated there. I lower down, replacing my thumb with my lips, letting my tongue taste him.

"Fuck, that's good."

Between my thighs, wetness pools as I listen to Griffin tell me how good it feels to be in my mouth. How well I suck his dick and how beautiful I look with my cheeks hollowed out, taking every inch he gives me.

I'm sucking him hard, wanting to push him over the edge like he's already done to me, but he doesn't let me finish. He pulls out of my mouth and presses me backwards until I collapse on the pile of pillows behind me.

"I need to be inside you."

I nod eagerly. "Yes."

His palm skates over my stomach, his fingers teasing between my legs. Two fingers filling me, stretching me so good.

"I've waited so long for you. I want you bare. Nothing between us."

"I'm on the pill. And clean."

"I'm clean, too."

He removes his fingers, then teases his crown at my entrance.

I reach up to pull him closer. I know his full weight isn't on me, but what is feels so damn good. I want to feel every inch of him holding me down.

He slowly presses inside, his thick cock stretching me until he bottoms out.

"This might be quick." He chuckles with self-deprecation.

"Because it's been so long?" I ask.

"No, because it's you." He pants like he's out of breath, his eyes rolling back with pleasure. He groans, then growls. There are a few expletives in there as well. It's like he's doing everything in his power not to lose his mind. "You feel fucking amazing."

After a moment of stillness, Griffin begins to move. The movement helps me adjust to his size.

I want him to come. I'm so focused on lifting my hips up to meet him, on watching him chase his orgasm, that mine sneaks up on me.

"Damn, you're squeezing me tight." He groans.

"I'm going to—" I can't even get the words out; the fullness of him and my impending orgasm steal my words.

"Let me feel you, sweetheart," he rasps. "I'm dying to feel my wife's tight pussy squeeze my cock."

I clench so tight around him it's almost painful, the contractions of my muscles pulling him in farther, which I didn't think was possible.

Once my orgasm subsides, Griffin places one of my legs over his shoulder and leans back, his eyes fixed on where we're connected as he continues pumping in and out of me.

His eyes move back to mine.

"God, you look so pretty with my cock buried deep inside you."

My hips buck off the bed when his thumb starts circling my clit.

He can't expect me to come again. But he does. He waits until I'm on the edge, then right as I'm falling, he buries himself deep inside me and pulses his own release. The chemical release from my orgasms coupled with the relief of admitting our feelings for each other has tears springing to my eyes while I start giggling.

Griffin hovers over me, wiping away a rogue tear. "Are you okay?"

"Yes, I'm deliriously happy. Or I might be crazy." I smile. "Either way, you're stuck with me now."

He laughs and presses a soft kiss to my lips. "Good, because I love you."

"I love you, too."

"And I love that you giggle after you orgasm." Griffin nuzzles against my neck.

"I do?"

"Yeah. You've done it every time I made you come."

"Huh, I didn't realize I did that." I run my hands through his hair while he peppers kisses along my jaw.

"It's my new favorite sound." He growls playfully. "I want to hear it over and over, again."

"I think that can be arranged," I tell him.

He reaches over to the bedside table to grab a bottle of water. "You should hydrate. It's going to be a long night."

I reach for the water but he's already tossed it aside and is climbing over me again.

"Too late, Mrs. Hart. The pleasure sword is coming for you."

He can barely say it with a straight face. I burst out in a fit of laughter, but it dies a second later with Griffin's lips on mine.

He pulls back to look down at me, his fingers playing with loose strands of my hair.

"Marry me," he says.

My lips pull into a wide smile. "I already did."

"Fine. Stay married to me."

"Is that your proposal? I'd have to argue mine was better." I'm being difficult and he knows it.

"Be a good girl and say yes."

"Hmm. I don't know." When I continue to tease him, he pins me beneath him and nips at my neck. "Okay. Yes!" I squeal from beneath him.

"I love you, Mrs. Hart." He kisses me slow and sweet, before pulling back to reveal a wicked smile. "Now get on your hands and knees."

CHAPTER 32

Griffin

"What time does the ceremony start?" Emma calls loudly from inside the shower.

"Two o'clock," I answer, stepping in behind her.

When my hands wrap around her hips, she jumps. She turns to open her eyes, then a smile spreads across her face. "I didn't realize you were right there."

"I couldn't resist my naked wife in the shower."

She shows her approval by wrapping her arms around my neck and pulling me to her for a kiss.

For the past two days, I haven't been able to take my hands off her. After Chloe and Barrett's wedding, we returned to the city on Sunday and only left Emma's bedroom to accept the food delivery we ordered, twice. If food wasn't necessary to keep our energy up, we wouldn't have bothered eating at all. Luckily her parents stayed another night in the Hamptons so we had the apartment to ourselves.

Yesterday morning we packed up and flew to Vegas. It's odd being back but everything about my life has changed.

While Emma had been looking at purchasing a condo with her realtor, we've decided to rent first so we can be flexible. Yesterday we filled out an application for a place we picked out together and plan to do a tour when we get back to the city on Friday.

Sophie's graduation is today and before that, I have a meeting with Terrence. I haven't told Sophie about my plans for moving to New York yet. I want her to enjoy her day, and I'll talk to her about it tonight.

My fingers tease between Emma's thighs, finding her slick from more than the water.

"I can't get enough of you." I groan into her mouth.

Emma wraps her hands behind my neck, her nails digging into my scalp as our kiss turns blistering. Soon, I'm lifting her up against the tile and pressing the head of my cock against her entrance. Her legs wrap around my waist and I thrust up into her. I'm still in awe of how good it feels to slide into her. To fill her up and claim her.

With long, deep thrusts, and my thumb rubbing her clit, it doesn't take long for Emma's back to arch and her pussy to pulse around my cock. I follow, shuddering my release inside her. Once we've caught our breath, we wash up.

Emma reaches up to massage the shampoo into my hair.

"I know today is going to be a lot. Your talk with Terrence, telling Sophie about New York." She presses a soft kiss to my lips. "I want you to know that I love you and we'll figure it out together."

I'm anxious about the conversations I have to have with Terrence and Sophie, but looking down at Emma in this moment, seeing the love and encouragement in her eyes, I know that I'm making the right decision.

While returning to Vegas with Emma by my side has felt surreal, so does the thought of telling my mentor that I'm moving to New York City and can no longer accept the job he's been holding for me.

I pull open the door at McGregor & Lange. Sonny, the receptionist, smiles as I approach her desk.

"Hi, Sonny."

"Griffin, so good to see you. I heard you were on a trip."

"Yeah, I was."

It's still hard to believe that I left Vegas three weeks ago to pose as Emma's husband, and I'm returning to Vegas to pack up my life and move to New York City to be with her.

"I'm here to see Terrence."

"He just got out of a meeting, so I'll let him know you're here."

"Thanks." I take a seat on one of the leather armchairs in the waiting area.

A few minutes pass, and then Sonny motions for me to head back to Terrence's office.

As I walk the hallway toward Terrence's office, I think about the life I had planned after the revue.

I knock on his open door.

"Hey, kid." He motions me in, then stands and circles his desk to give me a handshake and a hug. "Now I can congratulate you in person." He claps me on the shoulder. "You did good. I'm real proud of you."

"Thanks, Terrence."

"Grab a seat." He motions toward the guest chairs.

"Sophie got the flowers you and Rita sent for her graduation. That was very thoughtful."

"It's hard to believe she's grown up now, graduating. You both have done well for yourselves."

"I've always appreciated your and Rita's support. I couldn't have done it without you two. You know that, right?" I want him to know that the decision I've made has nothing to do with our relationship and the investment of time he's made helping me out over the years.

"We supported and encouraged, but you, son, you did all the hard stuff."

Sitting in front of Terrence now, I'm struggling to get the words out. To tell him that I appreciate everything he's done for me, but I've found a new path. I found Emma and a life we can share.

"I know I'll see you later at dinner, but I needed to talk to you privately."

"Sure. I'm all ears."

"The reason I wasn't able to start here earlier was because I had some business to take care of in New York." I explain everything to Terrence. Marrying Emma, going to New York to pose as her husband, and then, falling for her.

Terrence leans back in his chair. "Wow. I didn't see that coming."

"That's why I came here to tell you I have to decline the job you offered me."

He's quiet for a moment. His hands pressed together, fingers steepled against his mouth as he thinks. Finally, he lets out a light chuckle.

"Good for you, kid." He smiles.

"You're not upset?"

He shakes his head. "No. The legal counselor in me could give you a spiel on how fast you're moving, how you should proceed with caution. That's what I'd tell a client. But with matters of the heart, it's a whole different ballgame. And I know you. I know the man that you are and if you've fallen for this woman, then she must possess all the qualities that you desire in a partner. I don't see that there's even a case to argue."

"Yeah," I say, thinking of Emma. How perfect she is for me. How well we complement each other. "You're right."

We talk for a few more minutes, but don't say our final goodbyes. I'll see him later after Sophie's graduation. I leave Terrence's office with a weight off my shoulders, but I know that my talk with Sophie is by far going to be the most difficult.

After Sophie's graduation ceremony, we gather at Rita and Terrence's for dinner. Chad stops by to meet Emma and even a few of Sophie's friends make an appearance. Rita makes her famous enchiladas, and we all eat so much we can barely move.

On our way out, Rita pulls me aside. "I can see how happy you are with her." She hugs me tight. "I'm sad to see you go, but I love the direction you're headed."

I assure her I'll be back. That my new job will bring me to the area often.

Chad pulls me in for a quick hug. "I thought you might have a screw loose, man, but seeing you two together...it makes sense now."

"Thanks, man." We make plans to hang out again before Emma and I leave on Friday.

Me, Emma, and Sophie spend the rest of the evening relaxing on the couch and catching up. We are still full from Rita's enchiladas and she even sent us home with a whole pan.

Emma and Sophie have already become fast friends. I'm relieved, but also it makes me sad to think we won't be close to each other anymore.

"You're gorgeous and elegant. Are you sure you want to stay married to my brother? You know he drinks orange juice straight out of the carton? And he likes the pulp." She makes a gagging noise. "Disgusting."

"Thank you for enlightening me on his proclivity for pulp-laden orange juice." Emma's lips twist with humor. She gives me a sideways glance and I give her a wink. "I think I'll let it slide."

I told Sophie that Emma and I weren't going to get an annulment, but I've yet to have the conversation about me moving to New York.

Emma yawns and stretches. "I'm exhausted. I'm going to let you two catch up."

She gives me a soft smile and a sweet kiss on the lips. My hands grip her hips, wishing she could stay, but I know she's giving me this time alone with Sophie to talk.

When Emma's gone, Sophie turns to me. "She's perfect."

"Yeah, she is." I rotate the glass of water in my hand.

She props her head on her hand, then tucks her feet underneath her. "It's so wild to see you in love. But I love seeing it. I love that you're happy."

The tips of my ears go warm at her observation.

"You knew, didn't you? That's why you married her. That's why you went to New York."

I nod. "I went to New York to do the right thing, but I quickly realized I'd never be able to walk away from her."

"I always felt bad you never dated, never prioritized finding love, but that's how it was meant to be, because it found you." I can see the tears starting to form in Sophie's eyes. "You've been the best big brother I could ever ask for, giving up so much for me."

"That's never how I saw it," I tell her adamantly.

"Another reason why you're the best." She laughs as she wipes a tear. Fuck. Her tears are making this harder.

"Sophie, I—"

"So, when are you moving to New York?" she asks.

My eyes catch hers. It's like looking in a mirror. We both have our mom's eyes. And Sophie knows me better than anyone. I should have known she'd be one step ahead of me.

"I got a job offer there; it starts next week. It's with a real estate developer. The company is starting a project here, in Vegas, so it will bring me back regularly."

She nods slowly.

"I don't have to move right away. I know this is sudden. Unexpected. I'm still thinking I'm going to wake up any second and it will all be a dream."

She smiles and twists her blonde ponytail around her hand. "Speaking of dreams, I have some exciting news."

Sophie seems to be taking the announcement that I'm moving to New York well. I guess I'm the one who is struggling with leaving her behind.

"Yeah?" I ask, glad she's in good spirits about the whole thing.

"I got a paid internship at Marion Adler Events."

"Congratulations! I'm so proud of you, Soph." We meet in the middle of the couch where I wrap my arms around her, squeezing her tight. Then I realize something. "Wait, isn't that the one in New York City? The one you thought you'd never get in a million years but you applied for it anyway?"

Her smile is bright. "That's the one."

"So, you'll be moving to New York, too?" I sit back, stunned, because I can't believe how perfectly everything is working out, but then my protective brother alarm starts going off. "You'll need to move in with me and Emma."

She scrunches her nose like the idea is not appealing at all.

"In all your research of the city, have you looked at the astronomical cost of living? Even with a paid internship, you'll need some time to get on your feet."

"Yeah, I'll need some time to find roommates my own age," she says.

"That have been thoroughly vetted."

She laughs, but I'm one thousand percent serious. Then, I realize I'll need to make sure Emma is okay with Sophie living with us.

"I'll need to check with Emma, make sure she's good with it."

"That makes sense." Sophie nods.

"When does your internship start?" I ask.

"Two weeks."

"We'll be in our new place by then, so that should work."

"Oh my God, I love this for us!" Sophie jumps up off the

couch, grabs her phone and starts texting. "Maybe it's not what you had planned, but it's exactly what I've been working so hard for. My friends are going to freak out. I'm going to start packing. Oh, and don't forget to check with Emma, okay, goodnight!"

Sophie rushes toward her room. I hear her already talking on the phone to a friend.

"You're right, it's not what I had planned. It's even better." I'm talking to myself but it feels good to say the words.

A few minutes later, I walk into my room to find Emma curled up in bed reading a magazine. The light from my bedside lamp illuminates her soft features. I take a moment to stare at her. Sophie and I have been in this apartment for the past seven years. There's never been a woman in my bed here. Now, I'm taking in the view of my wife as she cuddles under the navy comforter, her hair spilling over my pillows.

Emma in one of my t-shirts is one of my favorite sights. She's so fucking sexy. In our rush to pack she thinks she forgot pajamas. In reality, I removed them from her suitcase.

She looks up to catch me staring from the doorway.

"How'd it go?" she asks, tossing her magazine onto the nightstand and sitting upright, anxious to hear.

As I make my way over to the bed, I pull my shirt over my head and toss it on the desk chair.

"How do you feel about having a roommate for a while?" I ask.

"Who?" Her brows draw down, but then her eyes light with realization. "You mean Sophie? She's coming to New York?"

"She got a paid internship at an event planning firm there."

"Which one?"

"Marion Adler, I think it was."

"Wow. That's huge. She's by far the most sought-after event planner in the city."

"She's worked really hard and I know she's dying to go, but her income—"

Before I can go into more detail, Emma interrupts me.

"Of course, she'll stay with us. For as long as she needs."

"I know you were excited to move out of your parents' apartment so we could have our own place, be as loud as we want."

"You already know I'm not a screamer."

She's right. Emma's orgasms are explosive, her muscles clamp down so hard on my cock, and I love watching her face when she comes, but she's not loud.

"True. And I can always cover your mouth with my hand or fuck you with your face down in the pillows. We do have options."

She scoffs, pushing her hands into my chest, but in one quick move, I yank the t-shirt over her head and toss it.

"No underwear?" I ask, taking in her nakedness.

She shrugs. "I must have forgotten to pack it."

I roll over her, pinning her to the bed. She arches up into me, her hard nipples rubbing against my chest.

"You're beautiful, Mrs. Hart." I kiss her softly. "And you're all mine."

Epilogue

EMMA
One week later

Like most of our relationship, the last week with Griffin has been a whirlwind. We returned from Las Vegas after Sophie's graduation, signed the lease on our new apartment in Gramercy Park a few days later, and now it's move in day.

Next weekend, Griffin will fly back to Las Vegas, help Sophie get all their stuff packed up and drive back to New York.

"Are you ready?" I ask, reaching for the door handle.

"Hold on." Griffin reaches for me. I let out a yelp as he lifts me into his arms. "Now we can proceed."

With one arm around Griffin's neck, I push open the door with my other hand. He carries me over the threshold into our new apartment.

Since yesterday, a few pieces of furniture we picked out together have been delivered.

"Oh, the dining table is here." I gasp at the sight of the

birch table and chairs that have already been placed in our dining room.

Griffin walks us over and gently sets me down.

"Isn't it gorgeous?" I lean over the edge to place my hands on the smooth wood, then look over my shoulder to find Griffin staring at me with heat in his eyes.

"Yeah. How long do you think we have before the movers starts bringing things in?" he asks, his hands sliding along my ass as he leans over me.

"Ten minutes?" I guess.

"We'll have to be quick then."

Griffin reaches under my sundress to yank down my panties before he lifts me up onto the table. "Did I ever tell you how convenient it is that you wear dresses all the time? You make it so easy to slide my hand under your dress and feel how wet you are for me."

He does just that, his fingers teasing at my opening while he yanks down his shorts and boxer briefs, exposing his hard cock. I grip his arms as he pulls me to the edge of the table. One hard thrust and he's inside me.

The delicious intrusion has a moan escaping my lips. I wrap my legs around his hips, relishing the feel of him pushing deeper inside me. His hands grip my hips tighter and his mouth captures mine with a blistering kiss.

"I can't wait until I can lay you out on this table and eat your sweet pussy. Fuck you on every surface in this apartment." He rolls his hips, his cock finding that sensitive place inside me.

"You're close, aren't you, Emma?" He moves his hips again, and presses a kiss to my neck, right below my ear. "Be a good girl and give it to me. Let me feel you come."

His words have me clenching around him, my orgasm sending shockwaves through my body. Griffin groans and pulses his release inside me.

"I love you, Emma." He drops a sweet kiss to my lips.

"I love you, too."

We quickly clean up and pull our clothes back into place.

When there's a knock on the door a few minutes later, I rush to open it.

"Mrs. Hart?" he asks, looking at his clipboard.

I smile and nod. "Yes, that's me."

GRIFFIN
Three months later

"Tonight was perfect." Emma sighs as she pushes my suit jacket off my shoulders. "Don't you think?"

Before tonight, I'd never stepped foot in a Bergman's department store. I already knew Emma Belle Bridal's exclusive contract with the luxury department store was a big deal, but tonight, with Emma's dresses front and center in the formal wear department, it became even more clear how amazing the achievement was. And listening to Emma talk to guests at the launch, explaining her inspiration and design process only made me fall more in love with her. Watching Emma be a bad ass businesswoman and achieve her goals is so fucking hot.

"You're perfect," I reply as she climbs into my lap where I'm sitting on the edge of our bed.

I kiss along her jaw. My hands roam over her bare legs, my thumb caressing the inside of her right ankle, over her butterfly tattoo. A month ago, she got it professionally colored in. It's pink with black on the edges of the wings. It's a nod to her romantic side and suits her perfectly.

After the dust settled on my official move to the city and my new job at Premier Real Estate, I finally had a moment to think about what I would have done differently with Emma.

Unlike Emma, I'd never put any thought into falling in love and getting married. It happened anyway. But I decided there is one thing that I want.

"You know what would make it even better?" I ask.

"An orgasm?"

"Yes, but first," I reach inside the pocket of my discarded suit jacket and pull out the small velvet box. Emma's eyes go wide.

"Griffin." Her voice is barely audible as her eyes shift from the box to mine.

"Emma Belle Warner, four months ago you stepped out on a rooftop in Vegas and I got my first look at you. Even in that moment I knew you were mine. You've said you wouldn't change our wedding or the way we fell in love for anything. I agree, but there is something I wanted to do. A tradition that I didn't realize I wanted until I fell in love with you." I pull open the box. Emma's eyes drop to the two-carat princess cut diamond set on a gold band that matches her wedding band.

Emma gasps. "Oh, it's beautiful."

I pull it from the box and reach for her left hand.

"I wanted to pick out a ring I knew you'd love and place it on your finger." I slide the ring into position over her gold wedding band.

Emma's eyes are filled with tears. "I love it." Her hands find my jaw as she drops her lips to mine. "I love you."

"I love you more every day and can't wait to see where life takes us."

Before Emma, I thought I needed to be at a certain point in my life to find love. To be able to share my life and be worthy of someone sharing theirs. To be worthy of Emma. But creating our life together, navigating the start of my career, finding an apartment together in the city, celebrating the launch of Emma's bridal line in Bergman's department store has been the best part.

My eyes snag on the framed picture on our dresser. It's

one from the bubble bath photoshoot with Kandi Kline. We have an entire album from that shoot, but our favorite photo is one we didn't even pose for. Me writing words on Emma's soapy back while she looks over her shoulder at me. It's sweet and sexy and perfectly captures the real us.

"Tu es á moi," I whisper in Emma's ear.

She knows the translation now and she knows every word is true.

You're mine.

This woman, and our life together was completely unexpected. But I'm grateful every day that she's mine.

THE END

Thank You

Dear Reader,

Thank you for taking the time to ready my book. There are so many books to choose from, so thank you for spending your precious time reading mine. If you have a minute, please consider leaving a review for Unexpectedly Mine. Reviews help indie authors so much!

XO, Erin

About the Author

Erin Hawkins lives in Colorado with her husband and three young children. She enjoys reading, working out, spending time in the mountains, reality TV and brunch that lasts all day.